THE FOURTH WORLD

Also by Dennis Danvers

END OF DAYS
CIRCUIT OF HEAVEN
TIME AND TIME AGAIN
WILDERNESS

THE FOURTH WORLD

DENNIS DANVERS

AVON BOOKS, INC.

An Imprint of HarperCollins*Publishers,*
10 East 53rd Street
New York, New York 10022-5299

Copyright © 2000 by Dennis Danvers
Interior design by Elizabeth M. Glover
ISBN: 0-380-97761-3

Library of Congress Cataloging in Publication Data:
Danvers, Dennis.
The fourth world / Dennis Danvers. — 1st ed.
p. cm.
1. World Wide Web (Information retrieval system) — Fiction. I. Title.
PS3554.A5834 F68 2000
813'.54 — dc21   99-052345

First Avon Eos Printing: March 2000

AVON EOS TRADEMARK REG. U.S. PAT. OFF. AND IN OTHER COUNTRIES,
MARCA REGISTRADA, HECHO EN U.S.A.

Printed in the U.S.A.

FIRST EDITION

QPM   10 9 8 7 6 5 4 3 2 1

www.harpercollins.com

For Sarah
El amor de mi vida

Neighborhood and place have been denigrated in the
modern world. We live instead in space, in global
space, media space, advertising space. But our place—
the block on which we live, the soil, the birds, the
history—is often totally unknown because people are
simply garaged there overnight. The next morning they
return to the great machine of late-stage capitalism,
which continues the pumping up of desire and
consumption.

—JERRY BROWN, Mayor of Oakland

Chiapas is not an article in a newspaper, nor the daily
portion of horror. Chiapas is a place of dignity, a
source of rebellion in a world pathetically asleep. We
should continue travelling to Chiapas and speaking
of Chiapas. They ask us to. Leaving the refugee camp in
Polho there is a sign which reads: "When the last of
you have gone, what is going to become of us?" They
do not know that when one has been to Chiapas, one
never leaves. Because of that we are all in Chiapas today.

—JOSE SARAMAGO, Zapatista Front of National Liberation

THE FOURTH WORLD

PART ONE

Bienvenidos a Ladrónvilla

Poor Mexico, so far from God and
so close to the United States.
—PORFIRIO DÍAZ

CHAPTER ONE

THIS WAS SANTEE'S FIRST TIME IN MEXICO, EVEN THOUGH he'd been working the border states, mostly Texas, off and on for the last six months. He was a reporter, or called himself one. For about a year, he'd worked for NewsReal, a virtual newsite specializing in news to get your blood racing. It was his job to be on the spot, experiencing and recording stories around the world so that people everywhere could experience the news virtually for themselves. At least that's what he'd been told when he was hired.

NewsReal got a tip of renewed hostilities in Chiapas, and Santee was the closest man to Mexico. NewsReal pulled him off interviewing mass-murder survivors at a Houston skating rink (a story sure to bring about the final demise of all but virtual skating rinks everywhere) and put him on the first flight to Mexico City. From there, he'd ridden most of the night on a bus to get to Chiapas, hiking out at dawn from Ocosingo to this valley dotted with pyramids and a huge military base. Except for the number of soldiers and checkpoints, you wouldn't think there was a revolution going on—had been off and on since January 1, 1994— twenty years come January. The Zapatistas and a few other dirt-poor groups (mostly Indian farmers but some *mestizo* laborers) were taking on the Mexican government, controlled by the same corrupt party since 1929 and backed by an impressive military, several paramilitary groups, and the wholehearted support of the United States. The whole lopsided thing was supposedly finally winding down.

He crouched in a grove of macadamia trees that afforded him a good view of the village where something was supposed to happen. Beyond, on the horizon, one of the watchtowers at the base peeked over the trees. As usual, the body stocking studded with jelly-bean-size sensors (for a full visceral experience) kept riding up his crotch. You could edit

3

out such distractions, but it was better if they weren't there to begin with. NewsReal was upgrading to little ones—a little bump on the back of the neck, the tiniest of scars—but he hadn't gotten his yet. He shifted his position and waited. This was the first time he'd done anything he'd call a real story.

When he'd interviewed with NewsReal, he thought they might like that he had acting experience, but that didn't impress them. They hired him, they said, because of his acute senses and strong feelings.

"We're always looking for a man who can cry," one of his four interviewers told him.

"I also think," he said, and everyone laughed.

"And," one of them said, "you have a sense of humor!" They were charmed; they hired him on the spot—the spot being (depending on your perspective) the NewsReal Corporate Site, Conference Room C; or his mother's home office where he'd been sleeping nights, between jobs again at thirty-two. As Santee's mother might say, he'd had trouble finding his niche.

NewsReal thought he'd be good with victims, so he went from tragedy to tragedy, talking to survivors, walking among the dead. His boss, Inez, explained his job this way: "People want to feel better. You can give them happy news, but that only makes them feel worse. They think, 'That's okay for them, but what about me?' Better to show them how awful things can be, so their own lives look better, and they *feel* better. Got it?"

He got it. He and his ilk were popularly known as *vultures*. NewsReal had the best, everyone agreed, and he was a rising star. *Why is it*, he asked himself, *that I always succeed at the things I loathe?*

Now, he looked down into this valley of little plots of cultivated land and tin-roof houses and waited for tragedy to strike. Smoke from cook fires rose lazily into the morning sky, still streaked with red. Roosters had been crowing for some time. In the fields, in the small yards beside the houses, dozens of people were already about their business.

They were Zapatista land invaders—they'd taken back this land from the *hacendados* who'd stolen it from their fathers, their grandfathers, their great-grandfathers. Not so long ago there'd been cattle grazing where corn and beans were now growing. The *hacendados* who owned the cattle—men who lived in Mexico City, Cuernavaca, Los Angeles, men who had contracts with McDonald's or Burger King or Taco Bell— wanted the land back, and they intended to take it back this morning.

All of this was in the briefing Santee had accessed on the way here. But it hadn't quite prepared him for the reality.

He'd passed several of the Indians, the land invaders, coming and going on the trail. They smiled at him in their shy way. They were small and thin, but not frail. They worked too hard for that. All of them, even the children, seemed to be carrying something—usually firewood or bags of corn—that weighed as much as they did. He was rigged with a Spanish translator, but half the time it didn't seem to work. Then he remembered from the briefing that a lot of the older Indians didn't speak Spanish, only their indigenous tongue.

They weren't what he'd expected. They were growing corn and beans in the middle of a war zone, but there were no cartridge belts, no guns, only hoes and machetes. Inez had told him when she gave him the assignment to keep an eye out for "one of those revolutionary babes— tits and an M16—young guys eat that stuff up. Remember that young men, fourteen to twenty-four years old, are a key component of our target audience for war-zone coverage." But these young women, while beautiful, were more likely to be carrying children or buckets of corn on their way to the *tortilleria*. Santee hoped the target audience wouldn't be too disappointed.

Inez had faith in him: "I know this is a lot different from the hanky-wringing stuff you've been doing, but I told them upstairs you could handle it. So whatever you do, don't flinch." She gave him a good-natured punch on the arm like a member of the target audience. "You wouldn't want to make me look bad."

He'd found the macadamia grove as he tried to elude a couple of young boys, Nico and Francisco, who'd taken a friendly interest in him. They'd offered to show him the *ganado*—a half dozen half-starved cattle in a stone corral that were apparently the pride of the *ejido*. He said no, but they tagged along anyway. But when he took the trail into the grove, they stopped and asked him if he was staying at *el rancho*, pointing up the hillside to a series of little cottages, apparently situated for the view. He lied and said yes, and that seemed to settle him. They waved good-bye, calling out *vaya bien*, and let him be. He hadn't been in Mexico long, but he couldn't help noticing that in the city they would've asked him for money, but here the subject never came up. He wondered if he should tell them, as he watched them driving their cattle out of the corral by pitching stones at their bony haunches, that according to a NewsReal informant, they were about to be attacked.

But that would upset the balance, ruin the story. He was never supposed to get involved.

He was beginning to think NewsReal's tip was false anyway. Through his binoculars, he could see that nothing seemed to be going on at the military base except for a couple of fellows lounging in the watchtower. If the *ejido* expected an attack, there was certainly no sign of it. The roosters kept crowing, dogs barked, and American oldies blared from an antique radio. A single wire went to the village from an unofficial looking splice onto the line that went up the hill through the macadamia grove. Children played a shrieking game of tag under a Zapatista flag. Nothing was going to happen.

And then they began to arrive—two caravans of shiny American pickup trucks from opposite ends of the valley, loaded with muscular young men with guns, who dropped out of the back of the slow moving trucks as they circled their target. They wore T-shirts and jeans and cowboy boots. Whoever they worked for didn't issue uniforms—only first-class hardware.

The trucks stopped, sunlight glistening from their lavishly chromed bodies, the only sound in the valley their motors smoothly idling in concert.

One of the truck horns gave three staccato beeps, and the men started firing. Santee dug his hands into the dirt, holding on as if he might fly off the planet, and watched. That was his job. He watched them murder women with children in their arms, old men on their knees. He watched them shoot Nico in the back, Francisco through the head. He watched them shoot everyone except a handful who managed to escape into the hills. And when everyone was dead or gone, he watched them burn every house, every field. He watched more than he could comprehend, more than he could stomach.

But, he told himself repeatedly, he couldn't turn away. People had to know what was happening here. He was the eyes and ears of the world, its conscience. As the killers rounded themselves up and made a pyre of bodies, he looked with tear-blurred eyes through his binoculars at the military watchtower, and a soldier seemed to be looking back at him through his own binoculars. But he wasn't looking at Santee. He was watching the carnage. Like Santee, he wouldn't intervene. To get here these trucks would've driven right by the army base in a caravan. Santee wondered if anyone in the base had waved.

Santee stared at the flames until he heard a crackling overhead. He looked up to find the tree he crouched under consumed by flames. The fire in the cornfields had spread, and the entire grove was ablaze. He had no choice but to retreat up the hillside.

As he emerged from the grove, there was a tall gringo with silver hair swept back in a ponytail slouched against a fence post like someone at a cocktail party. He had a dazed look as his eyes moved from the burning village to the burning grove. "*Buenos días*, good morning, whatever," he said with a tired smile, toasting Santee with an empty glass. Santee wondered if the man was drunk, but he didn't wait around to find out. Instead, he broke into a dead run.

SANTEE DIDN'T REMEMBER MAKING HIS WAY BACK TO TOWN and his hotel. Once he was behind locked doors, he backed up everything he'd recorded and transmitted it back to NewsReal for editing, fully expecting the world to witness these horrors within hours and denounce them. He showered, lay in bed, fell asleep for a couple of hours, woke up screaming, not from dreams but from memories of the slaughter.

They even shot the cattle.

He got online and went to NewsReal, but there was nothing there. He checked an hour later. Nothing still. After a bit of a runaround, he finally connected with Inez, and they went into her virtual office. It looked out on an idealized Atlanta skyline. She wasn't encouraging: "Preliminary word we have is it's a local dispute—feuding Indian clans—there's no story there."

Santee couldn't believe it. "Indian clans? What the hell are you talking about? The farmer clan and the bodybuilder clan? The hoe clan and the M16 clan? Did you see the stuff I sent?"

She put a hand on his shoulder, a kind, understanding, restraining hand. "Let it go, Santee. Nobody wants this one."

"What do you mean, 'nobody'? I fucking want it! People need to know what's going on down here."

Her hand squeezed his shoulder, a little too hard. "No, they don't. Nobody *has* to know anything. Nobody wants to know everything, and it's not our job to tell them. Don't get messianic on me, Santee. You've got good instincts. You feel deeply. It'll play real well with the right story. But, trust me, this isn't the right story." She smiled. "I know this must've been terribly stressful for you. Why don't you take a little time off? Get online. Have a wild time—company expense."

"The goddamn Web is the last place I want to be."

"The hand that feeds, Santee. The hand that feeds. Okay then: Get drunk. Find a friendly *señorita*. Shouldn't be too hard down there, eh?" She gave his shoulder a little shake—just one of the guys. "Just let it go."

"What if I can prove this wasn't feuding clans?"

She studied him for a moment. *You showed such promise,* she seemed to say with her look. She gave his shoulder a maternal pat. "We'll see."

AFTER HIS CONVERSATION WITH INEZ, SANTEE SAT IN HIS hotel room in Ocosingo, sorting through what had happened, waiting for things to quiet down, already knowing what he had to do, just waiting for the silence it required. Now it was two o'clock in the morning. Even the sound system in the lobby—cranked loud by Felix the desk clerk as a courtesy to everyone in the hotel who might want to listen to turn-of-the-century American rock—was finally shut off. The only sound was an occasional burble from the water bottle echoing off the courtyard tiles.

Santee had copied the massacre recordings before he sent them to NewsReal. He wasn't supposed to. In the twenty-page document he signed when he took the job, he promised, among many other things, never to copy NewsReal recordings. It was easy to do. The techie who trained him on the interface told him how, even as he told him never to do it. When Santee asked him why, he suggested Santee figure that out for himself.

There were several good reasons *for* backing up recordings, and most reporters did now and then, at least in the short run, especially in bad weather. Data could get scrambled in transmission, misdirected. He'd once lost a whole afternoon of interviews with mud-slide victims when the system crashed in mid-transmission. So why *was* the system configured to purge a file once it was sent? And why did NewsReal periodically ransack everyone's drives to see if anyone was hanging on to his work?

It wasn't copyright protection, which is what NewsReal said it was. Sell recordings to whom, for what? A recording wasn't going anywhere unless it went through the WebNet satellite network where it would be identified as recorded by NewsReal equipment, the fees assessed and automatically deposited in NewsReal's accounts, or, if there was no account to pay for the posting, the site would be shut down and prosecuted. You couldn't steal a NewsReal recording; you could only create new opportunities for NewsReal to make more money from it.

It wasn't the cynical theory popular among the reporters that News-Real feared what people might do if they discovered the yawning gap between unedited recordings and finished product. Fact is, any idiot could see the news was stuffed with blatant product placements and was gored up or down for different markets, but nobody seemed to care. Why should they? Nobody took the news seriously anymore.

Santee thought the reasons for NewsReal's ban on copying recordings might be more subtle. NewsReal was dependent on people like him to gather experiences for others and pass them on. But what would happen if reporters started hanging on to their work? They might replay their recordings, mull them over, quit thinking of them as just "raw product" (as Inez called them) and start thinking of them as experiences, their own experiences. Then they might get it in their heads to ponder them, try to understand them, maybe even do something about them. They might quit thinking of themselves as just cameras. They might start thinking they were witnesses. They might start thinking the truth mattered somehow—that there even was such a thing. Such notions—News-Real had every reason to fear—could be very, very bad for business.

Santee hoped so.

His recording interface could be used for playback, though it was a lot more intense than the usual virtual. Dangerously intense some said, and every reporter knew someone who knew someone who'd died of a heart attack or gone insane replaying some horror show he'd recorded.

He'd gone out earlier and bought a pack of cigarettes, taking out one and giving the rest to Felix. He lit it now, his first in five years. As he smoked, he drank a Scotch and water without ice. The computer was on the table in front of him ready for playback.

He sat by the open window. From here he could see up the valley toward the ruins, his view framed by the open courtyard. The smoke that trailed up into the sky most of the day had faded by sunset. Now the sky was thick with stars.

When he'd gone out earlier, he'd tried to get someone, anyone, to talk to him about what had happened just outside town. Even the gregarious Felix, leaning up against the wall beside the entrance, answered Santee's question about the plume of smoke with one of his own. "Do you like Sheryl Crow?"

"Everyday Is a Winding Road" was blaring in the lobby.

"Yes," Santee said. "Very much."

"Good song, no?" Felix looked up the road in the opposite direction from the plume of smoke.

Santee got the point.

HE PUT HIS CIGARETTE IN THE ASHTRAY AND THE SCOTCH beside it on the windowsill. With a trembling hand he struck a key to play back the massacre. He played it raw without any filters or toning down. It was set to play continuously until he told it to stop. He was aware that the whole business smacked of penance.

The first two times, he couldn't do anything. Paralyzed with panic and terror, it was all he could do to breathe, as if he were down there in the village being picked off, watching everyone he knew die before his eyes. His eyes filled with tears, but his vision in the playback was steady, relentlessly focused. His training had held, so that his eyes swept the entire scene periodically to take in everything. But he could take in nothing. He wanted to burrow under the earth and hide.

It wasn't until the third time that he began to notice those who were getting away. A wild-eyed man, shirtless and half starved, jumped onto a bicycle and rode it into the nearest gunman, leapt from the bike, and scrambled into the woods. A woman with a bullet wound in her shoulder crawled out a few feet at a time when she thought the gunmen weren't looking. When she reached the corn, she stood and ran for all she was worth. The kids playing tag—seven of them—ran off toward the ruins when the shooting started. One of them made it. The shortest. A girl no more than four or five. The gunman who sprayed them with bullets aimed too high. When it came down to the lone child, the gunman, to his small credit, turned away with a tortured look on his face.

Santee called up the virtual keyboard and took notes, made a count. Eleven people had gotten away. Five of them were wounded or injured in some way, two probably fatally. There were nine, maybe ten survivors. Besides the murderers themselves, the soldiers in the watchtower, and the gringo on the hillside, Santee was their only witness.

And then he began to count the dead. Those who stayed inside he couldn't be sure of until they were dragged out of their bullet-riddled houses for burning. One of the gunmen seemed to be doing a body count himself. Santee wondered if that's how they were paid. Certainly not by the hour. From the time the trucks surrounded the village until they drove away leaving it in flames, twenty-seven minutes passed. He had to replay it five times to get all the dead, to see each face (if he could) for identification, noting the cause of death and the apparent perpetrator for all 176 murders.

He took the greatest care with the killers, blocking out each one's face, storing it, enhancing it, tagging it for recognition. They made his task easier by standing briefly in formation beside the blazing bodies, apparently to see if everyone was accounted for. Other than the one who'd taken a bicycle to the crotch, there were no casualties. There were three gunmen whose faces he couldn't see clearly at all, another eight he couldn't be sure he'd seen clearly enough to ID. There were twenty-four he was certain he would know if he ever saw them again. With a grim bit of whimsy, Santee set the recognition software to shroud their faces in flames if he came across them when he was recording.

WHEN SANTEE WAS DONE, JOHN MELLENCAMP WAS SINGING for the hotel, and Felix was singing along. Roosters were crowing. The breeze through the window smelled like plants and disinfectant. Santee'd let three quarters of his cigarette burn up in the ashtray. Just as well. He took the Scotch and water into the bathroom and poured it down the drain. He rinsed the glass and drank off a glass of water before wondering if the water was safe.

Safe.

Vaya bien, Nico and Francisco had called to him, waving their arms in broad sweeps through the air. Literally, "go well." They were both dead now. Gone. He was still alive. Safe.

He broke down crying, sobbing, "Jesus God!" though he'd never been religious. He leaned his back against the wall and slid to the floor, rested his forehead on his knees. He couldn't stop crying. The hard tile walls echoed his sobs back to him. They almost sounded like laughter. He was pathetic, helpless. For a second he thought about getting online, going to a crisis intervention site, but the thought repulsed him: as if his pain were the crisis, when there were survivors out there in the hills. The enormity of their mourning filled him with shame.

The hand that feeds, Santee. The hand that feeds.

After a time, he curled up on the tile floor and slept, as if passing out from a night of drinking. When he woke, he felt strangely peaceful. He knew exactly what he must do.

*   *   *

WHEN HE'D ASKED INEZ WHAT SHE'D DO IF HE COULD DIS-credit the clan theory, he'd had no idea how he might do such a thing. He wasn't an investigative reporter. He was a hand wringer, a bystander with a sharp eye and a lump in his throat. Useless to all those dead people, even more useless to the living. But now he knew two dozen faces, two dozen men who probably lived around here.

He showered and dressed in shorts and shirt and backpack like any other tourist. He went out in the afternoon for a walk, looking at every face. He didn't have to stare. The computer in his backpack did that for him, processing the information a hundred times faster than he could. He headed south for the market, but it was mid-afternoon and there wasn't much going on. He looped back to the center of town, and crossed the *zócalo* diagonally, southwest to northeast. He glanced at a man on a park bench in the middle of the *zócalo* getting his shoes shined, reading a newspaper. He looked up from the paper as Santee passed, and his face burst into flames.

Santee stumbled on by, turning right at the corner, heading south so that the man, facing northwest, wouldn't see Santee loitering in the shade of a tree behind him. The shoe-shine boy was finishing up, buffing vigorously, snapping the cloth. The man stood, tossing the boy a coin, and headed northwest. Santee followed half a block behind. The man was dressed in a crisp white shirt and black slacks. His freshly polished shoes were quite a contrast to the boots he'd worn yesterday morning, boots that must be soaked in blood and mud and ashes.

They hadn't gone far when the man opened an iron gate and went into a private courtyard, closing the gate behind him. Santee could hear the muffled sounds of greetings from inside, shouts of laughter. There seemed to be a party going on. He looked through the scrolled grillwork of the gate and saw a courtyard crowded with people—men, women, and children. A birthday party, he guessed.

The man he followed was making a fuss over a little boy six or seven years old, calling him a little man, feeling his proffered muscle. Some-one noticed Santee at the gate, and it was as if the party noise was silenced with a switch. The man turned to face Santee. "May I help you?" the man asked in Spanish. Santee heard the translation as a quiet voice in his ear. He didn't use the translator to answer but his own college Spanish in an accent even his patient teacher would've found unbearable.

"Me llamo Santee St. John. ¿Cómo se llama usted?" He awkwardly snaked his hand through the gate, grinning like an idiot, a refugee from nothing more than Spanish class, and like magic the man shook his hand, told Santee his name, opened the gate wide, introduced him all around, and invited him to the birthday party of his nephew.

As the evening wore on, Santee asked him where he lived, who he worked for, who he worked with. Everyone enjoyed laughing at the foolish gringo with the terrible Spanish. They liked America; they liked Americans. He answered their questions with the stereotypes they all wanted to hear: He was rich. He owned a big new car. He had many women, real and virtual. His computer was the best money could buy and capable of near-magical operations. He was a naive buffoon who understood Mexican politics about as well as a dog understood vegetarians and cared even less. He was their future, a global man.

In an impressive display of generosity, *Tio* Roberto gave his nephew and all his pals a voyage on a virtual pirate ship. When the children were online, dozing in a row of little Weisiger interface recliners, Roberto treated the men, Santee included, to a place called Planet Whore, a "gentleman's pleasure site" run by the same group that did NewsReal.

Early the next morning, Santee hurried back to his hotel. He stood in the shower with his clothes at his feet, the water beating down on him. He'd met four of Roberto's fellow murderers while visiting Planet Whore. From them he had leads on a dozen more. The truth, it seemed, would be relatively easy to get at. It was living with it that would be hard.

Over the next few weeks, he found eleven more of the twenty-four in and around Ocosingo, plus the names of a dozen they worked with and for. He never mentioned the slaughter of Indians to anyone. He didn't have to. They tried to impress him with tales of how high up their connections ran, how powerful was their grip upon the country. But they would also confide how hard it was to make it down here, that they really had no choice but to work for the ruling party. The Zapatistas were ruining things for everybody. He should tell the people back home that the Zapatista lies weren't true. Santee wanted to tell them that most of the people back home spent their time, money, and energy with more fundamental lies than any the Zapatistas might tell. But he didn't.

*   *   *

HE GOT ON THE WEB AND DID ALL THE RESEARCH HIMSELF, though by rights NewsReal paid other folks to do that. Santee didn't want to take any chances. When he was through he had a list of twenty-seven names, all of whom worked for a landowner's association whose links with the ruling party and the president were so obvious that they didn't seem to think they had anything to hide. Most of the men had been arrested for serious crimes, including murder, rape, and arson. None had ever stood trial for any of them.

She stalled him, but Santee eventually got an appointment with Inez to show her what he had. He crunched it down into a fifteen-minute experience. She bailed after five. "It's too complicated," she told him. "It requires too much thought, and there're no good viscerals."

"You already got the good viscerals with the stuff you wouldn't run. Rich people are stealing land from poor farmers to graze cattle for American hamburgers. When the farmers fight back, the rich people murder them with hired thugs. What is so complicated about that?"

"Blah, blah-blah, blah-blah. Words, Santee. No one cares about words. I can give you two minutes, three tops. You show me what? A big mess with no answers—"

"What do you mean, answers? Is that our job?"

"Let me finish? No answers. Nobody wants to feel stupid and helpless. They can get that from their wife and kids. They come to us to be on top of things, to understand the world in fifteen minutes. Maybe they don't understand shit. That's not for me to say. What we're selling is that they *think* they do."

"Why can't you give me more time?"

"Haven't you heard what's going on?"

"People don't live online here, Inez."

"This is bigger than that. A twenty-two-year-old guy in Vermont has recordings of the President boinking him when he was *seventeen*! Which do you think the world cares more about? That some starving Indians get shot in Mexico or that the President's queer and faces criminal charges?"

"Which one do you care more about, Inez?"

"I got us five minutes of the actual recordings—the climax, the simultaneous climax I might add. Exclusive. We broke the record for total hits in the first hour it was up. NewsReal subscriptions are up a thousand percent. My bonus alone would put God in my lap for a month. I'm sorry, Santee. I'm sure your Indians are very nice, but they couldn't do that for me, or for you either. Maybe if it was slow, they could have their turn at being this week's lost orca, but it isn't, and I've got work to do."

"How do you know the recording was made when the boy was seventeen?"

"Santee, grow up! It doesn't matter. You're always trying to make things too complicated. Didn't you learn anything in school? Focus, Santee."

"Gimmick, you mean. Hook. Manipulation."

He'd gone too far. She crossed her arms, looked haughty and righteous. "The next time I see you I expect a different attitude toward your work. You're beginning to sound like you belong on some other site." She cut him off to leave him hanging, throw a scare into him. But he wasn't scared. The thought of losing his job with NewsReal seemed as threatening as recovering from dysentery.

SANTEE HAD DONE HIS JOB. HE'D DONE EVERYTHING HE WAS supposed to do and then some, but it'd come to nothing. It was time to head home, his tail between his legs. But he couldn't quite bring himself to do it. It'd been a week since Inez turned down his story in favor of the allegedly gay president, and Santee was still in Ocosingo, still editing, still figuring out new lines of inquiry, not willing to admit he'd hit a dead end. At least on the road he'd been traveling.

He'd made this story a cause, a litmus test of where his life stood. Smart boy, sensitive boy, he'd gotten a good education, a dose of idealism along with it—that was proving to be stronger than he'd realized. He'd thought he had no illusions about the news—sure, it was mostly just for show, just to make a buck—but when it really mattered, in the midst of all the hype, it got the truth out there. Now he saw that it was precisely when the stakes were highest that it *didn't* tell the truth, that it ignored or lied about anything that might upset business as usual. This wasn't a novel idea to Santee. He'd heard it a million times, but hadn't believed it. *You'll find out*, he'd been told, along with the usual predictions: He'd turn cynical—though he'd call it "realistic"—keep doing the job, moving up, moving on, getting over it, facing facts. Growing up.

His mom and dad were proud of their middle-aged boy, an oversensitive pain in the ass most of his life, who'd *finally* found, in his mother's lexicon, "his calling." As if he were some missionary. Which, in a way, he was—spreading the gospel of NewsReal far, wide, but not too deep: The world was what you wanted it to be in the privacy of your own home, fully customizable to suit your personal profile and lifestyle. There were misfortunes, calamities, disturbances, to be sure, but you were safe, sound, and well-informed here in the Web where the old virtues were tacked on to most every story. For the Victims—except those who'd Brought It Upon Themselves—there was Hope. Faith was available at a multitude of sites. Charity was seeking volunteers.

He should just quit, he told himself over and over. And do what? Feel bad? That did everybody a lot of good. He couldn't just walk away, but the thought of continuing with NewsReal made him feel sick.

He opened the curtains and threw open the window. The air was cool and dry. It was approaching dusk. He hadn't been out of his room all day. He went down to the lobby, which, like the entire hotel as far as he could tell, was empty. The film of water on the freshly mopped tile floors was evaporating before his eyes. Felix sat in the doorway, smoking a cigarette and looking out at the street. For once, the music was turned off.

Santee had learned that Felix didn't just work here, he owned the place. The "maid" Santee had seen a few times was Felix's sister. Usually, Felix cleaned the place himself. They'd inherited the hotel from their father and uncles who'd had high hopes for it once upon a time, selling their shares of *ejido* lands at the turn of the century to buy it. Felix's cousins had all gone north in search of jobs. His sister wanted to sell. But how could you sell, Felix wanted to know, if there were no buyers? Santee doubted the place broke even.

When he was a boy, Felix said, the hotel was often filled with Americans, Europeans, Canadians, many of them come to see *la guerra*, the war, perhaps catch a glimpse of the Zapatistas or even Subcomandante Marcos himself. But *El Sub* was gone, and nobody cared anymore. The only guests now were salesmen or farmers come to town for markets or festivals. But with little to sell and less to celebrate, there weren't too many of those.

Santee sat down beside Felix, expecting him to ask, as he did every evening, whether Santee intended to stay for another night, but Felix surprised him.

"A woman came looking for you this afternoon," Felix said.

"A woman?"

Santee's apparent shock made Felix smile. "Yes, a woman. She says she's a friend of yours. Her name is Margaret."

Friend. *Amiga*, he said. But that could mean anything from acquaintance to lover. No matter. "I don't know any Margaret," he said. "Did you tell her I was here?"

Felix shook his head. "When a woman comes looking for a man, is not always a good thing. Sometimes the man doesn't wish to be found. I didn't believe she was your friend: She offered me two hundred pesos to tell her where you were. But who pays to see a friend?"

"You should've taken the money and told her I was here."

Felix smiled. "No. I look out for you, señor. You are my guest." He shrugged. "She is a very foolish woman. If she wants to find you, it's not so hard. Besides, two hundred pesos is nothing anymore."

Santee's month-long residency here was probably some kind of record for this chronically empty hotel. Felix wouldn't want to jeopardize their relationship. But Santee didn't believe that Felix only saw him as the gringo who'd laid the golden credit card. They liked each other. As much as their maleness and language and cultural barriers would allow, they'd become friends.

"What did she want?"

"Love, business. *¿Quién sabe?*"

"Did she say anything?"

"She said, 'Tell him to meet me at Hotel Colonial this evening for dinner.' "

"But you told her I wasn't here."

He laughed. "She is an intelligent woman," he said admiringly. "She didn't believe me."

Santee caught the sexual charge in Felix's tone. "What did she look like?"

Felix grinned at the question, undulated his shoulders as if the music had started up. "She is very good-looking woman. But strong, you know? Not a little girl anymore. She knows what she wants. A woman like that, you got to be serious. A woman like that, you must be willing to give her your heart, nothing less."

"You can tell all that from a five-minute conversation?"

"You can't? You Americans think too much. You don't trust your feelings until someone else has them for you on the Web. You want your room for another night?"

"Maybe I should move to the Colonial." Santee attempted a leer, but his heart wasn't in it. Most likely this Margaret was a troubleshooter from NewsReal coming to check up on their investment. She was serious all right. Serious trouble.

CHAPTER TWO

THE COLONIAL WAS THE NICEST HOTEL IN TOWN, THE PLACE where visiting government officials stayed and most newspeople, back when more of them bothered to come here, or anywhere for that matter. The hotel's restaurant, while not the best in town, was definitely the most expensive. There were a few tables outside on a railed porch overlooking the *zócalo*. Nine or ten people were there. She was hard to miss. The only woman and the only American, she sat at one end of the porch all by herself, a ring of empty tables around her. She was pretty, as Felix said, with brown curly hair and large eyes. She reminded Santee of an actress from a film he'd seen in college, but he couldn't remember the name. A comedy, he thought. Silent.

But this woman, whose name might or might not actually be Margaret, looked to be on serious business. She wore a severe gray suit and a determined expression. A satchel leaned up against her chair like a loyal dog. Whatever she wanted to see Santee about was most likely inside that satchel. A NewsReal lawyer, he guessed.

He had on battered khaki pants and a collarless white shirt—both dappled with the stains sink washing wouldn't remove. He'd traveled light to Mexico, three shirts, two pairs of pants. He hadn't bought any supplies here except food, acting each day as if he intended to leave *pasado mañana*, the day after tomorrow. But he could never quite leave, could never quite shake the feeling he had unfinished business here. Maybe this stranger, who said she was his *amiga*, might just motivate him to get it done or let it go.

She hadn't spotted him, didn't even seem to be on the lookout for him particularly. He approached her from behind. Waving off the waiter, he circled around, pulled out the chair across from her, and plopped down, hoping to rattle her, to let her know from the get go he wasn't going to be pushed around.

"If it isn't my old friend Margaret," he said.

She was unfazed. She set down her wineglass, blinking slowly, smiling the tight-lipped smile of someone humoring a child. She glanced over his shoulder. He realized she'd been watching his approach in the window in front of her.

She stuck out her hand. "You're Santee St. John," she said. The smile broadened but didn't deepen. He felt as if he were in a Webplay, interacting with a scripted character for whom he really didn't exist, didn't matter, as if their significance, whatever it might be, wasn't taking place here and now, but somewhere else.

He took her hand, shook it quickly, and let it go. She was attractive. So what? It didn't matter. But her eyes startled him—a pale green, kinder than he would've thought, but guarded. "How do you know who I am?"

She gave a nervous laugh, riding a wave of manic gaiety he guessed wasn't her usual manner. "Your bio's posted at the NewsReal site, along with photo, samples of your work. I know all about you."

If she was supposed to be a starstruck fan, he wasn't convinced. She was trying to charm him, appeal to his vanity. Unfortunately, what vanity he'd possessed had atrophied since the massacre. "Then you have me at a disadvantage."

"I'm sorry. Margaret Mayfield."

"And you are?"

"I'm between jobs at the moment."

"And what sort of jobs are you between?"

She laughed. "All kinds."

"Is this where I make some lewd joke?"

"I hope not."

He wondered how long she'd keep up this silly patter, but he didn't have the patience to find out. Pretty she might be, but she was also the enemy. Had to be. No one else knew he was in Ocosingo. Now it was his turn to give her an indulgent smile. "Why don't we just cut the crap, Margaret Mayfield, and you can tell me what business you think it is you have with me."

The waiter was standing a couple of yards away, waiting to be summoned. "How about over dinner?" she asked.

"This place is too expensive. I prefer the *taquería* down the street."

"We'll go there then."

"Let's talk first, then we'll see. I'm particular about who I dine with."

That put a crack in the smile. Then she let it dissolve altogether. "That's not what I've heard. You've been dining with the bottom feeders lately."

"And why is this any of your business?"

She turned to the waiter and told him in excellent Spanish to come back later. She waited for him to leave before she spoke.

"Okay. I'll come right to the point. I believe you recorded what happened up near the ruins a month ago."

"Is that information posted on the Web as well?"

"If you know where to find it." She ticked her points off on her long, slender fingers. "You arrived here the day before it happened, right after NewsReal yanked you out of Houston in the middle of an assignment. NewsReal has you listed as being on vacation for the last month, but Ocosingo isn't exactly most people's idea of a vacation paradise, and NewsReal's not that generous."

"You know how it is with us world-famous reporter types—it's hard to get away."

"I'd say NewsReal was tipped about the massacre and sent you to get the story."

"If that was true, then it would've been on the Web, wouldn't it? I'd be back home by now, wouldn't I?"

"Unless NewsReal didn't want it, and you had other plans."

"And what does all this have to do with you? I somehow missed that part."

She studied him for a moment through narrowed eyes. "What's your price?"

"Price?"

"For the recordings. You made a copy, didn't you? That's what you're still doing here. You're probably thinking of trying to shake down some of the bad boys you've been palling around with, but I'd strongly advise against it. They're already getting suspicious of you, and your employers have already beaten you to it anyway."

There was a level of scorn in her voice when she said "your employers" that was hard to fake. He was pretty sure she wasn't with NewsReal. So who was she? What did she want? "What are you talking about?" he asked.

"You haven't heard the news?"

"I'm on vacation. Remember?"

She took a handheld out of her satchel, which on closer inspection was more of a streamlined leather backpack that didn't quite go with the suit. She opened the handheld, found what she was looking for, and put it on the table in front of him. It showed an item from NewsReal. They'd just been awarded an exclusive contract to handle the official Web presence of Mexico, both domestic and international, in a deal worth several billion dollars. "So you're saying they've been bought."

"That's a flattering way to put it. It's a toss-up as to who approached who, but my bet is NewsReal did the soliciting. They had something to sell to one particular buyer interested in keeping it quiet, something the general market would rather not have to think about anyway, so the only real money to be made was in *not* running the story. It wouldn't surprise me if that isn't the deal they had in mind when they sent you here in the first place."

"Do you see everything in economic terms?"

"No, the world does. Haven't you noticed?"

"And what would be your interest in these recordings—if they existed?"

"Does it matter?"

He lost it. He'd been holding in his rage for weeks. "Does it *matter*? Do you have any idea what's in these recordings?"

He was practically shouting. She shifted uncomfortably in her chair. "A fair idea."

"A fair idea. What I should do is wire you up and let you experience them for yourself for a few hours—give you a vivid idea of what it feels like to witness a mass murder. Then you can tell me what you think they're worth, whether they 'matter' or not, see if you feel like having a nice dinner after that, making some little deal."

He stood up and shoved in his chair. Her wineglass wobbled, sloshing red wine onto the tablecloth. "Now if you'll excuse me, I'm on vacation." He turned on his heel, vaulted the railing, and headed across the *zócalo*, not with any destination in mind, just to get away from Margaret as quickly as he could.

What's your price? It was all he could do to keep from strangling her.

WHEN HE COOLED OFF A LITTLE, HE REALIZED HE WAS PRAC-tically running and slowed his pace. A rust-colored dog, roused to its feet by his charging approach, peered at him, made a stiff-legged circle, and flopped back down in the dust. At the bottom of the street the last stalls in the market were closing down. The vendors went about their business in slow motion. It'd been another bad day. It was always a bad day. No one had any money.

You've been dining with the bottom feeders lately.

Almost no one, he corrected himself. Almost no one. Mexico was one of the richest countries in the world with dozens of billionaires. But it also had millions in abject poverty. The disparity between rich and poor had grown wider here than anywhere else in the world. Santee had come to understand what should've been obvious—that the two went hand in hand.

In one of his Web evenings with *Tio* Roberto and his pals, Santee'd found himself having a drink with an Italian economist, who explained what he called the facts of Mexican life: "In the eyes of the world, Mexico is cheap labor, cheap oil, cheap forests to grind up into toilet paper. The world gives Mexico lots of money for these things to a few cooperative men who mustn't share the wealth or the game is up. It is a well-known fact that the more prosperous a people become, the more likely democracy will take hold, and the people start making decisions for themselves. The next thing you know there goes the cheap labor, the cheap gas, the cheap toilet paper, and nobody has nothing. You understand?"

Unfortunately he did: The first world was full.

He thought about what Margaret had said. NewsReal probably had sent him here with no intention of ever running the story—unless they'd lost the contract they were after. He supposed he should thank her for stripping him of the illusion that he'd ever been anything remotely resembling a journalist. He was just a bit player in a business deal.

He decided to get a beer and some tacos at the *taquería* off the *zócalo*. A few locals were dining at the plastic tables and chairs, their eyes glued to the old TV set hanging on chains from the ceiling. The Veracruz *Tiburones* were winning another soccer game. On the Web, you could pick a player to "be," switch to some other guy mid-play, replay it from any perspective—from godlike to the bleachers. TV coverage looked like it was reduced to three workmanlike cameras. But no one here at the *taquería* seemed to mind what they were missing. Behind the players, the TV cameras revealed, were only a few sports reporters and a handful of old-timers sitting in the stands watching the game.

As he ate, he considered his options and decided he didn't have any. It was over. It was time to go home. Look for yet another job. Or maybe not. He'd saved up quite a sum in the last year, always on assignment, living on expense account. His most recent home was a rental he could let go any time. He took a mental inventory of everything in the place and decided there was nothing he'd miss if he never went back.

He'd finished eating and was starting to get interested in the game over a second beer, when Margaret showed up. She'd changed into faded orange pants and a turquoise T-shirt. Her hair was down. He'd thought she was attractive before. Now, she was beautiful.

Paulette Goddard, he remembered—the actress whose name he couldn't remember—in *Modern Times* with Charlie Chaplin. "You don't give up, do you?"

"May I sit down?"

"I don't want to do business."

"I don't either. I think I misjudged you. I've come to apologize."

He shrugged and gestured toward the Coca-Cola chair across from him.

She sat. "It was an honest mistake. I had you figured for the typical NewsReal guy. No conscience, no brain, great teeth. Do you know Clint out of Mexico City?"

She was trying to be light, friendly. He remained stone-faced. "We've met."

"He's the one who tipped me about you. He'd heard you were here, figured you were working some scam. I thought you were like him, another media jerk on the make. . . . You're not going to help here, are you?"

Whatever he thought he'd seen or hadn't seen in her eyes before had changed now. If he could trust his instincts, she'd been playing a role before and was being straight with him now. But what if his instincts were wrong? "I'm just waiting for you to come to the point."

"Okay," she said sadly. "There's not one, I guess. I'm just really sorry I was so insensitive a while ago. I've never met one of you guys who cared before."

"That's my specialty. Real tears. But you still haven't told me who you are or why you wanted to talk to me."

"I have an informal relationship with some of the human rights organizations. I travel a lot around Mexico. Sometimes I find information they can use."

"Like my recordings."

"Like your recordings."

"And who was going to make good on 'my price'?"

She winced. "Not me, certainly. That was just bluff. The good guys don't have any real money."

"So what happens now?"

"You still don't trust me, do you?"

"Well, no."

"Fair enough." She printed up a card with her handheld and gave it to him. There were several Web addresses on it. "These are the sites I would've passed your recordings on to if you'd given them to me. I've put in the contact person for each one. You can check them out and do what you want."

He recognized some of the addresses—Amnesty International, Human Rights Watch. He shook his head. "No one listens to these people. Without NewsReal's hype, I might as well post the recordings myself. They'll run it, the copyright violation is detected, NewsReal lawyers circle them like sharks, declare it a fraud, and bury it. All that will take a few hours at most."

"A few hours is better than nothing."

"A few hours *is* nothing. It would take a few years to get anyone's attention."

"So what are you going to do?"

"I don't know." He turned the card over in his hands, put it in his pocket. "I've got more than just the tapes," he said quietly. "You want a beer?"

HE TOLD HER ABOUT THE MASSACRE, WHAT HE'D WIT-nessed, what he'd done about it. What it'd done to him. Somewhere in the telling she'd reached out and put her hands on his. They were still there. "I know the truth about all those murders, but it's all based on that NewsReal recording. All NewsReal has to do is declare me a wacko and the recording a counterfeit, and it all falls apart." He shook his head. "The 'eyes and ears of the world' only see money, listen to money."

"Maybe it's not as hopeless as you think."

He turned his hands over, took hers. "So what about you, Margaret Mayfield? What brings you to Mexico?" Her bare arms were long and slender. She withdrew her hands and sat back in her chair, signaled the waitress for another beer.

"I came here after I graduated from college. Art major. I was just going to bum around awhile, sort of a last fling, ended up staying."

"Was there a man involved?"

"Now and then. Nothing permanent. I've been told I'm difficult, headstrong, bossy. What about you? Is there a wife or girlfriend at home worrying about you?"

"Not in a while. I do all my own worrying. Too much, I'm told. Do you work down here?"

"I've taught English, been a tour guide, even sold some art a few times. I inherited some stocks from my grandparents."

"You needn't sound so guilty about it."

"It's hard not to feel guilty about being the rich *gringa*."

"Why do you stay on here? I've only been here a month, and it all seems so hopeless."

"I love this place."

"You're kidding. Haven't you heard there's a war going on?"

She laughed. "I know. It's crazy. Did you ever live in California?"

He shook his head.

"Me either. But it's like that, I think—living on a fault line. Sometimes the war blows up. Most of the time it doesn't."

"But you always know the possibility is there."

"That's true wherever you are."

"You can't stop an earthquake. There's no question of right or wrong, taking sides."

"Then what kind of sense is it to abandon the place where you might make a difference and stay on where it's all in the hands of fate?"

He laughed. "None I guess."

"You're on vacation, right? You should see more of the countryside and the people while you're here. It's a wonderful place, really." She'd grown animated, sitting on one leg, leaning across the table toward him.

"I'll have to take your word for it." He remembered what Felix had said to him earlier, and he realized, he did take her word for it. He'd probably take her word for just about anything.

She sighed in frustration. "I wish I could just show you," she said. "You'd see."

"You offering to be my guide?"

She burst into a full, unrestrained smile. Margaret, as herself. It was the first time he'd seen it. He developed an immediate addiction. She tilted her head to one side and scrutinized him with such theatrical care that it was obvious she'd made up her mind to a question he wasn't sure he'd seriously asked. "Sure, why not?"

She sat up straighter as the waitress brought their beers. She took a swallow, full of the good cheer Santee would learn marked the prospect of any travel. "It's not a war, by the way. It's a revolution."

OVER A COUPLE MORE BEERS, MARGARET TOLD SANTEE THE story of how she'd first gotten interested in Mexico. She was fifteen and her global studies teacher, Ms. Tompkins, dedicated the first class after spring break to nineteen-year-old Jennie Pasquarella who'd spent her spring break from Barnard College getting kicked out of Chiapas for documenting human rights abuses instead of getting kicked out of some beach bar for barfing on the table. Ms. Tompkins pointed at the world map, hung so that south was on top. "Tell me where Chiapas is, and I'll give you an A for the day." Ms. Tompkins was that kind of teacher. Only Margaret took the dig seriously. She was that kind of student.

That night, she got on the Web and found out where Chiapas was, why Jennie Pasquarella was there, who the Zapatistas were and what they were fighting for, who Subcomandante Marcos was. She read his communiqués and thought they were the coolest . . . essays, stories, fables—she didn't know what to call them—she'd ever read. She was desperate to understand them better, but knew nothing about the politics. She'd never heard of any of this stuff before. She'd been ten in '94 when the uprising began. She snuck down to the kitchen and made a pot of coffee. When she went to school next morning, she hadn't slept, couldn't have slept. Her mind was buzzing with the Mexico she'd gleaned from the Web, a buzz that persisted for the rest of her life.

She found out that one party, the PRI, had ruled Mexico since 1929 with corruption and violence and greed, while the peasants' lives, especially the Indians', got steadily worse. Her own government, her own President, had no problem calling that a democracy.

She found out where Morelos, Chihuahua, Veracruz, Guerrero, Oaxaca, Aguascalientes, Torreón, Acteal were. She downloaded maps, photographs, music. Her room began to look and sound like a cross between a geography class and a Mexican bus. She met Hidalgo, Juárez, Diaz, Madero, Zapata, Villa, Carranza, Obregón, Cárdenas, Salinas, Zedillo. She read about NAFTA, GATT, and the IMF, about PRD, PAN, EZLN, CNI, CIOAC, and UNORCA. She'd halfheartedly skated through Spanish classes in the past. Now, she started teaching herself, struggling through *La Jornada*'s website every morning before school. Her senior year she tried to persuade the Spanish teacher to redirect the Spanish Club trip from Costa Rica to Chiapas but was told, "Chiapas isn't safe." Even then, Margaret knew her comeback, "Ignorance isn't safe," wouldn't get her anywhere, but she couldn't help it. It felt too good to say it.

She would be asked many times over the years, Why Mexico? What is the fascination? As one quickly former boyfriend put it, "You've got poverty, corruption, and disease right here at home. What do you need Mexico for?"

Her counselor—the one her mother sent her to—called it her encounter with the *Other*—which, Edith, the counselor, explained, was really an encounter with her Self, strongly implying that any old Other might do, because the true business of life was Self-Knowledge. Margaret disagreed. Here it was, the country *right* next door, and it was so mysterious and alien. It humbled her, she told Edith, who seemed to think that humility was a bad thing. "Envision yourself as powerful," Edith suggested.

"I am powerful," Margaret replied. "I'm a middle-class white American. I'm too damn powerful."

"Can't you see yourself apart from those empty social categories? As simply a human being?"

"I'm a human being who lives an incredibly pampered life without giving anything back, stuffing my face with burgers made from cattle grazing on land stolen from people starving to death without hope or rights or freedom. Why, just for us to sit here and talk for an hour costs my parents more than a Mexican making sports utility vehicles like the one you drive makes in two weeks. Just how much of that am I supposed to forget before I can call it 'Self-Knowledge'?"

Later on in life, in the less combative arena of a restaurant or living room, she'd say she set out to understand the world, one country at a time, but could never quite finish the first one. When she understood Mexico she'd move on to somewhere else—assuming she could still get around after a few hundred years.

The irony was, from the very beginning, that the more she studied Mexico, the more clearly she saw her own country, and the more deeply that troubled her. At the end of that first year in global studies, Margaret stayed after class and asked Ms. Tompkins, "What do you do when you decide your own country is on the wrong side?"

Ms. Tompkins was loading up a box with the contents of her desk. This didn't register on Margaret. "You keep your mouth shut if you want to pay the bills."

"You don't mean that. You don't keep your mouth shut."

"People don't want to listen, Margaret, and I don't have a job."

Ms. Tompkins' contract hadn't been renewed because of "unprofessional conduct." The new global studies teacher, Mr. Branwell, hung the map right side up and didn't take kindly to Margaret's caustic remarks about American foreign policy. But still Margaret didn't see the wisdom in Ms. Tompkins's advice. She became infamous for violating the school's rule against wearing clothing with "political content" dozens of times. Her going to a counselor in the first place had been part of a deal her parents struck with the school to keep her from being suspended.

When Edith declared her a hopeless case, Margaret came to school next morning wearing a shirt with a picture of the Earth, reading,

INDUSTRIAL NATIONS,

WITH 22% OF THE PEOPLE,

CONSUME

60% OF THE FOOD,

70% OF THE ENERGY,

AND 75% OF THE MINERALS.

She was suspended before she made it to her first class. She appealed the suspension, arguing that facts alone weren't political. She lost. She called the ACLU, who enthusiastically took her case. She wore her first amendment shirt to the trial. She lost. Her appeal was dropped as part of a deal to allow her to graduate with her class.

By this time, her parents had lost all patience with her, and her father had become seriously ill. She'd caused enough trouble, she admitted, just wanting her father to get better, though she secretly believed she hadn't caused enough. She went to college and helped look after her father. He died the week before she graduated. That summer she finally made it to Mexico, and she'd been there ever since.

Santee listened to her stories, told as if they were cautionary tales warning off any reasonable man, with the growing conviction that she was the most fascinating woman he'd ever met.

THE DAY AFTER THEY MET, SANTEE AND MARGARET STARTED traveling around Mexico together for what ended up being several months. He'd had his doubts that more of Mexico was what he needed, but she'd been right. He couldn't escape what he'd witnessed. He still woke up in the middle of the night, his heart racing, screaming out in horror. But he was beginning to understand where he was. It wasn't just some train wreck he'd found himself in the midst of. Or maybe it was, but it was better to wake up here than in some hotel room in Houston when the dead came to him asking why they'd died. He had no answers for them, but at least he was looking.

He was seeing almost everything differently. Time seemed to move differently. He'd never traveled like this before—with no plan except to go to the next place that caught their interest. It made the whole thing like episodes in a story. From Ocosingo to San Cristóbal to Carmen de Arcotete to Comitán to Tsimol to Tziscao to Tuxtla Gutiérrez to Teapa to Huimanguillo to Herradura to Malpasito to . . .

Margaret preferred the predominant Mexican mode of travel—the second-class bus from city to city, *colectivo* (old minivans with wooden benches for seating) to the smaller towns, footpath into the countryside. Some places, the usual transportation, called a *camioneta*, was a pickup truck with benches along the sides and an iron framework overhead for the standing passengers—by far the majority—to hang on to. Santee, who'd never even ridden in a Greyhound, found he actually enjoyed hanging off the back of a truck winding up a narrow mountain road, especially with Margaret beside him.

She took her guide role seriously, weighing carefully what she wanted to show him next. "You really should see this," she'd say, and off they'd go. Sometimes, he felt like someone being taken home to meet the family. Or families. They were scattered around the country—people who took her in as if she were their daughter. And even though she and Santee slept in separate beds, she took relentless teasing about having a *novio*. The translation varied from "sweetheart" to "fiancé," but the idea was clear. Margaret denied; Santee hid behind the language barrier. But more and more, he wished he were her *novio* in any sense she liked.

But it was as if there was an invisible barrier between them. Even when they went to some little town and shared a room with two beds to save money, talking late into the night, neither one crossed the room to the other. Even when Santee woke from one of his nightmares with her arms around him, he didn't kiss her lips as he longed to do.

Santee wasn't sure why. He kept remembering Felix's observation: *A woman like that, you must be willing to give her your heart, nothing less.* At first, Santee thought he might be afraid to risk such a commitment. But that wasn't it. He was afraid—as much as she liked him, or even *because* she liked him so much—that he would offer his heart and she would refuse it. He couldn't bear that.

Now, months and miles from where they'd met, he was sitting on the crowded porch of a country store at midday, his back against the wall, watching her talk with one of the locals. She sought directions to the nearby town of Candelaria where she'd heard there might be cabins to rent. She wanted to go there, as far as Santee could determine, because she'd never been. That was fine with Santee. Everyplace they'd been so far, even the tiniest village, Margaret had visited at least once, sometimes with some other man whose only role in the story was to turn the pronouns plural now and then, at least in the versions Santee was getting. He wanted to be the one who went someplace with her for the first time. He tried not to think about who might be hearing Santee's story in a few years. *We went to Candelaria. We traveled together for a while. I don't know where he is now . . .*

Her informant was a barrel-chested man in blue work clothes faded down to gray. His shirt gaped open where buttons were missing. The remaining buttons didn't match. He hadn't shaved in several days, and, like everyone else crowded onto the shade of the porch, he was drenched in sweat. He pointed at the line of four *camionetas* parked across from the store, then up the road, then beyond to the mountains, his hand moving back and forth like a fish. He had a nice smile, studded with silver fillings. Santee couldn't get over how friendly and helpful most everyone was. He tried to imagine this scruffy-looking man walking around the States asking strangers for directions. He'd be in jail in no time.

Watching Margaret's bright-eyed face as she chatted with the man, Santee believed she could charm anyone, anywhere. At the moment, they were somewhere near the intersection of the Tabasco, Chiapas, and Veracruz borders, but he wasn't quite sure which state they were in. Yesterday, when they'd been hiking out in the countryside, an old man with a frail herd of goats pointed out the three states from a high plateau. He didn't sound too impressed with any of them.

He was a small man, even by Mexican standards, with a handful of stones he shook like dice. Now and then he'd toss one at the goats to herd them. Like Nico and Francisco had done, Santee remembered, and the memory sickened him all over again. He looked out at the mountains and valleys. The whole country seemed to be nothing but mountains and valleys. When Cortés was asked to describe Mexico he'd wadded up a piece of paper and spread it on a table. The important boundaries in the countryside didn't seem to be latitude or longtitude, but altitude—the rich in the fertile valleys, the poor up here.

As the old man talked, the crackle of gunfire echoed through the canyons in such a way that it was impossible to tell where it came from. "La guerra," he said, shaking his head.

Margaret asked if there'd been much fighting in the area.

"'Fighting'? No 'fighting.' Low-intensity warfare," he said carefully in English, repeating the media euphemism. "En otras palabras"—he smiled bitterly—"solo los indios muerten." In other words, only Indians die.

Before Santee came to Mexico, he'd been vaguely aware of some "civil strife" in the country, nearly always linked with "narcotraffickers," "leftists," or both—dismissing the story before it was even told.

What he found was a government making war on its own people, but quietly, discreetly, so as not to upset potential investors. And the United States was providing the firepower. Even though Web drugs had pretty much dried up the American drug market, the United States still provided military hardware to the Mexican army, supposedly for the War on Drugs. There was no shortage of helicopters, Hummers, bazookas, rocket launchers, flamethrowers. Truckloads of heavily armed soldiers might show up anywhere at any time. American surveillance satellites tracked rebel movements for the Mexican army, while the American government deplored Mexico's human rights abuses for the news. It was a tired old dance, but no one seemed to care.

The rebels, seriously outgunned, kept a low profile. Any one of the people who filled this porch—men, women, and children—might be the "enemy." But mostly they were just people trying to survive. Everyone seemed to work all the time, including the children. What educational system there'd been had collapsed under the war. Margaret and Santee had seen more than one former school building riddled with bullets or reduced to rubble by a bazooka. Any teacher willing to work out here, the government reasoned, had to be an enemy sympathizer stirring up trouble anyway.

The media conspired in this drama by ignoring it. The important stories were the rise in oil prices, the dip in the Dow. Mexico, with a growing number of billionaires, was the poster boy of the global economy. These *campesinos* didn't know how good they had it.

Margaret came back across the porch and sat down beside Santee. He handed her a bottle of water, and she took a deep drink. "That's Antonio," she said. "He told me that all these people are here because the government was supposed to be handing out fertilizer today. But the fertilizer trucks are about two hours late, and all the *camionetas* are waiting to take everybody back home. He said if the trucks haven't shown up in another half hour, the *camionetas* will head up the mountain. The red one's the one we want." She poured some of the water on her head. "It's too hot to leave this porch anyway."

"Did you ask him about Candelaria?"

She laughed. "He said the place should be avoided at all costs, that it was full of *maleantes*, 'criminals,' *ladrones*, 'robbers.' "

"Doesn't that bother you?"

"You hear that all over the country."

"I'm not sure what I've heard," Santee said. He'd sworn off using a translator, trying to resurrect his college Spanish. There were times he thought he understood, but just when he grew more confident, he understood nothing. At first the accent around here had thrown him. Everyone dropped the *s*'s off the ends of words so that *buenos días* became *bueno día* or *además* became *ademá*. In the language tapes everyone talked like a newscaster from Mexico City.

"I'll show you," Margaret said and stood up. "Excuse me," she said in Spanish to a woman standing beside them. "Do you know Malpasito?" Malpasito was the town they'd just left. They'd stayed in a *cabaña* by a stream rented out by the *ejido* to the occasional tourist. In the evening, the locals would stop by to visit, usually with several children in tow to meet the Americans. Santee's favorite was a little boy who sat on the other side of the stream and held his hands to his eyes to form pretend binoculars. When Santee looked back in the same pose, the boy erupted in gales of laughter. They kept this up morning and evening the four days they were there. Santee's last view of the place as they walked out, children trailing along beside them, was this little boy calling and waving, then holding his hands up like binoculars.

At the mere mention of Malpasito, however, the woman on the porch clutched at her chest and denounced the place in no uncertain terms. Santee couldn't follow everything, but he caught the words *ladrones, maleantes.* Margaret let the woman elaborate as she caught Santee's eye and winked.

"Only just last week a woman was raped and murdered up there," the woman said in Spanish, and Santee understood every word. "The robbers asked for her watch, and she refused to give it to them." Santee was proud to have navigated the pronouns, even as the story gave him chills. The woman made a slitting motion under her throat that needed no translation. "Where are you from?" she asked Margaret.

"The United States," Margaret answered, a faint smile on her lips.

The woman gasped. "She, too, was from the United States." She shook her head at the dark irony of it all.

Margaret thanked the woman, reassuring her they'd changed their minds about going to such an awful place, then slid down beside Santee and whispered in his ear, "How do you suppose she knew the detail about the watch? She must be one of the robbers, no?" They shared a quiet laugh. This little drama was supposed to persuade Santee of the foolishness of his fear, but it lingered just the same.

ABOUT AN HOUR LATER, WORD CAME FROM SOMEWHERE that the fertilizer would not arrive today after all. Perhaps Tuesday. The assembled farmers took it better than Santee would have, with only an occasional curse and a shake of the head. They'd lost a whole day's work, spent some of their precious cash to travel here and back home. Then they'd have to do it all over again on Tuesday. "They can't decide," one farmer observed, "whether they want to shoot us or help us, so they do both—but neither one very well."

Everyone who'd been on the porch climbed into the four *camionetas.* There were easily thirty people in each one. The benches were given to women with small children and old people. Everyone else stood except for a few young men who hung off the back and sides. The four *camionetas* lurched into motion and started the long climb up the mountain. Santee and Margaret climbed onto the last *camioneta,* the red one. Santee had a good view as the tallest person in the caravan.

One by one the others turned off and plunged into a valley as the rest honked their farewell.

Finally, the one to Candelaria was the only one still climbing. With each turn, the road grew steeper and narrower. At the steepest places, the young men dropped off and trudged alongside until the *camioneta* had revved its way up the rise and the driver had ground second gear into submission. Transmission repair, Santee decided, would be a survival skill in Mexico.

Rock slides made the road narrower still, and thunder clouds filled the sky and rumbled all about. Santee would've been terrified if everything hadn't been so beautiful. Huge blossoms sprang from the cliffs, a waterfall misted his face as they whipped around a curve.

When hard rain started falling, one of the men joked with everyone, "We're going to get a free bath! Did anyone bring soap?"

They were all soaked through, laughing. Packed in with all these people swaying like a stand of trees, Santee felt jubilant and alive. Margaret stood directly in front of him. He rested his chin lightly on top of her head. The smell of her wet hair filled him with longing. She smiled up at him. "Isn't this wonderful?" she said, and it was. She was.

THE RAIN SLACKED OFF. ONE BY ONE THE OTHER PASSENgers disembarked, disappearing into cornfields or forest, until there was only a woman and her two children sitting on one bench and Margaret and Santee sitting opposite. Margaret asked if they were from Candelaria, and the woman answered yes, but when asked if there were cabins to rent she said she didn't know. The children, slumped on either side of their mother, hovered between sleeping and waking. She shook her hips to rouse them.

They'd reached the very top of the mountain. The road played out, and the *camioneta* bounced to a stop in the middle of a rock-strewn meadow. A couple of burros on tethers grazed, noting their arrival with a stamp and a snort. The woman handed her children down to the driver and jumped to the ground. Margaret and Santee climbed down onto the rain-drenched rocks. The driver took their fare and pointed to a footpath. "Candelaria," he said. The woman and her children were already hurrying out of sight down the path. The driver started to climb back into the cab.

"*¿Cuándo vuelve, usted?*" Santee blurted out. When do you return?

The panic in his voice brought a smile to the driver's face. He held up the requisite number of fingers as he answered, to make sure Santee understood: seven in the mornings, five in the afternoons. "*¿Hay cabañas allá?*" Santee asked.

"*No sé.*" The driver spread his hands and looked around the meadow to indicate that this was the extent of his knowledge of Candelaria.

Margaret watched this transaction with apparent amusement. The *camioneta* turned around in the meadow and headed down the road leaving Margaret and Santee alone. The rain had stopped altogether, and the air was heavy with the scent of wet grass and wildflowers. The remaining clouds were reddening in the sunset.

"You speak Spanish fine when you have to," she said with a smile.

"Doesn't it bother you that the woman said there aren't any cabins?"

"She said she didn't know, which just means she didn't want to tell me for some reason. She'd *have* to know. It's a small place."

"Why wouldn't she want to tell you?"

"I don't know. Maybe she doesn't like the people who rent them. Maybe there aren't any, and she didn't want to be the one to disappoint us."

"So maybe there aren't any?"

"I thought you knew that already."

"I did, but I just thought . . ."

"What?"

He laughed, giddy and nervous. "I don't know. You've got these great instincts. You always seem to know where you are and where you've been, and then you get some notion and take off to see what's around the bend and it always seems to work out."

"This still might work out."

"I know. I didn't mean that. It doesn't matter, really. I've just been following along. It's been incredible. And here we are, just about as close to the middle of nowhere as I'm likely to get, and I just wanted to tell you . . ."—he took a deep breath and looked into her eyes— "that I would follow you absolutely anywhere."

She looked stunned, and for the first time since he'd known her, like she wasn't so sure where she was. She looked out over the valley, squinting as if trying to see something very distant, then back to him, offering her hand and tossing her head toward the path. "Shall we go check it out?"

When he took her hand, she held it tight and pulled herself into his arms, and they kissed for the first time.

THEY WALKED THE PATH TO CANDELARIA SIDE BY SIDE. IT climbed over a rise and descended into a bowl. The town itself lay below them along the banks of a rocky stream. Low log houses—Santee counted thirty—were scattered in the woods, their cook fires' smoke curling up into the sky. The path broadened into a narrow road and wound down to the stream, then across and up the other side. Women washing clothes downstream stole furtive glances at them, though their children stared openly.

Other children had spotted them first and shadowed them into town, running on ahead. Santee could hear their shouts—"*¡Turistas! ¡Turistas!*" The first adult to greet them was a woman who leaned out her glassless window and pointed up the road, answering Margaret's question before she could ask it: "*Allá arriba.*" A scrawny dog with a cowering grimace slunk alongside them. His companion, a waggy, darting fellow, led the way, beagling his excitement.

Coming down the road toward them was a man with a half dozen children from eight to sixteen. He was grinning from ear to ear.

"*¡Bienvenidos!*" the man called over the sound of the dogs, the children, and the rushing stream.

"*Buscamos a las cabañas,*" Margaret shouted back.

Santee knew they'd indeed found a place to stay for the night when the smallest boy danced in circles, transported with joy.

THE CABIN WAS MORE LIKE A SMALL DORMITORY DESIGNED for school groups, with bathrooms, cots and bunk beds, a propane stove and lanterns. Diego's children swept furiously, hauled in mattresses, scoured the sinks, mopped the bathroom floor. Diego sat at the ten-foot table with Margaret and Santee, apologizing for the mess. He explained that *eco-turismo* was supposed to have revitalized the town, but that they were the first tourists in eighteen months. The promised road had never been built. The electricity came and went. There was the war, of course. There was always the war. And now there was the Web. The children lifted up their heads at the word.

"I was told no one would come anymore. Do you think that is true? Are you the only ones?"

Santee wanted to lie to him, but couldn't justify it. "Yes. I'm afraid so."

"Well then," Diego said. "You must have a good time while you are here." His wife brought in a fried chicken, tortillas, beans, coffee. After they'd eaten, the family lingered and visited.

The oldest girl, Sylvia, put on Santee's translator and asked him about the United States: "Does everyone have a computer? How many cars do you have? Why do the big dogs go to school with the black children?" Diego explained that Sylvia watched the television when there was power. The youngest boy perched on Santee's lap and cautiously touched his beard, giggling as if it tickled his tiny fingers. Meanwhile Diego talked politics with Margaret at a clip Santee couldn't follow.

As if by some signal, the family gathered itself together by the door and said their good nights. For the following day's expedition Diego suggested a hike to *Las Cascadas De Enamorados*, the Waterfall of the Lovers, deep in the *pura selva*, the unspoiled forest, and Santee and Margaret enthusiastically agreed.

Diego wanted to leave one of the older boys with them for security, but Margaret negotiated with Diego in low tones—Santee couldn't catch it all—and the entire family left, smiling at Santee as if they knew something he didn't.

"Pretty nice *ladrones*, wouldn't you say?" Margaret said as she closed the door after them.

"They should call the place *Ladrónvilla*," Santee said. He followed her into the bedroom as she lit candles, pushed two of the cots together. "What were you talking to Diego about—*Luna de miel*? Moon of something. What's *miel*?"

"Honey," she said, stripping off her clothes and stretching out on the cots.

"Oh," he said.

He lay down beside her and took her in his arms.

"*Bienvenidos a Ladrónvilla*," she whispered. Welcome to Robbersville.

CHAPTER
THREE

SANTEE DIDN'T FORMALLY QUIT NEWSREAL UNTIL SOME months after he and Margaret left Candelaria. They were staying in Campeche. Lounging in bed after lovemaking, the daily afternoon thunderstorm raging outside, lightning flashing from their sweat-slick flesh— it seemed like a lark, an adventure, to accept an invitation to meet a *bruja*, a witch. Reynaldo, a tourism student who'd been showing them around the local ruins, had invited them. The *bruja* was his grandmother. Margaret was eager. She'd never met a *bruja* before. Santee was hesitant, suspicious even. And though he hadn't admitted it to Margaret, a little afraid.

But that was okay. She'd be there with him. He traced the contours of her back as she called Reynaldo and made the arrangements for the following afternoon.

THE *BRUJA* WAS AN ABRASSIVE WOMAN WHO LOOKED VAGUELY pissed off except when her eyes fell on Reynaldo, whom she obviously doted upon, grabbing his head and hugging it as if he were still a little boy, though he was a good foot taller than she. He bent over so she could reach him, grinning and blushing the whole time.

She made it a point up front to tell Santee and Margaret she never charged for her services, but she had to talk with them awhile first to see if they were worthy. She was like that, brimming with self-importance. She proceeded to tell a series of stories with the identical theme—how wise and infallible she was, and how gruesome were the misfortunes that befell those who ignored her pronouncements. Heartbreak, miscarriage, suicide, lingering painful disfiguring disease—nothing was too horrible for these fools, who richly deserved their fate.

It wasn't exactly Santee's idea of wisdom. He preferred Socrates humbly calling himself a fool (though admittedly he seemed to relish making fools of everyone else). The *bruja*, at least, had no desire to *make* a fool of you. She assumed you'd accomplished that before you showed up on her doorstep.

They sat in a garage that had been turned into a living room by covering up the door with paneling, scattering carpets around the concrete floor, and painting walls and ceiling turquoise. A skylight of green fiberglass made everything glow even greener. Margaret and Santee sat on a musty sofa that reeked of cat piss. Reynaldo and his grandmother flanked them in aluminum folding chairs. The cats, sleek and well fed, lurked on the periphery, occasionally weaving in and out of the *bruja's* legs. Somewhere in the back of the house the grandfather could be heard coughing the cough of a dying man. Neither cats nor husband distracted the old woman from her endless, self-important monologue.

When the preamble was done, she turned her attention to Margaret, who patiently listened to something about being "incomplete" or "behind" or something like that. He couldn't follow it and didn't want to. Margaret was a confirmed atheist—what was she doing listening to this nonsense? Why had he ever agreed to this? He struggled unsuccessfully to get comfortable on the lumpy pile of cushions, releasing a fresh cloud of cat stench. His stomach turned over. Would it be too rude if he just got up, excused himself, and walked out? He didn't belong here—not in this house, not in this country.

All of a sudden, the witch fixed him with a deadly stare. "*Y tú. Esperas, esperas, esperas. ¿Por qué?*"

And you. You wait, you wait, you wait. Why?

Or she could mean "hope." It was the same verb in Spanish. That made sense to Santee. Waiting always implied some element of hope or dread, didn't it? Or maybe that was his own neurosis. He didn't have to ask her what she was talking about. Maybe she didn't even know. It was enough that he did.

"*Sin razón,*" he told her. For no reason.

She smiled as if to say I told you so. Reynaldo held his head high, proud of his grandmother's performance. He'd told them she was a "true witch," *bruja verdadera*. Santee was convinced. He still didn't like her, didn't think he'd ever like her. But as she settled back in her creaking aluminum chair with that smug smile spread across her face, it was Santee who felt humbled.

＊　　＊　　＊

JUST AS THEY WERE FINALLY LEAVING THE BRUJA'S HOUSE, Margaret had decided she needed to go to the bathroom. Reynaldo was already in the back of the house. It was just Santee and the *bruja* standing in the kitchen. She looked him up and down. "*¿Quiénes mataste?*" Who did you kill?

He didn't think he could've heard her right. "*¿Cómo?*" Pardon?

"*¿Quiénes mataste?*" She enunciated each syllable with sarcastic precision.

This was too much. Who the hell did she think she was? "*Nadie,*" he snapped at her. No one.

She smiled her smug smile again. "*Mataste nadie. Lo diga.*" You killed no one. Say it.

He just stared at her, his mouth open. "No, you don't understand," he wanted to say. "You weren't there, you don't know."

"*Lo diga,*" she insisted.

One of the cats had jumped onto the kitchen counter and was drinking at the dripping faucet. Santee watched its quick tongue. "*Maté nadie,*" he said at last. I killed no one.

She patted his cheek as if he were Reynaldo. "*Escucha a tus fantasmas,*" she said. "*Te contarán.*" Listen to your ghosts. They will tell you.

At the sound of Margaret's return, she held a finger to her lips. *Our little secret.*

"WHAT WAS ALL THAT ABOUT YOU WAITING AND WAITING?" Margaret asked as they were walking home. They smelled like cinnamon and rosewater. The *bruja* had given them a *limpia,* a cleansing—the usual mumbo jumbo of chanting and dousing with herbal concoctions— for no charge as promised. Reynaldo had stayed behind to visit with his grandfather.

"I think she was talking about NewsReal."

"It's getting to be kind of a long vacation."

"Exactly. I'd say it's time to move on, wouldn't you?"

When they got back to the hotel, Margaret took a shower—*limpia* or no—and he went online to have it out with Inez. It didn't take long. When he told her he was quitting, she could hardly contain her joy. NewsReal hadn't fired him, afraid he might make trouble. Now that problem was solved. He resisted the temptation to make a pointless, righteous speech, and she promised to give him a glowing recommendation. "The news isn't for everybody," she reassured him, her virtual hand on his virtual shoulder for what he hoped was the last time, and he managed to stifle any of several snide comebacks that came to mind. But what would be the point? Inez wasn't the enemy.

Why had he waited so long to quit? For a while there he'd entertained the notion that he might somehow persuade them to run the story. He could see now that even if they had, it wouldn't have accomplished anything. They would've stripped the heart out of it, edited it down into some digestible misfortune like a schoolyard scuffle. Worse, their version would've become the received truth of the matter, unassailable by anything as paltry as an eyewitness. Their site counter would number in the billions, and who was he to argue with that? It seemed only fair—truth by majority rule.

But still he hadn't quit.

He wanted to think that it was for the usual reason—that he wanted to put off figuring out what to do with himself. The nightmares had slacked off. He was coming to terms with it, right? But just because he'd stopped screaming didn't mean he understood anything, and it certainly didn't mean he had a clue what to do about it.

He'd killed no one.

He'd known that, but he hadn't really, until he'd stood accused. That's what he'd been dragging around—guilt. When he let it go, he didn't have to wait anymore, he didn't have to wonder what he hoped for. He'd already started listening to his ghosts. Off and on he'd been working on a virtual fiction site he called Rincón. "Corner." As in backed into. He had a notion of how he might bring Rincón to life, but he'd been putting it off. The *bruja* had given him the nudge he needed.

After leaving Inez, he checked the sound in their hotel room and heard Margaret's shower still running. While he still had the momentum from quitting his job, he called on Woody, an old friend from college. Back then, no one could stand Woody except Santee. He was boorish, arrogant, shallow. Not much had changed, except that now Woody was also filthy rich. He'd invented a sim assembler reputed to be the very best. A couple of years ago, Santee had run into him at the second wedding of a mutual acquaintance. Woody had managed to annoy almost everyone there, but he'd given the bride and groom a pricey virtual safari, and so the guests put up with him, sucking up to his wealth. Woody camped by Santee all evening and bitched about their hypocrisy, driving away any other social contact Santee might've had. As they'd parted, Woody gave him his private address, making a big deal of it. At the time, Santee never dreamed he'd use it.

Woody's personal site was a nerve-racking place, a big city park with automobile traffic encircling it, honking and roaring and fouling the air. Helicopters swooped through skyscraper canyons. Sirens wailed and dopplered to imply disasters offstage. In Woody's world there was apparently no oil shortage. The drivers of all these vehicles were sketchy, like images painted on the windshields of toys. The main occupants of the site looked like derelicts, wandering up and down, sprawled on the benches, perched in the trees. Several of them were vaguely familiar. One staring into his footprints in the mud beside the duck pond looked exactly like Einstein.

Woody called his invention FACTS—Fiction Activated Cyber Thespian Simulator. He loved to explain it: "I simply taught it to read fiction, or more accurately, to read everything *as* fiction. Character and plot— a real Aristotelian. Doesn't matter what it is—the phone book, *David Copperfield*, Einstein. One of my most in-demand sims, by the way. Everyone wants to hang out with a genius—as long as he's not real." He jerked his head back and sniffed the air in a gesture that suggested his own genius had not made him popular.

"Anyway, after it reads something, anything—every word and image ever published on JFK, a few Aesop's fables, a Roadrunner cartoon, or a Chilton's manual, doesn't matter—it develops thorough simulations of all the characters."

"A Chilton's?"

He rolled his eyes. "Obviously you have to use the personification function."

"Obviously."

"But here's the best part—the character isn't bound to its story. So I can supply a particular character's role at any licensed site, and it will read any interactions there as fresh incoming plot and respond plausibly, convincingly, and *in character*, or your money back. You can always feed the character new texts, and it incorporates them into the mix for greater subtlety and complexity. Or you can instruct it to rely on a few key texts to the exclusion of all others—an Einstein, for example, based solely on his famous letter to Truman. After a while, not surprisingly, a sim needs closure or it grows stagnant or dissociative. So I replace them after a year—keeping a few special ones here with me. The customer can get a fresh Einstein or Barbie or whatever, or sign on for a new character altogether. I also have a character-of-the-day program just under way that's a real bargain, and a truly huge courtesan business—limited editions."

Santee said, "I don't want to buy anything, Woody. I want to make something—a novel I guess you'd call it." He explained his idea to Woody, who sat uncharacteristically silent, just listening. He didn't even roll his eyes again, his trademark gesture.

"You want to deliberately subjectify these sims."

"That's right."

"And you just want to use FACTS for *free?*" He almost choked on the last word.

"Consider it a donation to the arts."

"You going to get legal nonprofit status?"

"No."

Woody made a face. "Course not." He shook his head in dismay. "Do you need recording equipment, too?"

"I still have my NewsReal rig. I'm supposed to give it back, but it's custom-made. It'll only work with me. They won't bother to come after me if I hang on to it."

Woody nodded his approval at Santee's proposed theft. At least that part made sense. As Santee continued to explain what he had in mind, Woody shook his head, snorted in disbelief—his usual conduct at a seminar or dinner table. "You realize that FACTS can just take all this data in any form without you in the mix at all, don't you?"

"I know. That's not what I want."

Woody sighed heavily, thinking hard. Santee could guess the struggle going on inside Woody's head. On the one hand were the two principles he'd built his life on—intellectual property rights and greed. You didn't give anything away, ever. On the other hand, the product Santee described was totally worthless in Woody's eyes. It wasn't as if Santee would benefit in any way discernible to Woody. Somewhere in Woody's memory also must've been the many nights he'd crashed on Santee's sofa after being thrown out of yet another place. One of the communal houses had even gotten a restraining order to ban him from the premises—for *his* protection they said, since several vegetarian pacifists residing there had sworn to murder him with their bare hands if they ever saw him again. The only girlfriend Woody ever had in college left town her senior year after dating Woody for six months, and was rumored to have changed her name and moved to Fiji. Now, according to the press, Woody's only companions were his sims. A recent birthday party, attended only by his sims and reporters, had made for a bit of fluff news for a day or two, complete with interviews of his more wacked-out guests.

Finally, he decided. "Shit. Why not? If you want to waste your time, why should I stop you? I can download the software right now if you want."

"Thanks. You can check out the results on the Web."

"A freebie site, I suppose."

"Of course."

"If you want to write, you know, I can always use writers."

The Einstein sim had rolled up his white duck pants and was wading into the pond, then out again, backing up, carefully placing his feet in the same footprints, watching the results as he lifted them high with a sucking sound.

"Thanks, but I want to work on this. It's a labor of love."

The phrase seemed to amuse Woody, and he softened for a moment. "You have a girlfriend these days?"

"No. I have *the* girlfriend these days."

"Figures, doesn't it? Me—I've never labored for love."

Santee and Margaret continued traveling around Mexico on the cheap, living off Santee's savings and Margaret's stock income, taking the occasional translation job or putting together a website for a hotel in exchange for room and board. Santee didn't directly record their journey. Instead, in the evenings, he'd write about the day in his journal, recording himself in the process. He recorded himself reading everything he could get his hands on about Mexico, especially firsthand accounts by gringos like himself besotted with the place: Rosa King, John Reed, D. H. Lawrence. All these recordings were loaded into FACTS, along with his recordings of the massacre he'd witnessed and his journal entries since he'd come to Mexico.

He didn't know how he was going to make sense of it all, but he threw himself into trying. Unlike his experience in the real Mexico, Rincón settled into a country of one town, Ladrónvilla, rendered as a few blocks, Rosa King's hotel at the center of it—the now ironically named Bella Vista since it offered a view of nothing. Like Margaret's attempts at understanding the world one country at a time, his imagination had staked out one street corner.

During *siesta*, while Margaret usually slept, he'd go to Rincón for a few hours and hang out with whichever characters came forward of their own volition, and talk with them, question them, argue with them, or listen to their stories. He called this process revision.

Before long he saw that he wasn't making sense of Rincón, but Rincón was making sense of him and the world he escaped from. He hadn't had a Ms. Tompkins like Margaret—or maybe he had and just hadn't noticed. He would've been too dreamy to get the point of upside-down maps. The characters in his fictional dream, however, were fond of stripping away his illusions. Zapata, turned studious and brooding, told him stories and fables, but didn't care to hear much about the twenty-first-century state of affairs. John Reed, on the other hand, couldn't get enough of it, pounded the table as he railed against the capitalists. Then they'd drink and talk about women they loved.

Nico and Francisco played in the streets, down the alleys, calling to each other, pitching stones against the bullet-pocked walls. They only let him get but so close, and they would never speak to him. Once, he chased them into a dead-end alley, only to find nothing there but a pile of burning furniture.

Shortly after reading Rosa King's account of the Mexican revolution, Santee had tea with her in Rincón on the verandah of her hotel, a much leaner vision than he'd imagined as he read, but she seemed content with it.

"It's quite gone, you know. What it once was. I rather think it's better that way, don't you? All that money and finery when so many had so little." She'd been a British widow trying to run a hotel in a foreign land when all hell broke loose around her in 1910. And even though she lost everything and was forced to make a terrifying flight through the mountains—fleeing Zapata's rebels—her sympathies were with the downtrodden peasants who'd suffered under one bully after another, ever since Cortés. As Santee had read her book *Tempest over Mexico*, he kept thinking how little things had changed in over a century. She told him, "We are on the wrong side, you and I, the moment we set foot here, despite our best intentions. We, therefore, must be particularly careful to do the right thing. It's such a temptation merely to deplore this and question that. But in the end, we must do the right thing."

This speech haunted him. The war, once sprawled over most of Mexico, had been contained in recent months to Oaxaca, Guerrero, and Chiapas. A particularly bloody assault with helicopters and armored vehicles on rebel strongholds in Oaxaca and Guerrero had left the only active resistance where it began—in the mountains of Chiapas.

A century before, the revolution had come to Rosa King. Santee had no such opportunity or threat. Increasingly it seemed to him, if he were going to do the right thing, he had to go to the revolution, to return to Chiapas, where a little over a year ago now he'd witnessed the slaughter of 176 men, women, and children, an event still officially written off as feuding clans in a world that arrogantly saw itself as a "global village."

So one night in Cuetzalán, he told Margaret what he'd been thinking and she hugged his neck. "Let's do it," she said. "It was okay in my twenties to just wander around with my heart in the right place, but I've seen too much for that. Let's find the war and enlist."

SHORTLY THEREAFTER THEY APPLIED FOR JOBS WITH INtrepid Explorers ("Wherever you want to go, we've been there first!"). One of their headhunters had approached Margaret and Santee in Tlaxcala about working on the Mexico update. They were desperate for help, especially from those willing to travel in the wartorn south. The fact there was a war going on made it all the more attractive to IE: People liked going places they couldn't go in the real world; it made them feel important and adventurous. At first they'd said no, but the more they thought about it, the more it seemed like the perfect cover, allowing them no-questions-asked travel at company expense with sophisticated recording equipment. They hoped to supply information to the human rights organizations, eventually make contact with the rebels and offer their services to them. As it had been from the beginning, the war in Mexico was waged as much or more with propaganda as with guns.

They'd been worried IE would be suspicious of Margaret's politics and Santee's quitting NewsReal, but those things didn't seem to matter in their interviews. She knew her way around Mexico, and he had recording experience—that was all IE seemed to care about.

A couple of weeks after their interviews, Santee came offline one evening, and Margaret told him, "We got the jobs." She had a bottle of Champagne and their tin travel cups ready to celebrate. "They just called on the phone."

"On the phone?"

She laughed. "I know. Weird isn't it? Josh—that's our, ta-da, *Regional* Supervisor—says he finds the phone 'more personal.' "

"He does, does Josh? We have a Regional Supervisor?"

"Most definitely," she boasted. "Why, I bet there's even a *Continental* Supervisor."

"A *Global* Supervisor?"

"Absolutely."

"Get out of town! What about a *Galactic* Supervisor?"

"Oh yeah. We're bad: There's an *Intergalactic Universal Supreme* Supervisor."

"Jeez. Who's over him?"

"Her. The CEO, of course."

They laughed, popping the Champagne and toasting their new careers as travel correspondents. "There's something I have to tell you," Margaret said. "Our first assignment is Friday. They want us to go with some meditation group to record their experience of a 'power vortex' on top of some pyramids."

"Sounds like it might be good for a laugh."

"The pyramids are outside Ocosingo."

Santee felt a rising panic, but fought it down. "That's right where we wanted to go."

"They have us staying at the Rancho Estrellita. That's the place you told me about, isn't it? The man in the macadamia grove? He must be Zachary Taylor Hayman. According to Josh, Zack and his wife, Edie, own the place."

Santee lay back on the bed. "Jesus." He studied her face. This was the break they were looking for, legitimate entry into the heart of the war zone, a center of known rebel activity. It was almost too good to be true. The next assignment could just as easily be wheezy old Cancún—Gringolandia, as Margaret called it—worse than being deported. Still, she wouldn't pressure him to go, careful and protective of his delicate feelings.

He sat up and drank off his Champagne, poured another cup, and topped off Margaret's. "Tell Josh we'd like to get down there early to scout it out before the vortexers arrive. What the hell's a vortex anyway?"

She smiled at him, her eyes full of love, held her cup aloft, and proposed a toast. "¡*Bienvenidos a Ladrónvilla!*"

They clicked mugs—"¡*Bienvenidos a Ladrónvilla!*"—and drank.

"Are you the supervisor of Ladrónvilla?" *she asked in the role of earnest ingenue.*

"Certainly not," *he replied brusquely.* "We're all anarchists here in Ladrónvilla."

"Except those who aren't."

"Pre-cisely."

GEORGE, THE LEADER OF THE MEDITATION GROUP, WAS born in Hong Kong but grew up in Atlanta. He billed his expedition as a fusion of the mystical traditions of East and West—the Mysterious Orient meets the Ancient Mayans. Most of his clients were middle-class white Americans in their thirties looking to add to their stockpile of meaningful experiences that someday in some way would coalesce into some personal theology or vision or both. Santee had no problem with that, but it wasn't *his* vision, and soon George lost all patience with him.

Every morning for a week, Santee, with fifteen of the faithful, trooped up to the top of the tallest pyramid at the right time of the morning, aligned himself with the energy flux lines George said were coursing through these old stones like subway trains, did the series of breathing exercises and physical contortions George guided them through—but nothing happened.

From atop the pyramid, Santee had a clear view of what had been the land invaders' settlement. There was little sign that it'd ever been anything other than a pasture. Black cows munched lazily on grass fertilized by the blood of murdered Indians, and Santee felt anything but transcendent.

Everyone else in the group was wide-eyed when it was over, babbling excitedly as they disentangled themselves from their pretzel shapes and headed down the pyramid for some hearty chow and obtuse debriefing at the Estrellita. Santee felt nothing except low back pain and a little hyperventilation dizziness. Listening to the others gush about their vortex experiences, Santee alternately wanted to scream or sleep. Sleep usually won out. Unfortunately for George, no matter how transcendent a time everyone else was having, Santee was the one doing the recording. Without a decent recording, neither George nor the Rancho Estrellita would find their way onto the IE site. They could continue to drum up real participants from the dwindling pool of real live travelers, or they could tap into the swelling torrent of virtual adventurers and be rich. Enlightened or no, they wanted the bucks.

Zack was an unlikely innkeeper. From what Santee could glean, Zack, a transplanted Idahoan, had been in Mexico since before Americans switched from real to virtual drugs. He had a certain stoned charm, a "whatever" philosophy that treated war, famine, plague as water off a duck's back. Only Santee knew what Zack'd witnessed standing in his burning grove. You could see it in the contracted corners of his eyes when the conversation dwelt upon the war, and he'd stand and clear dishes, freshen drinks, slip out into the yard for a toke. They never spoke of their encounter, and if Zack recognized Santee, he never let on.

Zack did allow one evening, when he'd cornered Santee in the kitchen, that he wished things were going better with George. He suggested that Santee might get more out of George's sessions if he smoked a litte pot or ate some mushrooms first, but Santee declined the offer. Edie, for her part, offered Santee her own therapy by getting drunk every night and coming on to him.

After a week of this, Santee and Margaret went for a walk in the valley. She said she had something to tell him. He stood in the middle of the green pasture, using the watchtower at the army base and the Estrellita as points of reference.

"This was the middle of town," he said. "The way I figure it, they bulldozed everything under, bodies and all." He kicked at the ground where the soil seemed to arc and revealed a rusted bicycle rim. He looked off toward the hills wondering if there was still anyone there who'd survived that day. He imagined them watching him—the witness returned to the scene of the crime.

Escucha a tus fantasmas. Te contarán.

"If we stay here another day," he said, "I'm going to lose my fucking mind."

She put her arms around his waist and laid her head on his chest. "*Then* maybe you can experience enlightenment?"

He groaned, "Fuck enlightenment," and kissed the top of her head.

She nuzzled his chest. "I detect some negative energy jamming up your chakra. 'Deep, healing breaths, deep, healing breaths.'"

She did an excellent impression of George. He smiled, barely. She was trying to cheer him up, and he didn't want to be cheered. Then he remembered and said, "You had something to tell me?" more to change the subject than to find out. "Please tell me that Josh says we can give up on this Georgia Grasshopper and get out of here."

"Better," she said, looking up at him. "While you've been having fun getting your energy overhauled, I've made contact with the Zapatistas."

"You're kidding. Who?"

"Hermalinda, the maid here. She approached me, actually."

"What did she say?"

"She says Subcomandante Marcos wants to meet with us."

"Marcos?" He finally had the whirling sense of vertigo he'd been seeking all week. "Marcos is dead."

"Apparently not. He found out about us through your site."

"Rincón? Marcos has been to Rincón?"

"As a matter of fact, that's where he wants to meet us tonight."

"Tonight?" was all he could manage. He couldn't help wishing he'd revised more.

MARCOS HAD BEEN THE INVENTION OF RAFAEL SEBASTIÁN Guillén Vicente during the first Zapatista uprising in '94. He was the spokesman for the group for many years, and was popularly known as the first revolutionary to use cyberspace. Without their high visibility on the internet, the Mexican government would've squashed the Zapatistas immediately, would never have negotiated with them. In fact, it was doubtful that the Zapatista insurgency would've ever become real in the eyes of the world. But that was a long time ago. Both the Web and the revolution had changed. The Web, like everything else, had become a booming capitalist enterprise with little patience for idealistic and bad-for-business revolutions. The quaint notion that the Web would make the world a better place had been about as prophetic as similar pronouncements about television. Though calling it a web had been unintentionally insightful.

Marcos had dropped out of sight in the midst of Mexico's brief flirtation with democracy at the turn of the millennium. Some said irrelevant, some said dead. But before the collapse of the Mideast under a radioactive cloud, before the U.S. invasion of Venezuela when they attempted to nationalize their oilfields, before the Mexican ruling party was put firmly back in the saddle by the United States to "promote stability and the rule of law" in what by then amounted to an American labor colony and oilfield—there'd been Marcos.

So when the Zapatistas rose again, so did he, though in the meantime the Weisiger interface had transformed the Web. Marcos had been a poet—perhaps something of a windy one—but a poet nonetheless. He was a creature of words, and cyberspace had lost interest in words. A man in a ski mask talking and smoking a pipe? Who cares? Where's the experience?

There were many who said this new Marcos wasn't really Vicente anyway, but a stand-in. There were rumors of competing subs popping up around the Web. It scarcely mattered. He'd become quaint. His reappearance on the Web was treated as if it were the nostalgic revival of a TV show or a pop singer. He promptly vanished from public view for the second time. There were a few who claimed he was still alive, still the brains behind the Zapatista cause, that he had gone into hiding for the good of a revolution that desperately needed to be taken seriously. But scarcely anyone believed these claims.

He was gone. Like Che or King. That's what Santee had thought. Until now.

He'd read all the Subcomandante's writings into FACTS, but Marcos had never presented himself as a character in Rincón before. Santee had wondered why not, given his enormous opinion of the man, and now he knew. Santee had set the FACTS preferences so that it wouldn't replicate himself or any other real visitor to the site. He didn't want to meet himself just yet and didn't imagine other people did either. So if the real Marcos had been visiting the site as Hermalinda said, a fictional one wouldn't appear. It wasn't too hard to figure how Marcos would've gotten the address. He'd have a webwatch out for any new site dealing with Mexican culture and politics.

The bizarre thought crossed Santee's mind that this Marcos could be a FACTS-generated sim and—true to the ironic persona that had inspired it—was choosing this convoluted means of stepping into the plot. He shrugged off the idea, laughing at his paranoia. He'd been up on that damn pyramid a few too many times. Woody's program was clever—he was constantly learning its subtleties—but it wasn't *that* clever. And, besides, Marcos had contacted them through Hermalinda, not in Rincón.

AS IF HE DOUBTED THEY WOULD TRUST HIS AUTHENTICITY IN any other guise, Marcos waited at the Bella Vista for Santee and Margaret wearing his trademark ski mask, pipe in mouth. Helene Pontipirani, Romanian journalist and spy during the first revolution, sat across the table in her riding clothes. There were no horses in Rincón, but she was usually dressed to ride, right down to the crop.

She was saying to Marcos in her deeply accented, sultry voice, "I find that when things happen, it is generally because someone has made them to happen!" She was very erect, as if on horseback. Her cheeks were flaming, and her eyes were bright. It was a shame there wasn't a wind to blow her hair back. "That is what I like in people," she said, "the power, the force, that make things to happen!"

Marcos laid his pipe on the table and pulled off his mask, tossing it on the table in front of her. "You should like this then," he said with an amiable smile. "Masks make things happen."

Helene, apparently uncertain whether she was being made fun of, tossed her hair over her shoulder and noticed Santee and Margaret standing in the street. She spoke to Santee. "What are you doing here?"

"We've come to speak with the Subcomandante."

She stood, tall and willowy and restless, slapped her thigh with the crop. "Very well." And then to Marcos, "You and I, we will speak again soon." She walked through an archway into the hotel.

Marcos, too, had stood. He watched her go. "She is quite something," he said. "It's easy to see why Zapata was in love with her."

"Not all historians accept that as true."

Marcos chuckled. "But in Rincón it's true, is it not?"

Santee laughed. "Yes, I guess it is."

"She didn't accept your gift," Margaret said, pointing to the mask still lying on the table.

"I didn't think she would. It was a test."

"Did she pass or fail?"

"It wasn't that sort of test." He held out his hand. "I am Subcomandante Marcos. Ms. Mayfield, Mr. St. John, I am honored." He shook their hands in turn. "I thank you for meeting me on such short notice. Shall we sit?"

Santee couldn't help noticing that they'd been here only moments, and already Marcos had taken charge in the politest possible way. They sat at a table and spoke of drinks and food as if the place were real, deciding by consensus to forego an imaginary repast. Perhaps another test.

Marcos was a handsome man with thick hair and mustache, now

grown gray. His skin was smooth but for sunlines around the eyes. Smooth and white. Marcos himself was not an Indian, but dedicated his life to indigenous rights, though he probably wouldn't have seen it that way. If democracy excludes anyone, it's not democracy, not for anyone. Santee remembered Marcos's disarming refrain: *Para todos todo, nada para nosotros.* For everyone everything, nothing for us.

"I don't wish to be rude," he said, "but I can't risk staying here long. There are still those who make it their business to determine my whereabouts. May we get down to business? Hermalinda tells me you wish to help, and that you work for IE. We have information that IE is developing a new recording interface. Have you heard of it?"

Even before they started working for IE, Santee and Margaret had heard rumors of a new technology under development—a completely internal nanoassembled interface that would not only record the senses but also the subtleties of perceptions, thoughts, and feelings. Current recordings would be cartoonish by comparison, particularly in the realm of emotions. It was rumored to be ready for beta testing.

"I've heard of it," Santee said.

"I want you two to volunteer for testing. We have a use for such an interface."

"To document the fighting?" Margaret asked.

"The fighting is over. We can never win by force of arms. There is only one way. For too long the camera has been aimed at the victims. It's time the victims became the camera. We hope to give everyone in the Web the experience of being one of us, direct and unedited. We hope to shame the world into justice by installing this interface in thousands of poor *chiapanecos* and flooding the Web with their lives. Will you help?"

It took them a second to comprehend the enormity of what Marcos was proposing. When it hit them, almost simultaneously, they gasped at such an incredible act of faith in humanity. They wanted so much to believe humanity was worthy, how could they possibly say no?

CHAPTER FOUR

ALMOST TWO YEARS LATER, SANTEE WAS FINALLY CHOSEN to field-test the new interface. This was no surprise to Margaret. He was the emotional one, the one who could see a poem in some rusted-out bus overgrown with vines or be moved by fishermen casting their nets. And that's what the new interface was all about—the complete experience, feelings and all, the stronger the better.

"Intensity's what we're after," the tech told Santee. "Passion!"

They don't know what they're letting themselves in for, Margaret thought. She certainly hadn't. His passion was contagious. She'd always thought of herself as levelheaded, a poor candidate for being swept off her feet. And she hadn't been—she'd leapt. She'd gotten along fine on her own for years. She hadn't been moping through life, longing for some man to make her life worthwhile. But now she didn't know if she could stand the loneliness without him.

For her part of the plan, she'd requested a reassignment to a straight editing job in the States, claiming she was burned out on being away from civilization. To sweeten the story, she hinted to Josh that her romantic relationship with Santee had cooled, and he seemed to buy it even though he'd seen them together many times since they'd been working for him, and they were obviously crazy about each other. But people were always ready to believe that things fell apart.

Santee ingested the interface inside a fine-tuned Weisiger field inside an impenetrable concrete bunker inside a mountain somewhere in Nevada with every molecule monitored and accounted for. After a couple of weeks of testing, they sent him back to Mexico to wander about and feel deeply. They even encouraged him to witness "military actions" as long as they didn't present a personal danger to himself and the IE property that resided in his nervous system.

A temporary loss of signal from a men's room in the Mexico City airport didn't seem to concern them, however.

With the installation file in the thing's memory and a sample of Santee's blood—drawn and downloaded in a bathroom stall—some techs Marcos recruited reverse-engineered a copy. They passed it to Margaret on her flight to DFW inside a tiny Chivas Regal bottle that showed up on her tray during a trip to the bathroom.

She took it to a nanofabricator in Dallas, who made it on the sly between more legitimate runs. It was a slow process—a few hours stolen here, a weekend there. When a batch was done, she sent it to Santee in Mexico disguised as an allergy medication. For the most part, Margaret's job was to wait and wait and wait in a rack-and-stack. With their cover story of a love gone bad, they were advised it would be risky to even see each other on the Web unless it was strictly business, performing a chilly show for whomever might be watching. They'd worked out a simple code before she left, so they could warn each other if something was wrong or blow each other a kiss, but it was no substitute for love or sex. She pretty much hated everything about her new home. It was like moving to hell.

Dallas was the most soulless place on the planet, the heart of the heartless global economy. If the love of money was the root of all evil, Dallas was evil's arboretum. Its Web presence was huge, state-of-the-art. It hadn't been a real place for so long, a shrine to disposable architecture that could go anywhere and went nowhere, it was no stretch to move lock, stock, and barrel onto the Web. The old skyline—a dense stand of glass and steel penises thrusting high into the heavens—was growing shabby from neglect in reality, but it still looked good from the air, and the Web version was the envy of every boy in the schoolyard.

Technically she resided in the town of Collinsville, though Dallas-Fort Worth was one big indistinguishable sprawl of rack-and-stacks all the way to the Oklahoma border. It was amazing how a place packed with so many people could appear so lifeless. From the airport to her new residence by Smartcab, she didn't encounter another living person out and about. She was the odd one, turning off the Web in the cab, looking out the thick, heavily tinted windows with about as much to see as from a bullet traveling down the barrel of a gun. Whoever kept all this up and running stayed out of sight. Margaret already had a pretty good idea what they looked like—dark and poor and not from around here.

She'd never lived in a rack-and-stack before. Hers was Harbour Haven—"The Very Finest In Online Living." She rented the place online, giving it a virtual once-over and surrendering her credit number. The reality was even worse than she'd imagined, and she'd told herself it would be awful. She paced it off, then just paced. The damn Weisiger chair sat like a throne in the middle of the room. She managed to wrestle it into a corner. She tried to shove the PowerStroller out the door, but the thing wouldn't budge. There were no windows, of course, but even propping the door open proved problematic. A chime and a concerned voice warned her the door was ajar and she risked robbery and/or assault. She spent an afternoon trying to disable the contacts on the door but only succeeded in convincing the voice that the door was open whether it was or not. She found the speaker in the ceiling and plunged a screwdriver into the heart of it until it fell silent. She would not be getting her deposit back. But if all went according to plan, that would be the least of her worries.

She figured the only way she could stay sane was to make herself a real life out of whatever came to hand, establish some sort of routine. She found her way up to the flat roof, which offered a vista of some miles in all directions. There wasn't much to see but range grass, mesquite trees, concrete, and asphalt. Virtually identical boxes dotted the landscape. The jumble of an abandoned shopping district lay to the southeast. On a clear day, the Dallas skyline glistened on the horizon like the logo for this wasteland. Except for the mostly driverless vehicles out on the smart road, there were no signs of human life. It was the same no matter where she looked.

But there was air and sun, the moon and stars at night. Birds, mostly vultures; coyotes occasionally; crickets and cicadas; spiders, flies, and ants; lizards. She was grateful for any evidence the planet was still alive. She made her meals up on the roof on her single-burner solar stove, ate picnic style on her poncho spread out on the warm tar. She strung up sheets to provide some shade from the brutal sun, walked or jogged laps around the perimeter a few miles a day, downloaded novels— though they were increasingly hard to find—and read. From memory and photographs, she sketched scenes from all her years in Mexico and, too often for her own good, portraits of Santee. She stuck them up on the walls of her cell and talked to them.

Months and months went by. It was getting close to the end, with one more batch of the interface to be sent to Santee. She waited for the fabricator's delivery. And then one afternoon, just before dusk, she thought she saw someone else on a rooftop like her own a couple of miles away due south. She hurried down to her place and returned with her binoculars, but by this time the light was fading quickly and details were murky. She couldn't be sure which rooftop she'd been looking at, but she patiently studied a cluster of them. Just when she was about to give up, she was rewarded with a glimpse of light, coming and going, seeming to dance about. A flashlight beam. She hurriedly sketched the cluster of buildings, marking the one with the light with glow lines like a lightbulb in a cartoon. In the morning she rose early and began to watch the place.

There was no one there. She had, perhaps, been deceived by a trick of the light or her imagination. But what else was she going to do? So she kept on staring at the one box among dozens. It was like chanting a mantra. And then, when the sun was high and the rooftop was bathed in light, she was rewarded with an oddity—a glimpse of green. The rack-and-stacks themselves were pastels—powder blue, lavender, pale pink, aqua. Some of the older ones had the names painted on the side in huge letters, but the new ones were largely anonymous. Who was going to read them? But on the roof of this one, an uninspired beige, there was a patch of bright green, a couple dozen square yards or more. Her binoculars weren't very powerful. The Texas sun made everything shimmer as if about to evaporate. She couldn't be certain of anything at this distance. But she thought she knew what she was looking at, especially when, in a gust of wind, it swayed back and forth. She could almost imagine the sound it made. Her neighbor was growing corn on the roof of a rack-and-stack. This was someone, she decided, she must meet.

She had a Smartcar at her disposal through IE, but accessing it was no simple process. At least twenty-four hours before she wanted it, she was supposed to submit a route request stating her destination and business, both of which, in this case, she'd have to lie about. IE wouldn't regard making a face-to-face call on a total stranger part of her job. She didn't bother. She decided to head out cross-country. She got on the Web and pretended to be shopping around for a new place. After a half-dozen virtual tours, piecing together aerial views into a map of sorts, she was fairly certain the place she was looking at was called Renaissance Square West. Unfortunately, a smart road cut a swath between her and her destination. It would be easier to make wings like Icarus and fly than to cross a smart road on foot.

CAUTION: FENCED AND SECURE FOR YOUR COMPLETE AND TOTAL SAFETY, the roadside signs claimed, and they were deadly serious. The electrified fence went deeper into the ground than a bunny could burrow, higher into the sky than a deer could leap. If anything bigger than a field mouse moved anywhere inside the roadway without a trip code on file, it was vaporized with a laser weapon that was the only real success of SDI. Its short range made it useless for star wars or even orbital wars, but it could fry a rattlesnake or a person across twelve lanes of traffic with no problem. And if there was a problem, with the flip of a switch miles away, the whole thing could be shut down and made accessible to Authorized Personnel only, whoever they might be. She'd seen the cops screaming past while all the other vehicles sat perfectly still like a field of stones. Every tenth one, more or less, had a life inside.

Even if you weren't actually stuck on the road, they were the only way to go anywhere, to get out of the burbs, or even go from one to another. Margaret and all the rest of the rack-and-stack populace were prisoners whenever the road was shut down. And, since they weren't the ones with their hands on the switch, they were as good as prisoners all the time. A little exploration was in order, she decided. More than anything in the world, Margaret hated to feel trapped. She wanted—she needed—to find the back door. Besides, if she didn't get to set foot on real ground soon, she'd go crazy.

When she visited her mother on the Web, she let slip some of her feelings of confinement. Her mother suggested a bike ride up some volcano in Hawaii. "I did it last weekend, and it was marvelous!"

"It was a website, Mom. You didn't go to Hawaii."

"Oh, what's the difference? It was real enough for me, I can tell you. You should lighten up, Megs, and enjoy life."

"I'm glad you had a good time, Mom. I'll keep it in mind."

Her mother knew she was being brushed off but let it pass. They'd both learned a lot over the years about getting along through careful editing. Her mom didn't have the faintest clue what Margaret was really doing with her life. When her mother asked about work, Margaret imagined telling her the truth:

Yeah, Mom. Work's fine: I'm working with Mexican revolutionaries, stealing top-secret state-of-the-art hardware from a major multinational and handing it out for free to dirt-poor peasants. If my employer finds out

I'll go to jail for the rest of my life, unless the Mexican government shoots me first.

What she really said was, "Yeah, Mom. Work's fine. I really enjoy working at home." She didn't feel guilty for keeping the truth from her mom. She only hoped her mother had her own secrets she wasn't telling.

Margaret studied the map again and found a creek running under the smart road a couple of miles east. If she couldn't cross the road, she'd go under it. As she imagined the journey, she felt a rush of excitement and anticipation. She had to smile at herself. She'd found an excuse to get out and about. She could stay caged up for only so long.

HER FIRST OBSTACLE WAS TO MAKE IT TO OPEN GROUND. No allowances had been made in Harbour Haven for anything so quaint as a pedestrian. The local tram would take her to the Harbour Haven Marketplace and Pharmacy or to the smart road access, both dead ends on foot. The roads used by the delivery vehicles were a possibility, but they had their own security cameras and ID codes she'd rather not deal with.

Instead, she lowered a rope from the roof (her clothesline twined and knotted together), and climbed down to the ground below. She hadn't done any climbing since college, and it was kind of a kick. There was a stockade fence about ten yards behind the building for who-knew-what reason that was leaning at a forty-five degree angle. The remnants of a hurricane had blown through here last year, and no one had gotten around to fixing the fence. She walked up it like a ramp, and it pitched over farther. She walked to the end, and hopped to the ground three feet below. Ahead of her for as far as she could see was mesquite and sand. She checked her compass and headed toward the creek.

The plan was to follow the creek south, under the smart road, then another mile or so south, then head back toward Renaissance Square. Renaissance Square West was actually the southwest building of the north, south, east, west square of buildings. Other than the smart road, her biggest problem would be to distinguish Renaissance Square from the other rack-and-stacks. Maybe she'd have to listen for the rustle of the cornstalks.

She'd started out at dawn to avoid the heat. There were other animals about with the same idea. Jackrabbits bounded across the landscape like tiny kangaroos. Horned toads skittered out of sight with surprising speed.

Despite the optimistic twittering of the birds, the air already felt hot and heavy, the ground still radiating yesterday's heat as the new day began. By the time she reached the creek, she was drenched in sweat.

The creek itself was a disappointment. Any resemblance to a real creek had been obliterated with piles of basketball-sized concrete-gray boulders dumped inside to channel it. Somewhere under this rubble, a trickle of water flowed, but it would take a good hard rain before it was visible. So much for her fantasy of cooling off in the water. The air above the boulders shimmered with heat. About a hundred yards away, a rattlesnake sunned itself where fish should be swimming. If it was rattling, she couldn't hear it over the sound of the smart road just over the horizon to the south.

She walked along the bank for as long as she could until dense scrub forced her down into the ditch full of boulders that made up the creek. It was hard on her feet, and she was always on the lookout for snakes, but she made good time to the smart road. It stretched from horizon to horizon and was as loud as the ocean. Where the creek crossed under it was a chain-link fence with No Trespassing signs attached every few yards. Electrification and running water didn't mix, so at least it wasn't hot. She got up close to one of the signs and read the paragraph of legalese below the main message. This was a highway right-of-way, it primly advised, the property of the State of Texas and under the jurisdiction of the Highway Commission. It never said why, but it made clear in its awkward way that you could do time for cutting this chain-link and slipping under the road. As if to make clear how much they didn't care, person or persons unknown had already cut the chain-link and peeled it back neatly to either side making a triangular doorway like the entrance to a teepee. This was the first good sign she'd seen all day.

She thanked her wire-cutter-toting benefactor and passed under the road. The shade was delicious, but she didn't dare linger. Security cameras panned the shadows. There was no avoiding them, so she waved instead. "Just passing through," she called. A matching doorway parted the chain-link on the other side, and she stepped into the sun again with a sense of triumph. She was past the damn road, and others had come this way, too—others she could find if she put her mind to it.

Her original plan had been to continue down the creek, but she'd had enough walking on boulders. Besides, going up the side of the western bank was a trail to the top. At the foot of it, someone had patiently lifted the boulders off the creekbed and piled them in a ring to form a small pool of open water. She cupped some in her hands. It was silty but smelled clean and fresh. She drank to demonstrate her solidarity with whoever had made this pool, refilled her water bottles, and splashed her face and body. She chugged up the trail with renewed energy.

The trail continued at the top, angling southwest through a small stand of oaks and pecans, roughly in the direction of her destination. She followed the trail as it wound through the woods, past rack-and-stacks and service roads, through cracked and weed-grown parking lots, skirting civilization and following its seams. She wasn't surprised when it led her to Renaissance Square West, and a brown metal door with MAINTENANCE stenciled across it.

It was locked. She did the only thing she could. She knocked.

Nothing.

Locusts sang in the oppressive heat.

She knocked louder, with conviction.

Nothing.

She stepped back and looked up. A dark face overhead abruptly withdrew. She tried to figure out what she'd seen—man, woman, adult, child—she had no idea.

She cupped her hands to her mouth and hollered. "Hello! I live across the smart road to the north. I've come to visit."

Nothing.

"I just want to make friends."

Nothing.

"Please! It's hot. I've come a long way."

Nothing.

"Fuck it," she muttered to herself. She leaned her back against the door and slid to the ground. She looked out at the baked landscape and pondered her options. It was about noon. The temperature was in the low nineties and climbing fast. In the building's shade—four feet wide and shrinking—it was only barely tolerable. She'd have to find better cover, maybe in the tiny oak woods, wait till dusk to set out, slinking back to her hole at nightfall. Fortunately, she'd brought her flashlight. She took a drink from her water bottle. It was almost empty, but she had another in her pack. She had a can of tuna, some crackers, and an orange. She wasn't going to die, not from this trek anyway. This place though—this godforsaken warren of zombies—that could make her wish she were dead, even if it was too cowardly to kill her outright.

Sometimes she thought there wasn't a place on Earth where she belonged anymore—an educated, upper-middle class white American girl who hated the Web. It seemed obvious to her the thing was evil. It had created a world that confused solipsism with individualism, capitalism with democracy, information for thought. No, she reminded herself, it wasn't the Web that did all those things. It was only the means. The people on the Web lived the lives they wanted, the lives they thought they deserved for being born in the right place. They just chose to ignore that almost everyone else in the world was struggling just to survive.

There wasn't a problem, she'd often been told, that couldn't be solved by sitting in that damn Weisiger chair and going online. She pictured her own, bought and paid for—rented at least—waiting just a few miles away. "Here, hon," it seemed to say, "sit down. Take a load off."

No. She couldn't give up so easily. She had seen a face. She was sure of it. She closed her eyes and tried again to picture it. She had a vision, a hunch, or wishful nostalgia—she couldn't be sure which. She stood up again and cupped her hands to her mouth. "*Vengo del otro lado del carretera inteligente. Soy amiga.*"

The face appeared again briefly, then vanished. She was sure this time. It was a man, a latino, twenty-five or thirty. Fifteen minutes passed and Margaret slumped dejectedly against the side of the building. No one was going to let her in. Why in the world would anyone invite an obviously insane *gringa* into his home?

She stared into the sky. High above her, pilotless planes circled silently, waiting to land at DFW with paper clothes made in China or car parts from Brazil. She imagined herself boxed as cargo in the belly of one of those planes, flying back to Mexico.

And then the door opened. The man she'd seen before leaned out and beckoned her inside. He glanced over her head, and she followed his gaze. A camera sweeping the area was headed back in their direction.

She didn't hesitate to follow him, closing the door quickly behind her. Beyond the doorway was a stairwell. Her host was already a flight above her. He went all the way to the top, and she followed. When she stepped onto the roof, she found herself inside a shelter fashioned from old tarps—blue, green, yellow—strung from the stairway entrance. In front of a plank table set for a meal stood the man, a woman, and two children. Behind them, on the north side of the roof, stalks of corn waved in a raised bed. They were real after all.

The man, Sebastian, introduced himself and his family—Beatríz, his wife; Manuel and Blanca, his children.

Margaret introduced herself.

Everyone beamed, and Sebastian invited Margaret to join them in a simple meal of beans and tortillas. She almost wept for joy. The delay in answering her knock had been to ready their home to receive a guest.

"I would love to," she said.

This was the sort of thing that was only supposed to happen on the Web, one of the supposed advantages of virtual reality—getting what you wanted when you wanted it. But she hadn't virtualed her way here. She'd found it, serendipitously. True serendipity was a rarity on the Web. It was too easy to think you knew what you wanted and just go there, doomed to the exercise yard of your own imagination.

They ate off disposable plates, battered with age, salvaged from richer folks' trash. There were no utensils except a wooden spoon in the pot of beans. Beatríz cooked the tortillas on a piece of corrugated metal hammered flat in the middle, the heat source a smoldering fire and the blazing sun. A sweet tea Margaret had never tasted before was served in clay bowls the same orange-red as the landscape. The children— Manuel looked to be about four and Blanca a year or two older—ducked their heads and giggled whenever Margaret smiled at them. She was completely enchanted.

She resisted the temptation to quiz them about their lives, as if to call them to account, but bit by bit she found out their story. They were Guatemalan. Sebastian's brother Salvador had originally been the maintenance man for Renaissance Square as well as the adjacent complexes Victorian Manor, Sherwood Green, and Colonial Village. Sebastian came north to stay with his brother and look for work, but his brother died. Sebastian took over the job, and no one seemed to notice the change.

Sebastian complimented her Spanish, and Margaret told him he was much too kind. She told them she worked for IE, and though she couldn't detect any reaction, she couldn't help wondering what he thought of this admission. IE had a reputation for cowardice, for seeing only what the powerful wanted it to see, a reputation it richly deserved.

Are you married? they asked her, somehow less personal than her work, and all she said was no, feeling vaguely guilty for not acknowledging, married or not, that she had a mate, a mate she wished were here now beside her.

"Where did you two meet?" she asked Sebastian and Beatríz to deflect the subject from herself.

"*El Mall,*" Beatríz said squeezing Sebastian's hand, and Margaret wasn't sure she'd heard right. *El Mal* would mean "the evil." Then it struck her what they meant. "The mall." A shopping mall. They dotted the suburban landscape like the bleached bones of deceased dinosaurs, rendered irrelevant by the Web. Margaret had heard they led a new, clandestine life as gathering places for the underclass. The media treated them as a social problem in need of correction, a breeding ground for crime and drugs and depravity. Margaret was filled with curiosity. As if Sebastian and Beatríz could read her mind, they asked if she would like to go. *Al cine,* they added hopefully. To the movies.

The children cheered at the prospect.

BACK WHEN THERE WERE BUMPER STICKERS AND EVERYONE had at least one private car to put them on, a favorite in Dallas read A WOMAN'S PLACE IS IN THE MALL, and there'd been plenty of malls to choose from—dozens before it was over—sprouting up at the intersections of increasingly bloated freeways built to "alleviate congestion," a practice not unlike treating anemia with leeches. The precise name of this mall was lost in the smog of time. It was simply, to Sebastian and his peers using a half dozen different languages, the Mall, and it was packed. Quite unaware of the fact, Margaret had chosen a Sunday to come calling, and it was market day.

She'd had to argue with Sebastian to let her carry part of the load in her backpack. She was a guest, he said, and though he didn't say, a white woman. Even Manuel and Blanca had their burdens, and the bag of clay pots Beatríz waited to hoist onto her back must've weighed as much as she did. Margaret insisted. It was Beatríz who finally settled the impasse by placing her hand on Sebastian's forearm and squeezing. He turned to her, and she furrowed her brows and gave him a little nod.

Margaret could carry the spoons, he said, and they would be forever grateful.

So her backpack was filled with wooden spoons Sebastian had fashioned from the tops of school desks salvaged from an abandoned grade school near Renaissance Square. They'd rustled pleasantly like some percussion instrument as they walked the path back to the creek and up the other side, then on another mile to the mall.

The entrance of choice was through a ruined department store. The stock was long gone, but the naked mannequins, impossibly long and lean, towered over them in the dark, or sat squat, headless and limbless torsos cast from translucent resins. The children quickened their pace in the darkened store from fear or anticipation.

Beyond it lay the central core of the mall, bathed in light. It had been a huge place with four levels of shops. Four stories up, the ceiling was made of glass. Some of the panes were broken, and there were almost as many birds as people. The stores themselves were mostly dark and closed up. The action was in the open spaces, the broad promenades and walkways, the escalators demoted to stairs, and around a dry fountain that looked like a giant had thrust a fistful of rebar into a pool of wet concrete.

They found a place on the third level next to a Somali family and spread out their wares. Beatríz and Blanca, it turned out, would see to business, while Sebastian and Manuel took Margaret to the movies.

As they made their way through the crowds, she offered her hand to Manuel, and he took it. Sebastian greeted his neighbors, mostly brown and black, though there were a few Asians. Most everyone spoke Spanish with lots of English thrown in. "Hi" was the most common greeting, and almost everyone offered it to Margaret. She was one of the few white people in the place. No one asked her what the hell she was doing there.

She expected an old movie theater, but they walked right past one of those without stopping. The lobby was a sea of shattered mirrors. They went instead to what had apparently been a sports bar. One wall was a huge television screen with halves of football helmets glued to the wall around it. Homemade benches filled the bar and fanned out into the mall. Young men worked the perimeter, pitching the next show, selling tickets. The seats filled up fast, and Margaret and Sebastian were lucky to get two. Manuel sat on Margaret's lap. When the benches were packed full, one of the ticket sellers ran down and slid a disk into the player.

It turned out to be *The Postman* with Kevin Costner, dubbed into Spanish. It was doubly strange to see an apocalypse that hadn't happened and to hear Costner speak of *"Los Estados Unidos"* with a wistfulness it'd never deserved in Margaret's lifetime. She wondered how many of the people back when they made this movie would recognize the apocalypse that *had* happened—that was happening even back then—as an apocalypse at all.

She looked around. The audience—from Guatemala, Pakistan, Nicaragua, Cambodia, Zaire, Bosnia—watched with rapt attention. She wished she could see it through their eyes. They must identify with the inhabitants of a world in ruins.

The film left Sebastian very thoughtful. As they walked back through the mall, his face was somber. He glanced at Margaret several times, as if she were the problem he struggled with. When they came in sight of Beatríz and Blanca, he sent Manuel on ahead to join them and took Margaret aside.

"*¿Quién es?*" he asked her. Who are you?

She knew what he meant, and she told him. The truth. Hiding nothing. Maybe she was crazy, but if he was the enemy why wasn't he rich? He asked a few questions about the interface, about the logistics of the thing. He didn't seem to think it was a crazy idea at all. He laughed and shook his head. "*El Sub es un buen hombre.*" He looked back to his family, who were openly watching their conversation, then to Margaret. "*Yo quiero la interface por mi familia.*" He gestured around the hulking ruin of a mall. "*Por todo el mundo.*"

I want the interface for my family. For everyone.

Fair enough. She could try to get an extra batch for them. This one day alone was worth that. Margaret stuck out her hand. "*Viernes,*" she said. Friday. Just enough time for them to get onboard, she figured.

They shook on it. Later, she long regretted that she hadn't been able to make good on her promise.

SHE STAYED THE AFTERNOON, EVEN BOUGHT A PLANT TO liven up her place. When she got back to her rack-and-stack, a package from Phelps Nanotronics had been delivered, another batch of the interface ready to be sent to Santee. She sent Phelps a message, requesting another for Sebastian and was told it could be delivered on Friday. In the morning, she took the batch she had to her local pharmacy, one of the few businesses no one had figured out how to replace on the Web. People's bodies still went to hell lying around in their Weisiger chairs. The pharmacist, whom she understood to be a Zapatista sympathizer, took the caplets as usual and packaged them up as an allergy prescription for Santee St. John. The paperwork was impeccable. It all looked perfectly legal. This was to be the last. She and this pharmacist had been going through this charade for almost a year now. As he slid the package across the counter, Margaret broke her silence and said softly, "Thank you so much. This will do a lot of good."

"Don't thank me. I get paid plenty. I'm not in the 'good' business. Next."

Margaret mailed the package next-day international to Santee's hotel and rode the tram back to her place, all the while wondering: If the pharmacist was in it for the money, where was the money coming from?

She added this to her stockpile of questions for Santee, if they ever had the chance to speak openly again. He was scheduled to contact her on Thursday to let her know in code that he'd delivered the interface in Ocosingo, but he wouldn't touch her, wouldn't hold her, wouldn't kiss her. Even some virtual affection would be better than nothing. She chided herself for whining. It was as hard on him as it was on her, harder. No one was likely to shoot her around here.

She'd been worried about him lately. He complained of fitful sleep, bad dreams. He looked awful. But everything was going according to schedule, and soon, very soon, it would all be over.

Wednesday night she dreamed she and Santee went to the mall, but it was empty. The fountain had become *Las Cascadas de los Enamorados* and the roar of its waters, crashing down from floor to ceiling, filled the place with sound and spray. They swam naked in the chill waters and made love in the shadows of the department store, all the mannequins watching.

The next morning she couldn't shake the feeling that something wasn't right, and that night she didn't hear from Santee. She contacted his hotel but was told that he hadn't come back Thursday night. She looked for him at Rincón, but he wasn't there either. Somehow she had to get to Mexico.

THURSDAY NIGHT A CARNIVAL WAS GETTING UNDERWAY IN Ocosingo. Ancient Ferris wheels, Tilt-A-Whirls, games of chance. Most of the rides weren't set up, and those that were were still dark and motionless. But there was already a big crowd. Along one whole side of the *zócalo* were folding tables set end to end, covered with computers, twenty years old or more, bought up in the States at yard sales and

Salvation Army stores, the rusted blades of cutting-edge technology. Fat jumbles of wires wrapped in duct tape spilled off the tables on all sides.

At every computer young Mexicans huddled over the keyboard, jostling for a view of the screen, trying to explore the Web through an interface that'd been dead in the States for at least ten years—not even virtual, much less wireless. They could look, but they couldn't touch, like peeking through the windows of a mansion so you could pretend you were seated at an elegant feast inside, listen to the dishes and silver clink and imagine you were eating.

There were several soldiers in the crowd, some off duty, some not, all armed, all young. They wore a bewildering variety of uniforms— brown, blue, drab. Santee could never sort out all the police and military organizations that made up the armed presence in Chiapas. Though it was the ones who didn't wear the official uniforms you had to watch out for. These boys were simply a distraction—someone for government officials to point to, saying, "See, we're not killing anyone."

From his park bench in the middle of the *zócalo*, Santee watched six of the soldiers at the computer directly across from him playing around with a hump site, little more than dirty movies without a virtual reality interface. They were laughing at the one they called Ruiz, slapping him on the back, as he typed frantically, vainly trying to pick up a woman in cyberspace. The antiquated computer translated his poetic Spanish into nonsensical English, delivering it in a robotic monotone. "*My blood becomes a turkey. . . . You are a heart attack. . . .*"

Four men passed quickly in front of Santee, blocking his view of the soldiers for a moment. He looked after them, all in black T-shirts and black jeans stretched tight over lean, muscled bodies, and his heart froze. Down the line of tables, Jorge was moving toward him, glancing unconvincingly at the screens as he passed, not as if he really cared, not as if he was really just another kid out for a good time. If Santee hadn't known, if he'd been asked to guess the young man in the crowd on Zapatista business, he would've chosen Jorge, no older than seventeen or eighteen, a revolutionary from birth.

Jorge looked up just before they reached him, and the four men covered him like a black umbrella. Perhaps only Santee, from his low angle on the bench, could see the knife blade flash and disappear under Jorge's ribs. Perhaps only he saw Jorge fall face first, the four men moving past him like water flowing around a rock. Perhaps everyone saw, but like Santee they had to pretend it didn't have anything to do with them, that they didn't care much one way or the other whether this particular Indian, or any Indian for that matter, bled to death in the center of town. It'd happened before. Plenty of times.

Santee forced himself to watch the hapless Ruiz's progress on fuckalot.com, until there was a loud shriek from a woman who stumbled over Jorge's body lying in a pool of blood. All the computers were abandoned as the soldiers moved toward the screams, and most everyone else hurried home. Then and only then, Santee rose to his feet and looked off at the scene with a degree of curiosity appropriate for a drunk gringo at a carnival, and no more.

He headed off toward his hotel, hoping there was no one following him. He hadn't had a drink, but he feigned a stagger so that no one would think it suspicious when he stopped a few blocks from the *zócalo*, leaned over the curb, and threw up.

When he was done, he could hear soldiers' boots jogging on pavement, but he couldn't see them, couldn't place which direction they came from or where they were headed. Every dog in town was barking furiously. A woman was wailing inconsolably. It couldn't be Jorge's mother. She'd been murdered years ago. He wanted to sink to his knees and wail with her, whoever she was, howl with the dogs. For almost a year now Jorge and others like him had been meeting with Santee, taking the interface back to their villages, waiting for the big day.

He had to get a grip, get away. He thought better of returning to the hotel. They'd probably searched Jorge's body by now and, more than likely, found a room number, a phone number, maybe even his name. Or if they knew what Jorge had been up to, they already knew about Santee and would be waiting for him.

He had his computer. Everything else was expendable. He wished he'd brought his jacket—there was a chill in the air—but he could get along without it. He wished he could get online, but he didn't dare risk it. His silence would have to be message enough that something had gone terribly wrong.

The taxi drivers were on strike again, and half of them were informants anyway. He was better off on foot. He headed away from his hotel with a purposeful, unhurried stride. The town was only a few blocks across. It didn't take long to reach the edge. A path ran for six or seven miles through cornfields, pasture, and woods, out to the ruins and the Rancho Estrellita. Fortunately, there was a moon, and he knew the way. He'd been there before. A couple of times.

PART TWO

Tierra y Libertad

*One's homeland, I would add, is also made up
of those foreigners who are concerned for our
country as we, Mexicans, are concerned about
what happens in Chile or Argentina, Cuba or
Algeria, Ireland or California. There is a great
homeland of intelligence and love from which
no one can be expelled.*
—CARLOS FUENTES

CHAPTER FIVE

WEBSTER WEBFOOT—NOT HIS REAL NAME—LOVED HIS JOB stocking food units. He had a lot of privacy, a lot of time to think while driving his route. He'd see some other service folk out, but nobody got too close, and the customers were nearly always online or asleep or both. If a customer should perchance have a problem—a pickle, a jam, a fix, a hardship—Webster was only authorized to pass on the Bruce's Drive-To service rep address, so that the customer could have a virtual tantrum with someone who had "problem" in his job description, someone in management—what a joke—which was most everyone above Webster. There was nothing below but machinery and Developing Nations. They had their share of problems, which was why, apparently, they never seemed to develop anything but more problems; but as for Webster himself, he didn't believe in problems.

He was only seventeen, but it seemed to him that most people, most of the time, made their own problems, pumping them up, inciting others to lend their hot air to the cause, and pretty soon there was an organization, league, or society full of people who didn't have any real problems, dedicated to whining about the Global Crisis in X. People with real problems, Webster figured—starving, dying, getting-shot-at kind of people—didn't join societies, or if they did, they were labeled terrorist groups or fanatical cults—merely entertaining, if you liked that sort of thing—wiped out, if they actually managed to upset the status quo.

Webster, however, didn't have a problem, didn't want to upset anything. He had 576 units to service tonight, and he was racked and ready to roll. It was smart road out past Collinsville, where his route began, so he passed the time, as he often did, listening to a vocabulary-building program, while he practiced juggling. Tonight, it was oranges and adjectives. In the tiny cab of the trike, the challenge was not hitting the ceiling with them—the oranges, not the adjectives. He hoped the discipline of juggling in a cramped space would keep him focused and improve his concentration. The vocabulary program was one he'd done before—he needed to get some new ones—but he didn't care. He loved words.

"*Zealous*, z-e-a-l-o-u-s : Ardently active, devoted, or diligent. Frank is a zealous champion of the global economy. . . ."

They were Ms. Mayfield's oranges—the only fresh fruit on his route—mostly a meat-starch-veg crowd, who did their culinary adventuring in the Web. The oranges were supposed to be riding in the back with the rest of the food, but he'd spotted them in the inventory and liberated them. Oranges were too classy to ride in back with the common comestibles—the so-called "prepared food." "Tortured food" was more like it—dehydrated, reconstituted, irradiated, emulsified, processed, compacted, vacuum-packed—the sort of food only astronauts used to eat. They still called it Astronaut Ice Cream, and it still sucked.

Webster watched the oranges moving in a counterclockwise orbit, and smiled with satisfaction. He waited for the optimum moment and tried reversing direction, but one of the oranges grazed the dome light, bounced off his knee, and fell between the seat and the door. He managed to catch the other two and stowed them in his pockets.

He looked down beside his seat and could see a thin sliver of orange. He groped around trying to get a grip on it, but it kept rolling in place like a ball bearing. He changed his angle and lunged. He almost had it. Shit. He withdrew his wet, pulpy fingers. The cab smelled like an orange grove.

"*Scurrilous*, s-c-u-r-r-i-l-o-u-s : Low and vulgar. The ungrateful worker made scurrilous remarks about his employer. . . ."

This was a dilemma. He could log a DIT (Damaged in Transit), blame it on some mechanical malfunction, back order an orange . . . but he'd done that a couple of weeks ago, and more than likely nobody believed it then either, just entered it into his file. Nobody cared why, how, or whatever: When you screwed up, you got a strike; when you had enough strikes, you were out. There was some disagreement among the drivers about how many strikes you were allowed, but no one argued with the reality. One day you had a job, the next you didn't. One day you were on the schedule, the next you weren't. Bruce's prided itself on not allowing "interpersonal intangibles" to enter into personnel decisions, thus ensuring the highest possible degree of "equitability." Though

Webster doubted *equitability* was a legitimate word, he wasn't about to discuss that issue with Bruce's.

He used to be pretty conservative about such matters: If it wasn't in the dictionary, it wasn't a word. But lately he'd come around to sort of a tribal notion of language: If a group of people uses a word, then it's a word. But certain groups, Webster had noticed, liked certain kinds of words, so it wasn't so much the word *equitability* he didn't like, but what you might call the equitability tribe. A tribe that would, without hesitation, bust his ass over an orange.

If it was another Chicken Santa Fe or a Snickers, who the hell would notice? But a fresh orange was a different matter. Before Ms. Mayfield's oranges, Webster had only seen oranges in the Web—where he'd also seen unicorns and petted them. That's the sort of thing he grew up with. His mom believed that unbridled fantasy was what made life worth living. Still did, as far as he could tell. He didn't see her much.

"*Winsome,* w-i-n-s-o- . . ."

Webster shut off the vocabulary program. He wasn't feeling particularly winsome.

You had to wonder why somebody who ate fresh oranges lived in a rack-and-stack logged in except to eat and shit. Food unit, bed, interface chair, exercise machine, computer, bathroom—all in an eight-by-ten box with no windows. Because, Webster answered his own question, oranges notwithstanding, she was normal, this orange-eating Ms. Mayfield. Bruce's Drive-To (*Why drive-thru when we drive to?*) brought her food, Disposa-Clothes dressed her, Potty Pumpers did their thing. If she was some kind of health nut she might spend a couple of hours a day on the PowerStroller, instead of the typical fifteen minutes. She worked in the Web, hung out there, partied there, fucked there. If she didn't waste her money on a real house, she could live pretty large in the Web. A rack-and-stack was the smart thing, they said. Cheap, low maintenance. If you wanted to go anywhere, you'd just log on and do it anyway, so what difference did it make where you lived?

Webster sucked the orange juice and pulp off his fingers, stuck them in again, and licked some more. There was this porn site he remembered from a couple of years ago, licking orange juice off this woman's body. . . .

He ought to just knock on Ms. Mayfield's door. "Here's your orange," he'd say, picturing it: Leaning against the doorjamb, holding out the orange like John the Baptist's head at Bibleland where Mom parked him Sunday mornings. "There was a little . . . accident." She'd be so unnerved by his nonvirtual presence she'd forget the whole thing. He had some California Fruit Sticks he could give her to smooth things over if she wanted—twenty-seven vitamins and minerals, six designer colors—like chewing on flavored candles.

Or she could just get pissed. She was the one who ratted on the last guy on this route—got him fired—or so he claimed. Webster knew him to be a prevaricator and a dickhead, wallowing in the Web with Barbies and Brain Fries. *A pulsing frying pan dances over a burner—an egg flies in low over your right shoulder—splat, sizzle, rainbow spray, you go numb from scalp to toenails—"Your brain on drugs! Any questions?"* Pulse, *splat, ahhh, any questions, pulse, splat, ooh. . . .*

Webster shook the Brain Fries site out of his mind. Once again he congratulated himself for renouncing such scurrilous Web pleasures. He smiled to himself. "Scurrilous," he said. "Scurrilous, scurrilous, scurrilous." He laughed and deepened his voice. "Scurrilous scoundrel! Scurrilous scalawaggy scoundrel!" It'd been a good week for S's.

The smart road was running out, and the trike advised him to prepare to take control of the vehicle. "Attention," it said in its stern little voice. "This is very important."

He grabbed hold of the stick. He liked to pretend the trike was a spacecraft instead of an electric three-wheeler with a big aluminum box on the back—like an egg sac on a rectilinear spider—stuffed with Bruce's food packets. In spite of the trike's serious tone, there was no real urgency. If he were asleep or passed out, it would simply park itself at the exit.

While the road wasn't smart here—you had to steer—the trike knew all the speed limits and every pointless stop sign, so that even if Webster wanted to careen wildly about the moonlit streets in a fit of pretend intergalactic abandon, he'd have to settle for wheezing along at thirty miles per hour, coming to a full and complete stop at every deserted intersection.

He saw only one other vehicle out tonight. It was a couple of miles away in Harbour Haven III. (He was in Harbour Haven V). By the pattern of lights, Webster guessed it to be the TrashVac. Selena, the driver's name was. He'd dogged her once, and they had a brief encounter at a four-way stop. It seemed to be going well, and he told her she was pulchritudinous. She told him his site was the stupidest place she'd ever been in her life.

Webster Webfoot's Website, well-known in certain circles, was a stone dungeon, damp and chill, where nothing happened. Water dripped somewhere in the gloom. You were alone. You waited for something to happen. Finally, you started to leave, and a voice whispered your name, followed by a randomly generated string of naughty words—*fuck, cunt, bugger, bang* or *tit, screw, cocksucker, hump.* What could it mean? you asked yourself. You stayed a little longer, you started to leave, a voice whispered your name. And so on.

The whisper never changed—librarianesque was the effect Webster hoped for. Nothing else happened. Ever.

It was a shithole, a roach motel, a dumpster express: a deliberately inane site posted to protest the stupidity of the virtual Web. His longest hit was three weeks, and there was a guy in there now who looked certain to shatter that record. Regulars came several times a week. It'd been listed as a coolsite at least a dozen times. At first this was an ironic dream come true, confirming his lowest opinions. But it was hard to feel good about that sort of triumph for very long. Selena was right: It was stupid, and it was made no less stupid by the fact that it was *supposed* to be stupid.

He decided to run his route backwards so Ms. Mayfield's block would be last. Harbour Haven blocks were made up of two dozen housing units stacked three stories high, eight across. Webster pulled into the first block, and it clamped ahold of the trike. As the trike moved on a track from dock to dock, loading three units at once, he opened the trike's door and freed what was left of the orange. The skin was ruptured from pole to pole by a juice-oozing canyon. He would've thought the juice would be oranger, more opaque. He set the orange in the cup-holder with the crack pointed up, and it looked like the globe at his high school geography site, only it didn't spin, didn't talk.

He usually had nothing to do but drive from block to block. At the sixth block, however, the trike ran its tests and told him to change out the carbonator in 720. Mr. Sildanik had apparently been drinking flat Coke for four days. He hadn't noticed or hadn't mounted the energy to call service. Webster got out of the trike and walked down the catwalk to the door. RESIDENTS AND AUTHORIZED SERVICE PERSONNEL ONLY the sign on the door read. Webster put his hand on the knob. The door ID'd him and opened onto a grid of metal catwalks and stairways serving three parallel lines of doors, two by two like couples (some actually *were* inhabited by couples, living next door even though they only got together in the Web). The carbonators were in clusters of four behind service panels between the pairs of doors. Webster ascended the stairs to the top row of units and found 720's.

The metal access panel banged and echoed. He changed the carbonator module, tossed the bad one in the TrashVac receptacle. Suck this, Selena, he thought. He whistled loudly the whole time, stomped his feet as he left, slamming the door behind him. All in all, he raised a rowdy rumpus. But no one looked out to see what was going on. If there was anything at all to steal here, he could've made quite a haul, but there was nothing but pipes and wires and concrete.

The rest of the route there was nothing to do but listen to the trike pump food into the food units. Several sexual metaphors came to Webster's mind, but there was nothing erotic about this mechanical insemination. There was a rhythm to it though—*click, click, click, click, click, clank—click, click, click, click, click, clank—whirrrrrrrr—click, click, click, click, click, clank.* . . .

Stop listening, he advised himself.

He accessed the Customer Information Profile on Ms. Mayfield. She worked for an outfit called Intrepid Explorers—high-end travel adventures. He'd heard of them—exotic far-flung destinations edited for the Web. She probably didn't do the traveling, just cleaned up the raw data. She was thirty-five, had had an account with Bruce's for a little over a year, and had no relatives that Bruce's knew about other than a mother in California. Webster trusted Bruce's to know if she did. Family was good for increasing the customer base. Bring someone else to Bruce's trough, and you got a price break. Once they knew you had somebody to feel obligated to, they played it for all it was worth: "Give your loved ones the gift of food!" they caroled every Christmas, sending you a complimentary suggested gift list for your nearest and dearest. With one command you could turn them loose dispensing cheer. He had to make extra runs, squirting fruitcakes so that Selena could suck them out after New Year's.

When he got to Ms. Mayfield's block, he had a decision to make: Short her an orange, or put this violated citrus sphere into her food unit. Either way he knew who'd get blamed—him. Not because it was his fault—which it was—but because he was the lowest life on the food chain—a seventeen-year-old webkicker working blue-collar to make a statement and pay for a modest supply of drugs and a hopeful supply of condoms. He wasn't even third world, where people might not have anything, but they had the good sense to long for what they were missing. He was bright, savvy, perfectly capable of making a good living in the Web, and still he turned his back on it, threw his life away. He was an irredeemable reprobate, deserving of his fate.

He went back to his brash fantasy of a rap upon Ms. Mayfield's door, and a bit of face to face. "Ma'am," he'd drawl, "I'm powerful sorry I wounded your orange, but I was practicing my humble craft of jugglery so that I might become an accomplished performer, hoping someday to finance . . ." College? Mother's operation? A brain transplant? It wouldn't work. Nothing would work.

He looked down the valley of windowless concrete boxes, like so many square boulders in the moonlight, and saw that Selena was in Harbour Haven IV now, headed his way. He remembered her tossing back her glossy black hair, looking at him with those dark eyes. "You seem smart, Webster," she'd said. "Why do you waste your time on such stupid shit?"

He turned on his heel, went around to the door, and inside the block. Ms. Mayfield's door was right in front of him. He planted himself squarely in front of the peephole and knocked before he had time to lose his nerve. The door opened quicker than he would've thought—he hadn't even figured she'd open the door at all, that he'd be pleading through an intercom. The first thing he noticed was that she was wearing real clothes, cloth clothes. And not just a robe, but jeans and a T-shirt. There were words on the front of the shirt, but he couldn't make them out because her arms were crossed over them. Lean, strong, tanned arms. Curly brown hair hung around her shoulders. There was more to this woman's eccentricity than just the oranges. He found her alluring, which vexed him sorely (since she was old enough to be his mother, or, since his mother had him when she was sixteen, his mother's older sister).

"Ms. Mayfield?" he asked, trying to sound resolute and forthright.

"Yes?"

He held up the dripping fruit. "I damaged your orange in transit. It was an accident, but I accept complete responsibility. I'll bring you another tomorrow. I'm deeply sorry this misadventure has befallen." How he would possibly get his hands on another orange he had no idea, but he was hoping she'd just let the whole thing go, like George Washington's dad and the cherry tree at Amerisite.

She smiled slightly. "That's quite all right. How did it happen? I thought you didn't actually handle the food. Your ads . . ."

She didn't need to remind him of the ads. *From field to food unit, hygenically pure.* Most people took that to mean that a tatterdemalion such as himself went nowhere near their food. "I'm not supposed to. I was practicing my juggling." There, he'd said it, told the truth, full disclosure, conducted himself with moral rectitude. If she wanted to get him fired that was her problem. Webster didn't believe in problems.

She looked as if she were deciding his fate on the spot, her head cocked to one side, her eyes in a half squint, thinking hard. Then she tilted her head the other way, her eyes opening wide as if something had just dawned on her. "How'd you get here?" she asked.

He stared at her blankly. "Beg pardon?"

"How did you get here? Do you have a car?"

"Oh, I see," he said, not seeing. "I'm in the big silver trike—delivery vehicle for Bruce's, you know? I'm with Bruce's."

She didn't seem to be listening. "Can you give me a ride?"

"A ride?"

"A ride. Can you give me a ride to the airport?" She spoke slowly and distinctly as if he might not understand English.

"The airport?"

She rolled her eyes and grabbed his arm. "Show me your trike, Webster."

"How do you know my name?"

"It's on your ID."

He looked down at his photo ID tag hanging from around his neck. His tiny little face smiled sideways at him. She stepped out and locked the door behind her. She had a backpack over her shoulder. "I can't take you to the airport," he said as they navigated the catwalk. "I'm not authorized to carry passengers. I could lose my job." By this time, they were standing beside the trike.

She put the pack down and leaned over, looking critically into the cab. "Not much room, is there?"

She possessed an enticing posterior. He cleared his throat. "Did you hear me, Ms. Mayfield?"

"I heard you. You're afraid of losing your job." She straightened up, put her hands on her hips. "Give me a ride to the airport, and I forget about reporting the orange. Deal?"

He could read the writing on the T-shirt now. It read:

"Don't Mourn, Organize."
—*Joe Hill*

He didn't know what that meant, didn't know who Joe Hill was, but thought it wasn't a good time to ask. She tossed her hair away from her face, and the wind caught it, streaming back. There was a light over the catwalk on the wall just above her head. It was as if she was standing under a spotlight. He realized for the first time that she wasn't wearing any makeup. She had freckles across the bridge of her nose, sun lines at the corners of her eyes. If she got out so much, why did she live in a rack-and-stack? This was like some mystery/suspense/adventure/intrigue site. A midnight ride to the airport with a woman of mystery. The Site of the Citrus Siren . . .

"Webster! Deal?"

He came back to reality, and looked her in the eyes. "Yeah, sure," he said, trying to summon the unruffled demeanor of a debonair man of intrigue. "Get in."

DFW AIRPORT WAS SMART ROAD ALL THE WAY, AND MOST OF the traffic was headed the other way. Most vehicles didn't have drivers. Several unmanned Bruce's trucks were headed toward the warehouses, where Webster's trike was loaded every day with food flown in from factories in Mexico or Chile. There were plans to automate more local delivery, including Webster's route, putting him out of a job, but he figured there'd always be rural routes in Texas. It was a big place. He also didn't plan on spending his entire life working delivery. He didn't have an alternative plan, but something was bound to turn up.

Ms. Mayfield didn't say anything, just kept her eyes straight ahead hugging the backpack to her chest. They were thigh to thigh on the lone seat, but Webster was fairly certain this was a lot more distracting to him than it was to her. The muscles in her legs were hard and firm. She definitely spent a lot of time on the PowerStroller. More to take his mind off her proximity than anything else, he started asking questions. "Where're you flying to?"

"Mexico."

"Isn't there a war going on down there or something?" Webster used to hang around in some of the battle zones when he was twelve or thirteen and into violence, cataclysm, and mayhem, but he hadn't kept up with them.

She looked at him for a moment, looking sad or disappointed or something along those lines. Webster felt like a total idiot, which he resented. He was only seventeen. How was he supposed to know everything? "Yes," she said. "There's a revolution going on. It's been going on for about twenty-five years now."

"Isn't that long for a revolution?" This time he knew it was a stupid question, but it was the only one he could think of.

She laughed out loud, and he felt himself blushing. She put her hand on his arm. "Yes, it's long," she said. "Too long." .

"So why're you going? Isn't it perilous?"

She looked away. "I have a friend down there. I haven't heard from him. I'm worried."

"Does he work for Intrepid Explorers too?"

She turned back to him, her eyes narrowed. "How'd you know where I work?"

"It's in your file—with Bruce's."

She shook her head at the flat, featureless landscape, sighed, and muttered to herself. "Even a delivery boy knows every detail of your life."

He started to contradict her, to say he didn't know every detail by any means. Like this male friend—he hadn't known about that. But that might imply he was overly curious. "I'm sorry," he said. "It's none of my business."

She shrugged. "It's okay. You've got to be where you are, right? You drop my orange, so you look up my life. Yeah. We work together." This look passed over her face, and for the first time Webster realized how nonplussed she was. "He's my boyfriend," she added, like it was an afterthought, but her voice quavered, and her eyes were teary. Perhaps it was a good time to change the subject.

"It's a singular occurrence for a customer with your socioecomonic rating to requisition oranges," he observed.

She smiled as she brushed at her eyes with the back of her hand. "Oh, is it?"

"You're unique in my experience. May I ask . . . ?"

"Why I eat oranges?" She laughed. "I don't know. My grandmother would always give them to me when we visited her in Tucson. There were several orange trees in the yard, and a lemon. I remember one Christmas. I was about your age. There was a bad frost coming, and everyone in the house was busy online except for my grandmother. She came and got me, told me I had to help her save the oranges. We went around with big blue tarps and covered them up, tied them down to stakes in the ground. I found out later they weren't even her trees, but the neighbor's."

He tried to picture all this. Running around outside in the cold in a real yard with trees. The closest thing in his experience was the Hansel and Gretel site he'd visited a couple of times when he was little. But it was never particularly cold. Arctic Adventures was cold, but there weren't any trees.

They entered the airport transportation grid, and she asked him to take her to ticketing. Shipping and Receiving was clogged up, but the passenger area was practically deserted. He waited for her as she went to the ticket kiosk, fully expecting her to wave him on once she got her ticket. She could take the peoplemover to the plane. Instead she came back to the trike empty-handed, slamming the door behind her.

"All flights to Mexico are canceled until further notice," she said in a bitter singsong, mimicking the cheerful voice of the kiosk.

"Is that because of the war?" he asked.

"Revolution," she snapped. "Do you know the difference?"

Of course he knew, or thought he did. But he knew enough to keep his counsel. He set the trike to go back to her place and pretended to be interested in the containers rolling out of the belly of a plane, the queue of trucks to haul them away.

"I'm sorry," she said after a while. "Thanks for taking me to the airport."

"That's okay. You're welcome."

She hunted around on the door. "Does this window open?"

"No. Would you like more air?" He reached for the environmental controls.

"No, it's fine. You through for the night?"

"Yes, ma'am. I went to your place last—on account of the orange."

"Have you ever been to Mexico, Webster?"

"Oh, sure. In global studies we went everywhere. Chichén Itzá, Acapulco, Mexico City."

"I don't mean on the Web."

She said *on* the Web, like most people her age. He'd grown up with the WebNet slogan seared into his brain—*Don't just get on, get in.* She'd turned in the seat so her back was up against the door and she was knotted up like a pretzel. She was looking right at him. A chill went down his spine, and he laughed nervously. "The trike has." He tapped the little metal strip on the dash—HECHO EN MEXICO. "I've never been any further than Waxahachie myself."

"Would you like to?"

That laugh again—*titter, snicker, chortle*, he didn't know what to call it—kept bubbling up. "Sure, I guess, but I don't have that kind of money—"

"It doesn't take money. It just takes guts."

Guts, moxie, verve, spunk, gumption. He was giggling now. That's what it was, a nervous giggle.

"Take me to Mexico," she said. "And I'll pay you."

His heart was racing. This wasn't happening. Go to Mexico? "I'd really like to," he said. "But I can't. I've got a route. If I were to embark on some smart road I'm not authorized to traverse, and the vehicle's reported stolen, we'd both just get incarcerated." He looked at her with a forced smile pasted on his face. The cab seemed to be closing in around them. He wished he had to steer or something.

She nodded her head, drew in a breath. He could tell she didn't quite believe him, but if he didn't want to do it, she'd let it go. "Can I ask you something?"

"Sure."

"Why do you talk like that—*embark, incarcerated, traverse?*"

He felt himself blushing again. "I like words. It's kind of a hobby."

"An avocation."

He nodded cautiously, wondering if she was making fun of him.

"That's nice," she said, apparently serious. She settled back in the seat and watched the countryside. He was off the hook.

AS THEY RODE ALONG IN SILENCE, MORE WORDS PARADED through his mind: *coward, poltroon, pantywaist, recreant, craven, dastard, milksop.* Some rebel he'd turned out to be. He renounces the Web—for the most part anyway—and the first chance he gets to have a *real* adventure instead of some made-to-order illusion, he practically wets his pants. What was it he hoped to experience in the world if not something exactly like this?

It was true what he told her about the trike, but there was always a way around that sort of thing. Machines were much stupider than people, and you knew exactly what they would do in any given situation. He looked at the little strip on the dash again. LINCOLN MANUFACTURING,

MATAMOROS, MEXICO. A long vehicle ID number ran the length of the strip.

Elsewhere on the dash, the odometer read out the miles as they zipped along. The fuel cells' good health made a bar graph glow green. The GPS told the world where they were. As he watched, the odometer turned 100,000. Somewhere Lincoln Manufacturing monitored the trike and took note. It was the law—for recalls, police investigations, traffic control.

It came to him how he could drive this woman to Mexico. He'd lose his job, but he'd probably already accomplished that, and he could always get another one. He probably wouldn't have another chance like this. He thought about it for maybe two minutes, then said, "I know how we can take the trike to Mexico. But I need to get in the Web first."

She turned to him, smiling in surprise, which made him feel like a valiant champion. He explained how he had a friend working a satellite maintenance hitch, who could route a counterfeit message so it looked like it came from wherever you wanted. He'd just issue a recall on the trike as if it came from this plant in Matamoros, and when the onboard computer swallowed it, he'd set the trike on automatic, and they'd be in Matamoros in five or six hours at the most. He laughed again, but this time it was deeper and stronger.

WHEN THEY WENT INTO HER PLACE, HE DIDN'T KNOW WHAT to expect—except that it wouldn't be ordinary—he was sure of that. He wasn't disappointed. There were maps all over the walls, not projections, but paper ones taped up. There was a big one of Mexico beside the interface chair. The lights were already on when they walked in, the brightest place he'd ever been. Sitting on the PowerStroller was a plant in a pot. In the house. Webster had never seen such a thing in his life. There was a cord strung diagonally from corner to corner with clothes draped over it—the panties made him nervous. She was taking the clothes off the line, stuffing them into the backpack.

The chair was the standard lounger though. He sat down, felt the tingle of the Weisiger field, and waited for it to boot up.

"I figured you for a webkicker," she said, "since you're working delivery."

"I am mostly, but I've still got friends I can only see in the Web."

One friend actually. Girlfriend to be more precise. But he didn't need to tell her—Ms. Mayfield, Margaret—that. Did he?

He was online before she asked too many questions. She'd left it bookmarked for startup on some site named Rincón. A dark-skinned man with a big sombrero sat on the verandah of what looked like a hotel. *"Bienvenidos a Ladrónvilla,"* he said.

Webster figured it for a tourist site, maybe something she was working on for Intrepid Explorers. He didn't hang around to find out. *"Adios,"* he said and left for Starr's private address, a rendering of the little house in the country where she claimed to have grown up, one of her more transparent falsehoods. He had the address to the living room. It took her a while to show up. She came in from the space station, leaving the door open behind her, and he could see into her real room. It made a rack-and-stack look luxurious, but there was a window with quite a view.

He didn't have time to gawk, however. Starr was glaring at him.

"I thought you were working nights," she said.

"I am. I need you to do me a favor."

"I'm busy. You can't just show up like this, Webster, after weeks of not coming around, and say 'Do me a favor.'"

He looked past her, trying to see through the doorway at whatever had her so busy. "Why not? We're friends, right? What are you so busy doing?"

"I have a life, you know."

"I'm not saying you don't. So will you route something for me, make it look real? I've got somebody waiting here."

"You're not staying?"

"I thought you just said you were busy."

"Who's waiting?"

"A customer, okay? I fucked his order, and if I do him this little favor, I keep my job. Please?" He had a little whine to his voice that, for reasons entirely mysterious to Webster, she seemed to find irresistible.

She put her hands on his chest, balled up his shirt in her fists and let it go. "Okay."

It didn't take long. Starr had the knack for getting one machine to communicate with another, like a sixth sense. By the time Margaret had changed clothes and stowed her pack in the empty food compartment, the message came through on the trike's display: RECALL ORDER. Webster, using the password he'd included with the counterfeit order, notified the trike, Bruce's dispatching, and the appropriate road routers that the trike was homeward bound, with two technicians from Bruce's on-board to oversee the work. He was proud of that last touch. He was going to tell Margaret about it as they headed south at 110 mph, but she'd already fallen asleep. The sun coming up to their left turned everything a golden red, like the Martian site where Starr hung out all the time.

He figured that's where she'd been when he showed up. She was going to be piqued when she found out where he was, but she'd forgive him. She always did. Just like his mom.

CHAPTER SIX

ZACK FIGURED THAT THE BODY OUGHT TO AT LEAST BE dressed like a gringo if he was going to say it was a gringo. So he had it in one of the *cabañas* trying to wrestle it into one of his two suits. Even though the suit was several sizes too large, it wasn't easy. Rigor mortis had set in, and it was worse than dressing a mannequin, something he used to do when he was stupid enough to work summers in his father's men's clothing store back in Boise—but that'd been high school, more than thirty years ago now.

Idaho seemed more like a million years ago. Zack and his wife, Edie, moved down to Chiapas in '93 after an unbelievable trip the year before when they came up to this mountain valley for the first time—nothing there but some ruins and cattle ranches. When they missed the last *colectivo* headed back into town, they ate the mushrooms they'd bought in Palenque off some guy who popped up out of the weeds like a fucking jack-in-the-box. Scared the crap out of both of them. But, anyway, after those mushrooms—best sex they ever had. Edie had some kind of rash for a few weeks after—some kind of Mexican poison ivy or something—but even she—who didn't agree to much these days—still agreed it was the best sex they ever had.

So the next year, when the contracting thing didn't really pan out, and this gung ho prosecutor in Moscow, Idaho, was trying to make a career out of a few dozen plants in the national forest, and Zack's father up and died leaving Zack a few thousand dollars in one piece, it seemed like the logical time to split, and this was *the* place to go, like it was meant to be. Rancho Estrellita—Star Ranch—they called it. Their dream come true was what it was—lying out under the stars saying how cool it would be to have a place here, a little guest rancho, and then, like magic, they did.

Edie went along. At least that's how she put it now. Jumping for joy is the way he remembered it. But neither one of them had quite counted on the whole Zapatista thing. Ski masks in Mexico—what was that about? He didn't even wear the damn things back home in Idaho. Not that he could go back there. Even if he thought the cops wouldn't notice, his sister would blow the whistle. She was still sore about the insurance money, said it was a burial policy and that Zack had betrayed the memory of their father. (Where did she get this shit?) Semantics. Zack just didn't see the point of giving perfectly good money to some ghoulish mortician so he'd perform his barbaric, outmoded rituals over somebody who clearly couldn't care less anymore. Besides, would his father have *wanted* his only son to go to jail?

Zack straightened up, took a toke, and decided that wasn't a rhetorical question he should entertain just at the moment. His back was killing him. He was exhausted from getting the corpse into the pants and shirt. He eyed it critically. Fortunately Zack'd had a white shirt with short sleeves, which made it easier to maneuver. It was left over from his donut-making days (yet another shit job of renown) but it'd pass for a dress shirt. The jacket would cover up the stains and his name stitched in red over the pocket. He went by *Zee* in those days. And even though the suit pants were about eight inches too long, he'd rolled the cuffs under so they looked halfway decent. The jacket, however, was turning out to be a royal pain in the wazoo. He couldn't get the arms into the sleeves with the stiff lying on its back. But his own back wasn't up for flipping it over.

He wondered how this guy'd died. He wasn't one of the locals. Probably from Chamula or the next valley over. Good-looking guy. You could see that even dead. Twenty, twenty-five. It was hard to tell with these Indians. He took another toke. There wasn't any point wondering about another dead Indian. The cause of death was Mexico, pure and simple.

Zack remembered the early days. Ninety-four was scary as shit. The government hauled out all that War on Drugs hardware to put down the rebels, so these big helicopters came swooping down the valley, itching to shoot something. Then after they put down that first uprising, the soldiers moved in for good, threw up a huge base directly across from the entrance to his place. Not exactly the ambiance most folks looked for when they got away from it all. Then the land invasions got cranked. It got so crazy the invaders were invading army land! He and Edie sat on the roof with a pitcher of margaritas watching the soldiers watching the land invaders burning army land like they were getting ready to throw in a crop of *frijol* on it—just to fuck with, just to see how far they could go. What a circus.

And then there were the land invaders themselves—right down below—their rows and rows of goddamn corn, hardly worth more than the dirt they planted it in. Put that in a brochure: *Come to Zack and Edie's and see the subsistence Indians scratching out a living!* He put in an orchard of macadamias to block the view of poor Indians, knowing it'd take years before they would form a proper screen. And then, as abruptly as they'd shown up, the Indians were gone, the grove burned up as well. He never replanted. A persistent drought had settled in, so there wouldn't have been much point anyway.

Zack grasped the jacket on either side of the back vent, and yanked, splitting it up the back seam to the collar. He pulled the arms on and slipped the collar over the head, tucking in the back on both sides like making a bed.

Not bad. It'd look better if it had the hands folded across the chest like they always do at funerals, but it was a little late for that. He . . . it. It needed a tie. Where'd he put that tie? He searched his pockets and found it stuffed in a hip pocket with his handkerchief. He shook it out and wrapped it around the guy's neck. You'd think they'd try to find somebody who looked a *little* bit like Santee, who looked like he *might* be a gringo, but they didn't bother. Too damn arrogant. Too damn macho. He remembered Huerta in his linens. "Zack, *mi amigo*. I desire a small favor of you." In the yard, two of his goons were already lifting a body out of the Lincoln Town Car trunk. Huerta handed Zack a paper bag. "These are his personal articles." There were a few clothes inside—none of them anything you'd want to get buried in—and none of them fit the stiff any better than Zack's did. Besides a few toiletry items, there was a plane ticket back to the States for Santee St. John. Proof of identity. Especially when you slipped a few thousand pesos in there with the ticket. The few thousand pesos alone would do the trick. For that, this dead Indian could be Ronald Reagan as far as the Mexican authorities were concerned.

Fuck this tie. He jerked it off the corpse and wrapped it around his own neck. Only a woman could tie a tie around somebody else's neck. He stalked across the yard to the bathhouse. It still smelled nice from the stick of pachouli he'd burned this morning. Nicest bathhouse in Mexico. Enormous claw-foot tub. Huge mirror he picked up in Tuxtla for almost nothing. It was a nice place. It would work out. Had to. They had everything sunk into it. People had a good time here. They had little cabins, good wine, good food, reefer for those inclined, and, of course, some guests brought those same 'shrooms from Palenque. Some things never changed.

It took him a couple of tries, but the tie looked pretty good.

He'd ridden out all this Zapatista craziness and was still making a go of it. This Santee nonsense was just another blip on the screen. It was this virtual shit that was eating him alive. He'd get past that too. Had to. If you can't lick 'em, join 'em—make the Estrellita an official Intrepid Explorer site, sit back, and collect royalties. At least that was the plan until Huerta showed up with a body. Zack didn't think saying their man Santee had died at his place would get him on Intrepid Explorer's good side. If he said, "Don't worry, it's not him" that could put him on Huerta's bad side, where people had a tendency to die.

After Huerta left, Zack had gone up to the top of the big temple to smoke a bowl and figure out a plan for dealing with things. You could see the whole valley from up there. Nothing came to him. It was an energy vortex site—at least that's what George told the people he hauled up here to sit in full lotus for several hundred dollars a pop. But what did George know? Being born in Hong Kong when it still belonged to the Brits and watching *Kung Fu* reruns didn't qualify him as a mystic in Zack's book. But he was good for business. The group of fourteen he was supposed to bring up yesterday would've booked him solid. Some sort of liberal Christian men's group—they'd run into a blockade—who the hell knew what for this time—and had gone to San Cristóbal to sip espressos with all the Eurotrash until the trouble blew over. Which was probably never. Not in his lifetime.

But he had to keep the faith. Couldn't let all this shit bring him down. No matter what he thought about it, he still had to haul this fucking stiff into the church and say it was Santee St. John, because Huerta asked him to, and Zack figured out a long time ago that his presence in this valley was totally dependent upon the goodwill of Huerta and his pals.

Zack didn't even know Santee, not really. He stayed at the rancho a few years back, had a woman with him then. Zack had figured that for his break into IE, and they stayed a good long while, but nothing came of it. Then Santee showed up out of the blue last night, getting Zack all excited because an IE man was at his place for a follow-up.

Stayed a couple of hours, and then he was gone.

Most likely, Zack figured, Huerta'd found him and killed him. Hell, he could've plugged him in the forest, buried him over there under those sorry-ass coffee plants that never seemed to produce but didn't know enough to die. He wasn't about to test out any of his theories on Huerta unless he wanted the same for himself. Still, he had to wonder why Huerta would want some gringo travel operative dead. Using a stand-in for the funeral wasn't hard to figure. Santee's body probably wasn't fit for public display. Or maybe they couldn't find all the pieces.

He went back to the *cabaña*. The new Santee St. John patiently awaited him. Zack slipped the tie from around his own neck and put it on the corpse's. Not bad. Big white flowers—gardenias he thought they were—the tie he got married in a long, long time ago.

Unfortunately, he'd reached that point in the morning he'd been dreading. He couldn't get the corpse into the truck by himself. He'd have to ask Edie for help.

EDIE HAD ONCE BEEN BEAUTIFUL. ZACK HAD PICTURES TO prove it. Back when she was happy. You could see it in the pictures— those smiles you couldn't fake. She never looked like that now. She'd gotten fat, but that wasn't it. Fact is, Zack didn't think she really weighed that much more. She just looked fatter because she was letting go, loosening, spreading out. Or maybe she was just diluting herself, margarita by margarita, into one miserable, pissed-off ooze.

Zack didn't know whether she drank because she was unhappy or she was unhappy because she drank. Either way, it was those giddy smiles that made her beautiful, and those were dead and buried in her own little plot before this dead Indian was even grown.

"Who is this guy, Zack? What dumb fuck thing are you getting us into this time?"

She was holding the feet, the lighter end, standing there planted, while Zack tried to get the head swung around and aimed for the doorway. "Can you back up a little?"

She didn't budge. "You've got room. Who is it, Zack? Can't you answer a simple question?"

"Santee St. John," Zack said, lifting up the head to clear the dresser and mule-kicking the screen door open, setting one foot down on the first step.

"Z-brain, check it out. This isn't St. John."

He hated the expression *check it out*. He suspected she used it just to piss him off. He was positive that's why she hauled out the old nickname. "Don't call me that. If Huerta says it's St. John, it's St. John."

"Huerta can kiss my fat ass," she said, but under her breath. One of the tarantulas or lizards might run tell. She dumped the feet on the end of the bed and fished her cigarettes out of her bra. "Do you have a light?"

"Can't you wait?"

"He's heavy. I want a cigarette."

"I know he's heavy. Believe me."

She patted his shirt pockets, found his lighter, and took it out. "You spending the night in San Cristóbal?"

"Could you hurry up with the cigarette, please?"

She lit the lighter and held it there, an inch from the end of her cigarette. "Are you?"

He tried not to whine, but he was standing there with a corpse in his hands. "Hell, I don't know. Probably. The roads are a mess. I don't think I can take that drive twice in one day. All the hassle."

She leaned toward the flame, lit the cigarette, and dropped the lighter in his pocket. She looked him in the eye, and blew smoke into the air. Before he could say a word, she gathered up the feet and started pushing him through the door.

"Hey, watch it," he said. He stumbled backwards down the steps with the faux Santee bearing down on him like a runaway train so that he almost fell on his butt with a corpse in his lap.

Fortunately, he had the truck right there, the tailgate down. He did a little sidestep, a real torero, and let the momentum carry the body on in, sliding into the pickup like a fence post, bouncing off the front of the bed with a *bong*. He wondered if a corpse could bleed. He didn't think so. He straightened it out with a yank on the feet, and threw a blanket over it, jammed the tailgate closed with a screwdriver.

He never did anything like this before he came to Mexico. Never *dreamed* of doing anything like this. Now he'd spent most of his life here. And it'd never worked out, never come right. He'd had a vision, clear as anything—how it was going to be, how it *had* to be. But the fucking place had let him down. It was just fucked up is all. Would always be fucked up. He was never getting out. He shook his head. I guess that makes me a Mexican, he thought. ¡*Viva México!* *Viva* fucking *México.*

Edie put her hand on his shoulder, and he practically jumped over the truck. "Be careful," she said. "I don't want to have to bury some poor Indian and say it's you."

He plucked her offered cigarette from her hand, took a drag, and gave it back. "I appreciate your concern, but I'll be okay. Santee was into things, up to something. I'm just doing a man a favor is all."

Edie's scowl was all the editorial she allowed on that bullshit. She knew he didn't even believe it himself. "Are you spending the night?"

Why did she keep asking? "I don't know. I told you: It depends on how I feel, what the roads are like."

"Yeah, right. The roads." She flipped her cigarette into the dry grass by the *cabaña* and headed toward the house. Didn't even turn around and wave good-bye.

He found the smoldering butt and ground it out with his heel. He couldn't blame her. She knew he had a lover in San Cristóbal, had to know. He'd tried to tell her straight out more than once, but she didn't want any part of his confession.

The last time he tried to sneak up on the subject. He said, "What would you do if I fell in love with another woman?"

"I don't want to talk about this," she said.

"What would you do?" he persisted.

"No, you don't get it. I wouldn't do anything, because I wouldn't know anything about it. I'm over fifty years old. I've got no friends, no life. Even my parents won't talk to me anymore, Zack. I've lived in this shithole with you for almost half my life now. So don't tell me anything I don't want to hear. Are you following me? Do what you want, feel what you want, but I don't want to hear about it."

It wasn't exactly a rational train of thought, but Zack could follow it. He knew what she meant: Don't rock the boat because I might drown. They were all just treading water anyway. Let her keep thinking there was a boat to rock if she wanted. He owed her that much.

IT WAS A BEAUTIFUL DAY, AS IT USUALLY WAS UP HERE IN THE mountains. Even now with the environment a mess, the forest all but gone, it still managed to be beautiful. At least as beautiful as a day could be when the soldiers outnumbered the *campesinos*. Idaho was no stranger to olive drab, but that was nothing compared to this place. The price of gas was through the roof, but there was still plenty of Pemex to keep these truckloads of soldiers zooming back and forth, as much for show these days as anything else—at least that's what he liked to think.

On the other side of Oxchuc, he was admiring the mountain wildflowers, when he rounded a bend and there was a line of rebels lying facedown beside the road, soldiers standing over them aiming rifles at their heads. Zack instinctively slammed on the brakes. He wondered if they were being arrested, or whether the soldiers were about to pull those triggers when he came around the bend and spoiled things. The soldier in charge—the one not doing anything—looked up and recognized Zack. "*Buenos días, Idajo! Adios!*" he said with a big, friendly smile on his face, waving Zack on with a little flick of his hand. *Don't bother yourself,* it seemed to say.

Zack still had the '93 Idaho plates on the truck. Soldiers at the checkpoints started calling him *"Idajo" (Ee-dá-ho)* and now it'd gotten around to all the soldiers. Zack didn't mind. They were always friendly as hell. If he'd gotten out of the truck and talked to this guy with half a dozen Indians lying in the dirt at their feet, the captain or colonel or whatever he was would've been absolutely charming, delighted to see the funny gringo with the rancho, as if being about to shoot several people had no bearing on whether it was a good day or not. Zack was in the hospitality business, but for Mexicans it was like some kind of religion or something. *Mi casa, su casa* even if a couple days later they might burn *su casa* to the ground. He'd never understand these people.

Zack tried to get a look at the rebels in the rearview mirror as he rolled slowly by, but he was around the curve before he had a chance to get a good look at them all, to see if any were women. He should've turned on the radio, stepped on the gas, put as much distance between himself and those Indians as he could. But he cranked down the window instead, coasted down the mountainside, listening, holding his breath, snaking slowly around one curve after another. He'd almost begun to think it wasn't going to happen, when it startled him, caused him to swerve onto the shoulder—the crackle of death echoing from the mountains, from everywhere all at once. He jerked the wheels back onto the pavement and stepped on the gas, his heart pounding.

But he could only run away from the present. The past was inside him. He remembered standing in his burning macadamia grove, that same sound crackling through the valley, watching all those people die, shot in the back, burned up. A bullet through a child's eye. A woman with her hair on fire.

And he did nothing.

He'd cursed them, those damned Indians, complained about them to any sympathetic ear. They spoiled his view, jeopardized his investment, sent the wrong message. And then they were gone. Huerta only weeks before had suggested to Zack that a *cortafuego* might be a good idea between the land invaders and the macadamia grove. Zack didn't know the word, and Huerta explained it to him. Growing up in Idaho, Zack understood the concept. A firebreak.

"They are such splendid trees," Huerta had said admiringly. "It would be a shame if they were caught in a brush fire."

Now here he was, driving around with a dead man. Zack hadn't been so scared since he'd driven from Moscow to Boise with five trash bags of fresh-picked plants in the back and stumbled on a driver's license checkpoint without his wallet. He'd gotten himself out of that one by talking high school football, pretending he'd seen The Officer play. *Wide receiver, wasn't it?*

Running back, actually.

Yes, that's it. You made that incredible touchdown. Damn, who were you playing?

The dumb cop ended up drawing plays in the dirt—didn't even write him up for no license.

But they didn't speak bullshit down here, not his dialect anyway. Huerta's name would probably get him through to San Cristóbal, but there were factions within factions here. A guy like Huerta had to have enemies, rival thugs he'd screwed over, who'd just love to get their hands on one of his errand boys. And then there were the Zapatistas. If they stopped him, he was a gringo hauling a dead Indian around. No political discussion would be necessary to get him shot for that one.

He shuddered and swerved to avoid a pothole and realized he was going too fast down the mountainside. He eased up on the gas. "What shall I say he died of?" he'd asked Huerta.

"In-flu-en-za," Huerta'd said with a laugh, dragging out the vowels, relishing the sound of the word. Zack had made an unsuccessful attempt to laugh along.

So now he was an accessory, an accomplice or something. To murder. Influenza didn't give you those nasty bruises on the neck, didn't make your head sit a little crooked on your body. He glanced in the rearview mirror at his passenger and caught a glimpse of his own eyes. Nice eyes. Puppy-dog eyes, Edie called them. *Look, I'm not such a bad guy,* he said to himself. *There's a lot worse guys than me. It's this place. You can't tell who's crooked here and who isn't.*

He couldn't convince himself. This wasn't a question of crooked or straight, naughty or nice. This wasn't liquoring up some slimy official and letting him stare at Edie's tits all night so he'd hand over the permits he needed. This was *murder.* Or murders. One for certain under that blanket, probably two counting Santee.

Okay, the Indian was *maybe,* arguably, a victim of war, and Santee was *possibly* a spy or an agent. These people died in the course of things, right? It was their choice in a way. They died for a cause. He tried to fit himself in there honorably somewhere—like an ambulance driver for the Red Cross—but he couldn't do it. He had a murdered boy in the back of his truck, and he was helping the murderer dispose of him and cover up another murder.

It was bad enough to know that he could just stand around and watch it without doing anything. Now he was helping out. Now he was one of them. His sister used to say he had no shame, but she didn't know him. He was filled with it. It was coming out his ears. But that apparently wasn't enough to stop him from doing things like this. His sister overestimated him. He wasn't clueless, he was—no surprise to anyone—just a coward.

THERE WAS NO SHORTAGE OF CHURCHES IN SAN CRISTÓbal. Driving in, Zack counted the crosses among the tilting planes of tiled roofs. They were about as useful here as they'd been back in the States—a good prop if you were making a vampire movie, not much good at making the world a better place. At least that's the way it was since the new bishop was installed. The old bishop—whom Huerta credited with single-handedly creating all the social unrest in the state of Chiapas and possibly all of Mexico out of nothing—had died in an "unfortunate" auto accident in the mountains, widely believed to be murder, though no one was ever charged. There was a big cross there too. By the highway. Scared off vampires for miles around. The new bishop was a senile, ineffectual idiot who would probably live to be a hundred.

Zack found the right church—the one Huerta "suggested"—and

pulled up in the back into a narrow alley. There were a few tourists walking around on the street. Nothing like there used to be. It was hip for daring college bums—French, Italian, English—to tramp the third world wired, mooch off people whose annual income wouldn't buy their hiking shorts and panamas, then go home and throw up a personal site of their adventures, edited to make them look even leaner and cooler than they were. They could visit the old recordings again later when they'd settled down with too many responsibilities to risk slumming in the real world. It was enough to make you miss home videos. American kids didn't do it so much. From what Zack could tell, they just stayed virtual practically from birth. Or if they did do some real travel it was to someplace like Cancún that'd never been a real place to begin with.

The tourists created a wake of kids selling shoe shines, artifacts, Zapatista dolls, wallets, newspapers, pottery, chewing gum, hammocks, or just plain begging. School was a luxury here. Both groups left Zack alone.

He went into the back door of the church and found the sanctuary. At the back there was a Mary carved from some kind of white stone, looking like she could've come from Idaho, even though the Jesus over the altar looked decidedly Indian. Zack studied the pain-twisted face on the cross. Make Jesus's beard a mustache, and it could've been Zapata himself. Somehow this was supposed to make the Indians feel better by suggesting a kinship between the betrayal and murder of their hero and some poor Jew a couple thousand years ago. Zack could never figure Catholics out either.

As if out of thin air, a slight fellow in a priest suit was at Zack's elbow, startling him. Everything seemed to be sneaking up on Zack today.

"May I help you?" the priest asked in perfect English. The priest was crisp and neat. His clothes looked brand-new. His hair was swept back, making him look like Tyrone Power in a Latin mood.

"Are you a priest?" Zack asked.

He smiled and looked Zack up and down. "Are you a cowboy?"

Zack laughed louder than he should've. *Come on, be smooth,* he told himself. "Sorry. I'm just a little rattled. I run a little guest rancho outside Ocosingo—maybe you've heard of it? Rancho Estrellita?"

The priest didn't commit to any knowledge one way or the other.

"Well, anyway. I had a guest die. Awful thing. So far away from home. Anyway, I wanted to give him a proper funeral, you know. Señor Huerta, a close, personal friend of mine, suggested that you people here might be able to help me out—conduct the service, handle the paperwork, all of that."

At the mention of Huerta's name, Zack could see the little click of compliance there behind the eyes. This guy wouldn't give him any trouble. Mind control was what it was. The old-fashioned kind: Scare the shit out of everybody, and they do what you say. He wondered if this guy was really a priest. That made it worse, didn't it? Nobody expected a guy like Zack to have any principles, but a priest . . .

"You have the deceased with you?" the priest asked.

"In the alley out back."

The priest was headed toward the door before Zack had a chance to point. Zack sauntered after him. The two of them hustled the body inside and put it in a room behind the altar. The priest didn't waste any time ushering Zack back into the sanctuary and down to business. "You have his personal effects, perhaps? Some proof of identity?"

Zack reached into his jacket pocket and found the envelope with the money and the plane ticket. He pulled the bills out, leaving the plane ticket inside. "How's this?" he asked, holding out the money. Zack wasn't sure what'd gotten into him, but there was something about this priest that pissed him off.

There was a little static on the line, a flicker in the eyes, a momentary glitch of conscience or dignity. "That will do," the priest said and took the money. It disappeared behind black cloth. At least he didn't count it. "What is his name?" he asked.

"Santee St. John. That's S-a-n-t-e-e. Señor Huerta suggested a virtual service. He has offered to make all the arrangements, and to notify Mr. St. John's survivors."

"That is most thoughtful of him."

"Isn't it though. You haven't asked me how St. John died."

The priest's mouth compressed to a tight little line. "No, I haven't."

"Or how it is somebody named St. John looks even more like an Indian than that ridiculous Jesus you've got hanging up there."

"Perhaps, it's time you left, señor."

"Zack, just call me Zack." He held out his hand. The priest glared at it, but didn't take it. Zack had been pushing, just to see where the priest would draw the line. And now he knew. He drew the line at touching Zack's hand. Couldn't say he blamed him. "What time's the service?"

The priest looked surprised. "You plan to attend?"

"I wouldn't miss it."
"One o'clock, tomorrow afternoon."
"Why the wait?"
"So that there is time to notify the survivors."

OUT IN THE STREET, ZACK DIDN'T KNOW WHAT IN THE HELL
had gotten into him saying he'd come to the service. But now he'd have
to. He wouldn't want to give the little priest the satisfaction of knowing
Zack was just showing off when he said he'd come. Besides, it was
possible that there'd be some IE people coming to the funeral, and he
could introduce himself, offer to show them the Estrellita. . . . He shook
his head. Sometimes he disgusted even himself.

He went to his favorite *taquería* and got something to eat. He struck
up a conversation with Anna Flores, who owned the place, and asked
her if she'd heard about any trouble near Oxchuc. There were a half-
dozen other people in the place, none of whom seemed to be paying
any attention to their conversation. "There is talk," she said, "but I don't
always listen." She picked up his plate, wiped the green Formica table
with a wet towel. "Don't worry," she said quietly. "She was not
among them."

"Is she in town?"

"No, señor," she said loudly, straightening up as three soldiers walked
up and sat down. "*No hay chorizo, hoy. Mañana, tal vez.*" There's no
sausage today. Maybe tomorrow. Anna took the soldiers' orders, let them
flirt. Zack wondered if they knew she was Zapatista.

ZACK CHECKED INTO HIS USUAL HOTEL, LOS TRES PIN-
guinos, whose name was a complete mystery. Paulo, an Italian bumming
around twenty years ago, had started and named the place, but he'd
sold it to the current owner, Gildardo, after only a few years. Gildardo
kept the name because he liked the mural of penguins in the lobby,
now chipping and flaking like snow.

As the shadows were lengthening, Zack smoked a bowl on his balcony
and looked out over the tile roofs, ranging in color from cantaloupe to
rust to almost white. From here, you couldn't even tell there was a war
going on, couldn't even see the ring of soldiers that surrounded the
town. He looked into the hills. She was out there somewhere, probably

bandaging some brave warrior or crouching in the dirt to get a good shot or to keep from getting shot at. He winced at the thought.

The church bells started up as they often did in San Cristóbal. They sounded for all the world like crazed people strategically placed around the town, furiously beating on scrap metal with sledgehammers. Calling the faithful, sounding an alarm, or just blowing off steam—¿quién sabe?

In spite of himself, Zack liked Mexico. Back in Boise, they'd never ring a bell like that in a million years. Down the street from where he grew up there was a church with terribly sweet electric bells that played Christmas carols every year from Thanksgiving to New Year's. Just like at the mall. "Come, All Ye Faithful Shoppers. . . ."

It was like being trapped in some Disney ride for weeks. These San Cristóbal bells, however, were out there, sounding wound up and half nuts. Zack tried to amuse himself by making up carols for them:

"Joy to the World Bank!"

"Feliz NAFTA-dad!"

"Santa Claus Is Running Your Town!"

It would've been funnier if his lover had actually been there to share it with him, instead of taking up every corner of his mind with her absence. Or maybe not. Nothing seemed very funny anymore. Especially himself.

CHAPTER SEVEN

LINCOLN MANUFACTURING WAS A HUGE, RAMBLING SHEET-metal cavern stuffed with rails and wires and lit up by halogens high above. There were no windows anywhere Margaret could see. They could be anyplace on the planet or under it. The road had ducked underground before they reached the border. Somewhere along the way, a computer had noted the trike's presence and verified its logged route. Such was customs. It was more like being on an assembly line than crossing a border. The trike had come to a stop in a queue of trikes, next to a concrete walkway. The only indications they were in Mexico were Spanish signs, mostly warnings of danger, and the brown workers, mostly young women, who scrupulously ignored their arrival.

Webster's phony recall had gotten them into Matamoros as promised. It was up to Margaret to get them out of this factory and into Mexico. Webster had told her his two-technicians-from-Bruce's cover story, and she'd have to play it. She just wished he hadn't used her real name. If they checked on her thoroughly, she and Webster might get sent home with more than just a spanking. With any luck, no one had noticed the trike until it showed up a minute ago, and hadn't had time to check it out.

Margaret and Webster stepped out as if they were at a rest stop on the Jersey Turnpike, stretching their stiff muscles, looking around for the Coke machine. She'd changed out of her Joe Hill T-shirt. She was in her border-crossing clothes—charcoal gray suit with pleated trousers, a coral silk blouse, an artsy-looking pin made out of different colored beaten metals—something her mother might have worn. "I want them to think I'm important and powerful," she told Webster as they headed into the factory. "You play the foot soldier; I'm the four-star general. Got it?"

"Four stars is good, right?" It was only when he winked that she realized he was kidding. He was wearing a stained workman's jumpsuit with old name and logo patches all over it—ROACH-KILL, LEO, SID'S SERVICE CENTER, TROOP 376, MITZI, BOB'S DO-NUTS. It was high web-kicker fashion, but not likely to impress here.

Their welcoming committee was already assembled. She'd been hoping for Mexicans, so she could play her gringo privilege to the hilt. What she got was an American, whose ID said he was a Product Security Chief named Blaine Clute; a Mexican suit with no ID; and two security guards who looked like they might be Salvadoran, American sidearms on their hips. Blaine was out front, spokesman for the group.

"Welcome to Lincoln Manufacturing of Matamoros," Blaine said in a most unwelcoming tone. "Perhaps you two could shed some light on what you and this vehicle are doing here." He had the ominous smile of a cop, which he probably had been back in the States. These *maquiladoras*—cheap labor assembly plants along the border—used a lot of bad-boy American cops. If he was typical, his main job was union busting, though they always called them "security." He could probably smell her politics coming out her pores.

She gave Blaine a perfunctory smile, walked around to the back of the trike, and opened up the hatch. When he followed her, she turned up the smile and the condescension. "Would you get my bag for me, please?"—she squinted at his ID—"Brian? After the ride I've had, I don't dare trust my back."

This is where she'd find out if he knew who she was or whether he was still trying to figure that out. He blinked a couple of times, took her backpack out of the trike, and set it at her feet. She wished she had something with a more executive look, but she'd never owned a briefcase.

"Thanks," she said.

Webster played his part to perfection, shadowing her like a manservant. He silently picked up the pack and held it before him as if it were fine luggage, awaiting orders. Noting an imagined Blaine thumbprint on one of the D rings, he wiped it clean with his sleeve. Margaret suppressed a smile.

"*Blaine* Clute," Blaine said, finally extending his hand. "I'm in charge of plant security here."

"Margaret Mayfield." She shook his hand. "Pleased to meet you, Bla-a-ine." She stretched the name out and laughed to acknowledge she'd gotten it wrong before. She didn't apologize, however. It wouldn't do to apologize to some factory cop, would it? An important woman like herself?

"Now could we *please* get to our hotel? I won't be good for anything until I can get a shower and a cup of coffee." She sighed, laughing humorlessly. "I don't mean to be difficult, but I *really* must insist on separate transportation the next time I make one of these trips."

Blaine's face was stuck in a tentative smile. His entourage had reassembled like a chorus behind him. His eyes were tight and nervous. He didn't know whether to cuff her or grovel at her feet. "And what trips might those be, Ms. Mayfield?"

Margaret let the question hang in the air for a long time, as if it were indecipherable, or uttered by a parrot who didn't really expect an answer. Then she did a long, drawn-out double take. It was hard to overact self-importance. A certain hamminess made it all the more convincing. "Excuse me?"

Squinting slightly, her fingertips rising to a furrowed brow where a vicious headache threatened, she repeated, "Excuse me? Am I to understand that you didn't know we were coming?" She bit her lip, summoning patience, tolerance, suppressing a seething rage already pushed to its limits by hours of riding in that . . . that . . . contraption. "How is that possible? *Your* people issued the recall orders. This cramped little deathtrap is *yours*, isn't it?" She dismissed the trike with the back of her hand. Webster had assured her there was no way they could trace the source of the recall. So Lincoln would have to take responsibility for it or admit an unforgivable security breach. She might as well play her one card and see what happened.

Blaine opened his mouth, but no words came out. The Mexican suit stepped into the vacuum. "Allow me to introduce myself, Ms. Mayfield. I am Simón Paz, Public Relations Facilitator. *Bienvenidos!* Welcome to Mexico! I will show you to your hotel personally, and arrange for anything else you may need while you are here. I do hope you will be staying with us for more than just a few days so that you might enjoy the riches our beautiful country has to offer."

"*Muchas gracias, señor. Usted es muy amable, un buen caballero.*" Margaret acted on a hunch that Blaine's Spanish wasn't too good, and she was right. His eyes glazed over as she chatted on with Simón, who obviously enjoyed upstaging the boorish Blaine. She took Simón's proffered arm, and soon she and Webster were in the back of an old limo with Simón, on the way to the hotel, which Simón assured her was the very best in town.

MATAMOROS WAS A BORDER TOWN WHOSE REASON FOR EX-isting seemed, at first glance, to lie entirely to the north. The street connecting the sprawl of factories and the town might've been shipped in from the States. Which, in a way, it had been. There was an occasional old building that hadn't been scraped off, but most of it was infested with the last desperate spasm of prefab-American franchise architecture of eight or ten years ago. Desperately polychromatic aluminum and plastic, beamed in from a future that would never exist, the buildings were sun-bleached and dusty now, either boarded up or converted to more modest enterprises, like the Circuit City stuffed with bales of used clothing or the KFC that was now a bicycle repair shop.

But the town itself was unmistakably Mexico. The streets, named after revolutionary heroes, were filled with people. It didn't matter that the revolutions had never made them free or that anyone with true power wasn't down here in the street, or even in the country. History wasn't just a subject here, a site on the Web; it was where you were, like it or not. Even in this border town, there was a *zócalo*, a place to gather at the center of things. As they drove by it, she wished she could just step out of this limo and take a bench there beyond the newspaper stand and read the paper, watch the comings and goings, strike up a conversation with a perfect stranger.

Most of the traffic was made up of *colectivos*. As the limo driver rolled slowly through a bottleneck of them discharging and taking on passengers, Margaret watched two women and a young girl boarding a quarter-century-old Previa already bulging with passengers, who shouted encouragement and rearranged their sacks of corn and boxes of belongings to make way for the newcomers. When there simply wasn't room, two young men clambered out a glassless side window, stood on the rear bumper, and clung to the luggage rack, banging on the roof to signal the driver. The whole lot of them were laughing when the van lurched into motion. On the dash, the Virgin stood and Choc Mool reclined, both no doubt smiling as well. Along the top of the windshield was the driver's lament in metallic script—*Tú o Nadie*. You or no one. Margaret felt a rush of emotion like coming home. She loved Mexico.

"Bruce's has long been one of our most valued customers," Simón was saying trying to lure her away from the window, fishing for her role in the scheme of things.

He seemed like a nice enough fellow. Unfortunately, she had to give him some lie to believe in, if she didn't want him checking her out. A big one. She might as well be his worst nightmare. "I'm new with the company," she said. "They brought me on board to oversee a complete reevaluation of the entire range of efficiency issues (particularly as they relate to the delivery infrastructure), recommend a reconfiguration strategy, and implement whatever modifications are deemed appropriate at this point in time and in the short and long terms." It depressed her how easily she could parrot this gibberish, even uglier in Spanish somehow than in its native English. "Naturally, when this recall order came in—given the huge fleet of Lincoln Manufacturing vehicles owned and operated by Bruce's—it was a no-brainer that I should jack into it to get some hard data." *No-brainer* and *jack into* she said in English, like everyone else in the world. In Margaret's mind, they were practically synonymous.

Simón was a bit dazed. "Naturally. If there is any way I may be of service—"

She cut him off. "I've more than likely accessed all the information I need at this juncture. I have a meeting this evening at nine to review our options and settle upon an appropriate course of action." Too late now, buddy. You've already blown it.

"A meeting?"

"On the Web, of course."

"Of course," was all he could manage. He bought it. Terror shone in his eyes.

Earlier she'd noticed him sneering at Webster in his tacky clothes. "It was my idea to bring along Webster here. Cute, isn't he? He's actually one of the Bruce's delivery team. He's spent *hours* in those little cars of yours. Can you imagine? He's been an absolute fountain of information. Nothing like hands-on, no?"

Webster smiled vaguely at the two of them, like a dog who knows he's being spoken of but not what's being said. Simón smiled back rather desperately, hoping all was forgiven.

S IMÓN WOULDN'T LEAVE UNTIL HE WAS SURE THEIR ROOMS were secured—*the very best rooms* he repeated to the desk clerk at every opportunity. Margaret dismissed him at the elevator with an icy smile. When the doors closed, she slumped against the wall of the elevator and sighed her relief, laughing out loud at her performance.

Webster finally spoke. "Do we have rooms here?"

She couldn't stop laughing. She was actually back in Mexico. "Yes, but we can't use them. We just bought a little time is all."

"Ms. Mayfield, where are we going? What are we doing?" His eyes were wide, and he was biting on his tongue. Margaret used to have a cat who did that when he was stressed out. It hit her she was dragging him into all this much further than he needed to go.

The elevator stopped at their floor, and the doors slid open. "I'm sorry," she said. "I wasn't thinking. Let's see about getting you back home." She pressed the lobby button. "If you just walk back across the border and say you've been for the day—"

He put his foot against the open doors. "No," he said. "I'm not saying I want to go back. I just don't know what's going on is all. I don't know any Spanish. On the Web it's all translated. And everything's so . . . unedited here. It's great, it's really great, but it's . . . overwhelming. I can't keep up. I don't know what we're doing."

"I know. I'm sorry. I'm really grateful for your help. You can't imagine how much it's meant to me. But you should be heading home now." She put her hand on his shoulder, and he shrugged it off.

"No!" She was startled at the intensity of his response. "You asked me if I wanted to go to Mexico, and I said yes. I'm not going back now. I just got here. Why should I go back home? It's a . . . a *hovel.* I probably just lost my job anyways, which means I'll have to call my mom and see if I can crash there like some pitiful milksop, get some infocrap job webbed in all day like some automaton." He shook his head vehemently. "No, I did what I said and got you here. You can't just send me home."

"It's dangerous, Webster."

He rolled his eyes. "I figured that much out already. If it wasn't, it probably wouldn't be worth doing, right? Logging on isn't dangerous. Squirting food into zombie condos isn't dangerous. Webbing around Mexico without ever getting up off your butt isn't dangerous. Right?"

He reminded her more and more of herself. "Right. But this is the real thing. You don't know what you're getting into."

"I'm already in it. So why don't you tell me what I'm in? You're a spy or something, aren't you?"

She stepped into the hallway, and he followed her. The elevator doors closed behind them. She looked up and down the empty hall. "Yes," she said.

"I knew it." He seemed quite pleased with himself. "And your boyfriend too, right?"

"Yes. I can't tell you what we're doing."

He laughed. "I probably wouldn't understand it anyway. You're on the side of the revolutionaries here though, right? The . . . the . . ."

"Zapatistas."

He smiled, taking that as a yes. He was a smart kid. She liked him. Their traveling together wasn't a bad cover either.

"So what now?" he asked.

"Since we have the rooms, I thought we might as well use the bathrooms. These could be the last toilet seats we see for a while."

He beamed. "Sure. What then?"

He wasn't listening to a word she was saying. She couldn't help feeling like a hero, probably a dangerous emotion if there ever was one. *Send him home*, she told herself, but said, "Migración, Immigration. They might have some information on Santee—my boyfriend. And we need tourist cards."

"Who am I supposed to be this time?"

The question startled her, though she knew what he meant. He was much too cheerful about the whole thing. He thought he was in some Web adventure. She really should send him back. If he stayed with her, sooner or later, he was in for a rude awakening. But then, that was better than sleeping his whole life away in the Web, wasn't it?

"My son," she said.

"Cool," he said. "Exquisite."

WHEN THEY WALKED INTO MIGRACIÓN, IT WAS LIKE STEPping back in time. In little cubicles, a dozen bureaucrats stared at monitors, clicked away on keyboards, raising a clatter like some swarm of insects, silent in the States since the Weisiger interface. An air conditioner stuck in the wall probably sixty years ago, somehow chugged on. Mexicans, in Margaret's experience, never met the machine they couldn't repair. Spare parts were for sissies; new equipment, for the rich. Webster watched the comings and goings in the office with wide-eyed curiosity. She guessed he'd never been in an office of any kind in his life, much less one filled with antiques. "I'll be speaking Spanish," she warned him. "Just be patient. I'll fill you in when we're alone."

"I will comport myself with the utmost equanimity," he reassured her.

They sat before Federico Aristos, who listened to Margaret's story of a wife and son in search of a missing father with a kindly, concerned smile. He was a pleasant, fiftyish fellow with a quiet voice and the settled-in look of someone who'd been in this cubicle for some time. In a Plexiglas frame next to the ashtray and his pack of American cigarettes, was a photograph of him and another man seated on a sofa, a white poodle standing on their knees.

"I will search our system for any information we may have concerning his whereabouts," Federico told her, and turned to his keyboard.

As Margaret waited for him to finish his search, she hoped there were no results. If immigration had any new information on Santee, it wasn't likely to be good. He could be arrested, hospitalized . . .

Federico turned from the monitor, with a deeply apologetic wince. "Forgive me, señora, but according to our records, Señor St. John is not presently married, and I must ask your relationship to him. Our files are confidential, and I can only divulge their contents to members of his immediate family."

She held her head up and looked him in the eye. "*Somos enamorados—sin casarse*," she said. We are lovers—without marriage. "*Es mi vida. Mi corazón.*" She cast her eyes toward Webster, who didn't have the faintest clue what was going on. A tear broke free at the corner of her eye and ran down her cheek. "*Nuestro chamaco*," she whispered. Our little boy.

Federico pursed his lips in sympathy, placed his hand on hers. "I am profoundly sorry, señora, but Santee St. John died only yesterday. His funeral is to be tomorrow at 1 P.M. in San Cristóbal de las Casas."

A sob rose up inside her, but she fought it back. It wasn't true. Couldn't be true. She'd know if he died, instinctively perhaps, but electronically for certain. He'd configured the IE interface, which monitored all his vital signs, to send a signal to her computer if he died, a signal she hadn't received. She couldn't fall apart, not now. He might be hurt, he might be in some hellhole of a jail, he was almost certainly in grave danger, but he was *not* dead.

The whole story didn't make any sense. What was he doing in San Cristóbal? There had to be a mistake. Her voice shook, but she held herself together. "How did he die?"

"An illness—it does not say exactly."

"Who reported his death?"

Federico put his hand over his heart, touched by her bravery, assuming no doubt that her probing questions were simply denial. He looked back at the screen. "He was brought in by Zachary Taylor Hayman earlier today. Señor St. John was apparently a guest at Señor Hayman's hotel when he died. There is no other information."

Zack Hayman? His place was miles from San Cristóbal, and he was hardly the Good Samaritan.

All Margaret had been able to find out since Santee failed to check in with her was that he wasn't at his hotel. She figured that he'd gone to meet Jorge, but something had gone wrong. He could've gone to Zack's, but he wouldn't linger there, unless he was hurt, which still didn't explain whose funeral Santee was getting the credit for. She gave Federico a brave smile. "My son and I wish to attend the funeral. May we please have travel visas?"

Federico spoke softly and carefully. "The funeral will be virtual, señora. You can access it at the cathedral here in Matamoros, or at home in—"

"No! Please, I beg you."

"But, señora, it is not recommended to travel in Chiapas at this time. You will be much safer here—"

She put her fingers to his lips. "Please, señor. You must understand. Your heart isn't stone. My love is dead, and you speak to me of safety?" She slid her passport and Webster's ID from Bruce's across the desk toward him and pulled her hands away.

He hesitated for only a moment and picked them up. He eyed Webster's ID. "Webster Webfoot?"

"He had his name legally changed."

Federico smiled his understanding and sympathy for the mother of an American teenager. He propped the card and Margaret's passport behind the keyboard. He put his fingertips briefly together over the keys as if praying, then typed in quick bursts. Their visas sputtered out of an ancient printer. Federico lit a cigarette and offered her one, which she declined. The visas lay on the desk between them. "The director must sign them," he explained, checking his watch. "He will arrive in twenty minutes." They sat and waited for the director as Federico smoked. Margaret asked for directions to the bus station, and Federico drew her a map on a half sheet of paper.

Webster, looking bored to distraction, pointed at the pad and gave Federico a questioning look. Federico handed it to him. Webster tore off three sheets of paper, wadded them into tight balls, and started juggling them.

Federico, at first slack-jawed, asked Margaret softly, "The boy, he does not speak Spanish?"

"No."

"So he doesn't yet know about his father?"

"No," Margaret said. "I will tell him when we're alone."

Federico clasped his heart. "*¡Que lastima!*" Webster smiled at what he took to be an expression of admiration for his performance. He reversed direction.

The director arrived, and Federico hurried after him with the visas. Margaret turned to Webster. He was juggling the three balls of paper with one hand. "Very good," she said in English, and they cascaded to the floor.

"Sorry," he said, getting on his knees to round up the balls. "What did you find out?"

"Get up off the floor, Webster." He ignored her. "I'll make this quick. I don't know how much English Federico knows. According to his information, Santee is dead, but I know for a fact he's not. Somebody, however, is having a funeral tomorrow in San Cristóbal, and I'm going to attend. It means riding all day and all night in a bus on mountain roads. There aren't any smart roads here, and we're heading into a war zone. You *sure* you don't want to go back home?"

Webster was still crawling around after the third wad of paper. "Got it," he said, sprawled full-length under Federico's desk. He straightened up, banging his head on the underside of the desk, and staggered into his seat. He looked over at her and grinned. "I've never ridden on a real bus," he said.

He was giving that as a reason to go instead of a reason not to. How could she say no? There weren't enough Websters in the world as it was. He didn't ask how she knew Santee was alive, probably figuring she just didn't want to believe he was dead, and for now she let him think that.

Federico returned with the visas and placed them in Margaret's hand. They all stood at the threshold of Federico's cubicle as if before a grand hacienda. "*Vaya bien,*" he said, and waved as they crossed the carpeted plain.

As they were descending the stairs, Webster asked her, "What would you have done if he hadn't given us the papers?"

"Gone anyway."

"Cool," he said. "Audacious."

THE BUS STATION WAS SEVERAL BLOCKS AWAY, BUT MARGA-ret felt like walking. She'd have more than enough time to sit on the bus. Besides, she wanted to introduce Webster to Mexico. He'd probably never walked through anything more exotic than a rack-and-stack or an abandoned shopping mall in his life. Worse, he'd been trotted through all the websites and been told he'd been somewhere. *In global studies we went everywhere. Chichén Itzá, Acapulco, Mexico City.* She had a hunch, in spite of that, that he was going to like the real place. In the past, she'd judged more than one person on the basis of their reaction to Mexico.

Webster was a head taller than anyone else on the street. He bobbed up and down dodging shop awnings, turning this way and that, trying to take everything in all at once. She had to warn him a couple of times not to step off the high curb.

They were off the main drag now in a quieter neighborhood. The walls were colorful planes of concrete—blue, orange, green—sometimes painted with advertising, both political and commercial. Across the street, a man on a scaffold had painted an eight-foot red circle on the wall and was lettering the message inside in white. SIEMPRE, he wrote along the top. Always. There seemed to be an inexhaustible supply of sign painters in Mexico. When the elections were on sale, they were everywhere, covering every flat surface with the acronymns of parties, each one identified with a color. The blue, the gold, the red—all bit players in the democracy show the ruling party put on for the world every few years. The ruling party was known as the tricolor; they claimed the red, green, and white of the Mexican flag as their own.

Webster came to a dead stop in front of a small store. Margaret came up beside him and looked inside. It was filled entirely with disposable diapers.

"What is this place?" Webster asked.

She pointed at the store's name painted over the door: PAÑALES DE-SECHABLES. She translated, pointing to each word: "disposable diapers."

The dappled walls were painted with the logos of several brands. Webster pointed at one of them. "That's the kind I wore."

"*Hecho en Mexico*," she said. She pointed out the phrase *por adultos*. "Bet you can translate that."

He laughed and looked up and down the street. There was a home electrical supply store with a plywood display of switches and outlets on a sandwich board; a store full of brightly colored plastic buckets and tubs; another filled with picks, shovels, and hoes. All three sold machetes. "This is so . . ." Words failed even him. "Different," he settled on.

"A lot of these stores are part-time businesses," she explained. "The family lives in back. They turn the front room into a store. Maybe they have a connection at one of the factories to get a particular item cheap. They've got other jobs at the factories or across the border, sometimes seasonal. . . ."

They had walked on as Margaret held forth, and she hadn't noticed he'd stopped to watch an *helado* vendor pedal past on a three-wheel bike. When she realized she was talking to herself, she turned back to see Webster a half block behind her, just as a little boy (maybe six or seven years old) crossed the street, vaulted the waist-high curb, and moved in on Webster with his hand out. "*Un peso, señor. Un peso. Un taco. Tengo hambre. Un peso. Un peso . . .*" Webster backed into the wall looking wildly about for Margaret to rescue him, his hands in the air as if the kid were holding him up and the outstetched palm had a gun in it. She headed toward them.

"What does he want?" he called to her.

"He's begging. He wants a few pesos."

"Tell him I don't have any."

"No is the same in both languages," she said quietly as she reached them.

The boy turned to her. "*Señora, un peso—*"

"*No lo tenemos. Somos Americanos, tenemos tarjetas plasticas solamente.*"

The boy eyed her suspiciously, but moved on.

"What did you say?" Webster asked.

"I told him we don't have any cash, that we're Americans and only use plastic cards."

"Isn't he supposed to be in school?" Webster asked.

Margaret stared at him a second. She didn't know where to start.

"Yeah. That's where he's supposed to be. This is the real world. Things are rarely what they're supposed to be."

They walked on in silence for a couple of blocks. "Are you mad at me?" Webster finally asked.

"No. I'm just mad."

"Where are we going?"

"To put a plastic card in a machine and get money."

SHE FOUND AN ATM AND GOT A FEW THOUSAND PESOS. SHE handed Webster some of the bills. "So you'll have some money in case we get separated."

He examined it carefully, held it up in the air to look at it in the light.

"You might want to put that away."

He jammed it into a pocket. "I've never really handled cash too much before."

"Ever play Monopoly?"

"Virtual. When I was a kid."

She didn't point out that wasn't so long ago. "It's the same as that. We should get something to eat. It's going to be a long haul."

SHE ASKED FOR DIRECTIONS TO THE MARKET AND FOUND IT. They stepped under the tarps strung to block the midday sun, and there were tables of fruits and vegetables, freshly butchered meat, piles of chickens, stacks of bread and rolls and cookies. Webster gasped. She guessed he'd never seen so much real food in his life. He walked up to a pig's head, dressed and ready to cook. "Is this what I think it is?"

"Yes indeed."

"What are we going to eat?" he asked eagerly.

This kid was too much. "Not pig head just yet. Do you like spicy food?"

He nodded, his eyes dancing. There was a row of lunch counters in the market that competed for their business as Margaret and Webster approached, rattling off their menus. Some of the women smiled at Webster, and he smiled back. Margaret, meanwhile, chose the cleanest and ordered *chilaquiles con pollo* for them both.

As they were eating, Margaret thought she sensed someone watching her and turned to see. A man in a pale yellow *guayabera* smiled and turned away, disappearing into the market.

"This stuff is great," Webster said. "What do you call it again?"

"*Chilaquiles con pollo.* It's fried tortillas, chicken, cream, and a spicy sauce."

"Cream like from a cow?"

"Yeah. Like from a cow."

He shook his head in wonder.

As they were leaving the market, Webster spotted a table covered with electronic gear and headed toward it. When Margaret caught up with him he was trying out a cheap translator. It looked like an old telephone headset plugged into a box the size of a deck of cards with an LCD on one side and a speaker on the other. You could put it in a pocket or wear it around your neck. Whatever was said was translated into English through the headphones and scrolled across the screen in both languages. Whatever he said into the microphone would come out the speaker in Spanish.

"Incredible deal," the vendor was saying in English. "You understand everybody. Everybody understand you."

Margaret had a natural aversion to these gadgets. Language was too subtle for a machine—especially a cheap piece of junk like that—to translate. "You don't want one of those," she said.

But he already had the thing on his head.

He was dialing through the selection of voices, all tinny, saying "One, two, three," as the translator echoed him in Spanish, "*Uno, dos, tres.*" The voice was determined by selecting certain variables—age, sex, nationality, region. He chose a Mexican accent, male, adolescent, called *Paco,* and looked into her eyes. "Margaret, you are a beautiful woman." *Margarita, tú eres una mujer hermosa.* He made a face at the youthful voice and selected age sixty-five and over, called *Abuelito,* grandaddy, and tried again. He looked pleased with the gravelly voice and kept it there.

"Thank you," she said laughing. "I think."

"How much?" *¿Cuánto vale?* He asked the vendor, pulling out the entire roll of bills she'd given him like an idiot.

But the vendor didn't seem to notice. He was looking past Webster up the street. Margaret followed his gaze and saw the man in the yellow *guayabera* leaning in a doorway watching them. When he saw Margaret looking his way, he quickly melted into the crowd.

Margaret named a price, and the vendor didn't even bother to haggle.

She advised Webster to get used to listening with the translator on, so he fell silent as she hurried him along. She stole glances over her shoulder when they rounded corners and caught a glimpse of a flash of yellow a couple of times, but she couldn't be sure it was the same man.

At the station, Margaret bought their tickets and they waited. Webster pulled the oranges out of his pockets, and they both laughed. As they ate them, Webster asked her, "Have you and Santee been together a long time?"

"Almost six years."

"Whoa! How come you never got married?"

"We want it to last."

He nodded his understanding. Maybe he wasn't as green as she thought.

As they waited for their bus, he entertained himself with his new toy by listening, with what appeared to be rapt attention, to two men discussing the price of corn. He asked if he could wander around the bus station and listen some more, and she told him to go for it. He was full of little surprises, or maybe she just lacked imagination. Her first impressions were none too reliable.

She'd certainly been wrong about Santee. *What's your price?*

THEIR BUS HAD ORIGINATED IN BROWNSVILLE AND WAS ALready near full, so there weren't two seats together. She directed Webster to a seat up near the driver so he could see better, while she headed to the back.

The bus was ancient, paneled in stained, polished wood throughout. The windows were covered with dark turquoise curtains aged into a color both cozy and dignified. The seats were worn and tired and comfortable. The wall between the driver and the passengers had a framed hole for a television and a VCR. As they started backing out, a movie came on. She smiled. The last time she'd seen a movie was on a Mexican bus. This was Steven Seagal's last film in which he played an aging environmentalist in the Himalayas who beat up everyone who crossed his path. The Spanish voice dubbed for Seagal sounded a lot like *Abuelito.*

Margaret wished Santee were here for this. The motor hummed. The bus rocked gently as it maneuvered into traffic. He wasn't dead. She knew he wasn't dead. But why was someone going to all this trouble to make it look like he was?

A couple of blocks from the bus station, she saw the man in the yellow *guayabera* standing on the curb watching them go, talking into a phone. Someone wanted her to think Santee was dead, and someone wanted her to know she was being followed. It made no sense.

She leaned out and looked up the aisle to check on Webster. She felt guilty for dragging him into this. He was already chatting amiably with a Mexican woman across the aisle from him. Something exploded on the screen, and they both stopped talking to watch. When the flames died down, Webster started talking again. The Mexican woman laughed.

Apparently Webster was doing just fine.

CHAPTER EIGHT

STARR'S NAME WAS REALLY STARCHILDE, BUT SHE HAD IT LE-
gally changed when she turned eighteen. She didn't want some fantasy
New Age name. She wanted the real thing—the stars themselves. And
she had them, more or less. She lived in space—a dream come true—
or almost true. The *J. P. Morgan*, the dinky little WebNet repair station
where she worked and lived wasn't exactly what she had in mind, but
she only had five months left on her contract, and she'd logged more
hours in space than most so-called astronauts. If everything went according to plan, she wouldn't have to sign up for another hitch. She'd
be on her way to Mars.

When Webster'd shown up, asking her to rig a phony recall, she'd
been, as usual, looking out her window at the *Morgan*'s closest neighbor,
the Mars Colony ship, the *Mariana*, being built a few kilometers away.
It was enormous, big enough for everyone, she thought. Even me. She'd
dreamed of being a colonist since she was a kid, when the discovery of
rich mineral deposits made a Martian colony a serious idea for the first
time. Growing up poor, realistically she didn't have a chance of being
selected, but realistically she should've been dead, pregnant, or in jail
by now. Realistically didn't get her off Earth and wouldn't put it behind
her. But that ship could, and watching it take shape made anything
seem possible.

When she first got to the *Morgan* the window cover in her quarters
had been shut, and nobody could tell her how to open it. It was computer controlled, of course, and the default was closed—end of story.
She'd poked around in her abundant spare time and found the routine
to open it, wading through endless shrill warnings in a condescending,
frostbitten white-bitch voice no real person could ever possibly have and
survive to tell about it—warnings about ultraviolet, mental illness, re-

duced efficiency, sexual potency. She loved that last one. A big issue up here a thousand miles from flesh to flesh unless she was nutty enough to consort with one of the other crew members.

The first time she got a look out her window as the cover slid open, revealing a vivid swath of stars, it was like their light wrapped her up in a web and pulled her in, and it was like she was one of them. Not floating, because there was no water, no nothing. Like a jewel with no setting.

She'd been drawn back into the *Morgan* by a loud whirring, warbling up and down, scraping, thumping, grinding, then silence. The window cover had stopped a few centimeters shy of completely open. A chewed-up gasket marked the boundary of window and cover like a bright blue rubber ruffle. It wouldn't close, which was just fine with Starr. She convinced the station's computer it was closed, the only opinion that mattered, so there was zero chance of anyone coming to fix it. She dragged a mat from the gym into her cabin and leaned it up against the window when the sun got too intense. On a bad day her place smelled like sweat and burning plastic.

By the time she got rid of Webster, the sun was at a bad angle. She covered the window and decided to get some work done. She opened the bay and hauled out a LOWNR (low orbital WebNet router), pronounced like *loaner* or *loner*, take your pick. It was about the size of an ancient window air conditioner like they had in her last earthly residence, a correctional facility in Goochland, Virginia, where she learned about electronics doing slave labor for Motorola (though they called it Rehabilitative Job Training). The bosses didn't teach her much of anything. They'd just give her some task: Microsolder part A to part B, pass it on to inmate C. She didn't even know what they were making. But, she discovered on her own, the computer always had help files, online tech manuals, diagnostic routines, library access. It went on and on, and as long as she made her quota and had a good attitude, they left her alone. She had a lot of time to study.

Anyway, the LOWNR, fashioned from ultralightweight alloys and stuffed with paper-thin circuit boards, didn't weigh much of anything, especially in the half grav of the station. She had it sitting in her lap. It didn't even weigh as much as Webster. Those old air conditioners were incredibly heavy. She once helped push one out a window during an escape. Not her escape. She thought her confinement would help prepare her for space. And since it was a juvenile facility, they told her, she'd be coming out with a clean record and the probability of a good job. She sure didn't want to blow that. Turned out they lied about a lot of stuff.

The LOWNRs lived to be upgraded, which is where Starr and the hundreds of other techies in orbit came in. It was cheaper to put techs where the satellites were, rather than make house calls with shuttles or round up the satellites for service at the hulking international space station, where the environmentals had gotten so bad the shuttle astronauts refused to get out of their suits when they were on board. Far better, WebNet decided, to scatter these flimsy prefabs around and hire people who, for the most part, didn't see much difference between working here or anywhere else, since their real lives were in the Web. They were cheaper than robots; and if one broke down, you just found a replacement on any city street. And when you ran out of those, you skipped a step and bought them up right out of prison before they ever got back on the street. Some of them had even had Rehabilitative Job Training.

Working orbital wasn't a bad way to get a little ahead. The pay was pretty good, and there wasn't much to spend it on since the company paid all your Web bills except for the really expensive luxury sites. They had to, if they wanted anyone to take the job and stay sane doing it. Some days, Starr thought she could sit and look out the window all day, but not every day for very long. Except for a few laughs now and then, she spent most of her Web time at the Mars site where you could actually experience the terraforming going on. They said in a few weeks you'd be able to breathe there without a suit if you were in good shape.

So she used all her private rec time working out, mostly running in circles and swimming in the stationary pool. The gym cycled through the four crew members' access codes, so most of the day only one of them could get in there at a time. There were two scheduled common times each day when it was open to them all so that they could socialize, build a community, pursue their common interests, form lifelong friend-ships—just like the recruiting ads. In short, the gym was empty twice a day.

Unless the place was going to blow up, crew members kept their distance, and probably even then. Especially if you were a woman. Orbitals didn't exactly attract the best types. Almost half of them were actually doing time on some incarceration contract. So even though there was one woman for every eight men, it wasn't a place you'd want to go looking for a date. There were some pretty gruesome stories. Starr used to think those women were just being stupid. Going real with somebody wasn't something to try in a place where all exits led to a vacuum. If you're closed up in orbit with a bunch of gorillas, you lock your doors. You don't go calling with a bushel of bananas. Her first hitch she found out that locking the standard door lock wasn't enough. Ever since, she smuggled up one of those plastic fold-up shotguns taped to her thigh, and kept it handy, made a point of letting the rest of the crew know she had it. This was her fourth hitch, and she hadn't had any more problems.

Her love life was strictly Web, no exceptions, and she kept that manageable. She was older than Webster—twenty six—but she presented younger to him in the Web, by about ten years. She liked to look younger. She felt safer with younger guys. They didn't want to get involved, and, after all, she was going to another planet. Of course, Webster might be lying about his age too. He could be forty for all she knew. Though he definitely acted seventeen. When she got to Mars, she told herself, she'd take the time for something real.

Starr couldn't complain. This job had gotten her into space just about the only way somebody like her was going to get there. When MarsCorp decided to build the *Mariana* on the other side of the planet from the international space station, that pretty much spelled the end of the public space program, such as it was. That was okay with Starr. They wouldn't even give her an interview. She took their stupid tests, and that was it. The math and science were so easy she couldn't believe it. She knew she'd aced them. Must've been the psychologicals.

But that was history. WebNet was upgrading all the LOWNRs in this sector, and she'd worked her own little improvement into each one, slipping her computer's address into the router—hard-wired it in so nobody could mess with it without getting their hands on the satellite themselves—so that once she had enough of them configured, all info going to and from Mars or the *Mariana* would pass unedited through her computer first. She would know everything there was to know about Mars, including the criteria for colonist selection. No battery of tests was going to stop her again. She belonged in space. Not in this orbiting wad of tin foil either, but out there on another world.

Only an authorized WebNet tech could open up the guts of a LOWNR. The access hatch had a magnetic strip tuned to a subcutaneous nanotransmitter in the right index finger of authorized personnel.

SmartButton they called it. They were always calling really stupid things *Smart*. People had some weird ideas about what was smart. Her cabin was called a smart environment because the whole thing was inside a Weisiger field, so you could spend *all* your time in the Web if you wanted. Lots of techs worked on the beach, sipping fruit drinks. Not Starr. She had her window.

Before she did any modifications, she had to take the LOWNR out of the grid and instruct the other LOWNRs to take up the slack. She entered in the codes and watched it cycle through the routine. When it was done, the LOWNR powered down. She pulled out the old circuits and set them aside. She was supposed to burn them, but she'd cannibalize them first. She put in the new board and powered up the computer, started running the diagnostics. As she worked, she couldn't help thinking about Webster and that phony recall he had her route. There was part of that story he wasn't telling. But so what? They got together in the Web, had a few laughs, had sex—and he was a willing learner in that department, unlike a lot of younger guys. But there was no commitment there, at least on her part.

Still. She was curious. She smelled another woman in it somehow—just the sneaky way he'd acted. She closed up the LOWNR and slid it into the launching bay, where it would await reinsertion into orbit when the computer decided it was time. She'd goosed the orbit just a bit to give it a broader range and had configured it for station-level priority, so that it could tell other LOWNRs in the grid what to do. That way she wouldn't have to modify so many to snare the information she wanted. She was dying to test it, but she didn't want to play her hand too soon. When this one was in place, she might just have enough to pull it off.

She ate a dinner bar or a lunch bar or a breakfast bar. It all tasted the same. Sort of a cross between beef jerky and peanut brittle with a cardboard aftertaste. She wouldn't have to taste it at all if she'd just web into a nice restaurant. She could be tasting steak and french fries. Well, there wouldn't be any steaks on Mars, any Web either. She washed it down with some water—still no substitute—but wished she had a Coke. She didn't figure it'd take long before there was Coke on Mars: There was Coke everywhere.

Somehow that thought made her feel lonely. Now would've been a good time for Webster to show up—and not just to ask a favor and leave. It kind of got to her that he pulled that. Maybe he had a good reason, like he said. It'd be easy enough to check out. The sun would still be blazing against her window for another hour or so, and she didn't feel like doing anything else.

She called up the address of the phony recall. It was some factory in Matamoros that made little smart cars and motorcycles for delivery, like Webster had said. She got inside their main computer using her WebNet service code, checked out the computer's peripherals, and there were a few dozen cameras. She let them cycle through the mindless drudgery of the assembly line. When she saw a guy with a suit, and a familiar jumpsuit-clad beanpole beside him, she zoomed in for a closer look. So, he really is seventeen, she thought. There was a group of folks, standing by a Bruce's trike. Her head buzzed like she'd just fallen off a building, and her stomach churned as if she were trying to digest herself. There was Webster with the person who had to be his customer—a woman he was following around like her personal slave. She was dressed like some corporate bitch with the dark suit and the feminine but tasteful blouse. Starr brought up the audio and listened to her yammering about a hotel for her and Webster. About then, the woman started speaking Spanish, and Starr's computer asked if she wanted a translation.

But she didn't need one. It was simple. This was the customer Starr had made happy as a favor to her boyfriend. Webster had used her to hook up with another woman, and Starr was . . . go figure . . . jealous. She contemplated turning on the Lincoln Manufacturing sprinkler system, but it was just too pathetic. If that's the way it was, that's the way it was. Fine. She was going to have to dump him anyway when she went to Mars. This just saved her the trouble. If she'd known Webster liked older women she could've looked forty all this time, or at least her own age.

As she watched them leaving the plant and the reach of the cameras, she wondered who this woman was, wondered where Webster was when he'd called. She'd put a webtracer on him, so she could catch up with him when she wanted to see him. She checked on his whereabouts when he called her and found he'd come from a site called *Rincón*. She looked it up, but there wasn't much on it—some kind of interactive fiction posted by somebody named St. John. It was free, which told you right away it was probably a waste of time. The Web was full of this crap, and Webster usually heaped scorn on it.

✻   ✻   ✻

SHE POWERED UP THE WEISIGER FIELD AND WENT TO Rincón. She wasn't sure what she expected, but it sure wasn't this. There was a street that looked like it'd been bombed into rubble. There was just enough left of the buildings, including a patchy mural of an army of peasants clad in white, confronting an enemy that was no longer visible, for her to guess this was supposed to be somewhere in Latin America. The only intact building was a hotel called the Bella Vista with a broad verandah. There was a man sitting at one of the tables who rose when she arrived, and bowed. *"Buenas tardes,"* he said.

"English," she said and the translation murmured in her ear.

"Your translation program won't be necessary. I'll speak English, if you like." He was a striking man. Very handsome. Dark, with this thick black mustache and eyes that could look right through you. He wore old-fashioned Mexican clothes with one of those huge hats lying on the table in front of him. "Are you real?" she asked him.

"It is difficult to say," he said. "I am Miliano."

Difficult to say. So there might be more to him than just a sim. There might be an actor behind him. That seemed awfully ambitious for a free site. "Starr," she said. She accessed her profile—set up to meet with Webster—and made herself look her age. There was no sense looking like a kid if she was going to be talking with a man.

"Estrella," he said. "What brings you here to Rincón?"

The way he said her name in Spanish made her feel a little woozy in the knees. She'd never thought of Spanish as sexy before. "What is this place?"

Miliano shrugged. "It is an old hotel. From another time and another place. Now it's part of a novel."

Starr had heard of places like this but hadn't figured she'd like them. She wasn't into art and stuff like that. She looked around. Everything was pretty sketchy. She had the feeling that if she walked a block in any direction she'd run out of virtual in a hurry. But Miliano was another matter. He sat silent with his long sensitive fingers resting quietly on the table. He was a graceful figure of a man, with a kind of natural elegance. He was dark, with beautiful white teeth beneath his heavy black mustache. She found him captivating. She shook it off. Too bad he wasn't real.

"I was looking for someone, actually. A guy named Webster came through here early this morning."

"He stayed but a moment."

"He didn't say where he was going?"

"He said nothing. I'm sorry I can't help you. Perhaps you'd like to stay a little longer while you sort out your thoughts and join me in a coffee?" The verandah was filled with inviting mission chairs and Boston ferns. A pair of black and yellow birds sat in a cage, twittering, hopping from perch to perch, nuzzling each other.

"Sure. Why not? What am I knocking myself out for looking for him? Let him look for me."

This seemed to please Miliano no end. "I quite agree."

She sat down in one of the chairs, and the cushion sighed, the wood creaked. But no memory was wasted on a waiter. The coffee just showed up on the arm of the chair. No illusion was spared on its aroma and taste, however. She liked Rincón. The way it was real and it wasn't at the same time. "So is this some kind of historical site?"

"It is imagined—past, present, future. Like all history."

Starr laughed. "That's easy enough for you to say. You're a character in a novel. I've got little bits of history that are more than just imagination." She unzipped her jumpsuit and showed him the scar on her sternum—twenty-seven stitches.

"And what do you imagine that scar to mean?" he asked with a twinkle in his eye, brushing back his mustache with his fingertips. "What history have you imagined for it?"

He was sly all right. "Good point," she said. "And what is it you do here?"

"That depends on what the visitor is looking for. You came seeking Webster, but he isn't here. Perhaps I could entertain you with a story to pass the time?"

Sim or not, she was sitting here with her jumpsuit unzipped down to her navel, and he had eyes you could get lost in. She zipped herself up and sipped the strong coffee. "Sure, why not?"

"It is a parable I call *Los Gamelos*, The Twins:

"There were twin brothers long, long ago who were left a magnificent castle by their mother and father. The parents were old and sick and wanted to provide for their sons when they were gone, for they had always done everything for their children, as loving parents will do. But when they died, the funeral had no sooner concluded and the brothers were alone, than the first brother seized the castle for himself and shut the second brother out in the wilderness that surrounded the castle walls. And in that moment, as if the gods blessed his iniquity, the first brother began to grow larger and larger, while his unfortunate brother grew smaller and smaller.

"And each day, the first brother, now a giant, sat atop the castle's highest tower and watched his shadow stretch all the way to the horizon—where the second brother toiled all day in his pitiful *milpa* to feed himself and his family and his children—and the first brother was quite content with himself.

"But as hard as the second brother worked, he could never prosper, for when harvest time came, the giant plucked the corn and beans for himself. He took his brother's chickens, his cows, the pig who would never be fat anyway. Everything went to the giant's table. He burned the forest to warm himself in the winter, drank the rivers dry in the summer.

"Fortunately, by this time the second brother had grown so small he could feed his family on a grain of corn, feed the entire village with a great rat roasted over a pine cone. He drank the dew in the morning, rode upon a breeze like a speck of dust into the castle halls at night.

"There, in the great hall he overheard the giant pacing up and down cursing his fate: always eating, but still hungry, brushing the high ceiling with his head, squeezed out of all the smaller rooms, unable to sit down and rest, unable to sleep, to breathe. The giant wailed to the heavens to rescue him from his sufferings.

"And when the second brother heard this—the tiny, diminutive brother, no bigger than a few molecules perhaps, a few particles or waves—he began to laugh. He couldn't help himself. The laughter grew louder and louder, so loud, as tiny as it was, because it was so very, very funny, that even the giant could hear it. And though it took a long time for the sound to travel from his enormous ears to his enormous brain, and a longer time still for him to figure out what this incredible sound could be, when he finally understood it, he went into a mad rage. There beneath his feet, in the cracks between the stones, his brother mocked him in the dust.

"The giant fell to his knees, tearing at the stones, ripping up the floor, the walls, until the castle fell down around him. Then he crushed the stones into powder and sifted it through his fingers, desperately searching for his brother. But search as he might, he could never find him, and soon matters became too desperate for him to continue his search.

"For now he had no shelter, and winter was coming on. He had become too big to feed himself, dress himself, lie down even in the great broad world without coiling himself around it like a snake. He became so desperate he called out to his brother that all was forgiven and could he please help him with a tortilla or a plate of beans. But deep inside the Earth, the second brother waited, smaller than a thought you can't quite remember on a hot summer afternoon. Until finally, the giant drank the last bit of water but a drop or two clinging to his huge mustache. He breathed the last air but the slightest puff that roared out of him as he expired. He fell the length and breadth of the Earth, covering it entirely, dying an enormous death mourned by no one.

"In the morning, the second brother came out of the Earth to claim his brother's corpse, and to give it to the people to live upon. For out of the rotting corpse sprang corn. Out of his mouth came the cattle and the chickens and the pigs. From his eyes, the waters flowed again. Birds nested in his hair. And in the great windy vaults of his empty skull, there was room enough for everyone."

Miliano flashed a smile to mark the end of his fable, and Starr burst into enthusiastic applause, stamping her feet. "That was wonderful!" she shouted. She imagined herself as the second brother, the whole world from the time she'd been old enough to duck, as the first.

"I'm going to a new world," she told Miliano proudly. "I'm going to Mars," not caring for the moment that he wasn't real. "To start a new life." It was better that he wasn't real. He wouldn't laugh at her.

"*Tierra y libertad*," he said, and she tapped on her ear to remind him to speak English. "Land and liberty," he translated.

"Exactly," Starr said. "That's it exactly."

SHE LEFT A MESSAGE FOR WEBSTER WITH MILIANO AND went back to her room. She was psyched. She hadn't exactly advertised her intentions to the world, and to have the charming Miliano's enthusiastic support made it all more real and immediate, even if he was nothing more than a sim in a virtual. He looked familiar, but whether she'd seen him in a history class or in a restaurant ad she couldn't be sure.

There was a whining noise as the outer hatch of the launching bay opened. The station had reached the insertion point for the LOWNR she'd just modified. It was a routine event, but she switched on the exterior cameras and watched it maneuver out of the bay. Then with a little spurt of its thrusters it moved off like a fish darting into the deep.

She did a little calculating as it continued on its course. She could, with what she had in place, snare the transmissions from Mars to Earth without too much difficulty. If she could just maintain a reasonably steady flow of data, no one would be the wiser. Going the other way was a little too busy to handle just yet. She didn't expect to see much she hadn't already seen, but it gave her a chance to test things out before she got a lock on the flood of data coming up from Earth.

A cheerful white-woman voice advised her that the LOWNR had been successfully inserted into its new orbit and was powering up. *Tierra y libertad,* she said to herself, trying to roll the *r*'s like Miliano, and initiated the program that would make her the gatekeeper of all data coming out of Mars. Her LOWNRs informed the others in the grid of the new instructions. It took a few minutes for the network to reconfigure itself. She watched the progress on her monitor with growing suspense.

She knew the Mars she got on the Web—that everyone got—was edited, at least to the extent that you couldn't get access to all the data all the time. There were at least nine recorders: There was one in an equatorial orbit that posed the place like a globe, where you could watch the clouds being born, the storm systems swirling around, the hues shifting toward green and blue. There were two at each of the poles— one that monitored the machines' action and progress like athletes going through their paces, and another on the evolving world of ice and snow that did a breathtakingly beautiful prismatic dance with the Sun. A couple flew around, some kind of drone planes, swooping through storms into valleys where rivers flowed and the banks were spongy with ashen green mosses as plump as loaves of bread, zooming in on genetically engineered guinea pigs scurrying about their new world, destined to be one of the staples of the colonists' diet. Finally, two at the site of Freedom City—one high, one low—revealed a place so lively even the buildings were being grown. Through it all, anonymous workers moved about in white suits like baggy-pants angels under a sky the color of a giant conch shell.

But you couldn't select which recorder you tracked. It just cycled through—not at random she didn't think. Somebody was deciding what was interesting to the folks back home. And there were lots of times when some of the cameras seemed to be out of the loop. She wanted to see all the recordings all the time. She thought there might even be some special recorders aimed at who knew what that weren't shown on the Web. She didn't figure MarsCorp was trying to hide anything particularly. It was just PR to them.

She had no idea it was all a lie.

What she'd thought was the work of nine recorders turned out to have a single source. It was being sent from the *Mariana* to Mars, where it was sent back to Earth. It was bullshit. A total sim that played with itself in some AI sim generator onboard the *Mariana*. She checked it five times. In the process she came upon another data stream on another band, heavily compressed and encrypted. Her newly cooperative LOWNRs, however, opened it up for her and showed her the real Mars.

There were indeed several recorders keeping MarsCorp posted on its property. They were like the "before" pictures everyone knew: a rock-strewn landscape unimaginably harsh, bitterly cold, swept by sandstorms. The terraforming machinery like blisters on the poles. A hell waiting to be reborn as heaven. Only it was stillborn. The only effect of the months of terraforming appeared to be an increase in the polar ice caps.

There was indeed a Freedom City, but on the surface it was a tiny thing. Most of it was underground—a cavernous facility like an extensive mining operation awaiting workers. It was all decidedly low tech, labor intensive. There were barracks stretching for acres. Or at least she called them barracks at first. She knew a jail when she saw one. Most of the people on the planet looked like guards waiting for someone to lock up. They carried shock rods on their belts that would bring an ox to its knees. This was more like a penal colony than a new world. Then she remembered the history of the so-called New World on Earth, and she had to ask herself why she was even surprised, why she ever thought rich pigs like MarsCorp would ever build anything else.

She went down into the cavernous cellblock and switched over to full virtual. The air was painfully thin and left an oily taste in her gasping mouth. A concerned white woman's voice advised her she was emulating a lethal experience which could result in emulatory shock. Did she wish to edit her inputs to recommended survival parameters?

"Fuck you," Starr said. "Fuck all of you."

FOR SEVERAL HOURS SHE INDULGED IN HER RAGE. SHE WENT to a fight site where you could hand to hand without rules or warnings in a landscape of endless alleys and burned-out buildings. She punched and kicked and clubbed a few, then switched over to lose. But even the experience of her skull shattering against a brick wall was no release from her mental anguish.

She had long prepared herself for continual disappointments in her quest to reach Mars. It might be years and years, she'd told herself, before she set foot on the red planet, the land of her dreams. But that it was all a lie, that her hope was all based on some fiction—*that* she couldn't bear.

She stared out at the *Mariana*. It was named after the MarsCorp CEO's daughter, a skinny blond who drowned off Cozumel a few months before construction began on the ship. For a while there, the Web was filled with gushing testimonials to her do-good activities helping the hungry, though she looked pretty hungry herself. Starr had never been able to swallow her sainthood, figuring it was just another soap opera to show the world what splendid folks rich people were. And yet she'd swallowed the dream of a Martian paradise—a new planet where people like her could maybe for once, finally, get a decent break. She swallowed that one hook, line, and sinker.

Her first temptation was to turn this reality loose on Earth—override the damn sim and show Mars for what it was. But she quickly overruled that idea. She wasn't strong enough yet, didn't have enough control to keep from being traced and shut down in a heartbeat once MarsCorp got wind of what she was doing. There were three more LOWNRs she was scheduled to upgrade this week, but that still wouldn't be enough. Unless she had an ally, someone on the station who'd modify his quota as well.

The crew communicated with one another, when necessary, through the station network. Every once in a while it got chatty, though Starr never went virtual with any of them. Still, after a while, you got to know stuff about each other. There was only one other crew member who was even a remote possibility as an ally and that was Powell. The other two, Crichton and Furay, were on penal contracts MarsCorp had with the federal prison system, and were doing time for armed robbery and child molestation, respectively. They both gave Starr the creeps. Crichton, because he was too damn pleasant and cheery for somebody who'd pistol-whipped a seventy-five-year-old Pakistani grocer, and Furay because he suggested they meet virtual every time she talked with him.

Powell was another matter. He seemed like an okay guy, kind of quiet and slow, who was up here trying to make a buck. They'd talked about the *Mariana* and the Mars colony, and he even acted like he was interested in her plans. But how did you know with guys whether they were telling the truth or not?

Maybe there was another way. If she could get over to the *Mariana* and disable the AI that was cranking out the bogus Mars, MarsCorp wouldn't be able to cover their ass when she started putting out the truth. There were service vehicles onboard that could make it over to the *Mariana*, and she was confident she could dock it. But as she considered that plan, she saw it would take two as well. Nobody legit would go zipping around in a service shuttle on their own. Her only chance to get at the AI would be as part of an authorized service technician team from WebNet.

Talking to Powell about it over the station's network was about as secure as talking on a street corner. Even personal webspace was probably too risky. If she was going to enlist Powell to her cause, she'd have to meet with him in person. He was a big, hulking fellow. His image crowded out of the edge of the monitor as if the camera were trying to take in the side of a barn. That was good in a way. If anyone on the *Mariana* needed some intimidation, Powell could certainly intimidate better than her hundred-pound self could.

But if he wasn't what he seemed, if he decided he'd rather take her back to his room as his plaything for the next several months, what could she do? Shoot him and the space station with her shotgun? That was suicide, pure and simple. They'd both be sucking vacuum in a matter of seconds.

But what did she have to live for anyway? She looked below the *Mariana*, below herself, to Earth. It was supposed to be beautiful from up here. Nice long shot that didn't show the dogs eating the dogs or the rich assholes betting on the outcome. There was nothing for her down there. Never had been. Never would be. She wasn't going back.

She checked the clock. The common time in the rec room was coming up in a few hours. She called up Powell and said, "I want to talk to you about something. Meet me in the gym?"

He ran his hand over his bald head, his thoughtful gesture. "Sure," he said.

She didn't ask him for any reassurances. She didn't want to hear him say like the last guy she'd met real, "I won't hurt you, baby. I won't hurt you."

PART THREE

Veinte y Dos de Diciembre

*It is better to die on your feet than
live on your knees.*
—EMILIANO ZAPATA

CHAPTER
nine

RAPID HEARTBEAT, RAPID HEARTBEAT, RAPID HEARTBEAT—
there was a word for it—Webster knew there was a word for it. *Hyper-*
something? Hyperventilation? No. That was breathing. Well, he was
doing that too. He tried desperately to think what it was. He turned in
his seat and looked back the length of the bus. Margaret was across the
aisle, one-two-three-four-five-six-seven seats back. Not exactly hard to spot
with her white face and light brown hair towering over everyone around
her. Webster had concluded he was the tallest person in all of Mexico.
They were the only two white people on the bus.

Everyone else was some shade of brown, their hair black or gray. All
real. Every last one of them. He remembered accompanying his mother
to a real party when he was little. Everyone there said, "You brought
him?"—absolutely incredulous. He'd slept under a pile of coats, wasn't
allowed to leave the room—not that he would've tried. He was too
scared, burrowing under the coats smelling of perfume and cigarettes to
hide from the cryptic noises seeping in under the door. He woke in the
morning in his own bed. He never knew what went on there, and his
mother wouldn't tell him. He sometimes wondered if it'd ever really
happened or whether he'd dreamed the whole thing.

But this was like a dream come true: a bus packed with dark denizens
of the third world going about their real lives, not a one of them online
as far as he could tell. Who were they? What did they do with themselves? Where were they going? There were suitcases overhead, boxes
tied up with twine, plastic bags with clothes peeking out, burlap bags
of unshucked corn, a television, a bicycle wheel—flat. The tiny blasts
and bleeps of an antique video game a few rows back interwove with a
dozen—two dozen—crazed baby chicks peeping like soprano popcorn—
too loud to pin down their precise location. He'd seen a little girl in

the bus station carrying a box with holes in it, little beaks thrusting out into the air. If this wasn't realworld, he didn't know what was. He was headed into the mysterious heart of another *country*. The thought gave him goose bumps.

Margaret told him he hadn't seen anything yet in this border town, that things got a whole lot weirder down south. She was trying to scare him, sure, but he knew she was right. He'd wandered around the bus station, listening to people, getting used to the translator, and it was like a global econ site—God, how he'd hated that class—only this was the real thing. There were businesspeople, tradespeople, vendors, farmers, soldiers—lots of soldiers. And beggars—blind, crippled, old, young. Webster wanted to talk to them. They no doubt had some stories to tell. But he felt guilty taking up their time if he wasn't going to give them any money, and since he didn't know how the bills in his pocket worked, he thought it unwise to take them out in a crowded bus station and ask a starving man if the red one would be enough. At first he drew the beggars like a magnet, but then the word seemed to spread, and they left him alone.

He settled into a steady round of eavesdropping, staring uncomprehendingly at a Spanish newspaper he'd found to make it seem like he wasn't listening. He found the farmers particularly intriguing with their talk of seeds and dirt and rain. The soldiers didn't talk about much of anything whenever he came around. There were also some American soldiers (mixed in with the Mexican ones) whose presence rankled Margaret no end. She said she'd tell him why later—when there weren't any soldiers around. From what he'd seen so far, that might be a while. It made him nervous being around all these real guns and bullets and grenades and knives. It was amazing what they lugged around all the time. They kept their helmets on, little headsets built into them. Webster wondered whether the noise that buzzed around their heads was the same American pop music that seemed to be everywhere or some secret soldier communication.

Though there weren't any on this bus, there were a few other foreigners around, most of them American businessmen. There were a few tourists, mostly old folks reliving some teenage adventure. Not too many young folks. He hadn't seen any other kickers. There were some kids about his age Margaret said were Dutch or Swedish or something, though she didn't tell him how she knew. They seemed to be into the whole otherness thing: recording each other recording each other in places where they didn't belong, though, as they might say, in the non-places of globalville nothing could be said to belong. Shit like that. They put together these huge spliced sites with things like a huge amphitheater with a starving baby crying and dying in every other seat, a marimba band on the stage doing ad tunes. Other brothers, as they were called, gave Webster a serious headache. They went places so they could say they hadn't been there. They were webbier than the Web. Webster didn't want any part of it. He was going to be a traveler, a wanderer, a wayfarer. A nomad, a vagabond, a pilgrim. A bold explorer. A Citizen of the *World*.

Most everyone in the bus station, if they talked at all, had talked about *la guerra*, the war—his first real Spanish word, Webster thought, other than the *adios* and *amigo* everybody knew.

Webster had hated Spanish class and failed to perform satisfactorily. That is, he failed. The sim instructor had pointed out Webster's off-the-scale aptitude for language arts and commanded: "You should like Spanish, Webster." But that was like telling Jimi Hendrix that he should take up the autoharp since he was good with stringed instruments. Spanish was a dead language. The Web ran on English and translators into English. Even the French had caved. Other languages were *over*. Webster figured it would take several lifetimes to get halfway good at English. Why waste his time on some language nobody used anymore?

That was before he was here in the middle of it. There was some English, sure. Songs on the radio. Even these big signs—billboards Margaret called them—with all the words in English, as if to say "If you're cool enough to read this, you're cool enough to buy our shit." But everything else was Spanish. It was like finding out that right next to the world you lived in was an entirely different one where the language was so different your mouth felt different when you tried to say it. It was like learning a new way to kiss.

He loved Spanish.

Sitting on the bus, the well-worn newspaper he couldn't read still in his hands, he thought about all the words—their sounds, their shapes. So far he'd figured out nouns mostly. *Helado*, ice cream (from a sign in the station). He hung around and listened to the vendor talk up business and figured out the *h* was silent; *tierra*, land; *salida*, exit; *billete*, ticket. He played with the words in his head like stringing beads on a thread, but he couldn't make a sentence. He needed some verbs. It occurred to him he could feed the translator sentences to translate by talking to himself.

"Good-bye, friend, I'm going to war," he whispered into the microphone.

"*Adios, amigo, voy a la guerra,*" the translator said in full voice. The man sitting next to him glanced over and away. Webster made two mental notes: 1) the translator does not know how to whisper, 2) *Voy a* means "I'm going to."

Voy a, voy a—voy a . . . what? It was about time, Webster told himself, to meet his fellow travelers.

He furtively perused the man sitting next to him. He was about twenty-five, in a dark blue suit and white shirt. His slender, uncomfortable-looking shoes shone with an ostentatious brilliance. His face glistened with sweat. And he wasn't presenting this. This was real. It was at least eighty-five degrees in this bus, and this man was wearing a dark suit. He was reading a Smartbook—*Getting What You Want in Cyberspace.* E. Paramount Briggs was the unlikely name of the author, a *nom de plume,* no doubt. The smiling American face on the cover seemed to be saying "I'm rich, and you're not." Webster leaned sideways to get a glimpse of the page and saw the text was set to Spanish. The man caught Webster looking over his shoulder and glared his displeasure.

"Hi," Webster said, smiling what he hoped was an engaging smile. "What do you do?"

"I am reading," the man said, or that's what the translator said he said. He had turned in his seat and was now reading with a vengeance. Webster thought better of saying that wasn't what he was asking.

The bus started up with a roar and settled into a quiet rumble. The arms of his seat, the floor beneath his shoes, vibrated ever so slightly. The sensation reminded him of the time in history class they did the *Lusitania.* He and Sissy Morris snuck down to the engine room and made out, missed the whole thing. It was a war or something. On the exam, he said it was a valiant voyage of circumnavigation, and the interrogator derided him mercilessly, calling Webster a polysyllabic sycophant. Webster mounted a spirited defense: There was too much knowledge, too much information. Everybody said so. How could one silly boat be that important? But he failed the exam anyway. Washed out of history. A lachrymose experience if there ever was one. But this wasn't some simmed tub wallowing in a phony ocean, this was a real bus headed into the third world. He wasn't studying history; he was in it.

A man started down the aisle taking tickets. His face looked like it came from the Mayan temples they visited in that same class. The guide had talked about human sacrifice and the number zero. Webster couldn't remember if there was a connection. He surrendered his ticket as Margaret had instructed him, and was given back a portion of it. Webster placed the remainder of the ticket—Margaret had called it a *stub*—in his pocket along with his visa and his money and zipped it shut. There sure was a lot of paraphernalia to keep track of in the real world.

The ticket guy was making his way slowly down the aisle. Some people were actually buying their tickets on the spot. Webster watched with fascination as the money changed hands, not just bills like he had, but coins as well. He couldn't wait to get some coins so he could jingle them in his pocket on a street corner.

The bus probably wouldn't be leaving, Webster figured, until the ticket guy was done. By leaning out into the aisle a little, Webster could see out the windshield. There wasn't much to see. They were still parked at the station. The driver was just sitting there, staring at nothing. Webster leaned around the partition between them and tapped the driver on the shoulder. He hadn't meant to startle him. "Hi, my name is Webster. What's it like to drive a big bus like this?"

The driver twisted around in his seat and eyed Webster suspiciously, looking him up and down. The only intelligible words in the driver's spirited reply were "shut up," "fuck," "old," and "gringo." Webster's translator had a limited capacity to handle obscenity, but Webster got the message and sat back in his seat. He thought the suit with the Smartbook had a chuckle out of it, but Webster didn't actually catch him in the act.

Maybe part of the problem was that the translator was still set to sound like *Abuelito*. The driver perhaps thought Webster impertinent, a perception not unusual in Webster's experience. He couldn't believe how he kept fucking up. At this rate, he would journey for days on this packed conveyance with absolutely no one to converse with. If he was going to get along in the real world, he told himself, he needed to be more real, more straightforward. He must eschew his webbish proclivity for irony. He set to work, sampling voices to himself, looking for mature, suave, and sincere all at the same time. Neither the driver nor the Smartbook reader, however, looked open to a tête-à-tête.

The television came on, and Webster jumped in his seat. He'd never actually gone face-to-face with a real one before, though in his youth he'd hung out at the TV Town site and met Gilligan, Lucy, Kramer, Ally, Howdy Doody, Uhura, Ted Koppel. He hoped for something Mexican, but it turned out to be an old American movie—*Because It Is There!* (subtitled *¡Porque Está Allá!*). Melodramatic music and airplane sounds swirled around Mount Everest during the credits. Webster burst out laughing when inside the airplane turned out to be none other than an aged Steven Seagal stuffed into an enormous yak jacket made, apparently, from several enormous yaks. He smoked a skinny black cigar and spoke Spanish. The voice sounded a lot like *Abuelito*, cranked high to be heard over the airplane noise. It was hilarious, risible, jocund.

The woman across the aisle laughed, too, and Webster looked over at her. "I thought he was only in the Web," he said. At the Fight Site Seagal's sim regularly pummeled a dozen armed ruffians who never fired a shot.

"In Mexico, he can't afford Web access. He still rides the bus like everyone else," she said.

She was joking with him. Badinage. A kindred spirit, he thought. She was about his age, her eyes the color of coffee. But they still managed to twinkle. "My name is Webster," he said and held out his hand, hoping that was the right thing to do.

She shook it. "Aurora," she said. The translator said "Dawn" in his ear. He preferred *Aurora*. "Dawn" was much too prosaic for this woman who managed to look exotic, noble, capable—all at the same time—despite her humble attire of worn blue jeans and a faded red T-shirt.

After his experience with the man next to him, he knew not to ask what she did. "Where are you bound?" he asked instead, one traveler to another.

"Home," she said. "My village."

"What's it called?"

"You've never heard of it," she said.

He tried to listen to the translator and the sound of her voice at the same time. She sounded pleasant enough, but she'd apparently seen through him already. "I'm sure you're right," he said sadly. "I've never been anywhere."

He hadn't intended to be funny, but she laughed anyway, though not in a mean way. "I wasn't trying to say that—only that *no one* has heard of my tiny village. It is called Twenty-second of December." When she told him the name, her voice dropped, as if she were confiding a secret. *Veinte y Dos de Diciembre.*

Webster laughed along, feeling mildly hysterical. "I've never heard of a town being named a date."

"We Mexicans do it all the time. Streets, towns. After important days."

"What happened on December twenty-second?" Webster asked cheerfully.

She ignored his question. "Where are you from?"

"Dallas-Fort Worth."

"I know that area," she said. "Whereabouts?"

¿Por dónde? Webster took note. "I have a room near the old baseball stadium. It's near where I work."

"What's the name of the town?"

"I don't know."

They were interrupted by an explosion on the screen. A huge fireball erupted into the air against a backdrop of snow-covered mountains. The soundtrack, full orchestra with electric guitar solo, distorted the speakers into rattling mush. Helicopters moved back and forth in the foreground to no apparent purpose. Webster and Aurora turned and watched it for a moment.

"You don't know the name of your town?" she asked, her eyes still on the screen.

"It's Arlington, I think. Do you really think all that arbitrary political-boundary stuff matters anymore?"

She turned back to him, a challenging look in her eye. "Only an American would say that. You live in your computers and forget every-one else."

"I don't. I'm a webkicker. I have a job, my own place." If you were really a webkicker, you didn't *call* yourself one, but here Webster figured it was just easier to come out with it.

"But you can't even tell me where your place is," Aurora said gently. "What does it mean—*webkicker?*" The word hung in the air untrans-lated. It only came in one flavor—American slang. That alone made her point, but she pressed on. "You pretend to work, you pretend to live in a real place. But it's all pretending. When you get older, and life gets harder, you quit pretending and become like your parents. I don't pretend to work. I have no choice, just like my parents."

Since he'd probably just thrown away his job on a lark, he couldn't exactly argue with her. "What if you had the choice?" he asked. "What would you do?"

She shrugged and laughed. "I don't know. I'm sorry. I have no right to criticize. . . ."

"Sure you do. No, really. If you could do what you wanted, what would you do?"

"Go home for good," she said quietly.

"Twenty-second of December?"

"You remembered."

"Of course." This seemed to please her no end.

The bus had settled into a steady, lumbering pace. Webster's long torso practically spanned the aisle. Aurora leaned toward him so that they might've been in some sidewalk café site having a chat. Bit by bit at Webster's urging, she told him her story.

Since she was thirteen, she'd worked in the U.S., at first seasonal, picking apples in Washington, grapes in California. Then she got a year-round job cleaning and maintaining retirement rack-and-stacks in Dallas-Fort Worth, then Charlotte. She sent money home to her mother and younger brothers and sisters, came home to visit once a year. "This is progress," she said. "It used to be only the men went north to work; now the women go too." She told him how her grandfather, while crossing illegally into the States, had died in a locked boxcar with twenty-three other men trapped inside. Only one man lived, and he later killed himself. A few years later, her father had been shot by American Marines patrolling the border, supposedly looking for drug traffickers. Her father had installed hot tubs in Virginia. He wasn't rich enough to have been running drugs.

She paid for good forged documents showing she had a day job in Brownsville, and always used public transportation to cross, so it was not so dangerous—though sometimes the border guards tried to shake her down for money or "other things." Once it took her a week of trying to get back across, and she almost didn't make it home for Christmas. Soon, in a few years she hoped, there'd be enough money saved to buy her family a decent house, and she could come home for good.

Webster tried to imagine the concept of being "home" for Christmas, but it wouldn't process. "Why don't you just stay in the U.S.? I know people in the Web who could get you work cards and stuff."

"I don't want to stay there. I'm a Mexican. I want to live in my own country, clean my own home, not always someone else's."

There was a series of grunts from the screen as Seagal kicked several men in the balls. Each kick gave Webster vertigo. Aurora's story had had a similar effect on his psyche. He turned back to her intense, beautiful eyes.

"How long has it been since you've been home?"

"Eight months," she said. "My mother asked me to come. She is frightened."

"Frightened of what?"

Aurora looked around her, as if one of the other passengers, all seemingly engrossed in the Seagal movie, might be a spy. "Life," she said with a rueful smile, her eyes tearing up.

La vida.

She thought he'd forgotten, but he hadn't. Now seemed like a good time to ask. "What happened on December twenty-second?" The translator said everything the same, but he hoped she could hear in his real voice that he was asking in the nicest possible way. You could see her deciding whether to tell him or not.

When she spoke, her voice was almost matter-of-fact, the sound of a speech handed down: "In 1997, in the town of Acteal, forty-five unarmed people were murdered by government paramilitary. Thirty-six of them women and children. No one was ever punished for the crime. The families who founded my village were refugees from around there."

"God, I'm sorry. I never heard of that." He felt like such a complete idiot. Of course, neither one of them had even been born in 1997.

"There's no reason you should have."

"I guess not," he said, though it made him feel sick to say it. There *was* a reason, lots of reasons. Every reason. He wanted to tell her this. He wanted—

She looked into his eyes. Without thinking, he said, "Your eyes are beautiful." It just came out. For a split second he wasn't even sure he'd said it out loud except for the echo of the translator—"*Sus ojos son bellos.*"

She drew back in surprise, gave him a level gaze. She didn't seem angry, but he couldn't be sure. "Do you always take such liberties with strangers?"

"Christ, I'm sorry. I was forgetting where I was. Not forgetting exactly. I *know*. But I've never really been anywhere, so I don't know what it means, how things work here. I've hardly ever talked to a woman in a real place. At a site, if I'm too fresh, a girl can edit me out, block me so I'm not even there. I can do the same to her. No hard feelings. Lots of sites the whole idea is to 'take liberties.' Something like this—a bus headed into the heart of a foreign country—I might as well be on Mars. But I really do think your eyes are beautiful, though I'm pretty freaked myself that I said it out loud. It would just really, really be terrible if saying it meant. . . . I'm just really sorry, truly penitent. . . .'' His voice trailed off.

He'd outrun the translator. So after he finally quit babbling, it continued on with his plea in mechanical Spanish. She listened with a faint smile on her face. She was beautiful all over, he decided, but thought better of blurting that out until the issue of her eyes was settled.

". . . *penitente*," the translator concluded. Four syllables. Webster chanted it silently to himself as he waited for her to speak.

"You don't have to apologize," she said. "I'm glad you like my eyes." She paused, looked into his eyes and away. His heart did a little tap dance. "What brings you to Mexico, Webster, on this long bus ride 'into the heart of a foreign country' besides flattering strangers?"

She was mocking him a little, but that was okay. He wished he could be straight with her, reveal his true mission, perhaps earn some respect from her, but he was a spy and must exercise discretion. He desperately needed, however, a more dignified cover story than traveling with his mommy. He sifted through what he'd learned about Mexico in school. There were rain forests in the south, he remembered, with species going extinct right and left. "I'm an ornithologist," he announced. She looked skeptical. "An ornithologist's *assistant*, actually." He pointed down the aisle to Margaret who smiled and waved as if on cue. "That's Dr. May-field," he said. "The chief ornithologist of the Global Institute of Ornithological Investigation."

He regaled Aurora with tidbits of information about species and ecosystems and forest understories as if he knew what he was talking about, as if he were back in school, impressing a proctor. For the life of him, however, he couldn't remember the name of a single Mexican bird and strung together Latin-y sounding syllables he hoped were convincingly scientific and birdish.

The man with the Smartbook got off in Monterrey, and Aurora took the seat beside Webster. He took this opportunity to divert the conversation back to her. His rain forest routine was running dry. Next, he'd be faking bird calls for his fake birds. She, on the other hand, had a real family to talk about, and he encouraged her to tell him about every single person in it. He heard about *hermanos, tias, primos, abuelos, bisabuelos.*

"Boyfriend?" Webster asked.

"No, no novio."

Bien, Webster thought.

But after a while she noticed the one-sidedness of their conversation and asked about *his* family. His clumsy attempts to change the subject only piqued her interest. "At least tell me about your mother," she insisted. "Did she raise you?"

"More or less. I was in the Web most of the time." He never talked about his mother with anyone, not even Starr. Mom was probably flying dragons in Pern about now. She'd gotten into that lately. She wouldn't mind Webster talking about her. She wouldn't mind at all. Would probably like it, as a matter of fact. Be nice, he told himself.

"She's my only family really." He looked for a word. "She's extremely chimerical, I suppose."

Aurora shook her head. "Chimerical?" The translator didn't know the word.

"Quixotic?" Webster suggested. That was Mexican or Spanish or something, wasn't it?

Aurora nodded vigorously. She knew and understood *quijotesco.* *"¿Cómo?* How?" she asked.

Webster heard both tinny translator and Aurora's rich alto and filed the information away: *Cómo* means how. She looked like she really wanted to know. He sighed and launched in.

"She's kind of a Web junkie. She's always saying it's better than the real world. She's been going through the same cycle since she was about thirteen, before the Web was even virtual: She gets hooked on some wild site—the weirder the better—then some guy at the site—also the weirder the better—then she gets real with them, gets pregnant, gets an abortion. Then she starts all over again. She broke the cycle with me— temporarily at least—because she met my father at a fundie site where the whole idea was to get hooked on fruitfully multiplying, which she did, long enough to get married and have me anyway. She and my father split up when I was still a baby. I never met him. She picked up again where she left off."

"Why does she do it?"

"She's a dreamer. She says the Web can be anything you want it to be, a place for dreams to come true."

"The Web is not a place."

El web no es lugar.

Webster started to correct her, to explain that it was a virtual place, millions of virtual places, but she'd just tell him again that he was talking like an American. "I guess it's just a dream, then," he said, borrowing a page from Mom's book.

"It's not even that. A dream, such as your mother desires, requires a place, like seeds require the earth."

He thought about this, and though his knowledge of *la tierra* and *las simientes* was strictly secondhand, it made sense to him. He'd never thought of his mother as doomed before, like someone trying to survive on imaginary food. He'd just thought that her way was not his way, that they were just different, on different paths, as she'd say. If what Aurora said was true, his mom would never be any happier than she'd always been, just pathetically hopeful forever. He felt a wave of sadness for her. In a strange way he was glad of it. He'd sometimes wondered whether he felt anything for her anymore. It was good to know he did.

"I'm sorry," Aurora said. "I speak too much. It's not for me to judge."

"No, this is good. I never get to talk to anyone like this, about something real."

"Do you have a girlfriend?"

"Yeah. Sort of."

He explained about Starr, how she worked in space and their whole relationship was virtual—and, well, mostly sexual. "I'm pretty sure she's older than she presents, and that's okay. It's kind of exciting, I guess. Or flattering maybe. But she can't be taking me too seriously, do you think?"

"Is she a prisoner?"

Preso. Webster knew where she got that idea. With cheap shuttles, it was hard to beat space as a prison locale, and people thought that's all there was up there. "Not everyone who works in space is a criminal. She had some trouble with the law before, but she went into space because she wanted to. She wants to go to Mars. She's kind of a fanatic on the idea. She says it'll be a whole new world."

Aurora smiled. "That's what they called Mexico five hundred years ago." She pointed out the window. "Does it look new to you?"

They rode along in silence. They were entering the high central valley, approaching the vast sprawl of Mexico City, the largest city in the world. You could barely make out the mountains that ringed the horizon where the air seemed to thicken and congeal. Even though it was still plenty warm, you could hear the sound of windows sliding shut throughout the bus, as if they could keep the brown air out.

Aurora was getting off in Mexico City to catch another bus east, then another south to her village up in the mountains. She drew a rough map of Mexico on his newspaper and placed San Cristóbal and Veinte y Dos de Diciembre for him. They didn't look that far apart, but she explained there were mountains in between. He knew she didn't have a site, so he asked for her phone number, but she didn't have one of those either. Even mail didn't come to her village, but she gave him an address in a neighboring town where her cousin held mail for her. "Good-bye, Webster," she said and kissed his cheek.

After she'd gone, and the bus pulled out of the station, he sat thinking about how someone could be real and alive but completely gone as if they didn't exist anymore. He drifted off, repeating to himself the time that was a place, *"Veinte y Dos de Diciembre."*

WHEN HE WOKE UP, SOLDIERS WERE BOARDING THE BUS, weapons at the ready. Margaret, who had apparently moved into the seat beside him when he was asleep, was shaking his shoulder. "Give the soldier your visa, son," she said, coming down hard on the last word to cue him.

He groggily sat up, unzipped his chest pocket, and reached inside. "Sure, Mom. I've got it right here." The visa was on the bottom, under the money and the stub. He pulled it all out at once, and the stub fluttered to the floor. Webster lunged for it, but froze, a gun barrel pressed against his neck, his fingertips hovering inches over the innocuous little square of paper.

"My stub," he said.

The officer in charge motioned Webster away from the stub with the back of his hand, bent at the waist, and swept it off the floor. Webster slowly sat upright. He could still feel the barrel against his neck, even though it wasn't there anymore. He'd had plenty of experience with guns, even had the barrels of automatic weapons pressed to temple, neck, forehead, testicles. But always, as Aurora would say, just pretending. He couldn't say that the actual experience differed from the virtual one in any sensory way. In every other way, however, they were nothing alike. His hands were trembling, and he couldn't swallow. He'd never been so scared in his life.

The officer examined the stub front and back, as if it contained all the secrets of Webster's life. "Why do you go to Chiapas?"

Why indeed? Why was he out here risking his life? Why . . . ?

"We are going—" Margaret began.

"I am asking the boy," the officer said, cutting her off with sharp, precise tones. He looked at Margaret, then at Webster.

"—to a funeral," Webster finished for his dear old mum. "My father's funeral." His voice quavered with what might be grief or terror. He sat up straighter in his seat, trying to be the brave young man, the good son.

The officer pointed at Webster's fist, still clutching visa and money. "Your visa." He opened his palm, and Webster placed the whole bundle there. The officer's hand closed around it. "Are you trying to bribe me?" he asked, smiling.

Webster managed a good-natured laugh. "No, certainly not." He held out his hand to get his money back, but the soldier ignored it and glanced over the visa. "Very good," he said, handing it back without the money.

"My money?" Webster asked tentatively, but the soldiers had already moved down the aisle. They hadn't even asked to see Margaret's papers.

"Smooth," Margaret whispered. "Was that all the money I gave you?"

"Yes."

"Next time don't keep it all in one pocket."

He felt awful, but Margaret seemed to find the episode diverting, which cheered him up a little. He'd faced real danger and emerged triumphant. It gave him a rush like no virtual experience ever had. He followed Margaret's lead and casually ignored the soldiers, pretending to read his newspaper. He found his word *guerra* several times, but he didn't know enough to figure out what was being said. The big story was wrapped around a photograph of *el presidente* shaking hands with a white-haired American named McCauley. The caption seemed to indicate this handshake had something to do with 1.4 billion dollars.

Webster stared out the window. Why was he sure this money would go to no good purpose? They were up in the mountains now, parked in a place that had once been a little village. Everything was blown up. The battered wall beside them had a few legible words still painted on it, one of which he knew—*helado*, ice cream. It was underscored with a line of bullet holes. The roadblock consisted of a couple of Jeeps mounted with machine guns parked across the road, a dozen soldiers lounging around.

Veinte y Dos de Diciembre, he thought.

The soldiers took two young men off the bus. They stood by the side of the road, their eyes down, but the soldiers didn't point their guns at them. "What will happen to them?" he asked Margaret.

"They're in the army now," Margaret said.

The bus started up again with a lurch. The driver didn't waste any time picking up speed. Pretty soon they were whizzing around hairpin curves overlooking precipitous canyons. It was like a wild-ride site. There was a shocked murmur from the passengers on the other side of the bus, and Webster stood to look out. A bus lay crumpled like a stomped Coke can at the bottom of the canyon. A bus painted the same as this one. At a site, he would've laughed, thinking *nice touch,* but this was real. The bus he was in whipped around another curve and he fell back into his seat. The windows were all open now, and the air smelled of pines and diesel and a bus full of strangers. His head teemed with vivid sensations—the taste of *chilaquiles,* Aurora's lips on his cheek, a gun barrel pressed against his neck, the glimpse of death in the valley—clear and unmistakable. He'd never experienced anything like this in or out of the Web. Nothing even close.

He'd thought he had a sense of direction before he met Margaret, that he was slowly and surely making his life real. But that was nothing compared to this. He'd thought real was real. That it was all the same. Like all the sites in the Web, when you got down to it, were all the same. Boy, did he have a lot to learn.

A real webkicker wasn't into any recording gigs, even if you stayed real yourself like this Santee apparently did. Like athletes spent most of their time real, slaving away to give the rest of the world the experience of being the strongest, fastest, most graceful whatever money could buy. There was a purity about professional athletes Webster guiltily admired, even if he couldn't condone their volunteering to live others' lives for them.

But Intrepid Explorers wouldn't be like that, would it? What if, like right now he was recording this bus trip and he put it in the Web—other people might say, "I've got to do that—go have some real experience in *another country!* If this *kid* can do it, I can too."

As they rode along, the idea grew in his head, until there was room for little else. When he could contain it no longer, he blurted out, "Margaret, do you think I could get a job with Intrepid Explorers?"

She had been looking out the window herself, with a sad distant look, apparently oblivious to the tosses and turns of their wild ride. She turned slowly to face him, shaking her head and looking at him as if he were totally demented. Her laugh was harsh and unkind. "That is a *thoroughly* bad idea, Webster."

He winced in anguish. He'd thought she'd be delighted to hear of his bold intentions. Wasn't she the one who made such a big deal of the real world? Instead she mocked him, deemed him unworthy. He didn't ask why, or what she meant exactly. Did it matter? Just another stupid idea in a long series of stupid ideas. He was just like his mom, no different for all his rebellion. Just another loser. Margaret had already turned back to the window as if nothing had happened.

He sulked for the rest of the way into San Cristóbal—with good reason, he thought. If she thought he was stupid, she didn't have to be so blunt about it. She didn't even notice he was upset, of course, acted like nothing was wrong. Pretty soon she was back to pointing out stuff through the window like he was some little kid on a field trip. She pointed out all the bad stuff—all the soldiers and the blown-up build-ings, the writing on the walls. She translated it all, of course, showing off how great she was in Spanish, but he made a point of not listening.

As they approached San Cristóbal, she started talking disparagingly about tourists like she'd never been one herself. Webster thought the town looked beautiful no matter what she said, as different from a row of rack-and-stacks as heaven was from hell. If he thought she would've cared, he would've told her that. But she'd probably just laugh at him again.

WHEN THEY REACHED THE CHURCH, WEBSTER WONDERED whether it was even the right place. There was nobody there, just a closed casket up front. By this time he'd settled so thoroughly into not speaking with Margaret, that he didn't even think to ask her what was going on. He just figured she'd tell him what to do. She was good at ordering people around. Finally, this priest with the long black thing—cassock?—and the whole getup, popped out of a side door hidden be-hind one of the many statues.

Margaret and the priest talked Spanish to each other too fast for the translator to keep up, and Webster shut it off. He didn't care about her dead boyfriend. He was tired, he was bummed, and he was hungry. Disconsolate was what he was.

He looked around while the two of them nattered on. The church was a trip. He'd been in Catholic churches before in the Web. Somebody'd told him you could meet girls there, which proved totally untrue in his experience. He'd always assumed the churches were enhanced for the Web with all the paintings and statues and gold leaf everywhere, but this was real and it was replete with baroque excess. The story of Christ getting killed was depicted in gruesome little scenes around the perimeter, and Webster longed to take a closer look. He especially liked the statues. Whoever had sculpted the faces around here could really do agony.

But the powwow was soon concluded, and the priest steered Margaret and Webster to the back rows of the church, where some first-class hardware was set up. Little Weisiger generators placed discreetly under the pews would Web in the back three rows Webster figured. He peeked under the pew and took a look at one. Nice stuff. The label on the side identified it as a rental unit belonging to MexNet, a division of WebNet International. It seemed like a lot of trouble for just him and Margaret. But in the midst of all this opulence, you had to figure somebody around here had some serious money.

"Are you ready to go in?" Margaret asked.

Webster shrugged. "Sure."

The priest powered up the generators, and they were in the virtual version of the church, just about identical in every respect, though this one was full of people, nearly all Americans it looked like, standing around talking to each other in English about dear old, dead Santee.

I didn't even know the guy, Webster thought. What am I doing here? Margaret rose from the virtual pew to mingle with the rest of the crowd loitering at the back of the church, and Webster tagged along.

A man broke from the group and bore down on them. "Margaret, this is so horrible. You have my deepest, deepest sympathies." He was a squared-off looking man—square face, square shoulders, square hair. Even his eyes looked square. Supposedly, this wasn't an enhancement and he really looked this way. Yeah, right. Webster recognized him as Cliff Carter, the anchor for NewsReal's *World at Large*. To a webkicker, he was the embodiment of the enemy, a deity in the pantheon of the Web. He was holding Margaret's hands, going on about her great loss, and she was taking what Webster thought was an inordinate amount of time to introduce her faux son.

Finally, she said, "Cliff Carter, I want you to meet a good friend of mine and Santee's, Webster Webfoot."

So he was demoted to "friend" now. Cliff shook his hand like it was supposed to be a great privilege or something. Webster thought of slyly confrontational things to say, but didn't waste them on this chiseled buffoon. He just shook the big square hand and stared at the man's square-tipped shoes. I can't believe I'm doing this, he thought.

"How did you know Santee?" Cliff asked in his square voice.

Webster looked around the crowd. Half of them were faces vaguely familiar from different newsites around the Web. "Tech," Webster said. He knew tech. He could do it if he had any desire to. He looked closely at Cliff's jaw. Squinted. "You might want to have your enhancements checked. Some of the lines look a little jagged to me."

Cliff rubbed his jaw with concern. "I'll do that."

Margaret was smiling when Cliff left. "That was beautiful," she said. "Couldn't happen to a nicer guy."

"Aren't you supposed to be grieving or something?"

"I told you—Santee's not dead. Did I say something to piss you off?"

He didn't answer. Another media type, a female of the species this time, came out of the crowd to comfort Margaret, and Webster decided to wander off toward Jesus lugging the cross through a hostile crowd. I know just how you feel, he thought. The music started up—wheezy church organ music. He'd rather hear cats scratching a blackboard than that ponderous cacophony.

I don't have to stay here, he reminded himself. I'm in the Web. He entered Starr's address. To his surprise, she didn't answer. She had to be around. She was always in her quarters except during her rec time, which were hours away. She was ignoring him, pissed for some reason. He checked his messages and was told a message from Starr waited for him at that Rincón site he'd popped in and out of what seemed like days ago. What the hell. He went there.

THE SAME GUY WAS SITTING IN THE SAME PLACE. THIS TIME Webster pulled up a chair and sat down with him. He looked just like the Jesus on the cross at the front of the church Webster'd just left, and he looked about as happy. "Webster Webfoot," Webster said.

"Emiliano Zapata," he said. "Welcome."

Webster had heard the name, but he couldn't really say what he'd heard about the man. "FACTS sim?" he asked.

The sim smiled and nodded. "More or less."

"A friend of mine named Starr left a message for me here?"

Zapata smiled at the mention of Starr. "A fascinating woman," he said. "She is strong, someone who will fight for what she believes in, but lovely and passionate as well. Don't you agree?"

"Hmm," Webster grunted. "Do you have a message or not?" Webster resisted the temptation to ask just what she and Emiliano had been up to when she was here.

"She says it's urgent that you contact her."

"Is that all?"

"I suspect she's angry with you."

"What did I do?"

"I believe she doubted your fidelity."

Webster considered the last time he'd seen her, in the midst of his silly crush on Margaret. Starr must've figured who his customer in need was and gotten it into her head to get jealous. It wouldn't be the first time. Even though she was the one who always said there were no commitments, no obligations, it rankled her if he showed the slightest interest in anyone else. It made no sense. He never understood women.

"What is this place?" he asked Zapata.

"Rincón. It's not a place. It's a fiction, a novel Santee calls it."

"Santee? Santee St. John?"

"That's right."

"I'm at his funeral with Margaret Mayfield. You know Margaret?"

"Very well."

"She's pretty strange, you know?"

"She is unique."

"You can say that again. One minute I was just going about my business, juggling oranges. The next thing you know I'm in another country—at the funeral of a total stranger with all these Web wonks. She seems pretty sure Santee's not dead, but a lot of other people seem to think otherwise. I don't know what to think. Do you know if he's alive?"

"I know very little of his real life these days. He hasn't been here in some time."

From inside the hotel came the sound of a piano. It seemed to come out of nowhere like someone had thrown a Chopin switch. The interaction here was really edgy, like this Santee didn't care whether it made any sense or not, maybe preferred if it didn't. Webster liked that.

"Is that another sim?" Webster asked.

Zapata smiled. "That would be Rosa." He cast his eyes that way to encourage Webster to introduce himself. "The proprietor."

There wasn't much to the parlor inside but a grand piano, a polished floor, and lots of potted plants. A woman in old-fashioned clothes played with little flourishes of her hands. She nodded at the bench beside her and Webster sat as she finished the nocturne.

He applauded when she was done.

"I am Rosa King. Welcome to the Bella Vista, Webster Webfoot," she said with a British accent.

"This is your place?"

"It was my hotel. It used to be in Cuernavaca during the Revolution until Santee moved it here to Rincón." She laughed. "Or rather, he invited me into his novel, knowing perfectly well my hotel must come with me wherever I go—along with my piano."

"What can you tell me about Santee?"

"Very little I'm afraid. He's the author of Rincón. I don't know him personally, only as one of his characters. I'm not even sure what he intends for me. It's not finished, you see."

"Well, if you see Santee," Webster said, "tell him I'm attending his funeral, and that Margaret and I are looking for him."

"I certainly will, Webster."

He tried Starr's address again. This time he did go somewhere, but it wasn't Starr's. It looked like his own site—a dark, damp little room. Someone in a ski mask, a red bandana tied around his neck, stepped out of the shadows with a gun.

"Why are you looking for Santee?" It was a woman's voice. Somehow that made it all the more frightening. He panicked and abruptly quit the Web. He looked around. Margaret was nowhere to be seen. The priest neither. The coffin no longer sat at the front of the church. The only sound was a pigeon cooing somewhere up in the rafters. In his lap was an envelope with his name printed on it.

"Margaret!" he shouted. "Where are you?"

Nothing.

Then he realized he hadn't heard the translator. He put his hands on his head. The translator was gone. He checked the envelope and found it'd been neatly slit open and was empty. On the floor at his feet was a folded up piece of paper. He picked it up and read:

Webster,

 Thanks for everything you've done. I appreciate it more than I can say. I hate abandoning you like this, but I have a lead on Santee's whereabouts, and I must pursue it. It's much too dangerous to take you along. Here's more than enough money to get you back to Dallas. Be careful.

              Margaret

 One by one he checked the many pockets of his jumpsuit: No visa. No money. Nothing but his ticket stub, and Aurora's friend's address. Even his Bruce's ID was gone. It didn't take him long to think of a word for his current condition. There was only one that would do. One that captured the essence of his predicament in all its horrific glory:

 He was fucked. Totally and thoroughly fucked.

CHAPTER
TEN

AS THE CHURCH FILLED WITH MOURNERS, MARGARET WON-
dered who'd notified all these people, and why so many had come. She
and Santee had been together for years. She knew everyone he'd want
at his funeral. None of them were here. Instead, the room was stuffed
with mere acquaintances, mostly co-workers from NewsReal and Intrepid
Explorers. Some she didn't know at all, and wondered if Santee did.
There were a few who actively disliked Santee. But here they were.
Why? Santee wasn't important enough in this crowd to elicit this level
of hypocrisy. She searched the faces, but didn't see Santee's parents, his
brother, his best friend—anyone he would've wanted to be here, anyone
who knew him intimately, who might give the lie to the whole
proceeding.

Except her.

As if this were all for her benefit. Maybe it was. By the time she got
to *Migración*, they would've had her in the system. Blaine Clute
would've run a check on her even if Simón thought she was the Virgin
of Guadalupe herself. Someone wanting it to look like Santee was dead
had put together this event to record and post on the Web. All the
better if his grieving girlfriend came to Mexico for the service. She
hoped Federico Aristos hadn't been in on the whole charade, that he'd
just been the dupe of the information he'd been fed, but she'd never
know for certain one way or the other. She chose to believe he was the
kind, helpful man he seemed to be. If no one could be trusted, anything
she did—life itself—was a waste of time.

And if there was one person you could absolutely trust, no matter
what, it made everything else worthwhile. She looked up the aisle. Here
in the virtual sanctuary, the coffin stood open. The mourners filed by.
They were all quite convincing in their grief, in their uneasiness before

the dead. Even here in virtual space, where feigned death was a commonplace.

From where she stood, she couldn't see who lay inside the coffin. Or seemed to. Of course it would look like Santee. This was a virtual. It could just as easily look like Mickey Mouse. It didn't mean anything. She felt oddly detached from herself as if she were looking down on the sanctuary like the dark Jesus on the cross. She started up the aisle at the stately pace expected of her. The crowd parted before her, their shuffling feet amplified by the stone walls, the pitch of their talk hissing down to whispers. She left a wake of sympathy—commiserating little grimaces, whispers to one another about what a "poor thing" she was. They didn't know. They didn't understand. "He's not dead," she wanted to tell them. "This whole thing is bullshit."

But what if the interface had malfunctioned somehow, and he actually was dead? She shook off the thought and picked up her pace. Her eyes ached to cry, but for some reason she held back. A voice in her head warned her as she drew closer to the casket: *Don't look down, don't look down.*

It was inevitable, wasn't it—the show they'd all come for—the widow wailing over the man she loved? The public surrender to death? *Don't worry, sir, I won't be no trouble no more, sir. . . .*

She'd reached the coffin. She placed her hands on it, gave the assembled congregation one sharp, defiant, over-the-shoulder look. *I'm no widow, for I was never wife. We're lovers.*

She looked down.

Santee lay inside, rouged and dead by all appearances. Her tears broke from her in great racking sobs, and she sank to her knees. The pain was unbearable. She knew this wasn't him, but that didn't matter. Someday he'd be dead, and now she'd have the memory of it for the rest of her life. In the manner of prayer, she closed her eyes, clasped her hands, and cursed long and hard whoever had done this to her.

She straightened up, turned away, and caught the priest watching her, not with pastoral concern but anxiously, like a chef watching a diner devour a week-old fish. He ducked his head and moved into the crowd, disappearing so abruptly he must've gone offline. She could think of no good reason, if this funeral was what it claimed to be, why a priest, a stranger to Santee but no stranger to funerals, should be anxious in his own church. If he knew this was all sham, she hoped his God existed so he could rot in His Hell.

She accessed her profile. *No tears,* she whispered and turned to face her audience, resisting the temptation to bow or give them the finger.

As she walked away from the coffin, she felt she was past the worst of it, had shed her tears, given them all a Touching Moment. Now it was time to get at the truth if she could.

AS ONE MOURNER AFTER ANOTHER OFFERED SYMPATHY, SHE tried to find out if anyone knew anything about Santee's supposed death, but no one knew a thing. They were an innocuous lot, all blurring together in a heap of formulaic platitudes near strangers offered up at funerals. There had to be someone here who knew something. She surveyed the crowd and spotted Josh. As their boss, he'd have to say something more than, "Isn't it a tragedy?" She wanted to ask him how he'd been notified of the death, why he hadn't notified her, when he'd last heard from Santee, what Santee had supposedly been working on.

She set out across the room to Josh, but after fifteen minutes, she still found it impossible to reach him. Whenever she got close, someone else would step in to offer condolences, and by the time she got free, Josh would've moved further away than ever.

An IE intern, who claimed to have worked with Santee recently, was the latest obstacle. Her name was Penny, and she gushed like a baby-sitter with a crush on Daddy. It was tedious and embarrassing. Margaret only pretended to listen, keeping her eyes on Josh. Someone bumped her from behind, and she took her eyes off Josh for a split second. In that instant he managed to move halfway across the room. He was a fake. Half the people here were probably fakes, including Penny.

"Why are you here?" Margaret asked her. "Is this routine supposed to plant some seed of doubt in my mind about Santee's fidelity?" Penny opened her mouth, closed it. Who's directing this thing? Margaret wondered. He's terrible, whoever he is. "Well, it didn't work. You're about as convincing as those breast enhancements." Penny beat a hasty retreat. At least she didn't zip across the room like Josh.

The swelling strains of a virtual organ announced the beginning of the service. She looked around for Webster, but he was nowhere to be seen. The priest stood at the front of the virtual sanctuary and raised his arms, the shepherd of the flock. The mourners started taking their virtual seats. She sat in the nearest pew, her mind racing. The priest began, but she didn't listen.

Nothing in this virtual world mattered. She was actually sitting in the back pew of an empty church in San Cristóbal with a coffin up front. Inside that coffin was the only glimpse of the truth she was likely to get. The priest turned his back on the congregation. Some strident soprano imported from the States began to sing 'Amazing Grace.' Poor Santee, she thought. He would've been livid.

Would be livid, she told herself, when she found him, when she held him in her arms again and told him, "They played 'Amazing Grace' at your funeral! Can you believe it?" and they'd laugh themselves silly as they had so often—and would, by God, again.

Enough of this.

She went offline.

Mourners and music vanished. In the blink of an eye, the sanctuary was empty but for the casket and the priest, Webster still sitting beside her. He had that dreaming-dog look people had online. Her face was wet with tears, and her nose was running. She sprang to her feet and strode down the aisle toward the priest. He must've heard her footsteps over the virtual din, or maybe whoever watched whispered in his ear, for he whirled about in a panic. At the sight of her, he fled the sanctuary, banging a door behind him. Pigeons fluttered in the echo.

The real casket stood open now, a portable Weisiger generator sitting unceremoniously on the foot of it. She forced herself to step up and have a look. An Indian in an oversized suit lay dead inside, a grotesquely ugly tie around his neck. The odd angle of his head told her his neck was broken. He was just a kid, not much older than Webster. Another victim of low-intensity warfare. She switched off the generator.

There was a scuffing noise behind her, and she turned, expecting the man in the yellow *guayabera*. Webster still sat where she'd left him, still online at some other site, unaware of anything going on around him. Behind him stood Zack, looking guilty, or maybe just embarrassed to be witnessing this sham.

"Hi, Margaret," he said. "Remember me? Zack Hayman?"

She wiped at her tears with the back of her hand and pointed into the coffin. "Who's the kid, Zack?"

Zack was the sort of man who was terrified of a woman's tears. His eyes danced around, and he rose onto his toes and down again before he spoke. "Terrible thing, isn't it?" He shook his head at the enormity, buying time. "You see, uh, Santee, he had this horrible accident—rock climbing—and he was buried up there in the mountains. And this kid here, uh . . . Juan, he died of influenza about the same time, so they used him for the virtual rendering. That way the poor kid, who otherwise couldn't afford it, could have a church funeral like they like, you know?" He looked around the sanctuary as if someone else might be hiding under the pews. "His mother was supposed to come, but she didn't make it. I don't know what could've held her up."

She walked toward him as he spoke. Now she planted herself in front of him. "How do you know all this?"

"Well, uh, Santee was staying at the Estrellita when it happened. You remember the Estrellita?"

"Of course. How's business?" Her tone was flat and hard.

He gave a nervous laugh. She wanted him to think she might do anything. It was working. "Just great. Couldn't be better. Sure was great to see Santee again. He told me that the time you guys stayed there— what was that? Five, six years ago?—he said that was a real special time for you two."

"He said that, did he?" She wanted to strangle him, but he was her one link to Santee.

"Oh, absolutely. The, uh, last time we talked. Look, Margaret, I'm really, really sorry about your loss. I really am. Santee was a great guy. And if there's *anything* I can do, you just name it. I really mean that."

That made it easy. Really easy. "Take me to the Estrellita," she said. "Take me back to Ocosingo with you."

His expression managed to say "oh shit" even if the actual words didn't come out of his mouth. "I'm not so sure that's such a good idea." He chuckled. "There's still a war going on, you know."

"I thought business was good."

He blinked. "It is. It is. Couldn't be better. That's just the trouble, you see. We got a group coming in, and every *cabaña* is full up. George—you remember George?—he's bringing in one of his groups for the energy vortex thing he does. I'm not much of a believer in that stuff myself. But people seem to eat it up, you know? I think it's just George they like."

She let him rattle on and walked over to Webster, still online. Some webkicker he'd turned out to be. If she went in after him, Zack might give her the slip. It was time to send Webster home anyway. Where she was headed, even gringo kids could get their necks broken. She took paper and an envelope out of her backpack, wrote him a note, wrapped it around some money, and put it in the envelope. She wrote his name on it and put it in his hands.

"I don't need a *cabaña*, Zack. I've got a tent and a sleeping bag."

He fumbled around, desperately trying to think of some other lie to tell. She saved him the trouble with one of her own. "While I'm down there, I can write you up for IE."

Whatever lie was about to come out of Zack's mouth lost its momentum. "You still work for IE?"

"Sure do. Want to see my IE ID?"

"Of course not." He laughed, what Santee had labeled the "innkeeper laugh"—deep and affected, reserved for paying guests. With the memory of Santee came the image of him lying dead, and every muscle in her body tensed.

She slung her backpack over her shoulder as if it weighed two kilos instead of twelve. "Where're you parked?"

He hadn't actually agreed to take her yet. That he hesitated at all implied he was plenty scared. But he couldn't pass up the chance she might be telling the truth. His thumb wagged over his shoulder with studied cool. "Right out back here." He chatted their way out to his ancient pickup. "It's kind of a mess. I wasn't expecting company."

He wrestled with a screwdriver and got the rusty tailgate open. He took her backpack and stowed it to one side, pressing it into place as if the laying on of his broad, bony hands would keep it from careening around the truck bed once they got up in the mountains. There was an old blanket beside the pack. He started to lay it over the backpack, glanced quickly at Margaret, then tossed the blanket to the other side of the truck.

As she got in, she admired the worn interior, running her fingertips across the rust-pocked dash. The seat covers were worn to a paper thinness. She wasn't immune to automotive nostalgia, though she hadn't driven since college. "Fixed up, this thing would be a collector's item back in the States." It seemed crazy to her, but people still collected things, posted their collections on the Web.

"People back in the States will collect anything," he said. He started up the truck. It idled with a pleasant murmur. "My sister had these little beanbag animals she supposedly bought for her kids all locked up in a safe deposit box. Each one had its own little certificate and shit. And she called *me* crazy." The innkeeper laugh again. She'd have to remember not to say anything that might evoke that laugh.

"You ever think about going back to the States?" she asked.

"No, no. Nothing for me there. I'm a Mexican now." He smiled sadly as he slid the gearshift into reverse. He looked over his shoulder and gave it gas, backing down the narrow alley and into the street without slowing down, sliding in a lazy arc on the sandy pavement, stopping just shy of a parked car. On the sidewalk, four tourists in glitzy recording gear—who'd been about to step into the alley—stared at them wide-eyed. "That'll enhance their fucking experience, eh?" He laughed again, but it was real this time, honed in various Idaho roadhouses Margaret imagined. She almost joined him. Whatever else he was, Zack was another crazy gringo who'd thrown his lot in with Mexico. It was a fatal attraction. You had to pity your fellow victims.

She let a silence fall as they made their way out of town. She never could make up her mind about Zack. Maybe that was because he couldn't seem to make up his mind himself. How could you live in the middle of a lopsided war for most of your adult life and remain neutral? She'd always figured him for harmless until now. But hauling corpses wasn't harmless. There was trouble around Zack. That was certain. Whether he was in it or part of it was anybody's guess. Either way, he knew more about Santee than he'd told her.

She knew Santee was alive. She figured he was either a prisoner or he was on the run. Prisoner didn't make sense. They'd just kill him. There wouldn't have been a sham funeral. They preferred the real thing. If he was on the run, he couldn't go on the Web without risking a trace, and they knew it. The funeral was supposed to make it look pointless and probably dangerous to come looking for him. But she was here anyway. So why were they just watching, letting her look? Maybe they didn't know where Santee was and hoped she'd lead them to him. At least that's the way she had it all figured for the moment.

There was also the possibility the funeral was bait and not a warning—a surefire way to lure to Chiapas the one person who could find Santee—because he'd want her to find him. Wherever he was, he knew she'd come looking for him, and he'd leave a trail only she could follow.

So she might be doing exactly what they wanted, and when she'd led them to Santee, Zack here would have a couple more corpses to haul. She looked over at him. It was hard to imagine him as a cold-blooded killer, but he did look a little stressed out, his hands gripping the wheel hard, then fanning out and gripping it again.

They were out on the winding highway now, threading their way through the mountains. She'd ridden in Zack's truck a few times before. Once, the ashtray had been left sitting open. She opened it now. There was Zack's little bowl, already loaded for the next round. It was a three-hour drive from San Cristóbal to the Estrellita, and Zack was a nervous wreck. He needed to relax.

"You have a light?" She held up the bowl like Eve proferring the apple.

He grinned. For some things, you could always count on Zack. His lighter appeared out of nowhere to light the pipe. She took a shallow hit herself, then held it to his lips as he drove. She waited until after he'd had two good hits to start asking questions.

"So are you friends with Juan's family?"

He rose from the fog. "Juan?"

"The dead Indian."

"Oh *Juan!*" He drummed his fingertips on the wheel. "No, no. Hardly knew him. Family either. Just some poor, unfortunate kid."

"Then why'd they ask you to bring in the body?"

He glanced up at the rearview mirror. "Bring in the body?"

"You didn't bring it in?"

His head switched back and forth from her to the road, from her to the road. He tightened his grip on the wheel. "Well, uh, yes-s-s. I did do that, as a matter of fact. But it was just a favor I did, you understand. For *Santee.* Setting things up. I told them after the accident when they said they'd buried Santee up in the mountains, 'That'll never do. We *have* to give him a proper funeral. It's only right.' " He got caught up in his own bullshit and took a moment to ponder what was only right. "And then the, uh, *priest* got the idea to use . . . uh . . . the Indian."

"Juan."

"Right, right. Juan. Juan."

"And his mother?"

He drew a complete and utter blank. He must've felt as if he'd fallen into stoner hell. He resigned himself to his ignorance. "What about her?"

"You said she was coming to the funeral."

"I did? That's right. I did. You see, the *priest* told me that. I didn't talk to her. Didn't even know her. No, I was just trying to do the right thing by Santee. That's *all*. Real nice guy. Sure wish he hadn't gone on that rock-climbing trip, though, and had that terrible accident."

She was supposed to break down in tears at that, but she was relentless. "How long did he stay at the Estrellita?"

"How long? Uh, about a week, I think. I'd have to look it up. It's been pretty busy." He looked at the ashtray, at her hands, finally spotting what he was looking for perched on her left knee. "Any more in the bowl there?"

"Sure." She held it up to his mouth, and he lit it, sucking out the last of the burning resins with a gurgle. The pipe grew too hot to hold, and she dropped it into the ashtray.

"There's more in the glove box," he offered, releasing a huge cloud of smoke into the cab.

"I'm fine," she said.

She gave him a break. Pretty soon he was smiling again. She always liked Zack better stoned. Fortunately, that was most of the time. "Thanks for all your trouble putting this funeral together."

He held up both hands. "It was nothing, really. The least I could do." They settled back on the wheel. "Hope the priest was okay. He was all I could get on such short notice. I didn't care much for him, to tell you the truth, but I'm not a particularly religious person."

"He was fine. Everything was fine."

He beamed as if he'd hosted a successful party, then settled into an all's-right-with-the-world torpor. She let him think the issue was settled long enough to navigate a particularly nasty stretch of hairpin turns on stoned autopilot.

"Who buried him?" she asked.

He ducked his head, glanced over at her, swaying from side to side. "Him?" It was almost a whimper.

"Santee. You said, 'They buried Santee up in the mountains.' Who's 'they'?"

"They're . . ." The answer was slow in coming. He pretended to be concentrating on the road, one of the few straight stretches since they'd left town. "Guides," he said finally. "A couple of guides do the rock-climbing stuff. Too dangerous for me, I can tell you." He laughed again, almost manic this time. The Idaho innkeeper was apparently afraid of heights.

"I'd like to talk to them—the guides."

He kept nodding as if he had a spring in his neck. "Course you would." He took a deep breath and gave her a sympathetic grimace to telegraph the bad news. "But they, uh, went home, *back* home. For good. They weren't local. Fact, I think they might've been Guatemalan."

"Guatemalan guides come up to Chiapas to show people around?"

"Oh absolutely. Work's awful hard to find down there."

Zack was lying. That wasn't too hard to figure. But even he'd have a better cover story than this if he'd been in on it from the beginning. He had to be making this nonsense up as he went along. The last time she heard from Santee, he was at the Hospedaje Felix, the same hotel he'd been in when they met. He must've come out to Zack's when something went wrong in town. Maybe Jorge had been arrested or killed. If Santee's trail led to Zack's, it wasn't hard to imagine him being strong-armed into a bit of playacting.

She started to feel sorry for him, imagining the local thugs pushing him around. But then she thought, no, if he was going to call himself a Mexican, it was time he took a stand. WHICH SIDE ARE YOU ON? one of her T-shirts had read. That one had been stolen from her by school officials, "impounded," they called it. Her counselor said it represented an outmoded notion of political conflict. But if it was so outmoded, Margaret wanted to know, why did they impound it?

WHEN OCOSINGO CAME INTO VIEW, SHE REMEMBERED THE time she met Santee, only yesterday and a very long time ago. They'd been through here a couple of times since. Not much ever changed except it was a bit more beat up. Whenever the war took a turn, there was trouble here. It never seemed to get much bigger or smaller. It waited for the war to end, though most days it didn't believe that would ever happen.

She said to Zack, "Would you drop me in the *zócalo*? I'd like to look around town before I go up to your place."

He looked as if she'd startled him awake. Maybe she had. "Sure. Be glad to." He pulled over. "You want me to wait?"

He was too eager. Now that she'd hitched a ride with him, apparently he didn't want to risk misplacing her. Maybe he was more involved than she thought. "I'll walk. It's a nice trail as I recall."

He was incredulous. "That's like six or seven *miles*."

"I know."

He glanced around, patting his pockets for cigarettes. She pointed them out on the dash. He shook one out and lit it as he spoke. "Uh, I was thinking about stopping in town anyway, tend to some business, go to the bank, you know. I could wait for you. Hour enough?"

"Suit yourself. I'll meet you here in an hour." She got out and watched Zack orbit the *zócalo* and speed north, away from any banks. She had to laugh to herself at his ineptitude as a liar. What possible business would Zack have with a bank anyway?

The Hotel Colonial was still on the corner of the *zócalo*, but the outdoor tables were gone. The railing Santee had leapt over had been clipped by a Hummer a few years back and never been replaced. As she walked across the *zócalo*, she spotted the man in the yellow *guayabera* sitting on a park bench eating an ice cream. She started to wave but didn't want to give him the satisfaction.

THE HOSPEDAJE FELIX HADN'T CHANGED. THE FRONT WAS painted sky blue. The freshly mopped tile floor was pumpkin colored. A boy slept in one of the lobby chairs; the other had a newspaper scattered before it as if someone had vanished in the midst of reading. Even Felix looked the same, standing behind the front desk, as he had years before when she'd offered him two hundred pesos to tell her where Santee was. It wasn't that simple then, and it wasn't that simple now.

She stepped up to the desk, and she saw he had changed—his face lined, his hair flecked with gray. The most striking change was in his eyes, now grown hard and sad.

"*Buenas tardes, señora,*" he said.

She answered in Spanish with her own pleasant good afternoon. "Do you remember me, Felix? I'm Margaret Mayfield. Santee's friend."

"Of course." His eyes darted from her, to the street, to the stairs, even to the sleeping boy. "I remember you very well. You have my deepest sympathies."

"Why is that?"

"I understood that Santee's funeral was today." His eyes pleaded with her to be discreet.

"Do you know why he went to Zack Hayman's place?"

He frowned and shrugged. "Perhaps the noise of the carnival. The violence in town."

"Violence?"

"A boy was killed in the *zócalo*. A knife fight. You know these kids. They talk big and someone dies."

"Was the boy's name Jorge?"

"I believe so, yes."

"How did you hear that Santee was dead?"

"Señor Huerta informed me."

"Do you believe it?"

He looked out at the street. "Señor Huerta believes it to be true. I wouldn't want to be the one to tell him that someone he thought dead was alive, or he might take it upon himself to correct his error."

"Could I look in Santee's room?"

"There is nothing there. They came and took everything in the room."

"They?"

He shrugged. "Friends of Señor Huerta's? I don't know. They didn't say."

"When did they come?"

"Immediately."

"Immediately after the boy was killed in the *zócalo*?"

Felix shook his head. "Immediately after Santee left the hotel."

"So they knew—"

He shushed her with a wave of his hand. "I don't know what you're talking about," he said. "I am very sorry for your loss. But he did not die here, *señora*." His eyes on the street, he reached under the counter and took out a faded blue bandana wrapped around something and slid it across the counter to her. "He left nothing for you," he said loudly. "They took everything."

She swept it off the counter and into her pocket. "Thanks for your help."

"I have not helped you. You asked me questions I couldn't answer, and I sent you away. *¿Verdad?*"

"*Verdad.*"

"*Vaya bien, señora.*"

MARGARET MANAGED NOT TO LOOK INSIDE THE BANDANA AS she walked around town and waited for Zack's return. From the feel of it, she guessed it was a small glass jar with a metal screw top.

All she learned in town was it wasn't a place to be asking questions. As she'd heard, the army was firmly in control. All Zapatista graffiti had been sandblasted from the walls, or the offending walls had been reduced to rubble. All the businesses she knew were run by Zapatista sympathizers had changed hands or had vanished altogether. The *taquería* where she and Santee had eaten wasn't there anymore. Down in the market, they denied there'd even been a carnival in town, much less a murder.

She bought a newspaper and sat in the *zócalo*, taking note of everyone who seemed to be watching her. There were four soldiers, one at each corner of the *zócalo*, a child on its mother's back, a newspaper vendor, and a young cowboy—pencil thin with a straw cowboy hat, getting his boots polished. There were others. How many were spies, and how many were just curious? Tourists went to San Cristóbal; fools came here. It was human nature to stare at a fool. The man in the yellow *guayabera* stayed out of sight.

AFTER ABOUT AN HOUR AND A HALF, ZACK CAME ROARING into town in a cloud of dust like a posse from a western movie. When she hopped into the cab, he was huffing and puffing as if he'd run here. "Sorry I'm late," he said. "Had some business to transact."

He looked awful. Whatever the business was, it had left him shaken. He looked as if he'd been crying. A couple of times he wrung the steering wheel and sucked in his breath as if something horrible had appeared in the road. But whatever he saw was in his head. She was almost tempted to go easy on him. She did wait until they were past the first checkpoint. The soldiers waved them through, calling Zack *"Idajo"* with boisterous laughter and a slap on the fender. He winced as if they were striking him. She'd never seen Zack so close to the surface before.

"Who's Huerta?" she asked.

He jerked his head around so hard he turned the steering wheel in the process, and the truck headed for the ditch. He jerked it back into the lane and shot her a look. "Where'd you hear that name?"

"Around town."

"Big name all right. Head of the party. Big rancher. What'd you hear about him?"

The party. That's what everybody said. Everybody knew which party you meant. The others were just extras in the democracy pageant they put on every six years. "Just the name."

He nodded his head. It was his turn to know she was lying. He scowled thoughtfully as they headed up the valley past another checkpoint and a military base, a row of American helicopters lined up on the tarmac, their heat-seeking guns hanging out the sides like spider legs.

As they turned for the Rancho Estrellita, he looked over at her, his face deadly serious. "Don't mess with Huerta, Margaret. He's really bad news."

"Is that what he told you to tell me?"

He shook his head and struck the wheel with his fist. "That son of a bitch didn't tell me shit. Huerta's no friend of mine."

She let it go, and he didn't say anything else until they got to the Estrellita. It turned out there were *cabañas* aplenty. George's group hadn't showed. Zack didn't even bother to act surprised at this news. "I can even put you in the same *cabaña* you and Santee stayed in that first time you were here," he said. "Would you like that? On the house."

"I'd rather have the one he stayed in when he was here last."

He slumped his shoulders and shook his head. "Yeah. Course. I'll have to clean it up. Could take a while."

"I'll take a bath," she said. "I remember your beautiful bathhouse." That cheered him up. Zack positively doted on his bathhouse.

THE OLD CLAW-FOOT TUB—AIRBRUSHED WITH A QUET-zalcoatl, the plumed serpent god of the Aztecs—was set in a tiled alcove, one wall of which was a stained-glass window depicting a mountain landscape much like the one a bather could've seen if the stained glass hadn't been there. He gave her a towel, washcloth, bathrobe—all over-size and plush and white. Would she like a drink? There was a bar in the bathhouse. He recited choices. A Coke would be fine. Incense? No thanks. Bubble bath? Shampoo? Bath powder? Hair dryer? As the tub filled with steaming water, and the bathhouse filled with steamy clouds, Zack scurried about trying to conjure up and then see to her every need. It took some time before she'd run him off and slid the bolt closed.

She took out the bandana and unrolled it. Inside was an Alka-Seltzer bottle. She opened it, and it was empty except for the styrofoam cylinder used for packing. She had to laugh. She knew immediately what she was supposed to do.

Santee had told her about the time his grandfather came to visit and woke in the middle of the night with a stomachache. In the medicine cabinet, he'd found a bottle of Alka Seltzer, empty but for the Styrofoam. Santee's mother found him in the kitchen staring forlornly at a glass of water that refused to fizz, a Styrofoam cylinder floating in it. She had told the tale on him for years thereafter. And Santee had told it to Margaret.

She took a glass from the bar and filled it with water, dropped the white cylinder into it, and set it before the stained glass, the late afternoon sun streaming through it. At first, it looked as if nothing was happening, but when she looked closely she could see the wakes of thousands of minuscule swimmers streaming out of the porous plastic. She stripped off her clothes and lowered herself into the steaming tub. She held the glass up to the stained-glass mountains and drank it off, lay back in the water and let the microscopic machinery she'd just swallowed do its work.

Her heart sped up and slowed down. There was a ringing in her ears that came and went and finally subsided. A headache seemed to move from one side of her brain to the other. Her sinuses started draining as if she'd just snorted a handful of ragweed. All perfectly normal reactions.

MARGARET COULDN'T GO ONLINE WITH HER NEW INTERFACE. Like all the other copies, it had to piggyback on Santee's original—encrypted with the access code. So the interface was useless without him. Along with the interface, however, a good deal of data could be installed, accessible to the user online or not. There was no map, no message to speak of, only one word, but Margaret knew what he meant.

When she emerged from the bathhouse an hour later, she felt perfectly refreshed. She found Zack in the dining room sweeping up. "Zack, is Hermalinda still living around here?"

"Hermalinda? Uh, yeah. I mean, no. Not here, here. She has a job in San Cristóbal."

"But you know how to reach her."

"Me? No. Edie might have her address around here somewhere. I can ask her. I think she's taking a nap right now though, but as soon as she wakes up—"

"Zack, cut the bullshit. Arrange a meeting with Hermalinda for me, okay?"

"Uh, sure. I can do that. A meeting with you and Hermalinda. I'll get right on it."

CHAPTER ELEVEN

WHEN ZACK DROPPED MARGARET OFF IN THE ZÓCALO, HE scooted on out to Huerta's place to tell him about her. He didn't see that he had much choice. He counted three guys standing around who'd sure as hell tell him if Zack didn't. Least this way he could put the right spin on it, maybe get Huerta off her back: *She's just a widow, man. Just another grieving widow. The country's full of 'em. You ought to know, asshole. You've made your share.*

Jesus, where did that come from? The mere thought of mouthing off to Huerta made his hands shake on the wheel even though this was the smoothest street in town. Señor Huerta's street. *Don't do anything stupid, Z-brain*, he told himself, wishing he were a whole lot more stoned or a whole lot less stoned — he wasn't sure which. Mostly he wished he was just somewhere else. He'd given up on some*one* else a long time ago.

Huerta called himself a rancher — wore the hat and the boots and now and again paraded a million-dollar horse at fiesta time lugging this silver-studded saddle that must've weighed as much as the horse — but he wasn't what Zack would call a rancher. He owned a humongous herd of cows — global-burgers on the hoof, grazing most of the valley, grazing wherever they took a mind to — but he didn't live anywhere near the smell of cow shit. Once a week up in Tuxtla there was an old lady did his hands for him so they were soft as Play-Do and his nails looked cast from Plexiglas. He had *campesinos* out in the valley to smell the shit and do the work. Shake hands with one of those guys, it was like grabbing hold of a board.

Zack parked the truck opposite a long white wall that ran on down the hill. Huerta's house was the other side of the wall. Broken glass bristled from the top of the wall, even though there were lasers that'd fry you before you ever cut your pinkies. But that Huerta, he was a traditionalist. The reason he had such a *casa grande* in the first place was to impress the peasants who couldn't be impressed by his Weblife and had to be intimidated the old-fashioned way. Not much had really changed in the global village when you got right down to it.

But Huerta knew where the real action was, so the house was also weisigered out the wazoo to show anyone of significance what a totally civilized webbed-in thug he was. Even Zack could've told him he was going over the top, trying too hard, that the big boys back in the States were living in sleek little auto-environs that fed you and scrubbed you and wiped your ass for you—all automatically, so you wouldn't have to condescend to haul your guts around. Little stim units took your muscles on a workout every night to keep you in shape while you virtualed your way up Everest or took a meeting with some Senators so you could tell them what to vote for. A big house just meant you couldn't afford decent hardware. A big flashy Website of your own just meant no one wanted you around, that you had no place to be.

But Huerta would never be one of those big guys anyway. In the end, he was just another muscle job exported to the third world—the steel toe on a bigger thug's boot, flashy and lethal. He was so good at it you could almost believe he didn't want to be one of those big guys himself, that he just flat out liked to kick people. Zack suspected, though, that there was no one he'd rather kick than his bosses. But being bosses, they never set foot outside the Web.

Zack clunked the knocker even though Huerta would already know he was here. By this time his sensors and databases had parlayed Zack's DNA into a positive ID and a detailed bio with an emphasis on black-mailable events. Least Zack didn't have to worry about that one. Huerta couldn't shame him. Zack himself had thoroughly covered that angle a long time ago.

The door swung open, and Zack stepped inside. The Weisiger field needed calibrating and didn't start up until about a foot inside the doorway, so you could see this little slice of the room where Huerta often kept him waiting, the usual red tiles and tan walls. You didn't always power up the virtuals for the help. Zack took another step and oozed into the virtual entry, a walled garden big enough to play soccer in. A mariachi band swathed in ruffles played "Cielito Lindo" over to one side. In the corner was a waterfall. With divers. Orchids bloomed everywhere. Crowds of butterflies fluttered through on their way to a Disney movie. A beautiful señorita with bronze cleavage looked discreetly out an upper window. She even had the fluttering fan. Toucans and iguanas hung out flashing profiles like bored teen idols.

Huerta was constantly messing with his system, constantly upgrading. This was one of those programs that read the features of any caller and adjusted its presentation depending on age, gender, and likely ethnicity. This was what scared Idaho hippies in their fifties got, Zack figured—tired clichés from a travel brochure, his dad's Mexico. Have a margarita. Check out the light show at Chichén Itzá. File stuff probably. He'd lived half his life here, and in the end he was just another old gringo fart.

Zack took a deep breath. He could smell the orchids—like one of those room deodorant sprays his father liked to dose the house with—but he couldn't smell the earth smell, that funky garden smell it would take to make him believe he was really where the program coaxed him to be. Cheap work. All form and no substance. A long time ago back in Moscow, he'd been an art major for three semesters. Had ambitions, opinions, taste. Now that seemed like some other guy on some other planet.

A sim manservant—an Indian dressed all in white, properly submissive—invited him to sit on an ornate iron bench painted whipped-cream white without a hint of rust or a single paint drip. Zack sighed and sat down. As his butt hit the iron, Huerta materialized across from him in a vine-shrouded grotto, looking twenty pounds lighter and ten years younger than he really was. But every bit as mean. He was wearing a slate-colored suit, which probably meant he'd been doing some business, and he looked about as happy as a kid spruced for church. Zack rose to his feet so Huerta could nod his permission for Zack to sit down again. Zack wondered if they taught that little routine in *cacique* school, but that's not what he said.

"The place is looking great," Zack started in, looking around with elaborate appreciation. "Haven't seen the virtuals in a while. Real nice. Real festive. Very welcoming.

"Just wanted to come by and let you know things went pretty smooth with the funeral thing. Can't say I cared for the priest that much, but that's probably just me. Priests and policemen, if you know what I mean.

"Anyway, there was one thing I thought you might want to know about. No big deal. But Santee's old girlfriend—I don't think they were even together anymore, to tell you the truth—she came to the church and tumbled to the fact that the body in the coffin wasn't Santee's. Well, she got a little upset. But I explained to her the body was just for the virtuals, told her that Santee was buried up in the mountains someplace, and got her calmed down on that score. Anyway, she wanted to come out here to the Rancho. Sort of have a last good-bye kind of thing. It was really a special place to them in better times, you know? So anyway—"

Huerta spat on the ground. "Shut up, Zack. I know all about the woman. She will search tirelessly for Santee until she finds him or dies trying. You will tell me when she succeeds."

"But Santee—he's dead, right?"

"Don't be an idiot. What I want to know from you is the whereabouts of the boy. Who is he, and where did he go?"

"The boy?"

Huerta sighed "She has been traveling with a boy who calls himself Webster Webfoot. Where is he?"

Huerta spoke the name as if he found it personally offensive. Zack thought it was kind of cute. "Oh *him.* She gave him bus fare, sent him north. He's probably halfway to Kansas by now. I don't think he's anybody important."

"He is not on a bus, you idiot. You don't think I can find someone on a fucking bus?"

Zack knew not to answer that question. He'd seen Huerta pissed before. The virtual Huerta looked fine, of course, but he figured the real one's fat face was good and flushed by now. This Santee thing was a big deal apparently, and the kid wasn't in the plan. "I'm really sorry," Zack said. "I didn't know the boy was important. Margaret wanted to come here, and she wanted to leave the kid there, so I left him. I could drive back up there and—"

"Shut up, Zack. I have intelligent, skilled people working on that. You are to keep an eye on the woman. Do you think you can handle that?"

"Well, sure. But I don't think she'll be staying long. I get the impression she's just going to have a good cry and head back home."

"Follow her."

"Well, I do have a business to run. If she leaves the area—"

"If you want to continue having a business to run, you'll follow her. Make note of everything she says, everyone she meets, everywhere she goes—and report it all to me. Is that clear?"

Zack was supposed to say, "Yes, sir!" But he didn't. He was never into that sir and ma'am crap his dad tried to cram down his throat. But he nodded, he gave in. He showed Huerta what he was made of, all right.

Huerta laughed. "Don't look so glum, my friend. Soon the war will be over, and your business should be booming. Everyone will want to meet the man who buried Santee St. John." He took Zack's hand and shook it, pulled him into his arms for an *abrazo*. Zack was supposed to feel honored—to be embraced by *El Señor*—but all he could do was ask himself how he'd ever sunk so low.

ZACK ANGLED ACROSS THE STERET AND HOPPED INTO THE cab of his truck without looking up. He cranked it with a roar and was rolling, when he sensed her or smelled her or whatever he did, and she raised her head up from behind the seat and told him to drive out to the countryside.

He was flooded with relief. The image of her lying beside the road, an M16 pointed at her head, hadn't left him since he'd driven by that business in Oxchuc. He said, "Jesus Christ, Hermalinda, you damn near gave me a heart attack. Why do you take risks like this? What if one of Huerta's men had seen you getting into my truck?"

"Don't worry. I wouldn't tell him I was your lover. I wouldn't want to admit it to anyone." He looked over at her as she climbed from behind the seat. If she wasn't so tiny, she wouldn't even fit back there. Her skirt rode up on a dark brown thigh. Her feet were bare and calloused hard. Just a harmless little peasant woman. He reached for her hand, and she took his in both of hers, holding it in her lap like a kitten. He loved her like he'd never loved another human being on the entire planet.

"I was terrified something had happened to you. I came up on this thing near Oxchuc—"

She squeezed his hand hard and shook it. "*Execution*, Zack. You can't even say it."

"Of course I can't say it. I don't *want* to say it. I don't want to think about anything like that happening to you. You've got to get out of this shit before you get yourself killed."

She released his hand and turned, facing the road, her arms crossing her chest. "Are you working for Huerta?" she asked.

When Huerta'd showed up with the dead Indian, the first thing Zack thought of was this moment of truth with Hermalinda. If he could've said no, this would've been why. But he couldn't or he wouldn't, and he went ahead and did it, knowing it was wrong. So now all he knew to do was waffle and hope she loved him half as much as he loved her.

"*Working* for him? I wouldn't call it that. He asked me to do him a favor, and I did, and I was just telling him about it is all."

"Don't lie to me. You helped him stage Santee St. John's funeral, didn't you?"

"You knew St. John?"

"He was a guest at the Estrellita when I worked there, Zack."

"Oh yeah. That's right. I forgot."

She glared at him. "You mean you didn't think one of your maids would get to know the guests."

"Now, Hermalinda, you know I don't feel like that. I just forgot is all. It was some years, okay?"

She nodded down the road. "Left up here."

He turned down an overgrown dirt road. "What was Santee up to, anyway? It doesn't figure. Is the guy dead or not?"

"Why do you want to know—so you can run tell your boss, Huerta?"

No. Huerta already knew. *Don't be an idiot,* he'd said. Easier said than done. What would an idiot do in this situation? Would an idiot do the right thing? The road petered out, and he stopped under some trees, yanking on the parking brake. "I told you, goddamnit, I don't work for that prick."

"What do you call it? Doing a friend a favor? Zachary Hayman—a friend to pigs everywhere." She spat out the window. He seemed to have that effect on people lately.

He laid his hand on her thigh, slid it under her skirt. "Come on, don't talk like that. He's a badass. He's been pushing hard. What am I supposed to do—get myself shot over some bad blood between Huerta and some IE guy?" She glared at his hand burrowed under her skirt, and he pulled it away. "So Santee's doing something for the cause, right? For the *Revolución*. How was I supposed to know that? I told you before, I don't get involved in that shit. I know you're in it deep, and that's cool. But it's got nothing to do with us."

"You know better," she said quietly. She got out of the truck and closed the door. The hinges sounded like a train derailing. The passenger door didn't see much use. She stood on the running board and leaned into the open window. "You remember how we met, Zack? Or has that 'been some years,' too?"

"Course I remember."

"Then don't tell me it's got nothing to do with us. You can't stand around anymore, Zack, just watching while the woods burn down around you. Something very big is about to happen. Everything is going to change. Whether you do or not."

"Nothing can change how I feel about you. I love you. You know that." He slid over to the passenger side and would've gotten out, but she was standing right in front of the door.

She laid her tiny hand on his cheek, looked at him like he was some little boy who just didn't get it. He expected her to say she loved him too. He knew she did. Couldn't say why. Best not go there. And she did say it, whispered it softly, her eyes full to overflowing with tears. But she didn't stop there. "*No basta,*" she added, tears breaking free, running down her cheeks.

It's not enough.

"Is that what you brought me out here to tell me?" he asked, his voice shaking.

"No. You're not ready to hear what I was going to say. I don't think you'll ever be ready."

She hopped down and walked off, and he couldn't doubt she was right. He hadn't been ready for what she did say. *No basta.* She'd never said that before. Hearing it now, he realized he'd known how she felt for a long time. She must love me a lot, he thought, to have put off saying it for so long. He wished he could get out of the truck and run after her. But there was no point in that unless he could tell her she was wrong about him, that he'd do *anything* for her, that he would never let her down.

He slid back to the driver's side and started up the truck, but instead of driving, he banged the steering wheel with the palms of his hands. What did she mean, it wasn't enough? It was everything. It was the only thing. He was absolutely loopy about her. This political shit didn't have anything to do with that. He gripped the wheel with both hands and shook it like he was trying to strangle it, slumped back in the seat, and reached for his pipe. He fished his bag out of the glove box and got a bowl filled, lit, and burned—wishing, just wishing the whole time, it would make things better, clearer, more focused.

But it didn't.

Wasn't the dope's fault. He was just wrong is what it was. Wrong as wrong could be.

He did a three-point turn and headed back to town. Out in the mountains there was a plume of smoke, probably some Indian burning off his tiny exhausted chunk of land.

You remember how we met, Zack?

He didn't just remember. It came back to him like a fist flying out of nowhere, right to the gut: He's standing in the damn macadamias. She's running with her hair on fire. He watches. Bullets rip up a tree trunk right by her head. She falls and rolls out the flames, then crawls inch by inch into the woods. While he watches. That's all. Like it was something on the news, nothing to do with him. A couple days later she shows up at the Rancho looking for work. Anything, she says. Edie, who hires all the girls, isn't going for it. The torn dress, the singed hair, the intelligent defiant eyes. Hermalinda definitely looks like trouble. But Zack wades in on it. Insists.

He never told her he saw her that day with her hair on fire. This was the first time it'd ever occurred to him that she already knew.

ZACK DIDN'T REMEMBER TOO MUCH FROM THE TIME HE LEFT Hermalinda until he got Margaret safely ensconced in the bathhouse. He was in his own head, just going through the motions most of the time. *Who's Huerta?* she'd asked. He remembered that. A question you didn't even *ask* for at least a hundred miles around. It seemed pointless to even try to explain it to her. Did they even talk about miles in the first world anymore? Turf? Territory? Didn't seem like it. "Local Customs," one of his guests told him, was the name of a Website.

He made himself busy, picking up around the place. Couldn't really say he thought about things, explored his conscience, all of that. It seemed like he just walked around and ached. He cleaned up the *cabaña* where he'd dressed the corpse. It was the *cabaña* she asked for, the one Santee'd stayed in Thursday night. He knew he could give her any damn one he wanted, and she wouldn't know the difference, but he didn't even consider it. Never gave it a thought.

She will search tirelessly for Santee until she finds him, Huerta'd said with absolute certainty. Zack had to ask himself: Who'd look for you— Mr. *No Basta?* Who'd look for you?

He checked the pantry and the fridge and figured there was enough for a few more days if Margaret liked eggs. If it wasn't for the hens, he'd have starved a long time ago. He remembered gathering eggs with Hermalinda when she'd been here. It was always early in the morning.

They were the only two up. She carried the eggs in her skirt. He told her about Easter egg hunts in Boise.

He swept out the kitchen and cleaned up Edie's blender mess. The trash had been building up for days. He usually waited till evening to burn it. But he gathered it up, stuffed it in the can, and got it blazing. He went to the truck without knowing what he was going for until he laid his hands on it. The old blanket, the one Juan had been wrapped in . . . no, not *Juan*. That was his bullshit Zack christening. His Z-brain name. Zack didn't know the kid's name. He wondered if Huerta did.

He dragged the blanket across the yard, trying not to breathe in its scent—soap or shampoo or hair oil—the kid's scent. He heaved it onto the fire, and the fire almost died. He waded into the clouds of smoke, poking furiously at the blanket with a rusty umbrella skeleton until the blanket whoofed into flames and seared his face with heat.

He stood close, letting the flames bake him like a lizard on a rock. War. Murder. Executions. Not exactly what he came to Mexico for. Might as well be honest though. He hadn't come to Mexico *for* anything. He just wanted to get away.

It wasn't Idaho.

He wasn't facing prosecution with a court-appointed lawyer who volunteered the opinion that marijuana was unchristian.

His sister would never set foot here. Her Spanish, after two years in high school, ran out somewhere between *taco* and *adios*. And any man darker than she was scared the sanctimonious crap out of her.

His dad wasn't buried anywhere around here. Though his ghost had showed up once, hitching a ride on some 'shrooms George gave him up on the pyramid.

"It's the vortex," George said, when he'd gotten Zack calmed down. "It opened a passageway to the Other Side."

"You actually believe in that shit?" Zack asked.

George thought about it hard in his own hallucinogenic fog. When he finally spoke, his voice was full of wonder and surprise. "No, not usually. Just now. Isn't that something?"

That summed up Zack's intense feelings and beliefs. He had them. But they came and went, like a sound system with a short in it, cutting in and out.

Except for Hermalinda.

When she started working at the Estrellita, he couldn't let her out of his sight, following her around, fixing up a little room for her off the old barn, stopping by all the time to make sure everything was okay, to ask if she needed anything. Edie said he treated her better than he did the guests, and maybe he did. His heart was more in it, anyway. He was eaten up with guilt, but it still made him glad everytime he saw her and knew she hadn't died, that she'd managed to make it even though he'd stood around and watched, doing nothing. Her family were all killed—mother, husband, son. He coaxed her story out of her on these visits. He stood in the doorway and listened.

It wasn't about sex. He thought she was pretty, beautiful even. But he couldn't begin to imagine she'd have the slightest interest in him— an old gringo pothead with a wife who talked to her like she was dirt— even if she didn't know he was a coward.

She told him later she thought he was just trying to nail her, but when she realized it was more than that, she was touched by his concern. He'd never told her where and when that concern was born, so he thought she didn't know. For some reason he thought it'd be better that way, that he wouldn't have to ever be responsible for what he'd seen, that he could just make his amends on the sly, so to speak. Now it seemed she'd known all along.

She'd seen him standing up there before, watching the *pueblito* growing up in front of his view. She told him the kids called him *espantajo*, scarecrow. Always standing in the grove, watching. She must've turned, expecting to find him there, hoping, perhaps, that he'd help her.

What he used to watch down there was Mexico—the people and the place right before his eyes, but a million miles away. He'd come here and built his Star Ranch, but it might as well have been a Taco Bell. About as Mexican as that stupid chihuahua in the old commercials, insulting on too many levels to even think about. He didn't belong here. Proved it by standing around and letting it burn to the ground.

When he brought her some old curtains to hang up in her one glassless window, she kissed him. Then really kissed him. He'd never been so astounded by anything in his life. And pretty soon, they were lovers. He still believed it was a miracle. If there was anything to George's vortex business, he had it all wrong. It wasn't about some *place*, some pile of rock, but about people. She was it for him. The center of the universe.

The flames had died down now, and he was standing in a dense cloud of smoke. He sliced the air with broad sweeps of his hat, thrust the umbrella into the smoldering blanket until it started breaking up, cinders drifting off toward the coffee grove. The stuff at the bottom of the barrel shifted, and the fire fell in on itself, sending up a rush of sparks. It soon settled into a quiet fire that would burn itself out.

HE WASHED HIS FACE AND HANDS IN THE KITCHEN SINK AND took the broom into the dining room. That's when Margaret showed up from her bath. She stood in the doorway, looking positively radiant, not like someone who'd just been to her lover's funeral. "Zack, is Hermalinda still living around here?"

He didn't know what he said next. He'd been thinking about nothing but Hermalinda for what seemed like days, and here was Margaret asking for her, asking to meet with her. George would've called it synchronicity or serendipity or some damn thing. Whatever it was, he saw the choice he had to make, clear as day. Margaret was in on whatever Santee was in on. Margaret wanted to talk to Hermalinda because she was Zapatista. Sure, Zack could set it up. And if he followed Huerta's orders and reported it to him, sure as the world, Hermalinda was dead. And if he didn't, most likely he was.

He was standing in the grove again. Watching it happen. He had a second chance.

Margaret had started out of the dining room, thinking their business was done, but he called after her. "Margaret, that boy you were traveling with, Webster?"

She turned back cautiously. You could see in her eyes she was wondering what he was up to, what bullshit was coming out of his mouth next. "Huerta's got guys looking for him. He also asked me to keep an eye on you. And something he said makes me think Santee's still alive somewhere."

She didn't look surprised at the news. "He didn't die rock climbing?"

Her tone told him he didn't have to answer that question. She'd known he was lying. Everybody seemed to expect it of him. He hung his head and shook it. "He showed up here and ran off. I don't know where he went. Huerta showed up next morning with a dead Indian kid to stand in at that phony funeral. You know the rest."

"Why are you telling me all this, Zack?"

He laughed. "Maybe you should ask Hermalinda when you see her. She might know."

✳   ✳   ✳

EDIE'S CAR, OR TECHNICALLY HER FATHER'S CAR — SHE STOLE
it the night they took off for Mexico in '93 since they couldn't fit all
their stuff in the truck and didn't want to spring for a U-Haul—had
been sitting on blocks for five years now. It was a red Saab convertible,
the old man's feel-young-again vehicle that he'd only driven a couple
of weeks before his grown daughter ripped it off. Wouldn't do him any
good in the States now anyway. Couldn't convert anything that old for
smart roads, even if you could get a permit. But Zack figured it'd make
it to the Mexico City airport where it could see out its last days in the
parking lot being savaged for parts. There'd be nothing left but a pile
of screws.

It'd been a bitch to keep running. Fussiest car he'd ever worked on.
Edie didn't help it any, driving the roads around here like she was
cruising some Interstate, when she wasn't running into a ditch three
sheets to the wind. So when the second starter died and he ordered
another one, he didn't tell Edie when it came in. She never even asked
about it. After a few weeks, he threw a tarp over the car, took the wheels
off, drained the fluids. Told her he couldn't get the starter, that they
quit making them. He had a big story ready with a strike and factories
shutting down and the whole deal, but she barely listened. "Fuck it,"
she'd said.

Now he got the starter down from a high shelf in the potting shed.
The cardboard was soft and pliant, and oily dust clung to it like brown
fur. He pried open the box, and the thing gleamed at him in its newness.
He put the Saab's battery on the charger and went to work.

A few hours later he had the car sitting out in front of the house,
running. Not exactly good as new, but good enough. The tarp had fused
itself to the convertible top, so it was wearing a little blue toupee. The
interior smelled like mouse piss. The timing was stuttery, but that would
smooth out on the road. He still needed to bleed the brake lines, but
he'd need Edie for that.

He shut it off and glanced up at the house. The bedroom curtains
stirred. She was up there all right. She liked to pretend she was out of
it all the time so she didn't have to deal with anything. That was one
of those things they had in common. But him resurrecting her car
without a moment's nagging had to have her wondering what was up.

He went to the kitchen and started a pot of coffee, went upstairs and
opened the door on the gloom of their bedroom, spoke to the sheet
pulled over her head. "Come downstairs, Edie. We need to talk."

She didn't stir.

He put his fingers to his lips and whistled, one of those earsplitting whistles that was an Idaho social skill. If she'd actually been asleep, he would've had to peel her off the ceiling. "I know you're not sleeping, Edie. Now would you please come downstairs?"

"Okay, okay," she murmured, barely audible.

HE HAD A CUP OF COFFEE WHILE HE WAITED, LISTENED TO her shuffling around upstairs. He didn't ask himself what she was doing, but how she was feeling. They'd lived together so long he thought he could tell such things just by the way she moved. She sounded scared. When she showed up a half hour later, she was completely dressed, something he hadn't seen in a while. She sat down at the table and lit a cigarette. She didn't say a word. She wasn't just scared, she was terrified.

He got up and poured her a cup of coffee, set it in front of her. "I'm in love with another woman."

She sighed. "Tell me something I don't know."

He laid Santee's Mexico City-DFW plane ticket on the table like he was playing a card. "You're leaving me."

"Fuck you, Zack. I'm staying right here." She blew on her coffee and took a sip.

"You can't."

"Hell I can't. This place is half mine."

He laid a fat envelope on top of the ticket. "Wrong. It's all yours. Here's the deed, all the papers. I signed it over. But you still got to go. It won't be safe here. I put most of the cash in there too—not that there's a lot, you understand. But it'll get you out of the country, back to Idaho if you want."

She looked at him for the first time since she'd come downstairs. "This isn't just about the girlfriend, is it? What are you up to, Zack?"

Her tone was almost kind. He wanted to try to tell her the truth. It'd been a while. "Hell, I don't know what it's about. It's probably mostly about her. *Everything*'s about her. It's like that, Edie." He stopped himself before he told her he'd never felt this way before. Not that it wasn't true, but saying it would be cruel. "I can't tell you what I'm up to because you don't want to know anything. All hell's about to break loose. You need to go back home."

She smiled at him. It wasn't what he expected. He hadn't seen that smile for longer than he could remember. "You taking a stand, Zee?"

"Yeah, I guess so."

"Good for you."

EDIE DIDN'T WASTE MUCH TIME PACKING. WHEN IT CAME right down to it, there wasn't much she wanted to take back to the States. Her parents were semiretired, living high on the Web. She'd visited them there a few times, using the cheap, single-occupant Weisiger rig they kept in the dining room for the guests who couldn't quite get away from it all. Zack didn't go with her, so he only had her sullen reports to go on, but to put it mildly, things hadn't gone well. But now that she was leaving Mexico and "that man," Zack was sure they'd welcome her with open arms.

He hoped she didn't hang out with them. Their gloating would get old in a hurry. But it wasn't his place to say anything. What was his place, anyway? Damned if he could figure it out. He hadn't loved her so much in years as he did watching her stuffing the same backpack she hauled down here in '93 with some of the same underwear and socks. He would've said they were like brother and sister, but he and his sister loathed each other.

They'd reminisced as they bled the brakes.

"Okay, pump it. Pump it!"

She started pumping the brake pedal like some drowsy señora milking a cow. "Remember when we stole this car?" she said.

"Sure." There'd been a billion stars in the sky. They used a hairpin and the tweezers from his Swiss army knife to pick the lock.

"Driving down here I just watched your taillights—"

Brake fluid spurted forth. "Stop!"

"Then I'd look in the rearview mirror for flashing lights—"

"Goddamnit, stop!"

"Back and forth. Back and forth. Mirror to taillights, mirror to taillights. I don't remember what we drove through." She finally quit pumping the brake pedal. Fortunately, he had plenty of brake fluid and clean shirts.

"Shame you missed it," he said. "You can't even make that drive anymore. It's all smart, high-tech shit now. Hurry, hurry, hurry. Faster, faster, faster. I hate that shit."

Edie laughed. "Well, it hates you, too, Zack."

SHE ZIPPED HER BACKPACK SHUT, AND HE REACHED OUT AND took it, slinging it over his shoulder. "I'll take this, ma'am."

She took his arm and they walked out to the Saab. It was nighttime now, not unlike the night they'd stolen it. At her insistence, he'd gotten the top down, though it was doubtful it'd ever rise again. He threw her backpack into the backseat and opened the door for her. The penetrating oil had done its job and the door swung open as silently as a bank vault.

She got inside, and he closed the door, pushing on it till it clicked. "You sure you want to drive at night? Might look suspicious. You could leave first thing in the morning."

"For me, Zack, *that* would be suspicious. This way I can tell the boys at the checkpoints that I had an awful fight with my husband and left him. They'll believe that. They might even offer to comfort me."

He bet they would. "You going to take them up on it?"

"Why do you ask?"

"I wouldn't want you to miss your plane."

"Don't worry."

He took something out of his back pocket that had been sitting there for hours, digging into his bony butt. He unwrapped his bandana from around it. It was chrome plated, shorter than his hand from wrist to fingertips. He didn't even know what kind it was. He hated guns. It had a safety, a trigger, you pointed it, and people died. Huerta had given it to him when the land invaders showed up, just to plant the idea they were for shooting. *It's loaded, my friend. To protect yourself, your family, and your land.* Why was it Mexicans were always going on and on about land? Zack wasn't about to kill anybody over a few acres of dirt. He figured that Edie still qualified as family, however. "You might want to take this. Just in case."

She wouldn't touch it. "No way. You keep it. Sounds like you'll need it more than I will."

"I'm not going to shoot anybody."

She shook her head and sighed. "Zee, they're going to shoot *you*."

*   *   *

WHEN SHE DROVE OUT OF SIGHT, ROUNDING THE CURVE BY the army base, he had his first taste in memory of doing the right thing. It felt good indeed. He smoked a bowl in the driveway to celebrate, looking up at the stars. There was no moon, unlike a couple of nights ago when Santee had come walking out of the woods into the moonlight with nothing but that little backpack slung over his shoulder.

The light was on in Margaret's *cabaña*. He walked over and knocked, but she wasn't there. He looked toward the ruins as he had the night Santee had taken off and saw the same thing he'd seen then—a small light moving around on the big pyramid, no doubt a flashlight from the Other Side.

CHAPTER TWELVE

AS SHE WAITED FOR HER MEETING WITH POWELL, STARR went to the WebNet Personnel Enhancement site and ran the virtual trainer for the onboard service/evacuation vehicle (SEV). She found out a long time ago she did this kind of thing best if she didn't think about it too hard and screw herself up. Better to play it by ear. Like dancing. So, as the perky sim launched into a lesson in elementary physics, she put her hands on the controls and let her mind wander.

Theoretically, crews used the SEV to make repairs to the station or to evacuate in case of approaching danger or station system breakdown. That's what it said in the book. In practice, no one ever used the things. Crews weren't paid to do repairs—and even if they were, most of them were scared shitless to be sitting out in space strapped into something that looked like a jungle gym with a few tiny thrusters bolted onto it— thrusters with just enough power to get you into serious trouble before you ran out of propellant and went into a roll. Everybody knew some-body who knew somebody who was "collecting permanent overtime," as they called it, in some slowly decaying orbit.

As for evacuating, no one ever had time to do more than say "oh shit!" before the emergency was over and the station and its occupants were just floating debris. WebNet had an "oh shit!" recording collection from all the rigs that'd tanked over the years. Seemed like NewsReal ran them every five minutes during the hearings.

There wouldn't even have been hearings if a couple of big WebNet rigs hadn't collided over Manhattan and put on a light show that was a little hard to explain away. It wasn't that WebNet was killing people that got the public upset, it was that they'd been forced to watch. After seeing something like that people had to work through the tragedy— through their pain and their suffering—like they'd been the ones burning up. The hearings only lasted long enough for everybody to say how "outraged" they were. That soon gave way to chest-thumping praise of the democratic process that had enabled the "bottom strata" of society to take on the most powerful corporation in the world—like David and Goliath. Though in this case Goliath didn't fall, he regretted deeply, and the couple dozen Davids had scattered their ashes over the eastern seaboard instead of slinging a lethal stone.

Then the hearings just stopped, the news moved on to something else, and absolutely nothing had changed except the number of jokes in the world with "oh shit!" as the punchline. Truth was, the whole thing was just a dog and pony show—a little ritual cleansing—and nobody was going to take on WebNet because of unsafe working conditions for space scum like her, even if they started making rigs out of chewing gum and old tin cans. If a few convicted felons died to keep the virtual life humming, what was the dif? Wasn't it a better gig than anything else people like that could get? They should be grateful was what it was.

Now it looked like MarsCorp was part of the same circle jerk as WebNet and NewsReal. They'd played the whole Mars story as a triumph for all the little people who never had a chance. The *Mariana* was the "new Miss Liberty," and there was a song and a virtual making the connection for you, blasting off from Ellis Island, setting down on the phony Mars, a ghostly Statue of Liberty lighting the way for all these smiling, beautiful, ethnically diverse people strolling through a red-tinted Eden. A stadium-sized choir, built on the foundation of strong black voices, proclaimed it a New World in several languages. She'd fallen for it, sure. Her throat had lumped on cue. She was one of the little people, after all.

The trainer had run through the basics, and the SEV was indeed a clumsy old cow, but Starr was starting to get the hang of it. You had to anticipate every move way ahead of time and account for inertia. She knew a lot about inertia from personal experience. She learned a long time ago that if you wanted something to happen you had to get off your butt and get moving. It took her a little longer to figure out you had to slow down once in a while or something would come along and stop you. Like a brick wall, or a cop, or a psycho with a knife.

Mr. Burton (call-me-Burt) Pangram who taught the Motivation Modification Module at the Juvenile Correctional Facility, talked a lot about inertia. He webbed in from Richmond once a week to teach the class in a cozy virtual living room with sofas that seemed to suck you into them. He made his motivational points more intense by putting his hand on your knee or your shoulder with a meaningful squeeze. If you were bucking for release and asked him for a letter saying how rehabilitated you were, he invited you to show him on his virtual sofa. Lot of girls did. They said it wasn't like they went real with him or anything, that it wasn't really sex. Starr didn't see it that way. That was like saying Pangram wasn't really a weasel because he just weaseled on the Web. He wrote the letters though. She'd give him that. Made you sound like the girl next door in a neighborhood you couldn't even walk through without getting arrested. He liked his girls to move on, to overcome inertia, to make way for fresh blood.

She entered the SEV mission she had in mind and waited for the trainer to set it up. She'd left an opening in the Weisiger field so she could look out her real window. Over at the *Mariana*, the workers zipped around on sleek little vehicles that reminded her of jet skis back in the days of cheap gas. She imagined inside those space suits were the same boys who'd cruised up and down the shoreline showing off. She hoped to give those hot rods a thrill when she lurched their way in the SEV.

The trainer informed her that the proposed mission was possible with a narrow margin for error, so narrow, in fact, that it should only be undertaken in the case of extreme emergency. No problem. Starr figured the wholesale deception of an entire planet could safely be described as an extreme emergency. Besides, these trainers were always twice as cautious as real pilots. The *Mariana* was only a few kilometers away. How hard could it be? She closed off the field, set the sim on high detail, and ran the mission.

It was easy: Open the bay, little spurt to get you clear, another and you were on your way, a couple of little bursts to correct the course, brake—brake—brake—nestle on the *Mariana* beside the workers' airlock, like setting a basket of eggs on a rock. She died several times before she got it right, of course, but that's what trainers were for. By the time a chime went off to let her know common rec time had started—time to meet Powell—she figured she could pilot the SEV to the *Mariana* blindfolded. She downloaded the sessions into the SEV's memory, so that when she took the controls in reality, they'd be like old friends.

She shut down the trainer, accessed the LOWNRs under her control, and set them to thoroughly screw up all the *Mariana's* communications at Starr's command so that they'd be delighted when WebNet service personnel came calling. It was Webster's phony recall that had given her the idea. And as long as the *Mariana* was cut off, they couldn't check her story. Now all she had to do was convince Powell to go with her. They'd have a few hours or so, give or take, to get the job done once she screwed things up and made their way over there. She wasn't sure what "the job" *was* exactly. She'd play that part by ear. She couldn't just sit around and do nothing.

SHE WAS FIRST INTO THE GYM. THE AIR WAS MISTY AND thick and smelled like a hospital. The environmental system dumped a cloud of disinfectant in here at the close of each session to prevent the spread of disease. Starr was more worried about the long-term effects of breathing this chemical crap. It was like being doused by a plant mister filled with a cocktail of mouthwash and bleach.

The punching bag, set up right across from her door, was still slick with Furay's sweat. He chattered nonstop while he pummeled it, dancing around the bag in the half grav like a musclebound gazelle—*The champ peppers the challenger with a left, a right, another left, jab, jab, jab, a vicious uppercut to the chin, the crowd is on its feet!* He even made the crowd noises, snapped his head back at the imagined counterpunches of his desperate, doomed opponent, then taunted him with mother insults or doubts about his gender. Furay was seriously arrested, which was probably why he liked little girls.

A couple of times Starr had watched him working out in his thong briefs on the security monitors that scanned the area outside her door, but hated herself afterward. They said it was guys who got turned on by naked bodies, that women were more romantic or whatever. She didn't buy it. In fact, there was kind of a turn-on about the fact that Furay's image on the monitors wasn't enhanced a bit, that he was just on the other side of her door in all his sweaty glory, pounding away. Going real had this dangerous, seductive thing about it for her, even though Web sex was better, longer, stronger, and always looked so incredibly good. It helped that Furay was such a slimeball, that she would never in a million years open a door between the two of them. She'd rather suck vacuum.

Powell's door opened above her. His place was opposite hers in the whirling donut that was the station. They'd both climbed "up" spiral

stairs from their quarters toward the center of the station to reach their
door to the gym. But the central core—where the docking bay was—
blocked their view of each other. She couldn't see his door from here,
but she could hear its echo in stereo. She'd said she wanted to meet
him at her place, and the seemingly ever-obliging Powell had agreed
without discussion. Was he not cautious because he was three times
bigger than her or because he was a trusting soul? Rather than sort that
one out, Starr just brought her shotgun.

She heard him approaching from the left past Crichton's door, and
turned to face him. His slippered feet came into view first, big enough
to make a sound even on a carpeted floor in half grav. He was truly
huge even from this weird, foreshortened angle. Six-eight, she'd guess.
He wasn't all bulked out like Furay, but he filled a jumpsuit without a
bulging gut. His head was bald as a baby's butt, dark black like an
African, though she knew he was from D.C.

She herself was an indeterminate mix of races. She didn't know her
father, had never even seen his picture. She remembered her mother
as looking kind of black, kind of Asian, maybe Indian or Mexican. There
were probably some whites in there too. They got into everybody one
time or another. But the last time she'd seen her mother, Starr was six
or seven, so what did she know?

People asked her what she was. She didn't know what to say. Even
the State, which made a study of such matters, had her pegged as
"other." She'd heard *mutt, mongrel, mulatto, mestizo, redbone, chigger,
racially diverse*. She really loved that last one. Just try saying to a shower
full of teenage felons, "I'm racially diverse. If I'm not mistaken, you
must be Spanish surname/African descent." The last few years she'd
taken to joking, "I'm a Martian, okay?" If you could make somebody
laugh, usually they didn't hit you.

She wasn't feeling particularly funny. When Powell was about four
meters away, she raised the shotgun, and he froze. She knew she should
say something, but her tongue was stuck to the roof of her mouth. It
was like her insides were trying to climb out through her pores. How
long had it been since she'd been in the same room with a real person?
She couldn't even remember. At least a couple of years. It was with the
doctor who sewed her up. And the doctor'd been a woman.

"You invite me out here to shoot me?" Powell asked, pointing at
the shotgun.

The security cameras were taking all this in, but she was convinced nobody Earthside monitored them. They were there so the crew could keep an eye on each other. Her voice shook, but she managed to speak. "I want you to go over to the *Mariana* with me. I've got something I need to do over there. If I go by myself, they'll know I'm not legit."

"The *Mariana*?"

"In the SEV."

"I didn't figure you wanted to walk. What're you planning on doing over there?"

"I'll do it all. You don't have to do anything except be there and look official." He shook his head. "I'll pay you," she threw in. Why not? It was just money. It wasn't doing her any good.

"I still want to know what you're doing."

"I'd rather not say."

"I see. You're asking me to help you steal a piece of WebNet equipment, take it to an off-limits construction site, and you're not even going to tell me what for?"

"It's not stealing. We're service personnel."

"Do you have a work order?"

"No."

"Then it's stealing as far as WebNet's concerned, trespassing as far as MarsCorp's concerned."

"They're all part of the same thing."

"Of course they are. And how does that change anything? You and I are not on their guest list. We're the help."

Stalemate. Shotgun or not, she still had to persuade him, and they both knew it. "How do I know I can trust you?"

He laughed and shook his head. "You're too much. You're the one pointing a shotgun in a space station in order to coerce me into commiting a felony, and you want to know if *you* can trust *me*? Shit. I think I'm the one with the trust issues here."

She lowered the shotgun, and he nodded his appreciation, but took a step back. She sighed. "I guess I have to tell you what's going on."

"Maybe not. Maybe I want to go back to my little room, Web a few virtuals, play my flute, meditate, and not worry about it." He hooked a thumb over his shoulder as he continued to back up slowly.

"Stop," she said. "Please!"

He stopped. He lost the ironic half smile he'd been wearing since he showed up.

She'd even startled herself with how pathetic she'd sounded. She imagined Crichton and Furay glued to their monitors, listening.

Powell took a step toward her, then another. She fought the urge to raise the shotgun. He leaned down, like a giant in a storybook, his hands on his knees so that the two of them were almost the same height. He didn't touch her, but he was close. He smelled like tree bark. "What's the matter, Starr?" he asked softly. "What's happened?"

They might've been in some virtual date site, and he was a made-to-order Nice Guy she could confide in and never see again. She held on to the comfort of that fantasy as she told him everything. Once she got started, she couldn't stop. She laid it out in one long rambling narrative, interlaced with her dreams and disappointments and good chunks of her biography, though the gist of it was simple enough: The whole Mars Colony thing was a pack of lies, but she was going to find out the truth of it or die trying. And she didn't say this part, though he could probably guess it: One way or another she was going to make the bastards pay.

"Show me," he said when she was through. By this time they were both sitting on the floor outside her door. She didn't say anything, so he thought she didn't understand. Actually she was a couple of steps ahead of him. "I want to see the real data," he said. "Will you show it to me?"

"It's on my computer. I can run it in my place," she said. It took her a moment to sort out whether that was a yes or a no, but he was already getting to his feet. She juggled her fears. Finally, she asked him, "If I show you the data, and it's like I say it is, do you promise to help me?"

He didn't hesitate. "Sure. If it's like you say it is." He offered his hand to help her up, but she pretended not to see it and rose under her own power, careful not to turn her back on him.

Maybe he was lying, maybe she'd be dead. Anything was better than sitting around whining and doing nothing. She had him stand well back as she thumbed the lock and opened her door. He waited until she'd gotten to the bottom of the stairs before he started down. He closed the door behind him, and the *snick* of the lock made her heart race. As he entered her room, he went right to her window and looked out, giving a low whistle. "Mine won't open," he said.

"Mine won't close."

"Is that how you spend your time, looking out this window at the *Mariana?*"

"And the stars."

That seemed to please him, which made her even more nervous. She didn't waste time on any hostess pleasantries, but made a place for him to sit and ran the data as a passive display.

She sat over to one side, watching him take it in. She didn't want to look at it again. It'd been hard enough the first time. A second time, and she might lose her nerve, her only asset, when you came right down to it.

A HALF HOUR LATER, POWELL'S VEINS STOOD OUT ON HIS neck like climbing vines, and each new bit of data brought a muttered stream of obscenity, so low you couldn't quite make out all of it, just enough to know you didn't want to hear the rest. She wasn't sure why he was so pissed. He'd told her once he thought the Mars colony was a collosal waste of money that could be better spent to help people on Earth. Not that he was so stupid to think that would ever *happen*. But she understood what he meant. But somewhere along the way he must've fallen for the New World hoopla, maybe not as gung ho as her, but on some level. In spite of his size, he was one of the little people too. Maybe he was just tired of being manipulated and lied to.

He pointed at her computer. "You mind if I have a closer look?"

"Be my guest."

He opened up a calculator and several reference sites, including some Starr had never seen before. One was a meteorological simulator and another had to do with soil analysis. For some reason he called up this fuel/oxygen combustion ratio thing that looked like it catered to vintage auto mechanics. As he explored the data, he paid more attention to the surface conditions than the living quarters, which he practically ignored. He did it all passively, not wanting the experience of asphyxiation or hypothermia. Then he spent a long time checking out some readings she hadn't bothered with since there weren't any visuals. Depth was a recurring variable, so she figured they were data from underground sensors. He kept going deeper and deeper, and she imagined him as a sleek black mole burrowing through Martian dirt as easily as a whale diving to the ocean floor.

"Can we get started?" she asked after a while.

He only grunted.

She asked again, louder this time.

"Don't rush me," he said. "I found something."

"It's all bullshit, right?"

"They're doing *something* there. Don't you want to know what it is?"

"Of course," she said, but she was more interested in getting over to the *Mariana*.

He produced some graphs in the air between them, showing the evolving Martian surface conditions—temperature, atmospheric density, oxygen levels, water vapor, winds. "Well, they're terraforming all right, just not nearly so fast as they want everyone to think. That's not what I'm trying to figure out. It's the power source that's too bizarre."

"There's uranium, right? Reactors?" That was supposedly one of the big discoveries, gobs of uranium, enough to power the colony for millennia, perhaps even enough for the energy-starved Earth.

He checked some figures, shut it down. "No. Oil. I've worked offshore, pipelines, refineries, you name it. They're pumping oil, making fuel."

"You're crazy. There's no oil on Mars. Can't be. For oil you need swamps and trees and plants from a billion years ago, right? It's organic. There's *never* been any life on Mars. They settled that one, remember? That's what makes it such a good place to colonize. There's no risk of disease. No ecosystem to screw up."

"That's what MarsCorp says. We've already determined they're lying about everything else. Why wouldn't they lie about this too? The discovery of organic compounds would complicate colonization tenfold. They must want the place pretty bad."

"For *oil?*"

"No. That would never be cost-effective."

Cost-effective. Tenfold. He sounded like a damn company wonk. "Who cares what the power source is? I want to know why Freedom City looks like a fucking jail. Did you see that place?"

"It's set up to be labor intensive. Lots of workers, not too much automated. It's cheaper, more flexible than machines. Not much of a life, but it's not meant for them."

"Then who's it for?"

He looked at her, amused. "Who do you *think?* Who is everything for? The Man. The one paying for all this with your money and mine. Trust me. No matter what's going on, follow the money and you can't go wrong. A year or two, when the terraforming's had a little time and it's starting to shape up, the Man will move in and take it over and say it was his all along."

She couldn't argue with that. "But what about these workers locked up in some cage under the ground? Why do it that way?"

"Ever hear of carrying a canary into a coal mine?"

A chill went down her spine. She had heard of that, actually. She'd also heard of the showers at Auschwitz.

AS THE AIRLOCK SLOWLY EVACUATED THE AIR AROUND them, they floated in their harnesses, waiting in silence. Starr was at the controls. Piloting had fallen to her after a brief discussion in which she wasn't entirely honest, but didn't exactly lie either.

"Are you trained to pilot this thing?"

"Sure. It's simple."

"Are you sure it'll make it over there?"

"Sure. No problem. I checked it out."

"I hope you know what you're doing."

"Me too. Ha, ha."

Neither one of them had been in a space suit since they were certified. Certification required a three-hour space-suit training session, fifteen minutes of which were actually spent inside the suit, clomping up and down under the supervision of a sim instructor who explained that things would feel somewhat different under zero-g conditions. What it felt like was being encased in pressurized panty hose with a trash can on your head—a trash can with a little window in it providing zero peripheral vision and no more than twenty degrees up or down, with the optical clarity of grimy plastic. Above the window on the inside of the helmet was a row of green lights that were supposed to make her feel secure. One of them turned amber, and she glanced up at it. It was labeled HEART RAT. She tried to enjoy the dark humor and spluttered out a nervous laugh, filming the inside of the window with spit. She lifted her hand to swipe it clean, and felt like a total idiot. Maybe she should've chosen the *suited* option in the SEV trainer to get used to it, but all she'd remembered about space suits was that she didn't like them. So she'd overridden the sim's default setting of suited. It shouldn't have given her the option. Why learn how to pilot a SEV suitless? What would you do, hold your breath?

As the last of the air was being pumped out of the airlock, she imagined some tiny detail from the instructions she'd forgotten or misunderstood that would soon mean her blue-faced death. (*Do not overtighten . . .*) Do not overtighten *what?* She couldn't remember. What did "overtighten" *mean* anyway? If you die, you've *over*tightened?

The bay doors started opening, and Starr jumped, quivering in her harness like Jell-O. She looked over at Powell, who looked as terrified as she felt. She tilted her head back to see up out of the bay, trying to imagine she was back in the virtual trainer where she knew what she was doing. Her heart was still racing about a thousand kilometers an hour, and her hands were shaking. Once again, it was time to overcome inertia. She'd given the command to screw up the *Mariana's* communications before they'd suited up. The clock was ticking. She'd played her hand. An hour or two from now, unless she did *something*, there'd be WebNet security swarming all over the *J. P. Morgan*, and everything she'd done would come to nothing.

Goddamnit, Starr, she scolded herself. *Just do it.*

She took a breath and squeezed, giving the thrusters a little shot, and the SEV started up out of the bay ever so slowly and not entirely straight. She had to correct even before they were out of the bay to avoid clipping the edge, and went into a roll. They came out of the station like a die coming out of a shaker. She desperately tried to find the right touch on the controls. It was all wrong, nothing like the trainer, way out of balance. Then she realized in some calm part of her brain not screaming in terror that she hadn't allowed for the mass of Powell and their equipment when she'd played around with the trainer. She also hadn't allowed for the fact that the trainer sim stayed immutable in the cocoon of virtual reality, while the real SEV had sat in the bay for ten years or so and let entropy have its way. Each little thruster was slightly off like an old shack in which nothing was plumb or parallel.

She thought about old houses, old buildings, cramped places tumbling out of control though they seemed to be sitting still. All the places she'd ever lived were like that, none of them by choice until this place, the space place. The Noplace. Nowhere, no gravity, no one. But her. And a fixed point. The *Mariana* would do. The pitch first, and then the roll and yaw. Until they were still. The stars fixed in their places. The SEV was stationary, Earth over their heads, the *J. P. Morgan* a dozen yards beneath their feet, and the *Mariana* a few kilometers dead ahead. They'd used a third of their fuel, and were no closer to their destination, but she was in control.

"You okay?" she asked Powell over the intercom.

"Peachy," he said in a shaky voice.

"Thrusters were a little off." She didn't dare look at him. She gave the SEV a little kick, and they started toward the *Mariana* only slightly off-kilter, hoping when the time came, she could stop.

S HE'D LEFT HER SHOTGUN BEHIND. S HE AND P OWELL WERE armed only with their WebNet service representative IDs and an impressive bunch of tools and testing equipment. Her sabotage had apparently worked. The jet skis were hovering about the communications array like bees around a flower. They wouldn't have any weapons either. They were workers, service personnel like her and Powell, only better paid. One of them took the low-tech measure of pointing at the approaching SEV, and in about fifteen seconds flat, she and Powell were flanked on all sides by jet skis. Starr flashed her ID like a cross before vampires, up, down, side to side.

At least she didn't have to execute a landing. They clamped lines onto the SEV and towed them over to an enormous bay big enough for a shuttle, though it was empty at the moment. She and Powell were hauled out of the SEV like cargo and floated into an airlock with a dozen of the workers. There were arrows everywhere to show you where to put your feet. As air filled the space, everyone else became heavier and settled to the ground while Powell and Starr continued to float. Starr had heard about this. The *Mariana* didn't use centrifugal force to fake gravity like the station did. They had a whole new artificial-gravity system. It wasn't really gravity at all but magnetic sites throughout the bloodstream drawn to special electromagnets in the floor, giving the illusion of weight. The AI controlled the whole thing.

A green light came on and the workers started taking off their helmets. Starr and Powell followed their example. With a wave of his hand and a few inhalations, the one who seemed to be their keeper indicated that Starr and Powell should take several deep breaths. They obeyed and gradually sank to the floor as the airborne artificial-gravity system installed itself in their bloodstream. Still no one spoke to them. Starr couldn't stand it anymore. This was too much like an arrest, not the tone to set.

"Bet you guys were surprised to see us. We're from the WebNet rig over there—the *J. P. Morgan*—got a notice your communications were down and we should check it out. We'll get you up and running again in no time." She smiled at them all, and several of them smiled back, but nobody said anything. One of them pointed over their heads just before the doors slid open. There was an array of sensors up there recording Starr's babble. The one who'd pointed took her elbow like she was a little old lady needing help with stairs and led her out of the airlock. A space suitless man in Disposa-Clothes casuals, the pricey kind that look like silk pajamas, was waiting for them. His ID said he was Terence Cassawalter, Admin. "Who are you, and what are you doing here?" he asked.

She acted as if she were delighted he'd asked her that question. "As I was just explaining to these guys, we're from the WebNet rig over there." She pointed over his left shoulder, though she had no idea where the station was from here. "The grid crashed in this area, and we came over to get you up and running again."

"We didn't request technical assistance."

She gave a condescending little chuckle. "Oh, but you didn't have to. It's part of WebNet's Full Service Plan—at the first sign of malfunction the system issues an automatic service request, followed by the prompt deployment of courteous and qualified service personnel." She resisted the urge to chuck him under the chin or pinch his cheek. For a brief while, Starr had supported herself by writing bad checks at a time when writing a check instead of using a Smartchip was a suspicious activity in itself. She found if you kept at it and were achingly sincere, eventually people believed almost anything you told them—to get rid of you as much as anything else. But she suspected that Terence Cassawalter, Admin, needed some sense of closure, something official, something, hopefully, scannable. Always give the customer what he wants. She unclipped her ID from her suit, unclipped Powell's from his, and handed them to Terence Cassawalter, Admin. "You'll want to scan these, I'm sure."

You bet he did. It was an empty exercise—the *Mariana* wasn't communicating with *anyone,* including WebNet. It'd be a while before WebNet would figure out their employees had started making house calls. All the scan would do was store their information in the system and check whatever database they had on board, which would only say they were who they said they were. Not exactly model citizens, but what could you expect with space help?

It proved to be a nice ploy. Cassawalter swiped the IDs at a terminal beside the airlock as if that settled the matter once and for all and handed them back, job well done. "Where do you need to get to?" he asked. There was nothing like delegating your brains to a computer to lay suspicions to rest.

"We'll need to start at your central computer to make sure that it's still properly configured and to rule out the possibility of viral infection. It's a long shot, but you never can tell. Then we may need to recalibrate the communications array. To tell you the truth, this is a pretty big mess. Once we have a look at the schematics online, we should have a clearer idea of the specific access required. Shouldn't take more than a few hours."

She was making this stuff up as she went. If you keep talking, so forthcoming it seems like you're going to start reading your diary to them next, then how can you be holding anything back? Wouldn't she be quieter if she was trying to be sneaky? If she'd told him short and sweet, "I want unrestricted access to your central computer," he'd have said no.

As they were being led into the heart of the ship—or more properly, the central nervous system—Powell caught Starr's eye and gave her a nod that told her he was impressed with her performance, though he might never believe another word she said.

STARR HAD SPENT MANY AN HOUR VIRTUALING AROUND THIS ship, fantasizing she'd be on board one day. Even with what she knew now, it was still a rush to be moving down these corridors. It was essentially a command module and common rooms on top with a gigantic parking deck for the colonists' shuttles down below, a big grid not unlike the SEV but on a much grander scale with elevator shafts running through it. In one of the media's favorite metaphors, the *Mariana* was like a big beehive hanging in orbit, designed to take on a swarm of colonists from Earth and transport them to Mars orbit, where they would fly down to their new garden. That much seemed to be true. As Powell had pointed out, even though the atmosphere on Mars wasn't breathable, they'd hiked the density way up so the big shuttles could land. Somebody was going to Mars on this ship, and by the look of things it would be soon. The ship was done. No one seemed to be constructing anything anymore, only testing, adjusting, calibrating.

Unlike the real and virtual Mars, the two *Mariana*s looked pretty much the same. The hardware was identical. In the virtuals, the crew was just decoration, deliberately generic to give the ship a lived-in look without being too much of a distraction. As they were led through the real ship, however, Starr studied the real people for clues. Most wore uniforms that looked like a cross between military and sports team uniforms, like in the virtuals but not as nice. Webster'd told her there was a big spin-off business in "official" knockoffs of these uniforms. There were five different colors, several different ranks and doodads. They came packaged with different burgers in your food unit.

Starr watched people's faces as Cassawalter went by. He didn't seem to be a particularly popular fellow. Most of them weren't crew members. The uniforms made it pretty obvious how they rated. Workers wore just-this-side-of-paper-bag jumpsuits that looked like they came out of a burger bag with their names stenciled on and the pants legs too short— always too short.

The crew had jackets that looked almost like cloth, with name patches sewed on. They were supposed to look "naval," the designer'd said in an interview. Whatever that meant. Starr thought they looked like waiters at a country club. The important people, the ones dressed "casual" in Cassawalter's price range, the ones he acknowledged as they passed, numbered about six or seven out of the hundred or so Starr guessed to be currently on board. They didn't pass anyone who outranked Cassawalter—since they all spoke first—so he was pretty high up the chain of command. He probably wasn't the top dog. That person was most likely in his quarters.

Studying the faces of the workers and crew, she doubted many of them had any idea what was really going down. They looked too cheerful for slavers, going about their work like it was opening night of the school play. The important people, however, looked a bit haggard, maybe even ill. Starr could sympathize. Lying wore you down, made you nervous. People got pissed off when they find out they've been lied to. The way Starr had it figured, there were no more than fifteen or twenty people on this ship who knew the truth. Maybe all it would take to really screw things up was to increase that number by one. Two, counting Powell.

THEIR DESTINATION, THE SHIP'S COMPUTING SYSTEM, WAS someplace Starr'd never been in the virtual. It was edited out for security reasons. The doors, the walls, the floor, the ceiling were emblazoned with warnings that only Authorized Personnel could enter. Voices in several languages chirped out the news as well. Starr and Powell stood in the din as the computer scanned them molecule by molecule. Meanwhile, Cassawalter negotiated their permission to enter by offering up the authority of his retina, his DNA, and his pheromone profile.

The doors opened, and they walked into a Weisiger field depicting a gray featureless cubicle ten meters on a side. The doors closed behind them. A sim of a muscle-bulging security guard stepped from the wall and asked Cassawalter to identify his guests. It had an odd, squeaky voice that made it seem even more ominous.

"WebNet service personnel to restore communications. Their identification has been logged and verified."

The sim looked as if it were actually listening, thinking. "Request verification from WebNet Operations," it said.

Cassawalter sighed. "No communications with WebNet Operations are available at this time. Override normal security protocol to deal with this emergency."

"Under your authority, Mr. Cassawalter?" the sim asked pleasantly.

"Yes."

The sim looked thoughtful again. "Access granted. Will there be anything else?"

"Show us where to jack in," Starr volunteered. Cassawalter turned to her in surprise, but she was ready for him. "This has to be a wired operation. We have security concerns of our own. Intellectual property protocol allows us to exercise whatever discretion we see fit in the deployment of protected equipment and software, including but not limited to the use of direct shielded access and the exclusion of non-WebNet personnel from the worksite."

Cassawalter smiled or sneered; it was hard to tell which. "You're telling me to leave?"

"I'm merely stating the terms of our service agreement. If you don't desire service at this time—"

"Okay, okay." He spoke to the air as he walked out. "I, Terence Cassawalter, authorize direct unrestricted access to computer system by logged WebNet personnel at this time for . . . How long do you need?"

"A few hours should do it."

"Two hours." The doors opened, Cassawalter left without even saying good-bye, and the doors closed behind him. The sim pointed to an access panel that had suddenly appeared in the wall. Starr opened it and plugged in her computer. She found the interface settings and shut off the Weisiger field. Cubicle and guard vanished.

"Mother of God!" Powell exclaimed. They were standing in an acre-sized room. Floating in the center of it was a constellation of hardware that would've dwarfed the *Morgan*. Starr couldn't speak. She knew it had to be big, but she hadn't been prepared for anything like this. She couldn't imagine all this was just to run this ship. They must have bigger plans for it, like running a whole planet.

"What now?" Powell whispered.

"We find out what's going on."

"Then what?"

"I don't know yet." She had the file structure displayed on her computer. This thing was immense, dense—God's computer, or at least Noah's. It wasn't hard to find Mars. She left the AI cranking out the Mars cartoons alone for now, and went for the dry data. She found a file labeled MISSION OVERVIEW. Like most of the files that looked interesting, it was labeled RESTRICTED. Now she'd find out how literally the computer took Cassawalter's rather broadly stated instructions. She gave the command and it opened up like a flower.

"You surprised me back there," Powell said. "I thought you were . . ."

She glanced up at him. "Crazy?"

"Shy."

He was looking at her differently. As if she were different, as if she really was the slick sister she pretended to be. "I am shy. Extremely shy. Just because I can string somebody along doesn't mean I'm not shy." She turned to watch the display. "Somebody you're trying to con, like Cassawalter, he's not real. He's not a person. It's like a play."

"To be shy you need another person."

"Yeah, exactly."

"Thanks."

"For what?"

"Saying I'm a person."

She didn't know whether he was making fun of her or not.

"Do you mind if I ask you something?"

"I guess not," she said, not looking at him.

"Are you always so intense?"

"Is that the question?"

"Yes."

"Only when I'm scared." *Which is most of the time,* she added to herself. But he could probably tell that already.

He was watching the display with her now, his arms folded across his chest. "I figure you're in charge on this expedition," he said. "If there's anything you want me to do, just tell me."

"Don't stand so close."

He sidestepped away from her, and she looked to see if he was pissy about it, but he gave her the nicest smile.

PART FOUR

El Nuevo Mundo

*I had learned a lot in the past two years.
I was no longer the woman who, because she was a
foreigner, thought this was not her Revolution.*
—ROSA KING

CHAPTER
THIRTEEN

BY THE TIME SANTEE REACHED THE ESTRELLITA ON THE
night of Jorge's murder, he'd reduced the mystery of Jorge's death to a
single conundrum. Why had his killers acted *before* he made contact
with Santee? They'd obviously known he was Zapatista and that he had
a rendezvous in the *zócalo*. Why murder Jorge before he had the contra-
band interface in his possession, before they could apprehend not only
Jorge but his contact as well? Were they simply inept, or did they have
another purpose? The only way it made sense was if they wanted to
prevent Santee's meeting with Jorge, while leaving Santee at large.

Jorge was from Tziscao, a village near the Guatemalan border, approximately a hundred kilometers as the crow flies, about twice that by road.
Santee and Margaret had stayed there years before when Jorge was a
boy. He worked around the hostel, watching old Mexican westerns on
television in the evenings and sleeping on a cot in the kitchen at night.
They'd learned not to inquire too closely about family. He might be
related to the adults who ran the place or he might not. Low-intensity
warfare had been particularly low and intense in the area, where rebel
support was strong and stubborn. What seemed to be a single family at
first glance could turn out to be the remnants of three or four shattered
ones. Santee was to have delivered two hundred doses of the interface
to Jorge to take back to such families.

Perhaps Jorge had had something for Santee as well. Information,
maybe.

He'd decided he would deliver the interface in person, see if he could
find out why Jorge had been murdered. Whatever the reason, the killers
were probably counting on him to let it be. That's what he was supposed
to do. In a shed out beyond the ruins, there was a car for Santee to use
if things turned sour, to run away, to go back home to the States. Was

that home anymore? He didn't know. He doubted he'd be any safer there. And if the government was really onto him, how far would he get heading north? How would he cross the border with all the nanoshit in his veins? He'd show up on electronic surveillance like a smart bomb with legs.

It didn't matter. He had to go south. He had to find out. He remembered Jorge's eyes. He'd spotted Santee, and they lit up with recognition. And something more? Relief maybe. The next instant Jorge saw the four men closing on him and knew immediately he was going to die. He wasn't surprised that four professional assassins had been sent to kill him. He'd known something important, something worth killing over. Santee had to find out what it was before it killed anyone else.

In the moonlight at least, it didn't look like Rancho Estrellita had changed a bit. The little *cabañas* sat in a row overlooking the valley. Zack's big American truck loomed beside the house. Everything was dark. He could sneak into one of the *cabañas*, steal a little electricity, and be on his way. He tried to tell by looking if one of them might be empty. They were all dark, but it was late. He'd just have to take his chances.

He needed five minutes to write a quick virtual to disk telling Margaret where he was going. The message he had in mind would only be intelligible to her. Unfortunately his computer's battery was low, and the backup was charging in his Ocosingo hotel room. When she received the one word message he'd left in the interface—*Vortex*—she'd know where to look next. Even under the circumstances, he imagined her smile at his choice of a hiding place and smiled it himself. Soon, very soon, he would see her again.

He started toward the *cabañas*, but as he stepped onto the caliche road, he heard a bemused grunt, turned, and saw Zack standing in the moonlight, his silver hair and white face making him look like a ghost on a ghostly road. The odor of marijuana hung in the air. He lit a cigarette with much clinking of his Zippo, and added a cloud of Marlboro to the mix. If he'd been startled by Santee's showing up in his backyard in the middle of the night, it didn't show. "Are you real?" he asked jokingly. "I was just thinking about you, and here you are."

Santee tried to match his host's studied nonchalance. He could understand how Zack could navigate the difficult male waters of Mexico. He was so laid-back he seemed almost macho, without ever having to fight anybody to prove it. "And why would you be thinking about me, Zack?"

"Are you kidding me? An IE man in town? Shit. Everybody in the tourist biz knows you've been staying at Felix's, recording this and that. How's he doing, by the way? Always liked Felix."

Of course. Zack was still angling for his big break. Santee couldn't help making an unflattering comparison with Rosa King. *We are on the wrong side, you and I, the moment we set foot here, despite our best intentions.* Whatever Zack's intentions, Santee doubted they were the best.

"Felix is fine. But I wanted something different, away from the hustle and bustle, and I thought of you. Do you have any vacancies?"

Zack doffed his floppy straw hat and swept it toward the *cabañas.* "Empty as a rich man's heart. Take your pick."

Santee nodded toward the closest one. "This one'll be fine."

"Excellent choice." Zack searched the ground around Santee's feet for luggage. "Traveling a tad light, aren't you?"

Santee pointed to his nearly empty backpack. "Just this. I like to improvise."

Zack chuckled. "It's a shame things didn't work out with you and George."

"I'm not very spiritual I guess."

"Neither is George. Would you like to take a bath before you turn in? A little brandy? Cuban cigar?"

"No thanks. I'm really exhausted." And he was too. Bizarre dreams had haunted his sleep for days. Sleep would have to wait, however.

Zack let him into the *cabaña* and turned back the bed. He paused at the door on his way out. "Should I put this on a credit card, or get it from the IE site, or what?"

Santee had some cash in a money belt, but that might further arouse Zack's suspicions, and he'd have more need of the cash later. He reluctantly surrendered his credit card. Might as well shoot up a flare if anybody was after him, but he shouldn't be here long enough for it to matter.

A HALF HOUR AFTER ZACK RAN THROUGH SANTEE'S CREDIT card, the phone rang. Zack was sitting in the kitchen halfway expecting the call and picked up on the first ring. He sure as hell didn't want Edie picking up.

It was Huerta. "You have a Señor St. John at your establishment this evening, my friend?"

There wasn't much point in lying to Huerta, but Zack didn't want to just roll over and beg either. He faked a big yawn that turned real on him, then mumbled, "Yeah, he's here. I'm sure he's asleep. What time's it, anyway?" Zack watched the digital clock on the stove turn to midnight.

"I want you to make sure he's sleeping well."

Santee's *cabaña* was still lit up. "I can see the *cabaña* from here. The lights are all off."

"Perhaps he lies sleepless in the dark, a victim of insomnia."

Huerta's voice had taken on that homicidal edge. Zack shouldn't push his luck any further. "Hang on." He went out the kitchen door, strolled across the road to the *cabaña*, and knocked on the door, phone in hand. He leaned over and peered into the window. He wasn't surprised to see the empty bed. "He's not answering. Like I said, must be asleep."

"Look inside."

Zack obeyed, making a racket of it for Huerta's benefit. The place was tiny with nowhere to hide. The bedclothes were slightly rumpled where Santee had sat down, but that was it. The back window was open. He walked over to it and looked out. From here he could see the top of the big pyramid, a flashlight moving around like a firefly. "He's not here." He shut off the overhead light to have a clearer view.

"Where did he go?"

"Don't know," Zack said, watching the light bob around and come to a stop just this side of the apex. "There's no sign of him."

Huerta made a fierce little noise like a Rottweiler hitting the end of his chain, but when he spoke again his voice was like velvet lining a casket. "I'm sure he'll turn up tomorrow."

FROM THE TOP OF THE PYRAMID, SANTEE WATCHED ZACK cross the road in the moonlight, the light wink out in his *cabaña*. It'd probably been stupid to come to Zack's at all, stupider to let him run his credit card. He was probably in the pocket of Huerta, the local *cacique*. Santee had met the man on a virtual skiing trip when he was nosing around after the massacre. Huerta wasn't quite at ease with their slick Mexico City hosts, but he watched Santee as if he knew exactly what he was up to. Maybe he did, but he didn't blow the whistle.

Instead he'd held on to the knowledge for future use. Memory was a tricky business in Mexico, long and highly selective.

Santee descended the back side of the pyramid, unrestored and overgrown. It'd been built by Indians centuries ago—conquered and humiliated, then remembered and glorified as if they were heroes from the revolution. Not much had changed: *They can't decide whether they want to shoot us or help us.* After some searching at the base of the pyramid, he found the trail that led to the stashed car.

More than likely, Jorge's murder meant that the government knew about the interface, knew of their plans. But what could they do to stop it? Trace thousands and thousands of peasants scattered throughout the mountains? Shut down the whole Web to silence the truth? No, as long as he was alive, this would work.

In a few days, he'd go online at the appointed time, hook up with those who'd installed the interface, and assault the Web with the reality it'd taken pains to conceal: That the global village had dirt floors and dysentery and children slowly starving. That while the Web might be Wide, it didn't go very deep, so that when you started spouting off about "universal access," you weren't talking about anyone around here. They lived in a different universe. In a few days, those who fancied themselves the World would get a vivid message from below. He could only hope they'd care.

As HE DROVE SOUTH, HE BEGAN TO DOUBT THAT THINGS were so simple. He was stopped at three checkpoints, waved through each time without even a cursory search. He had a phony ID, phony papers, but he never got the opportunity to try them out. No one asked to see them. He was a gringo in the heart of the war zone, driving around at two in the morning, and no one asked for his ID. And most incredibly, no one hit him up for a bribe.

Something was definitely up. They must know who he was and had orders not to delay him. But why? If they were just springing a trap they could've done that in Ocosingo. As Zack pointed out, everyone knew where to find him. For reasons he couldn't guess, it seemed as if they *wanted* him to carry out his plans.

He got a room in Comitán, parked the car in the car park down below. He zipped himself up in a contained Weisiger field and had the computer search every pore for bugs. As he expected, he was clean. The interface was skittish about other electronics poaching on the private reserve of his body. If he were infested with an invader, by now he probably would've suffered blurred vision, severe nausea, or piercing auditory hallucinations.

The car, however, was another matter, no doubt tagged at the first checkpoint. At least one wage slave, he was sure, had that car's image on a screen as his fulltime assignment. Santee had no desire to interrupt that person's tedium. The car would go nowhere. But if they had the car, they had the hotel, so traced or not, he was being watched from above.

In his backpack, he had computer, water bottle, compass, flashlight, binoculars, aspirin, poncho, and journal. Underwear would've been nice. He took a shower and dressed in the same clothes. He lay down on top of the covers to get a couple hours sleep. For the first time in days, he didn't dream.

FIRST THING IN THE MORNING, PACK ON HIS BACK, HE TOOK his post in the open doorway of his room. He let the maid pass by. She'd think he was just another lech. He nodded and smiled at an older couple on their way to breakfast as if he were just taking the morning air. But when the man next door, a small precise man with a thin mustache, passed in front of his room, Santee fell into step with him, draping his arm over his shoulders to make a single infrared blob for their audience above, and greeted him warmly.

"Buenos días, mi amigo. ¿Como estás?"

"Muy bien, gracias. Y tú?"

The man's Mexican politeness carried the two of them halfway to the street before he asked, "¿Dónde me conoces?" Where do I know you from?

Santee laughed long and hard at his instant friend's joke until he'd propelled them into a crowd of folk on the curb waiting to cross the street into the zócalo. "En ninguna parte," he told his confused neighbor. Nowhere. Santee crossed with the crowd and took a seat at one of the shoeshine stands. He called over one of the local kids, gave him some money, and asked him to go down to the market, buy two bicycles, bring one back to him, and keep the other one for himself.

Half an hour later, his shoes gleaming, Santee mounted his new bike—a Chinese heavyweight with huge whitewall tires and red, white, and blue streamers coming off the handle grips—and pedaled slowly out of town. As a last-minute inspiration, he'd also bought the boy's hat to give that authentic Mexican touch. Soft with age, it was a gray-and-blue cap with a star on it. DALLAS COWBOYS, it said. If they were looking down from their satellite perches, trying to spot him, as they no doubt were, they'd check it out in his profile and know the real Santee St. John wouldn't be caught dead wearing that cap.

SANTEE PEDALED BACK ROADS FOR SEVERAL HOURS BEFORE he came to the Lagunas de Montebello, a chain of limestone lakes and caverns of incredible beauty. Once a national park, it was now largely the province of the military concentrated along the Guatemalan border. Zapatistas, their weapons, and their sympathizers supposedly came back and forth across that border. But it was still hard to explain what all these soldiers, vehicles, and aircraft were doing here. The Mexican army looked as if it were preparing for an invasion by the combined military forces of Latin America.

Santee ditched his bike and took to the woods. He and Margaret had hiked the trails around here for weeks. There was one that zigzagged along close to the ridge above the highway all the way to Tziscao. His legs were still wobbly from the bike, but it felt good to be on foot again. The trail was steep, rocky, and muddy; but flowers bloomed in the most unlikely crannies, and roots made rounded stairs. It was an old trail, cut deep, heavily traveled by people and burros. Most locals didn't have cars or money for gas and like him would want to stay clear of the soldiers on the road in any event. He fully expected to meet someone on the trail, but there was no one. He told himself it didn't mean anything, that he was just being paranoid. But still, he kept an eye out for signs anyone had used this trail recently.

After a couple of hours, he came upon a bundle of wood that'd gotten away from somebody and lay scattered down the hillside. From the size of it he guessed a burroload. There was dung on the trail, but it was dry, several days old at least. The wood had been cut with machete maybe a week ago. What was it still doing here? One stick, right beside the trail, had a vine coiled around it, once, twice, three times. It was like finding money scattered on a city street. This was a lot of labor left to rot.

He looked up the trail. Over the next rise, if he remembered right, Tziscao would come into view. It was a tiny village—maybe three narrow streets by four or five strung along the south bank of an emerald-green lake. No more than a few hundred people at most. Nearly all of them cooked and heated with wood like this, hacked from the forest with machetes.

He jogged up to the ridge and looked down across the lake at the town. There were no fires, no smoke. No boats on the water.

He dug his binoculars out of his pack, and studied the streets and houses. The school. The tiny store. Though everything was intact, there was no one. No children hauling firewood. No women washing clothes. No one. Not even any soldiers. From here the trail descended to the shore of the lake, then a quarter way around the lake to the village. If there was anyone watching from that seemingly empty town, they'd see him coming long before he saw them. He didn't have a weapon, not so much as a machete. He didn't believe in weapons. As he headed down to the village, he had a new understanding of one of his father's phrases—having the courage of your convictions.

He couldn't shake the feeling of being watched as he tried to appear guiltless, nonchalant, strolling into town as if he had a reason to be there but was in no particular hurry. Another crazy tourist who might show up anywhere. He didn't bother with the binoculars again, but kept an eye on his destination. Still no one, nothing.

A half block into town, he heard a clatter from a house to his right and turned just as three dogs erupted from a window, fighting over what looked to be a corncob, and sprawled on the ground yelping. He shouted, and they scrambled to their feet, dashing up the hill in a panic. Santee scooped up a handful of rocks and walked the three-block width of the town. He saw no one except the dogs, who shadowed his movements at a safe distance to see if he might be good for a handout.

Few of the houses had locks. Many didn't have doors. He picked a house at random and stepped inside. There was a sour smell but nothing gruesome. As his eyes slowly adjusted, a perfectly ordinary house materialized out of the gloom. There was no sign of foul play. No blood, no overturned furniture. Everything looked perfectly normal, as if the people who lived here had just left. There were wooden bowls on the table. The porridge inside had dried to the consistency of custard. The rest of it congealed in a pot on the cold hearth.

He got out his flashlight and made a thorough search. There was no other food, no clothes. As far as he could tell, everything else had been left behind. There was a hairbrush, a jar with a few pesos, a photograph of a wedding, a machete in a tooled sheath. He could make no sense of it. Whoever lived here had left deliberately, taking time to pack but leaving behind money, and most mysteriously, that machete. He added a couple hundred pesos of his own to the jar, and tied the machete around his waist.

He went to the hostel, and it, too, looked deserted. He found an open window in the common room and climbed through. On one of the tables was a battered deck of cards, what looked like a two-handed game of gin or hearts in progress, two fans of cards faceup. A half-finished bottle of Coke sat on the table, a straw sticking out of it. Green and white rings of mold were forming on the surface of the liquid.

At first everything was as before—no clothes, no food, everything else left as if the inhabitants intended to return momentarily. But in one of the guest rooms was an old-fashioned guidebook to Mexico in English and a backpack filled with women's clothes. There was a handheld in the outside pocket of the pack. He turned it on and found a journal program, but couldn't read the entries without a password. He could read the dates, however. They left off four days ago. Before that, they stretched back uninterrupted for weeks.

He went into the kitchen and found some food under the counter— a box of packaged cookies and cupcakes for stocking the wire rack in the common room—apparently forgotten. He opened a package of Pinguinos, chocolate cupcakes with cream filling, and wolfed them down. Then another. He washed them down with a couple of canned juices, also lost in the clutter under the counter. He spotted a carpetbag hanging from a peg on the kitchen wall, directly over what had been Jorge's cot. He emptied the contents on the bed. Mostly clothes—a couple of shirts, a pair of pants, a bandana. Inside the bandana was an unlabeled prescription bottle. Santee recognized it as identical to the one he'd given Jorge on their previous meeting, with two hundred doses of the interface inside. It was empty.

There was also a little notebook and a pencil held together with a rubber band. Inside were pencil sketches, mostly incredibly detailed drawings of flower blossoms, lizards, faces. One of the last faces was a pretty girl about eighteen or nineteen. He remembered Jorge and Marga-ret had sketched each other one evening. Jorge had had talent, and it looked like he'd developed some skill. There were some more ambitious vistas—a view of Tziscao covering two pages from almost the identical perspective Santee had had from the trail, only there were boats on the water, children running down the streets, even a kite in the air. A few pages later was a view along the border where squat white obelisks made a dotted line as if on a map, the twentieth century's contribution to the area's monumental architecture.

Santee turned the page and froze. There was a detailed drawing of a spaceship, the new shuttle by the look of it, much in the news lately, the MarsCorp logo on the snout. On the next page was a rough drawing of what at first glance looked like a forest, but on closer inspection proved to be a valley full of spaceships.

The rest of the pages were blank. Jorge could've seen the shuttle on the television that usually played nonstop on top of the refrigerator. He could've copied these drawings from a magazine or newspaper left by one of the guests. Maybe they were just products of his youthful imagination. But if that were true, Santee reasoned, Jorge wouldn't be dead.

He put the notebook in his pack, and headed for the tiny store, closed up tight. He broke in the back door, and found the shelves still stocked with the same meager selection. He loaded his pack with cans of tuna, a bag of powdered milk, packages of crackers, a box of candles, a jar of Nescafé, and several bottles of water. The cashbox was under the counter, and he put the rest of his money in it. He left the way he came, trying to make the padlock look like it was still in place. There was probably no need to hurry, but he felt open and exposed on the streets, so he jogged quickly to the edge of town, where the street became a trail, and climbed up to the ridge and to the border and beyond. He had no idea how far he'd have to go. He couldn't be positive he was headed in the right direction. But he could make at least a few kilometers before sunset.

SANTEE GUESSED HE WAS ABOUT EIGHT OR NINE KILOME-ters inside Guatemala, but he didn't kxnow for sure. His computer's GPS would tell him, but without a map the information was useless and the maps were all on the Web. IE no doubt had a tracer on his computer, and who knew who else did. If he tried to see where he was, he risked being seen. He wished for the millionth time that Margaret was here. She always seemed to find her way. After all their travels together, maybe he'd learned something from her. He looked around at the darkening landscape, the first stars in the night, and calculated which way was north. He took out his compass and checked himself. He was

only about twenty degrees off—just good enough to get himself seriously lost.

In the dying light, he opened a can of tuna and ate it with a tube of
crackers. Wearing all his clothes, he stretched out on his poncho only
a few meters from the trail, his pack under his head for a pillow. As
the temperature plunged and stars filled the sky, he thought he'd be too
exhausted and scared to sleep.

Chilled to the bone, he woke at three A.M., stumbled to his feet, and
swayed at the edge of the clearing as he pissed. Staring vacantly into the
night, he realized he was staring *at* something, a glow on the horizon, as
if there were a brightly lit stadium a few kilometers off. He smiled to
himself as he finished peeing. With stiff cold fingers, he found a stick
and drew an arrow in the dirt pointing to the glow. For the rest of the
night, he lay shivering beside it, waiting for the sun to rise. At first light,
compass in hand, he headed toward the place in the middle of a mountain jungle, no towns for miles, that glowed.

THAT AFTERNOON, AS HOT AS HE'D BEEN COLD THE NIGHT
before, he trudged along with his sweat-soaked shirt tied around his
waist, his head pounding, wondering just how far he'd go before he
admitted he was just some dumb-ass gringo in way over his head who
ought to give it up and go back home. Trouble was he'd revised his
notion of "home" over the last few years so that home was with Margaret,
and by this time she was no doubt somewhere on the trail that led to
him, the trail he was on, and if he left it, she'd never find him, and
he'd never get home. At least that's the way it looked to him with sweat
streaming into his eyes. He'd lost his cap hours ago. He remembered
one of Margaret's tricks and made a turban of his shirt.

God, he missed her. He never got to talk to her anymore except their
stilted doubletalk on the Web. He conjured her ghost a hundred times
a day—Margaret would say this, Margaret would laugh just so, just now.
Can't you hear her absence? It'd been almost a year since he'd actually
heard her laugh, touched her flesh. And here he was, stumbling along
to his death for all he knew, and he might never touch her again. How
could anything matter if that were true? He wasn't supposed to think
this way. Everything was about the revolution. Doing the right thing.
Making something of himself. And what was he now? Journalist? Spy?
Snipe hunter? Fool?

He stumbled on a rock and stopped.

A very lonely man.

Shrugging off his pack, he let it drop to the ground. Insect sounds pulsated in the air around him, mocking him with their numbers. When all this was over, they were saying, we'll still be here.

He sat on the ground and wanted to cry. Why not? There was no one to see him, mock him, ignore him, sympathize with him, ask him, "Who are you? What are you doing out here anyway? Do you think you can actually change the world?"

The world didn't need change anymore. It had variety. Choice. *Freedom*, they called it. Don't like this world? Go to another one. He pulled open his pack and took out his computer, popping it open. It came on immediately, awaiting his touch, his first choice in the maze that led to other worlds: PASSIVE or INTERACTIVE. The global village awaited his decision. He could go anywhere, do anything—just watch and listen, or jump right in and have the experience. Choose your poison. He slammed it shut.

He drank some water, splashed his body with a handful, and washed his face. He dried off with his shirt and wrung it out. Fearing sunburn, he put it back on. As he buttoned, he remembered Margaret unbuttoning his shirt, spreading her hands across his chest, kissing his neck. He touched the remembered kiss. Those who called memory a virtual experience didn't understand experience or memory.

Margaret would've said: *Let's see what's around the next bend. The sun's getting lower. The worst of the heat's over. We've come this far.* If she'd actually been there, he might've snarled a reply, but she wasn't, so her ghost was persuasive. She helped him to his feet, and he kept going.

AN HOUR FURTHER DOWN THE TRAIL HE GOT A LUCKY BREAK. The wind switched directions, and he smelled human shit on the wind. A lot of it. He left the trail and, hacking a swath with the machete, made his way to higher ground, trying for a vantage point akin to the vultures' that circled the valley ahead. It didn't take long to find it. Jorge's drawing was depressingly accurate. He'd not exaggerated in the least. There was the valley of spaceships. From here he could also see the soldiers patrolling the ridge. If the wind had been from another direction, he would've walked right into their arms.

He crawled into the bushes and studied the valley through his binoculars. There'd been an addition since Jorge had been here, a chain-link enclosure like a dog run the size of a football field. The smell was coming from a ditch at one end. The rest of the space was filled with people he guessed were the residents of Tziscao, sitting on the ground, their bundles of food and clothes around them, looking as if they were waiting for a bus. There were no guards, just the fence, whose purpose seemed more to be to keep the swarm of vehicles from running over the docile prisoners than to keep them inside. They were expressionless, staring off into space, not speaking. They looked drugged. Or wired.

And then it hit him. They were wired. Wired with the interface he'd given to Jorge, to a dozen like Jorge scattered throughout Mexico, ultimately to thousands of *campesinos* just like the ones penned in this valley like cattle. A huge helicopter swooped in low and settled into the valley, buffeting them. They didn't bother to look up. The sounds and sensation were familiar. Santee looked around at the ridge, imagined it from their perspective. He'd been here before. In his dreams.

HE RETREATED BLINDLY FOR SEVERAL HOURS, THINKING OF nothing but putting as much distance between himself and that valley as he could. He felt like one of his own sims in Rincón, part of someone else's design. What he'd thought he was doing wasn't what he was doing at all. With his whole neurological system occupied by invaders, how could he be sure his thoughts weren't just scripts handed down to him?

Rosa had once complained, "We don't always understand what it is you want us to do."

He'd told her, "Don't think about what I want you to do. Be yourself." What bullshit. That's where this whole thing got started in the first place, in Rincón when El Sub himself sought them out and asked their help, and they couldn't refuse, couldn't even think of it: They were just being themselves, totally and predictably themselves.

But their Marcos obviously wasn't Marcos. The whole thing had been a setup from the beginning. That was the only way it made sense. He wondered if Hermalinda was really Zapatista, wondered just where the deception stopped and the truth began. One thing he was sure of, however, Jorge hadn't been in on it, nor had the whole village of Tziscao. They'd been tricked by their friend, their ally—Santee St. John.

When night fell, he kept going, shining his little flashlight on the trail, providing plenty of light to be seen but not enough to see. Screw it. If somebody wanted to shoot him, they could have at it. He wasn't brave, had never been, would never be. But he was awful damn tired of being afraid.

HE STUMBLED BACK INTO TZISCAO EARLY THE NEXT MORNing. The dogs were hanging around the hostel. He ignored their barking. He didn't know how to tell them that none of the people were coming back and they'd best move on. He climbed in through the common room window again without giving it much thought. He figured whoever was running this thing knew exactly where he was anyway. He cleared the table with the back of his hand, took out his computer, and powered it up.

Okay. If he was somebody else's character, it was time he gave the author a little surprise, showed him who was boss. No one expected him on the Web. He was supposed to be scrambling around in the mountains or running for his life. Smelling shit. "Fuck you," he said aloud and went to Rincón.

The Bella Vista smelled like darjeeling and Helene's perfume. He closed his eyes and took a deep breath. It'd been a long time since he'd been here. He opened his eyes and Rosa was smiling at him. "How good to see you," she said. "You look quite fit for a dead man. We were told you had a funeral."

A chill went up his spine. "A funeral?"

"Yes indeed. A visitor named Webster Webfoot said he was attending your funeral and that he and Margaret were looking for you. Would you care for some tea?" Rosa's eyes danced as she talked, fussing with tea things. She loved to play hostess.

"What did he say about Margaret? Is she all right?"

"She seemed to be fine, dear. It was you they were saying was dead."

"What else did, did, uh . . . "

"Webster Webfoot."

"Yes. What else did he say?"

"Nothing much. He passed through earlier and spoke with Miliano, I believe."

Helene leaned in the archway, her long legs stretched out before her. She propelled herself upright with a shrug of her shoulders. "I wore Marcos's mask and asked Webster Webfoot why he was looking for you, but he ran like a frightened bunny rabbit." Her voice was filled with disgust.

"I can't imagine why," Santee said.

She looked down her nose at him, her nostrils flaring. "This place bores me to distraction. When will something happen?" She stamped a foot and tossed her head like a skittish horse and glared down the road to the featureless horizon. "Every day I am here, but no one ever comes. Not even a soldier. Or a priest." She slapped the wall with her crop. "At least a bloody *horse!*"

This wasn't the first time she'd made this request. He'd always said no, said it didn't fit into his "vision" or something. What pretentious nonsense. Why the hell not, if that's what she wanted? FACTS came with a stock of cut-and-paste animals. He went for the obvious and plopped Bucephalus down in front of the Bella Vista. "Anything your heart desires," he told her.

She threw her arms around his neck and squeezed hard. She was almost as tall as he was and certainly stronger, and for a moment he couldn't breathe, but it didn't last long. She jumped back, mussed his hair, and dashed to her horse in quick progression. She never took long to get from one place to another. She always seemed to know where she was going, but found it nearly impossible to stay in one place. He started to tell her to figure out the tack for herself, but she'd already mounted the beast bareback and was trotting up and down the street.

MILIANO WAS AT THE FAR TABLE, ENGAGED IN A RECURRING obsession—poring over history texts, studying revolutions like a disillusioned lover looking for news of happy endings. At such times he became morose and withdrawn for days.

Santee approached the table and stood at a respectful distance until Zapata, tiny reading glasses perched on his nose, noticed he had company.

"Ah!" he said, taking off his glasses and tossing them onto the open tome in front of him as he rose from his seat. He scowled at the books as if they were difficult children. "Perhaps you can help me revise these, my friend?" He seized Santee in an *abrazo*. While Helene had practically wrung his neck, Miliano's embrace was like a passionate bear's. He wasn't a pounder like some, but wrapped his arms around Santee in an affectionate hug.

"It has been a long time since you were here," he said, when they'd settled into their chairs. "You have lost interest in us, perhaps?"

"No, not lost interest. Let's just say I've been trying to apply what I've learned from you."

"What you can learn from me is that it only takes one betrayal, and they shoot you down in the street for 'applying' what you've learned. Perhaps you're better off here."

"It's gone too far for that."

Miliano nodded. "One thing leads to another." He flipped the pages of the book before him. "And another and another." He furrowed his brow and spoke softly. "I'm glad to be out of it."

"You're not out of it," Santee wanted to say, but he didn't have the luxury of arguing with a sim that it was alive in the world as a symbol. "Rosa said somebody named Webster Webfoot talked to you?" he said instead.

This startled Miliano from his reverie, and he nodded as if giving the question careful thought. "Sí. He sought Starr, a beautiful woman with dreams. Later, she sought him, but he was gone. If you can't find Webster, perhaps she has found him or knows what he's up to." He wrote down Starr's address and handed it to Santee. "I told her a story; she went away. She is lovely. With the fire—you know?" He smiled as if remembering, and shrugged. "She promised to return. Who can say? You have troubles, my friend?"

Santee laughed grimly. "Just the usual: Things aren't what they seem."

Miliano brooded a moment. "Things are what they are," he asserted. "They seem different to this one and that. Perhaps the Author could help you find out how things seem to your enemies."

All the sims called Woody "the Author," provoking in Santee a twinge of jealousy, though he knew it didn't mean anything. Woody never let go of an idea. Anything created using FACTS saw itself as his no matter who else had a hand in it. Woody had won a royalties case a couple of years back when a much revised FACTS sim testified that as far as it was concerned, it was Woody's intellectual property and no one else's.

"I'm not even sure who my enemies are."

Miliano smiled. "Perhaps the Author knows—after all, he has many himself."

Whether Miliano suggested Woody because of some embedded command in FACTS or because he'd thought it out (insofar as sims could think) didn't matter. Miliano had a point. Follow the money, the saying went, and Woody was one of the prominent investors in MarsCorp.

"I can't risk going to him myself," he told Miliano. "Would you go ask him to meet me here?"

"Of course," Miliano said, "but I would suggest Helene for such a mission."

Helene had fitted Bucephalus with racing tack and was galloping up and down the street with a terrible clatter as if racing an invisible opponent. Santee called to her, and she reined in the horse. It pranced in place, its hooves sounding like castanets, as Santee shouted out his message and Woody's address. The horse reared up and took off.

As Miliano watched her galloping out of sight, he smiled his admiration. "If the Author is a man, he will come."

Santee wondered why these former lovers never seemed to get together in Rincón but decided to ask another day. "If Woody shows up," he said, "I'll be in Jack's room."

SANTEE LEFT MILIANO TO HIS READING AND WENT INSIDE the hotel, up three flights of stairs to Jack's room. Jack was sitting in front of his windows—thrown open to a view of desert sand and cactus that seemed to go on forever—writing at a small table. A vase of lilies sat on the table, bathed in sunlight. The heavy plaster walls were stark white, unadorned; the ceiling low and scored by dark beams. The bed in the corner was high and narrow as if it huddled there. It never looked slept in. There were chairs for visitors, a tattered rug on the floor. Santee'd never seen Jack outside this room since coming upon him by accident. While exploring the hotel, he'd heard humming in this room and listened at the door. It was "Yes, sir, That's My Baby!" Santee knocked.

He knew it was only an illusion, but sometimes it seemed as if he and Jack actually liked each other, that they'd become friends. Mexico had been Jack's first revolution, riding the train with Villa's forces as they pushed south. Some years later, Russia was his last. The real John Reed died there in 1920 three days shy of thirty-three. Here in Rincón, almost a century later, he looked to be somewhat older, about Santee's age.

"So what do you say, Santee St. J.?" He didn't raise his eyes from the page he was working on.

Santee sat down hard in a frumpy leather club chair that smelled of old pipe tobacco. "I think we've been fucked."

Jack looked up and pushed his pages aside. "What's up?"

Santee told him what he'd seen in the mountains. Jack listened carefully like the journalist he was, occasionally asking questions, but not with the objectivity a journalist was supposed to feign. With each revelation, his indignation grew, slapping the table with his palm so that the lilies jumped, exclaiming "God *damn* it!" When the story was done, he said, "You can't let these sons of bitches get away with this."

"Get away with what? I don't even know what's going on."

Jack was flabbergasted. "Santee! It's simple. It's capitalism, imperialism—what's that new one they got now?—*neoliberalism*. You have a valley full of spaceships, you've got poor people penned up waiting to be cargo, and you've got a revolution going on. I'd say the moneyed classes are enslaving undesirables and shipping them to the colonies to eliminate political dissent and to provide cheap labor. You can't figure that out? What planet did you grow up on?"

"The global one. You don't have to ship people around anymore, Jack. You fuck them where they live."

"Gee, somebody must've forgotten to tell that to the rich industrialists who built all those spaceships, then, huh?"

Now that Santee thought about it, the cost of what they were doing was incredible—even for "rich industrialists." What could possibly make Mars worth it? "The problem with your theory, Jack, is that it's not cost-effective. Those people could slave all their lives and never pay for one or two spacecraft. I just don't get it. Why bankrupt the empire for the sake of a colony?"

Jack thought about this, which is to say he accessed huge databases. Jack kept up with the news. "You're assuming the empire is alive and kicking. Perhaps the fatherland ain't what it used to be, perhaps rumors of the planet's demise ain't just gas. You have to figure they know something you don't. They always do. That's why you have to speak up, so the people know the truth. Because once the people know—"

The sound of clapping and a loud grating voice came from behind them. "Do I make good product or what? Sharp as a tack!" It was Woody, grinning at Jack like a proud father. He approached him, bent over, looked him in the eye.

"You going to ask me to say 'aahh'?" Jack deadpanned, and Woody, his eyes dancing, whirled around to Santee.

"He's *wonderful*, Santee. John Reed. Jeez." He shook his head appreciatively, then quickly gathered in his enthusiasm. Praise, in Woody's book, was a scarce commodity, any expenditure of which, however worthy, only made less for himself. He rolled his eyes. "I found the Zapata downstairs, however, a little too legendary for my tastes—if you know what I mean. And the Romanian Valkyrie, while very fetching—"

Santee had no time for literary criticism. "Tell me what you think some other time, Woody. I want to know what you know. Something big's going on. MarsCorp is spending a whole lot more money than they're letting on, and they're on record for trillions."

Woody eyed him cautiously, added a ladderback chair to the room, and sat down. "Why do you say that?"

Santee told the whole story beginning to end, with occasional promptings and commentary from Jack. Woody grunted occasionally, but mostly just stared at Santee as if he were completely insane.

By the time he was done, Woody was staring at the floor, shaking his head. Finally, he asked, "Why are you telling me all this? Why are you *trusting* me, Santee? Why are you being so fucking *stupid*?" He was practically screaming.

"So something *is* going on."

"Of course. And why is it I should tell you about it?"

"Because I'm your friend."

That was too much. Woody closed his eyes and pursed his lips, trying to summon the patience necessary to deal with such stupidity. "Okay then, *friend*. You don't want to know. Walk away, have a good rest of your life. Eat, drink, and be merry."

"What's so important about Mars, Woody?"

"The canals."

"There are no canals."

"I must've been misinformed."

"Fuck you, Woody."

"Okay, you want to know what's so important about Mars? Nothing. It's there. That's all. No secret. It's a real estate deal. Haven't you heard? Real estate is always a good investment."

"Since when do you need to make investments?"

"I'm looking toward retirement."

"You thought what Jack had to say about 'the fatherland' was 'sharp as a tack.' That's it, isn't it? One way or another, the Earth's going down, and there aren't enough lifeboats."

Woody studied him for a moment. "One, to be exact."

"You have a ticket?"

"Of course. Jesus! You are *so* stupid. Why do you have to push it? Do you have any idea what's at stake here? Give me one good reason why I won't blow the whistle on you, and have you killed?"

"Because you need me to initiate the interface and bring the slaves online."

Woody snorted. "A minor inconvenience. An insignificant delay, I assure you. They're practically on their way."

"All right then," Santee said. "How about because I never threw your sorry ass out of my house?"

"You haven't got a chance of stopping the process, you know."

"The *process.* Listen to yourself. Maybe I can't win, but you won't have me killed. That'd be like admitting everybody else way back then was right about you. And you couldn't stand that."

"That doesn't mean I'll help you."

"You already have."

"You think you're so smart. Well, let me tell you something. That stupid plan to tell the world the truth, make them feel the fucking truth right up their ass, and then things would be fair and good and true? It's stupid. The world already knows, St. John, they just don't fucking *care* as long as they get theirs. That's the way it's always been, and the way it will always be. So you and Revolution Boy here might as well forget about saving the world, because it doesn't want to be saved."

Woody vanished in a huff, chair and all, and Jack shook his head. "What a prick."

"I thought all you sims thought of him as Daddy."

"How do you feel about your old man?"

"I liked him."

"Lucky guy."

"What do you think it is that would make someone like Woody abandon Earth and go to Mars?"

Jack shrugged. "Radiation levels in the jet stream are way up. The new telescope has been suspiciously out of commission for a good while—maybe asteroids or aliens are on the way. Or maybe they're just running out of gas. Whatever it is, only rich rats get to jump ship."

"And their slaves."

"Just like home."

Santee left him to his writing. He was working on a poem he never finished, a poem he'd asked Santee not to read until it was done.

WHEN SANTEE CAME OUT OF THE WEB, HE FOUND BEDDING and the keys to the A-frames, and let himself into the one he and Margaret had stayed in. He set the alarm on his watch and stretched out on the mattress. Soon, Margaret would find him, and they'd figure out what to do. For now he needed a couple hours sleep. He was supposed to change the world tonight, after all.

Before the alarm went off, he woke to a rumbling noise outside. He opened the door a crack and peeked out. A Hummer bounced around the yard, making an arc. It stopped by the picnic table and two soldiers got out. The Hummer turned itself around and roared off. The two soldiers dumped their gear on the picnic table, propped their guns beside them, and sat down to play cards. They were no more than twenty yards away. He was trapped. Not that he had any place to go—in the real world anyway.

CHAPTER FOURTEEN

WEBSTER WAS SCARED SHITLESS AS HE SCURRIED THROUGH the streets of San Cristóbal in a blind panic. It was the unflattest place he'd ever been—up and down, twist and turn. The only thing that kept him from getting totally lost was that it just wasn't that big and it was in a bowl. At first he thought he was going in circles, since he kept coming up on a church. It took him a while to figure out it wasn't the same church or two. There were lots and lots of churches. An abundance, a superfluity. Too damn many. They spooked him with their dark, brooding interiors, and he felt like some scared little kid. In Dallas, most of the off-Web churches were way wacky. He kept expecting snake handlers, tongue talkers, or worse, bent on conversion or immolation, to come pouring out of the high old doorways, but no one materialized except mendicants. It was easy to turn them away. He didn't have anything. Not even *un peso*. But he did take note of their techniques for future reference.

At first he thought he'd catch some glimpse of Margaret and dash to her side, and they'd have a good laugh, and everything would be all right: rescued, redeemed, delivered. But he had to give up on that one. She was gone, just like she said. So that left, what?

Nada.

The word popped into his head like an unwelcome visitor, and seemed to tangle up his feet. He was in another *country*, another *world*. They didn't even speak *English* here. His stomach turned over trying to figure it all out. He slowed his pace, attempted to be cool. No use being so conspicuous. So, so . . . salient.

He looked around the streets, taking them in for the first time. He hadn't been noticing much since he fled the church except that Margaret was nowhere to be found. He'd been heading uphill for some time toward a long flight of stone steps to yet another church. He'd thought the bus station was that way, but now that he took a closer look, nothing was familiar. For lack of anything better to do, he took a right at the next corner.

There were lots of people out and about. None of them seemed to be paying any particular attention to him. No one looked American, but he wasn't sure you could always tell. Mostly they looked completely and thoroughly Mexican. None of them was wearing a translator.

He was screwed. He didn't even know where the bus station was, and even if he did know, he didn't have any money, and even if he had money, he still wasn't sure how to ask for a ticket. As he trudged along, taking turns at random, he felt increasingly despondent, crestfallen, woebegone. He said the word over and over to himself, dragging out the vowels, *wo-be-gone*. Not a word for everyone. *Whoa-bee-ga-a-a-w-w-n*. He clung to it like a life preserver in a stormy sea, and it buoyed him up. He was smart, especially with words, and that's what it came down to wasn't it, knowing the right words? He could do this—he had dash, verve, panache, brio—he wasn't just some dumb webbed-out kid. He'd figure it out. It was just words.

El web no es lugar, Aurora had said. And maybe it wasn't a place, but the *word*, apparently, was the same, and a question was a question, seemed like, no matter where you went. He started assembling the words one by one in his head from the stash of Spanish he'd been accreting since he arrived . . . yesterday. Just yesterday. That brought him up short. How could things change so fucking fast? How could he hope to keep up?

But step by step, word by word, he put together some sentences, got his confidence back, and began looking for just the right person to ask for help. He rejected anyone in uniform for obvious reasons, anyone too young because they wouldn't have any patience, and women because they might think he was hitting on them.

Up ahead was a man sweeping the sidewalk in front of a shop heaped with cloth goods—rugs, towels, bolts of fabric, those woolly looking shoulder bags he would've bought if he'd had any money. The man was plump, lots of gray, and he was whistling an old Disney tune from . . . *The Little Mermaid?* Webster couldn't be sure. Seemed like a good sign anyway.

He walked up smiling, planted himself, and delivered his lines: *"Buenos días, señor. ¿Cómo voy a el Web?"* His voice didn't shake too badly.

The man was startled at first but then smiled pleasantly, though he still looked totally baffled. *"¿Al Web?"*

"Sí. El Web. ¿Cómo voy a . . ."

They went back and forth several times, Webster trying to get the accent right, throwing in hand gestures like he was doing some kind of ritual dance. *Web* had him splaying his fingers and wiggling them in the air. Suddenly a light dawned in the man's face, and he chuckled, then smiled with understanding. It was a nice moment for Webster, to see that smile. Language was so cool. Now seemingly beside himself with joy, the man took Webster by the elbow, led him out into the intersection, and pointed down the hill. *"Allá. Siete cuadras."* He held up seven fingers. *"Hay restaurante donde está el Web. A la izquierda."* He gestured to the left. He swept his arms up and down as if he were trying to fly a single stroke. *"Una taza azul, muy grande."*

A restaurant, of course. On the left side of the street. There'd be some tourist place with a WebBooth. He could order, get online, jump the check. *Cuadras* must be blocks. He didn't know *taza azul*; it was *grande* whatever it was. *Just let it go*, he told himself. He had enough to find the place, and a deep sense of paranoid urgency prodding him on, though he didn't know what he had to be afraid of. That was sufficient to make him afraid. At least back home he knew.

"Gracias," he remembered to say as he took off. *"Muchas gracias."*

"De nada." The man beamed with satisfaction. *"Vaya bien,"* he called after him.

Vaya bien—something like check you later, Webster figured.

Bye. Adieu. Farewell.

Fare well.

Bien was well. *Vaya* must be fare or go.

Vaya bien.

Language was so fucking cool.

As he descended the steep blocks, Webster sank deeper and deeper into tourism. The number of Europeans and Asians, especially wired ones, shot up. He thought he spotted the same Other Brothers he'd seen before, plus a dozen more. He tried to figure out Margaret's trick of identifying where people were from just by looking at them, but soon gave up. What did he know? On the Web, everybody made themselves look like somebody else, except at history sites and such where famous people looked like themselves—the people that everyone else wanted to look like. So did that mean all Spaniards looked like Columbus? Or was he an Italian? He couldn't remember.

But it didn't take a great deal of acumen to remark all the folks who could afford to be ambling about for no good reason, and be heartened that he was headed their way: Civilization Dead Ahead. It was hard to miss the place once he got close. EL CAFÉ MUNDIAL, the sign read inside a big blue neon coffee cup. The familiar WebNet logo under the name told him he'd found the right place.

He grinned, remembering the man's arms, sweeping up and down. *Taza azul.* Blue cup. The very big blue cup. *Taza azul, muy grande.* Webster hit the door with a swagger. One cunning linguist was making the scene.

Inside were at least half the young tourists in town. That's why he hadn't seen more around out and about: They were all in here. They fell out in the usual tribes—Other Brothers, Mechanics, Actuals, webkicker wannabes. (If they were the real thing they wouldn't be in here, with WebBooths lining two walls and tech-shrine nowhere decor to make the webby feel right at home, slumming in reality.) There were a few moms and dads—about Margaret's age, but not as hip, though he bet none of them would've abandoned him in a foreign land.

Forget it, he scolded himself. *It'll just bring you down.*

And attitude, in a place like this, was everything.

THE WALL BEHIND THE BAR WAS THE MENU. IT UNDULATED with change as each item morphed from Spanish to English to several other languages Webster didn't know, some with alphabets he didn't even recognize. There were twenty-five different coffees from twenty-five different places, none of them, as far as Webster could tell, Mexico. But the menu was just for show.

The customers were being waited upon, with grave and fawning formality, by a dozen beautiful Mexicans—approximately the same age as the clientele, mostly but not exclusively male, wearing starched white shirts and black trousers. Even the trousers looked starched. They wore heavy-duty translators that made them sound like aspiring opera singers working their day jobs.

Webster's waiter was named Armando, according to the blue neon name on his shirt morphing through four alphabets. He seemed prepared, like the fellow a few tables over, to recite the entire menu if need be, but Webster saved him the trouble and ordered Greek coffee because a girl he once had a crush on, Zoë, made it at her website in a little metal cup with a long handle. He didn't know where she was these days. Worse, he'd forgotten what you called the little metal cup.

"Will there be anything else?" Armando wanted to know.

"*Tengo hambre,*" Webster said.

The pained look around Armando's eyes told Webster his Spanish must be pretty bad or such bluntness concerning bodily matters was not quite on here. Armando pushed aside the little mike on his translator and made a collar of the headset. "We have a wide selection of international pastries," Armando said in English, sans translator, much better than Webster's Spanish with one.

Show off. "*¿Chilaquiles con pollo?*" Webster persisted.

This deepened Armando's displeasure. *Is my Spanish that bad or what?* Webster wanted to know.

"We don't serve . . . that," Armando said.

In his mind, Webster stood the women in the market in Matamoros next to Armando, and thought he got the picture. It was a class thing. Like asking a French chef for ketchup. "Then what do you suggest?"

"The baklava—of course—would complement your Greek coffee."

"Of course."

Armando gave a convincing little bow, even though he clearly thought Webster a boorish cretin. As he headed off, Webster wondered whether his patter was scripted for him. His real name probably wasn't even Armando. For all Webster knew, there was a sim somewhere funneled through Armando's translator. Webster wondered whether it was the waiter he didn't like or the Café Mundial. Or the customers. Nothing here seemed real. It was like the whole point of the place was that you could achieve unreality even in the real world. Some newsflash, that. A definite *so what?*

What would Armando say about this place, Webster wondered, when he took off that starched shirt at the end of the day and drank a beer or smoked a joint or whatever they did around here? When you actually worked someplace, no matter how much you were supposed to act like a string of code in a program, the place got real. Did Armando have a thing for one of the girls that worked here? Or one of the guys? How many tons of coffee grounds did they generate in a day, and who hauled it out to the Dumpster or hosed it down a drain? Did he have ambitions to be the guy standing at the end of the bar, summoning his underlings with a crook of his finger? Or maybe he aspired to be one of the Webwonks above him who owned this place and hundreds just like it in a dozen other countries? Or did his ambitions not have anything to do with this place, or any other place he'd been able to find? Was he, in other words, just like Webster?

Once Webster walked the check and stiffed him, he wouldn't get the chance to ask Armando any of these questions. You could bet the money would be coming out of Armando's pocket and no one else's. Have to make those workers accountable, the guys with the money would say. One thing Webster'd noticed since he'd started working: Whenever you tried to cross the bosses, the only route ran right over a fellow worker. Webster didn't figure that was mere happenstance.

THE GREEK COFFEE WAS GOOD UNTIL YOU GOT TO THE BOTtom where it turned to sludge. Zoë's virtual stuff never did that. Baklava turned out to be a nut honey flaky thing sitting on a paper doily. It went pretty fast. It'd been a while since he'd eaten. He flagged down Armando and ordered a couple more. By the time they arrived, he'd hatched what he flatteringly referred to as a plan.

There was a guy in a chartreuse recording rig at the corner of the bar talking to himself in the mirror. Just beyond were the WebBooths, a row of eight of them, and two of them were empty. It could've been some place in Dallas or Hong Kong or whatever—wherever the Web weird hung out—and Webster didn't figure it'd be any different when he showed up here or there, real or virtual. He took his baklava to the bar and sat down next to the chartreuse Other Brother and slid one of the baklava his way.

"I don't believe I cued you," chartreuse said, sniffing.

Webster stuck out his hand, going for the radical gesture. "Webster Webfoot," he said, and the guy's eyes got big for a second.

"Cool," he said, a safe reply for over fifty years now, though he looked a little rattled in the presence of four-star Web celebrity. He took a bite of the baklava and chewed with enthusiastic concentration. "Thank you," he said. For the baklava or the handshake wasn't clear. Then he remembered he had a name too, even if he wasn't famous. "My name is Zorin," he offered apologetically, spewing baklava flakes.

"What's your address, Zorin?" Webster tossed his head nonchalantly toward the WebBooths, and pointed from head-rig to mirror to cue the shot he wanted, giving pretty much a view of the whole place with his booth in the middle of it. "I want to get online and watch the reflection of you watching me watching you. . . ."

"Watching me." Zorin grinned to reveal some retro taste sensors perched on his incisors like tiny ceramic tits smeared with baklava detritus. "Are you going to your site?" he inquired reverently.

"Yeah, sure." Webster was enjoying this in spite of himself. Zorin sounded German or Russian or something. He had the same accent as the robot in Scalded—the site that got busted for some kid bottoming out during the shish kebab thing. Course, Zorin might be faking the accent. How would Webster know the difference? But still, he was definitely from somewhere further away than Waxahachie, and he knew who Webster was. Surely that counted for something.

Zorin couldn't give over his address fast enough, and Webster thanked him with a regal nod and started toward the WebBooths. "Hey, Webster," Zorin called after him with a comradely leer, his last chance to impress: "Fuck, titty, cunt, piss."

Seemed like everyone in the place turned to look at Webster. His insides squirmed into a knot. Zorin didn't *know* him. Didn't know him any better than Webster knew his bogus accent. He knew Webster's website is all—in all its stupid glory. He swore to himself if he *ever* got out of this alive, the website was history.

He ducked into the booth like one of the rats at the warehouse diving down a floor drain. He could still feel the eyes on him, but it'd pass. Another fifteen seconds of fame.

He didn't have his card. But after a little dance with his mother's maiden name—an entertaining concept in itself—he got online and headed for Starr's. He didn't know who else to turn to. But he got a WebNet message that her address was "temporarily unavailable" without even an estimate of how long "temporarily" would be. But he kept trying. She might not be onsite, so he went for a direct link. (She'd given him the password when she was a lot more interested in him, and of course he'd saved it.) She might not be right by her computer, so he set it up to announce his arrival with his smiling countenance and a klaxon horn she'd hear even in the next room. A little rude, but it's not like she was ever anything but by herself.

He persisted because the next person on his list of who-might-help-Webster plummeted all the way to Mom. Would she even understand his predicament? Understand that he was actually in another country? He didn't want to find out. He was on the verge of surrender, when the WebNet notice dissolved, and he was in. Starr looked pretty pissed. But he couldn't help trying to see around her. Where in hell was she? Behind her loomed a mainframe the size of the old Hyatt, and a big black guy was surreptitiously lurking off to one side.

"Not *now*," she snapped.

What the hell did he do? She looked totally frazzled, befuddled, flustered, perturbed, and generally disquieted. She also looked a good ten years older, confirming his long-held suspicions that she was an Older Woman. Something singular was definitely afoot, but his own imbroglio demanded immediate attention. "I need to talk to you. This is an emergency. I'm stranded in Mexico. That guy Santee—"

"I've got my own emergency here, Webster."

"But—"

"Jesus, Webster. I'm not fooling around here. Call me back in an hour. Make that two. Bye."

She was gone. He'd defaulted back to his homesite. A voice whispered, "Webster Webfoot: wanker, sh—" He shut off the sound, though he ad-libbed the sequence in his head several times before he got a grip. He had to figure this thing out. He added a bench to the cavern wall and sat down.

She and the black guy had been wearing *space suits*. They had the helmets off, but there was no mistaking what they were. What were they doing in space suits? When Webster and Starr were first seeing each other and he found out she worked orbital, he'd asked her if she went out into space in a space suit and did spacewalks and stuff, and she'd laughed at him. "If you ever see me in a space suit, Webster, something has gone seriously wrong." He knew she'd just been kidding around, but still . . . And who the hell was that huge black guy with the shaved head?

This wasn't exactly turning out according to plan. Starr was supposed to be delighted to see him, listen sympathetically to his tale of woe and misadventure, and book him on a bus or train or plane headed back to Dallas, maybe in time to get his job back so he wouldn't have to move back in with Mom. Instead he was stuck in his own stupid site. He checked Zorin's feed running in a cube in his peripheral vision. He waved. Zorin waved a sad chartreuse paw. Jesus. The world-famous Webster Webfoot bootless and bereft before the whole World Wide Web.

His girl wouldn't even let him into her system before he'd defaulted back to nowhere. . . .

He contemplated where in the great Wide Web he might find his mommy, and it was depressingly predictable. She liked to roam from fad to fad, but you could always get word of her at the high fantasy sites. No. He wasn't quite ready to sink that low. He had some dignity left. He'd made it this far, which was pretty impressive when you thought about it. He had plenty of options yet.

Or at least one he could think of. It seemed to him Santee St. John was ultimately responsible for the mess he was in, and he could, by God, get him out of it. He went back to Rincón.

Nothing much had changed. It was as drowsy as the Café Mundial was frenetic. No one was sitting at the tables. The only sounds were some kids' voices, laughing and calling to each other in some language he was pretty sure wasn't Spanish. He followed the sound and spotted a couple of barefoot kids. He called to them, but they disappeared down an alley. He followed to find a leggy woman sitting astride an enormous black horse. Were all horses this big, Webster wondered, or was this a truly oversized beast?

The woman spoke.

In spite of the distraction of her slide from horseback to ground on the longest legs he'd ever seen, he recognized the voice and accent. She was the woman in the ski mask.

"You listening to me? Santee is looking for you, Webster Webfoot. You must find him."

"I don't even *know* him. What the hell is he up to anyway? So far he's gotten me stranded in the middle of a foreign country with no money and no way to get home and my girlfriend pissed off at me."

She sniffed the air. "Is that so terrible? What is money? What is home? Do you think you have met your last lover? My life would've been nothing if I'd thought like you. You are a boy. You should learn to be a man."

"You're a sim, and I don't have to take any shit off you, okay? Now can you tell me where to find Santee, if it's so damn important?"

"My name," she said grandly, "is Helene Pontipirani, and I take no shit, as you say, off anyone. Santee's in Tziscao."

"Where is that?"

"Is a town. Tziscao."

"Where is it?"

"Mexico."

"I figured that. I mean *where* in Mexico."

She shrugged. "I was never there. Can you do nothing for yourself? If you want to change the world, you must learn to change yourself."

This was too much. "I don't *want* to change the world."

"Why not? You think it's fine the way it is?"

"No. I didn't say that."

"Then you are a coward, no?"

Webster was getting pissed off, angry, indignant, wrathful, choleric, ireful, seething.

At a sim.

Whoever this Santee character was, he was certainly good at putting maddening women in his path. "Just tell Santee I want to go home, okay?" He couldn't help that he sounded like a little kid saying that. What was it his sim-counselor used to say? *Don't be so hard on yourself, Webster.*

"That might prove difficult," Helene said. She nodded toward the Other Brother feed. Zorin was now flanked by guys in black T-shirts, watching Webster watching them watching him. They had guns stuck in their belts. One of them had his gun stuck in Zorin's ear.

Jesus! What in the hell was he going to do?

He hadn't asked aloud, but Helene had a suggestion anyway. "Surprise"—she said with professional certainty—"is your only chance."

It was tricky. Timing was critical. First he had to line himself up with the WebBooth's door based on Zorin's sight angle on himself in the mirror. Then he had to go offline in mid-leap so that what started out virtual would propel him out of the booth and onto the floor, rolling, hopefully, into a run. It would help if he could remember where the door was in this place. It was somewhere outside Zorin's peripherals apparently. Webster'd been lost in his own little virtual back there at the door ten minutes ago when he walked in here, pretending he was a world-famous invincible dickhead, or he'd now remember where the stupid door was. He made himself tired, was getting tired of dealing with how tired he was. When was he going to grow up?

Zorin's feed vanished, and Webster decided to move, diving out of the WebBooth and rolling into a tall pedestal table, striking the chromed pedestal with his head, a blow that proved to be a good diversion, sending the table into a gyroscopic dance, knocking shit everywhere. As he scrambled to get free of the damn thing, he slung it out behind him and took out two of the guys with guns. He crawled frantically, slipping on a pool of blood that leaked from what was left of Zorin's head. He sprang off it in revulsion, driving the back of his head into something that felt like a chin and made a cracking noise, but he didn't stop to investigate. The door was a rectangle of light at the end of the bar. He ran toward it, propelled by the racket behind him. He hit the door full force, knocking another guy in a black T-shirt on his butt. Webster didn't think about kicking the guy in the head when he saw the gun come up. Game reflexes took over, and he just did it, hard; and the gun fell, and he was running down the street faster than he'd ever run in his life, real or virtual. Hell, if it was virtual, he'd have jumped off long before this.

As he rounded a corner, several hands reached out and grabbed him, pulling him from his feet. But he didn't fall. He just seemed to float into a dark room that got darker with the slam of a door at his feet. He was on his back, looking up, a few feet above the ground, and he flashed on the funeral—wondering if he was about to buy the farm, check out, meet his maker—when a dark face appeared over him and held a finger to his lips. There were other indistinct faces in the shadows Webster couldn't make out. Running footsteps clattered by on the cobblestone street outside.

In the ensuing silence, a half-dozen faces crowded around Webster. He could see now that they were young and old, male and female. A family, he guessed. "¿Ingles?" he asked hopefully.

They all shook their heads.

They turned him ninety degrees and set him on his feet. There was an old woman, a man, a woman, a couple of little girls, and a boy with the beginnings of a wispy mustache. Webster felt a little wobbly. His head throbbed, and he recollected the table he'd banged into and the thing that'd felt like somebody's chin. He remembered the gun coming up slowly, his foot kicking the head, not his head though, somebody else's. It just felt like he'd kicked his own head, like he was still kicking away. How truculent, he thought and turned around to tell himself to stop. He kept turning and turning until he was flying again into a cloud bank where he'd be safe. He circled DFW waiting for his shift when he'd be loaded into the back of his trike disguised as oranges and pumped into food units, safe from everyone but jugglers. After a time he felt the reassuring sensation of a vehicle in motion and fell asleep.

✻   ✻   ✻

HE WOKE UP WHEN A GANG OF JUGGLERS HAD HIM CORNERED in a church. *"Voy a la guerra,"* they chanted. He jumped, crying out. He was sitting up in bed in a small shadowy room. The wispy-mustache boy was sitting on the floor watching him. The floor looked like it was dirt. Swept dirt.

"¡Papá!" the boy cried out.

The little girls came flying into the room squealing, and the boy turned on them, snarling a stream of Spanish vituperation Webster couldn't begin to follow. They blinked their eyes as if he'd splashed them with water. Papá appeared in the doorway, silencing the boy with a look, and the girls slipped behind his legs.

"Buenos días," Webster said. *"Gracias. Muchas gracias."* The girls peeked out, and he realized they were twins. He smiled at them, and they vanished again.

"Buenas tardes," the boy muttered, and the man shot him another look.

"¿Habla español?" the man asked Webster hopefully.

"No."

His host couldn't mask his disappointment, and Webster felt awful for them both. He tapped his chest. "Webster," he said. "Webster." He felt stupid doing it, but he couldn't remember the name sentences.

But the man got it anyway. "Conrad," he said, tapping his own chest. He pointed to his son. "Elvis." Presented a daughter under each hand, "Alanis y Madonna."

A woman appeared in the doorway, holding folded clothes. Conrad pointed at her. "Taña Luz," he said, then pointed at Webster. "Webster," he told Taña Luz. They all knew each other's names now. Webster had his doubts how far that would get him. But Taña Luz looked positively cheered by it all. She held up the clothes. *"Ropa,"* she said, and handed them to him.

He looked down at himself and realized he was naked except for his underwear and socks. His work boots, sitting on the floor, looked like somebody'd cleaned them up. *"¿Mi ropa?"* he croaked.

Taña Luz winced apologetically and ran her hands down the front of her dress. *"Sangre."* Blood. She made a tearing motion with her hands and shook her head. His jumpsuit was bloody *and* torn. His jumpsuit was history.

Conrad hissed under his breath like a curse, *"Los asesinos."*

Webster remembered his hands sliding on blood-slick tile, Zorin's sightless eyes looking right through him: *fuck, titty, cunt, piss.* He flinched and fought down a wave of nausea, clutching the *ropa* to his chest. Conrad's hand gripped his shoulder, and Webster looked up. Conrad didn't try to say anything. What was there to say? Taña Luz was ushering the kids out of the room. Conrad stood, released Webster's shoulder, and pointed at the clothes, the *ropa.* They were leaving him alone to dress. Before he closed the door, Conrad made eating motions—"*¿comida?*"—drinking motions—"*¿bebida?*"

"*Sí,*" Webster said. "*Tengo hambre.*"

Conrad beamed at the news. "*¡Qué bueno!*"

THE CLOTHES MUST'VE BEEN CONRAD'S, PROBABLY HIS good ones, since they were a lot less frayed and battered than the ones he was wearing. They were used American clothes, or Chinese clothes made for Americans, or . . . whatever you wanted to call them. They were Mexican clothes now. Blue-green plaid sportshirt, khaki pleated pants. Polyester and cotton, heavy on the polyester. Obviously made before the oil shortage. He'd seen such clothes piled up on tables in the markets, people like Conrad and Taña Luz digging through them, holding them up to kids like Elvis and Alanis and Madonna. Nobody wore stuff like this back home.

In Dallas, Webster and his ilk kept a few antique apparel places going. The one he went to, Antique Antics, specialized in old workingman stuff—like the jumpsuit he'd just mopped up Zorin's blood with. It'd cost him a couple weeks' pay, and that was without the workingman patches he'd collected over the years—also not cheap.

Regular old cheap clothes like these, however, were worthless—you might as well wear disposables—so they ended up here. With what Webster spent on that jumpsuit, Conrad could probably clothe his whole family for years, though it'd take him that long to make the money. Webster'd been taught in global econ that—in the context of the larger economy—penurious wages were okay in the developing world. Okay for who? He'd bet it wasn't so okay with Conrad and Taña Luz. And even Webster'd figured out that the so-called developing nations just kept on developing and developing but somehow never got to be developed.

He put on the clothes. The sleeves were about six inches too short, and the pants hit him mid-calf, but other than that they were a pretty good fit. Good riddance to his jumpsuit—his uniform, his costume, his getup, his masquerade. Conrad didn't need an outfit to convince himself he worked. Who did Webster think he was fooling? *You pretend to work*, Aurora'd pegged him. *But it's all pretending*.

The room was small, with a bed and a battered dresser jammed into it. On top of the dresser was a photograph of a younger Conrad and Taña Luz in a wedding pose. They were both dressed in embroidered white clothes, and didn't look much older than Webster. Conrad had the same wispy mustache Elvis had now. Webster looked back to the bed, a lumpy double mattress on a rough wooden frame. It held the impression of two bodies. Christ looked down from the wall above. This was their bed, their room. Why were they doing this? They didn't even know him. He was some foreign kid running around with blood all over him, and they just took him into their house, laid him down in their bed, clothed him, and were about to feed him.

Then he thought he understood, part of it anyway. They'd judged him by his enemies. *Los asesinos*, Conrad had said bitterly. Assassins, had to be. And anybody those guys wanted to kill—which definitely included Webster—Conrad considered a friend.

Webster wished he knew *why* they wanted to kill him, not that it really mattered. He didn't need to know why to run like hell. He guessed it was because he'd been consorting with Margaret, and the *asesinos* presumed he was the spy he'd been pretending to be. Thus far, his career as a secret operative had proved less than exemplary. He'd managed to keep the secret, all right, even from himself. When you got right down to it, he didn't know much of anything about this business that'd almost gotten him killed and left him stranded in a foreign country without even the clothes on his back.

All because he'd fallen prey to a fleeting infatuation for an older woman.

What a buffoon.

Nincompoop.

Jackanapes.

Dumb shit.

But he didn't regret it, not much anyway. He'd just spent the most incredible two days of his life, and it'd all been *real*—how could he regret that? Except the infatuation for Margaret, which—the more he thought about it—was truly embarrassing. Not because it was any big surprise, but because it wasn't.

But he could log on for some counselor.com another day. Right now he needed to keep moving. *People want to* kill *you, Webster,* he reminded himself. He needed to get the hell out of Mexico, and for that he could use some help. Conrad and his family were real nice, but it's not like they could book him on a plane or buy him a bus ticket.

Starr'd said to call back in two hours, which'd probably long passed. It was a bad idea anyway. He'd almost died the first time. And if he showed up dressed like this, Armando wouldn't even give him a glass of water. Not that he could go back to the Café Mundial, but anyplace that was webbed would be the same. He'd be lucky to get in the front door, much less get away with jumping the check.

Besides, that's where they'd be looking for him. *Web*ster *Web*foot— duh—where do you suppose he might be? Those guys probably had a trace out for him, just waiting for him to log on. There'd be goons at all the Web hangouts for miles around, just waiting. No. Forget Starr. He'd have to handle this one without the Web.

Which ruled out Mom, too, of course. Not that she'd be any help. All she'd bring to the fray would be one of her credit cards, perpetually maxed into uselessness.

He had no idea where Margaret was, except she was looking for Santee, and Santee—if he could trust the leggy Amazon in Rincón—was in someplace called Tziscao, almost certainly deeper in the direction of trouble. Besides, Margaret had dumped him, hung him out to dry, abandoned him to the fates. He'd been forsaken, discarded, chucked in the ash bin (or was it ash *heap*; he wasn't sure what either one of them was exactly). In any event, Margaret had her reasons, he was sure, and he'd leave her to them. No hard feelings as long as he never saw her again.

He slid his hands in his pockets and recalled the piece of paper that wasn't there—the one Aurora'd given him with a friend's address. It was probably long gone, soaked in blood and torn to shreds, tossed on the ash heap (he was pretty sure *heap* was right). But it got him to thinking: He needed somebody he could trust, somebody who knew all about sneaking across the border. For all Webster knew, it was the Mexican government that was trying to kill him. Since Margaret and Santee were on the rebel side, it stood to reason. He didn't know whether Aurora spoke any English. They'd relied on his translator to communicate. But she'd worked all that time in the States. She had to know some. He remembered the sound of her voice, sexy and low, her dark, flashing eyes. *Sus ojos son bellos.* . . .

When he reached his decision, it seemed inevitable—a kismet—a word he'd never thought he'd be applying to himself. But there was something about going from juggling oranges to swimming in blood inside a couple of days that changed your perspective on things, made you do things that were downright *quijotesco.*

He practiced his questions. *¿Por dónde está el lugar Veinte y Dos de Diciembre? ¿Cómo voy allá?* I can always hitchhike, he thought. Hit the open road—without being fried by an electric fence. But first, his churning stomach reminded him, *comida* and *bebida* awaited.

HE CAME SHUFFLING OUT OF THE BEDROOM, DUCKING HIS head. This place wasn't built for anyone his height. The low roof was made from sheets of rusty metal supported by a complicated network of bowed two-by-fours. He found the high point and cautiously stood up straight. He was standing in a room twice as big as the bedroom but still plenty small. What light there was came through the open doorway, where scrawny chickens pecked the yard in what looked like late afternoon or early evening. The walls were planks salvaged from other buildings. The weathered colors made faded stripes like some old beach chair.

The twins giggled, and he spotted them in the shadows, sitting side by side in one of several hammocks drooping down like giant cobwebs. They waved at him, and he waved back. A woodstove—he could smell the smoke—was up against the wall where Taña Luz was cooking. In front of the stove, with a collection of mismatched chairs, was a table fashioned from a door on sawhorses of the same warped vintage as the roof.

Seated with Elvis and Conrad at the table was an old woman. "*Mi madre,*" Conrad said, introducing her to Webster simply as "Mamá." She was the oldest person Webster had ever seen in the wrinkled flesh. Her thinning hair was white, and she was toothless. He concluded, as Conrad shouted "Webster! Webster!" into her ear, that she was nearly deaf as well. You never saw old people back home—not that they didn't exist—but they presented younger in the Web. Unless they were too poor to get online, and then you didn't see them at all.

"*Siéntese,*" Conrad said, pointing to a rickety plastic chair beside Mamá. She was beaming at him, obviously pleased at the prospect, laughing a soft laugh that wasn't at all cackly. So far she seemed to find Webster's name, his appearance, his very presence, highly amusing. He liked her.

Comida turned out to be tortillas, fresh and warm. They weren't much like the ones that enshrouded Bruce's Tex-Mex Wrap, a foul gut bomb if there ever was one. These actually had a flavor. Which was a good thing since they were the whole meal except for some tiny green chiles that would melt your fillings. *Bebida* was a sweet tea with a cinnamony taste.

They were somewhere in the hills around San Cristóbal apparently. He didn't think they'd gone all that far. He had a million questions he wasn't sure how to ask. He caught Elvis's curious glances, and decided to take the plunge, returning Elvis's gaze and pointing at the floor. "*¿Dónde?*"

Elvis pointed out the door. "*San Cristóbal está casi veinte kilometros por allá.*"

Webster patted the air in a gesture he hoped meant slow down, and Elvis obliged, repeating the sentence word by word.

Webster almost had it. *Por allá* must be "over there" or "that way." But *casi*, what was *casi*? "*¿Casi?*" he asked.

Elvis scrunched his face in concentration, trying to come up with some way to explain it, but soon threw up his hands in frustration, giving up. Conrad, who'd apparently been watching this exchange, rapped the table with his knuckles to get Webster's attention and flashed his fingers twice for *veinte*, twenty, which Webster already knew from school. He wanted to say, "I get it all except for the *casi*, okay?" But didn't know how.

But Conrad rapped the table again, held his hands apart, and brought them slightly closer together. "*Casi no es todo—menos de todo.*" He flashed ten fingers, then ten again, but with one of his index fingers crooked in half. "*Casi veinte.*" He flashed Webster twenty again, "*Veinte,*" then the crooked finger thing again, "*Casi veinte.*" Then he did it again: "*Veinte. Casi veinte.*" He held his hands frozen in front of Webster's face, that digit still at half-mast, waiting for Webster to get it.

Webster stared at Conrad's nine and a half fingers for an eternity before it dawned on him. "Almost!" he fairly shouted, which prompted fresh laughter from Mamá and everyone else, even Elvis. "*Casi* is 'almost,'" Webster said. "It's *almost* twenty kilometers to San Cristóbal! *San Cristobal está* casi *veinte kilometros.*" Everyone cheered, laughing.

"*Casi, casi, casi*," Alanis and Madonna chanted gleefully.

Emboldened by his linguistic success, Webster blurted out his prepared question. "*¿Dónde está el lugar Veinte y Dos de Diciembre?*"

Silence fell as if the metal roof had collapsed.

Webster could see in their eyes that they knew exactly what he was talking about. It wasn't until that very moment that he formed a mental picture to go with Aurora's words: *In 1997, in the town of Acteal, forty-five unarmed people were murdered by government paramilitary.*

Forty-five people who looked just like the ones sitting around this table. Even Alanis and Madonna weren't safe. Their eyes roved now from face to face, knowing there was trouble, looking for an adult who didn't look scared. *Thirty-six of them women and children.*

When Aurora'd told him about the place and the time, 1997 had seemed long ago, like Vietnam or gas guzzlers or shopping malls—all those things that were over and done with. To these people, he realized, this massacre was only yesterday, because it could happen again tomorrow. He felt as if he'd matured a couple of years in a few seconds. "I'm sorry," he said. He struggled to remember the words, but could only remember one that might do. "*Penitente,*" he said. "*Penitente.*"

Mamá reached out a brown wrinkled hand and lay it on his. Conrad studied him thoughtfully. Finally he asked, "*¿Tú eres Zapatista?*"

Of course. That's why Aurora had whispered the name of her town like it was some kind of secret. It was a rebel town, a *Zapatista* town. It didn't seem like there was any escaping it. He didn't know what this war—revolution, or whatever it was—was all about, but he had a pretty good idea, and he definitely knew which side was trying to kill him. He definitely knew which side he was on.

"*Sí,*" he said. "*Zapatista.*"

Conrad smiled, spread his hands to take in his family, plus whatever village Webster had yet to see outside, then pressed his palms to his chest: "*Nosotros también.*"

Us too.

S OME HOURS LATER HE WAS ESCORTED INTO S AN C RISTÓBAL for a clandestine rendezvous with a truck that went to Veinte y Dos de Diciembre on a regular basis, a truck that could go anywhere without arousing suspicion. It was a big red Coke truck. *Siempre,* it said above the familiar red disk: Always.

He rode in back in an obscure cavity surrounded by cans and bottles of water and Coke. It was pitch-dark, jostling along with the incessant sound of sloshing. He wondered if any of the Cokes ever blew up. He popped open a can and downed it, which perked him up for a while. But pretty soon he grew drowsy and fell asleep.

He woke, flying into the air, and then came down hard. The whine of the engine revved in low gear drowned out the roar of churning soda. He clung to the necks of a couple of three-litre bottles and prayed for deliverance, imagining the truck hopping down the road on enormous springs, like a mechanical kangaroo. Then it started going backwards, forward, backwards again. When it finally came to a stop, the sloshing continued like waves lapping a pier. The engine died, and he heard the driver open and close his door. There was a ratcheting noise as the back came open. A case of bottles slid out of the way, and his tiny cubbyhole was flooded with light. The driver beckoned for him to come out. He crawled out onto the ground, blinking like a mole emerging from its burrow, tested his limbs to see if everything was intact.

Meanwhile, the driver unloaded a few cases of Coke and water. When he was done he pointed at the ground and winked to let Webster know this was the place, hopped back in the truck, blew his horn a couple of times, and drove off, bouncing back down the road. Webster sat on the stack of Cokes and waited.

He was at the end of a rutted road that climbed up from a valley below. A roofless church stood in the woods. Inside the sanctuary, a couple of goats were tied to a tree, grazing. Several trails radiated from here. Pretty soon a couple of boys with a hand truck approached on one of the trails.

Webster stood up and dusted off his pants. "¿Veinte y Dos de Diciembre?" he asked cheerfully.

The boys traded a look. Who was this guy?

"Zapatista," he said, tapping his chest. "Amigo de Aurora." He hoisted a couple of cases of Cokes and put them on the hand truck, as if to say, "You can trust me. We're in the same line of work."

They shrugged and let him help with the rest of the Cokes, though they didn't trust him with the hand truck on the winding trail. He followed along a few paces behind until they came into a tiny village. He waited beside the shack of a store, about the size of a rack-and-stack. Pretty soon Aurora found him, like he knew she would.

She laughed when she saw him. "¿No eres ornitologísta?"

"No," he said. "I'm in a lot of trouble."

She took his hand and gave him a sympathetic smile. "What's up?" she asked him, the first English he'd heard her speak.

She took him to her house, and he told her the whole story. He wasn't surprised when her first words were, "Santee's alive? We must go to Tziscao. Everything depends on him."

But he wasn't about to go anywhere until he finally got to hear what this Santee had been up to, what the big plan was—the reason, she told him, her mother had summoned her home in the first place. When she laid it out for him, his response was immediate and unequivocal: "It will never, in a million years, work." The Web would swallow up all their suffering with a belch and a scratch, and move on to the next thing. And then as he said it, he realized with equal certainty that it was never meant to work the way Aurora and Margaret and Santee had thought, that it was all a sucker play, an inveiglement, a siren song, a trap. You couldn't blame people though, all the stupid idealistic ideas they had about the Web, still had after all this time.

"You installed this interface in yourself?" he asked her.

"Only this morning."

If only he'd gotten here sooner, he thought, but he didn't say that. Instead, he said, "You're right. We've got to find this Santee before he goes online."

CHAPTER FIFTEEN

"SHE LEFT BECAUSE SHE DIDN'T TRUST YOU, ZACK. THE woman's not stupid." Hermalinda looked around the empty *cabaña* like she'd never for a second figured she'd find Margaret there. Before he discovered Margaret was gone, Zack had sent word to Hermalinda that Margaret wanted to see her. Now Hermalinda was acting like it was some trick to lure her out here. He wasn't stupid either. It'd take a lot more than another moony-eyed look from him to win her back. Before he could touch her, she slipped outside to the porch and stood looking up at the stars, her arms across her chest.

He'd told her that Edie was gone, that his marriage was over. She didn't say a word, didn't act like she cared. He followed her outside, stood behind her. In better times, he used to brush out her long black hair, thick and luxuriant. Sometimes he'd remember the first time he saw it, and he'd smooth it out with his hands, as if smothering the flames. Then he'd kiss the top of her head. He'd told her more than once that he worshipped her, and it was true. She could think everything else he said was a lie, if she'd only believe that.

Tomorrow another beautiful day would dawn. The first day of the rest of his life or some such bullshit, and already it was beginning to look like it was going to be like all the rest of them. This turning over a new leaf was like flipping a manhole cover with your pinkies. Imagine: You tell people, "I'm not a liar anymore," and they don't believe you! The nerve. His father used to torture him with sentences that began with "Nobody said it was going to be easy. . . ." Now he was saying them to himself.

"She asked me to arrange a meeting with you," he said. "She must've trusted me a little."

She turned and faced him. "She's desperate to find Santee. She loves him."

248

Even that sounded like some sort of accusation. He stepped toward her as if to take her into his arms. "Hermalinda—"

She held up her hands. "No, Zack. I came out here to see Margaret, to help her find Santee. It's important. I can't be bothered with you."

Can't be bothered. He let his arms fall to his sides. "What the hell *is* going on with Santee, anyway?"

"I can't tell you."

"Come on, Hermalinda. I might be able to help here, figure out where Margaret went. You want to know, don't you, or is that giving away too many secrets?"

"I already know. She's gone where Santee has gone."

"And where's that?"

"I don't know."

"I do," Zack said, sounding more certain than he was. "When he showed up here, he wasn't just scared, he had this look in his eye, like something was haunting him."

"Come on, Zack."

"No, I'm serious here. I know this look. It must've been how I looked after I dumped off that dead kid like a side of beef for that judas priest to serve up."

She looked away.

"Like I looked when you showed up here looking for a job."

"This has nothing to do with us, Zack."

"I'm saying Santee saw something there in town, maybe somebody killed, some Zapatista deal gone sour, and came running out here. That's it, isn't it?"

"What if he did?"

Bingo. The way she said it, he knew he'd been right. "Damnit, Hermalinda. Are you not listening to me? I'm a fuck-up, but I know people. He wasn't just running away. Something was eating at him, something he had to set right. Somebody died, right? Follow that corpse, and you'll find Santee."

She studied him a moment. "Thanks, Zack. I think you're right."

"So where'd he go? Who got killed?"

"If you really want to help, you can find out *why* he died, why the deal went sour, as you said."

"And how am I supposed to do that? I don't even know what 'the deal' was."

"Ask someone who knows. I believe he's a friend of yours."

She just wouldn't let that go. "You want me to talk to *Huerta?* You've got to be kidding."

She flew into a rage. "You rather *I* go talk to him? What do you think, Zack? Think he'll tell me? He's an old friend of the family, after all."

He held up his hands. "All right. I'm sorry. I'll talk to him. Where will you be?"

It took her a while to answer. She had turned away from him, looking at the back door to the house where the porch light burned. Was she remembering that day she showed up there? Her jaw was clenched, and he could tell from her breathing she was still angry. She hated to lose her temper. It brought back too much, or let too much out. He wanted to hold her but knew she wouldn't let him near.

She started down the porch steps. "I'll be following Margaret," she said, looking back up at him, in control again.

"And where's that?"

"Following Santee."

"At least give me the dead guy's *name.*"

"Jorge Trujillo. He was murdered in the *zócalo.* Santee, as you said, came here that night. Since then, he's disappeared."

"Is that the kid . . . you know."

"The one you served up to the judas priest? No. I didn't know him. Maybe Huerta just needed a corpse and picked one up on the way out to your place. As you know, there's no shortage in Chiapas."

That "as you know" wasn't lost on him. He wanted to tell her what he *knew*—that he loved her and would do anything to win her back— but knew also she wouldn't believe it—shouldn't believe it, for that matter—until it happened.

ZACK DIDN'T WASTE ANY TIME GETTING ON OVER TO HUER-ta's. No sense being all scared about it. Sure, Huerta'd be pissed Zack let Margaret get away, but not too bad. He probably knew anyway. Nobody could've gotten as far as Huerta had by placing important matters solely in the hands of someone like Zachary Taylor Hayman III. No. Zack'd done just about as well as Huerta'd expected him to. Huerta just liked pulling the strings is all, making sure they were still attached. Zack was *supposed* to fuck up, sort of like the court jester—good for a laugh, hardly worth killing.

He'd considered going to Huerta's straight, clear headed, ready to outmaneuver him with his dazzling wit. Instead, he smoked a bowl as he headed into town and got totally fucked up. Zack without his red eyes and hempen bouquet would be like Ronald McDonald without his nose and makeup, sporting an Armani suit. They wouldn't even let him in the playground. Zack had to be the same old Zack to put one over on Huerta.

On his way to Huerta's, Zack tried to figure out why Hermalinda had ever fallen in love with him in the first place. He used to think it was because he'd put one over on her, that she really didn't know who he was. But, as it turned out, she'd known all along he was a coward who hadn't lifted a finger to help her, to help her whole village for that matter. Maybe it was because later on, when he did help her, it was such a big surprise coming from a *no basta* guy like him, that it made him look better than he was. And back then she was a down-and-out homeless widow. Anybody would've looked good. Now she was a Freedom Fighter, Indigenous Rebel, whatever the fuck—one tough, committed woman who'd had too much of Zack months ago.

So'd Zack, for that matter.

But now, the way he had it figured, the only chance he had with Hermalinda was to surprise her again; and to do that, he'd have to surprise himself, surprise himself so much that it actually stuck for good. He slid in next to the curb, got out of the truck, and slammed the door. The metal thunk of the truck door echoed down Huerta's street and set all the dogs to barking, probably set off some sensors in the wall. Who knew what was already aimed at him, awaiting orders.

He could hear Hermalinda's voice echoing in his head as he crossed the street: *You rather I go talk to him? What do you think, Zack? Think he'll tell me? He's an old friend of the family, after all.* He'd never really put it together before that it was personal with her and Huerta, that he would've been the one who gave the order to take out her village, and she would've known that.

Before he came to Mexico, Zack thought of war as something big, impersonal, detached. Like a cruise missile or a letter from the draft board—who would you get mad at? But *guerra, revolución,* or leftist uprising, this thing here was *personal.* Which is why he always thought he should stay out of it. He knocked on the door. That and being a total coward.

The servant who answered the door was real this time and laying low.

It wasn't hard to figure why. Huerta chewing out somebody echoed from the back of the house like a television playing too loud, but there was one of those too, and he was drowning that out. There was a lot of fuck this and fuck that, but it'd gone past the point of making any sense. The servant, his head ducked down the whole time like a dog used to being kicked, led Zack into the real courtyard and made himself scarce.

There was no mariachi band here. No divers. No toucan. The ground was all dug up. Picks and shovels were lying about. The workers must've been run off or were hiding. Dozens of plants and trees sat around the perimeter in their burlap diapers waiting to be planted. Zack felt like he was at a party where all the other guests were plants.

This illusion was shattered when Huerta arrived, red in the face, snapping orders over his shoulder to flunkies. He was wearing cowboy clothes this time, dark blue jeans and a loud plaid shirt, his gut straining at the snaps. He was dressed for a barbecue, but didn't look to be in the party spirit. It wasn't just his usual meanness. He was wound up, edgy, preoccupied. Like a football coach on the sidelines. From the looks of him, it must be the fucking Super Bowl.

"Good to see you, Zack," Huerta said, not like he meant it, but like he couldn't be bothered thinking about it. Reminded Zack of a banker friend of his dad's back in Boise who always greeted him that way even though he hated Zack's guts. Somehow that memory, linking Huerta to a Boise banker, made it easier to take Huerta on.

"Good to see you, too, Señor Huerta. Afraid I got some bad news. Margaret Mayfield gave me the slip a couple of hours ago, jumped her bill and everything."

Huerta nodded his head up and down, so Zack knew the man heard him, but it didn't seem to piss him off. He looked like he was thinking hard, processing this new information, fitting it into the game plan. Finally, he said, "The woman doesn't matter. But this Webster Webfoot . . . Did she say anything to you about him?"

Zack got the impression that Huerta'd been thinking about little else since the last time they'd talked, though he couldn't imagine why some scrawny kid in a patchwork jumpsuit had Huerta so freaked. "No . . . not really."

Huerta nodded as if he expected as much. "He is clever, that one. I have learned that this boy, this Webster Webfoot, he is famous on the Web. A cyberterrorist. A skilled manipulator of the media. Run a Web-search on him, and the list is endless. Someone like that can be a dangerous enemy to have."

Zack wasn't sure what a cyberterrorist was, and maybe Huerta wasn't either, but he nodded sympathetically and muttered, "Yeah. That's really bad news all right. I'm sure he'll turn up. He kind of sticks out, you know?"

Suddenly, Huerta focused all his attention on Zack. "That's right. You have seen him. You know what he looks like."

"Well, I hardly—"

"You will find him for me and bring him here." Huerta looked quite pleased with this plan—takes a gringo to find a gringo.

Zack knew that "no" wasn't one of the possible answers. "Do you know whereabouts he might be?" he asked.

"Earlier today, he escaped from six of my men in a café in San Cristóbal. Café Mundial, you know it?"

"Six men? Jeez . . ."

"Do you *know* it?"

"Yeah, sure. Tourist place. Real nice. Not my kind of thing. Did he have a gun or something?"

"Apparently he didn't need one. Two of my men are in the hospital, one with a broken jaw and the other with a concussion. He got away on foot, so he couldn't have gotten far. Since you are a countryman, perhaps he won't be so quick to run from you, and you can win his trust. Do you still have the gun I gave you?"

Zack realized with a start that he did, stuffed into his hip pocket. "Yeah," he said. He didn't like where this was going.

"If you find him, and he won't come with you, you might need it to defend yourself, you understand?"

"Yeah," Zack managed one more time, swallowing hard. Huerta was telling Zack to kill this kid, but just in case the conversation was bugged, he could deny it. Force of habit with a guy like Huerta. I offered to get the kid before, Zack wanted to say, but you turned me down. *I have intelligent, skilled people working on that,* Huerta'd said. Guess they weren't so fucking skilled after all.

"I'll leave right away," Zack said.

Huerta almost looked grateful.

This is my chance, Zack thought. Maybe my one and only chance. I've got some skills of my own. He perched at the end of the high board, took a deep breath. "I've got something I'd like to run by you first, if I could."

Huerta, curious, gave him a tiny nod.

"Well, the thing is, my life's pretty screwed up right now. My wife just left me. The hotel business isn't for shit, and I'm burned out on it anyways. I'm not getting any younger, and I gave up on going back to the States a long time ago. I guess what I'm trying to say here is that I'm open to a new direction in life, you might say. And, I don't know— seems like something big's up with Santee and the war and everything, and I thought maybe you might need somebody on a more professional, long-term basis. Not that I'm not *perfectly* happy to do you any favor I can, as a friend and all. I just thought, you know, maybe I could get involved on a whole other level."

Huerta scowled as he listened and for a few moments after, then he burst out laughing. "You are asking me for a job?"

"Yeah." Zack smiled sheepishly at Huerta's wolfish grin. "Yeah, that's pretty much what I'm doing."

Huerta gave a big laugh, and his big beefy arm wrapped around Zack's shoulders, lifted him off his feet, and set him down. "I like you, Zack. You are a businessman who doesn't care so much what the business is, eh?"

Zack laughed along at what a slime he was. "What is the business, anyway?"

Huerta released him, leaned back, and studied him through narrowed eyes. But his smug look gave him away. He had a deal going he couldn't resist bragging to some gringo about, even if the gringo was Zack. He took out a cigar the length of Cuba, circumcised it, and lit it up. He offered one to Zack, but Zack turned it down and lit a Marlboro instead. He never could relate to the cigar thing.

"Land!" Huerta said reverently, passionately. "Millions of hectares of *land*!"

Of course, Zack thought. Was it ever anything else in this country? He said, "Wow! Where?"

Huerta puffed a few times. "I will tell you a secret, my friend: The conflicts which have plagued this country for many, many years, are about to come to an end. Very soon thousands of discontented *chiapanecos* will abandon their land, their precious *ejidos*, leaving a vacuum, one might say, that I will fill."

"Abandon" sounded like a euphemism for something more sinister. "You mean like a big military action?"

"No, my friend, they are leaving—going far away, never to return. A little bird will whisper in their ears, and away they will fly. All I will have to do is stake my claim." Huerta puffed on his cigar with an I've-got-a-secret grin.

"This is like thousands of people, right? Where are they going?"

The grin widened. They'd reached the punch line. He even raised his eyebrows: "Mars. They are all going to Mars." He blew a plume of smoke in the air as he made like a rocket with his cigar.

"*Mars?* You mean the colony? *They're* the ones selected?" Zack wondered if Huerta hadn't slipped a gear.

"Carefully selected, you might say. And who better? They are used to adversity, no? Scratching out a living from a harsh environment?" Huerta grinned. "Still, one might be forced to conclude that the colonist selection process is not the model of democracy and fair play it appears to be."

Course it wasn't. Nothing ever was. Sending all the rebels to Mars. It was crazy and awful enough to be true. And certainly Huerta didn't have any reason to lie to Zack. Why bother? But at least one thing didn't figure: Even if every Indian in the world was shipped off to Pluto tomorrow, how did Huerta think he was going to score? He was a big fish in this tiny pond, but this place was a teacup in the scheme of things. "Señor Huerta, I don't mean to doubt you or anything, but how will you get a shot at a deal like that? I mean, you got to figure that all the big multinationals'll wade in on it. Oil. Paper pulp."

Huerta slapped him on the back. "You are much smarter than you let on, Zack. It is true: Someone like myself wouldn't usually be allowed to feed at such a big, rich banquet. But that is the best part. As it turns out the multinationals won't be making any more long-term real estate investments, not *here* at any rate."

"Why not real estate in Mexico?"

"Not Mexico, my friend, the world. The wealthiest, too, are going to the new one."

"New what? What're you talking about?"

Huerta chuckled. "The new *world.*"

"The new world." There was a noise. Zack wasn't sure whether it was a bird trilling or his ears ringing. "Mars?"

Huerta laughed heartily. "That's right. So you see: They're leaving this one to me." He pointed his cigar at the ground beneath their feet. "They don't know it yet, but they are."

Zack's heart was racing. He tried a jaunty laugh, but it came out a groan. "No offense. But what's wrong with this world? Why the fuck go to Mars?"

Huerta smiled. "What is the expression the English use? Ah yes! I'm afraid we're in for a bad patch coming up. The details need not concern ordinary men like us—ozone layers, algae blooms. Let the *cientificos* worry about that. It makes them feel important and powerful." Huerta took another puff on his cigar and turned philosophical. "But these things, you know? They are never as bad as they say. And everything is better when you're rich, *verdad*?"

Zack struggled to keep a grip. Huerta had to be nuts. But Zack still hadn't found out what he'd come here for. "So how does Santee fit into all this?"

Huerta dismissed Santee with a wave of his hand. "He thinks he's saving the world—you know the kind of American who saves the baby seals and the little Mexicans. Don't worry about him. He is doing exactly what he is supposed to do. If Margaret finds him, they can die together." He gave a sentimental smile as if he actually thought that was sweet.

"What about Jorge?" Zack blurted out.

Huerta looked clueless.

"Some young guy killed in town the other night? I heard it had something to do with Santee."

"Oh, yes." Huerta smiled. "I had forgotten his name. He is not important. It was simply a matter of controlling the flow of information." Huerta laughed at his own joke, and Zack laughed along with no idea what he was talking about.

Zack sensed his time was running out, that Huerta's talkative mood was coming to a close, and there was no time for subtlety. "Where is it Jorge was from?"

Huerta laughed again. "*De la tierra*. From dust to dust, eh? Forget the boy. Now get going, my friend. We can discuss the terms of your employment when you bring me Señor Webfoot, one way or the other."

ZACK TOOK OFF FOR SAN CRISTÓBAL WHILE THE TRAIL WAS still warm. He remembered that silly kid in his getup. He'd stick out like a sore thumb. If he was still alive, Zack was probably the kid's only chance, though he did wonder how he managed to give the slip to six guys. But since Huerta had to get cute about where Jorge was from— *dust to dust*, what an asshole—Webster was Zack's only lead to Santee, his only lead back to Hermalinda.

He wondered what she'd say to this crazy Mars stuff. He probably should pass it along to the rebels right away, but he didn't really know anybody besides Hermalinda who'd take him seriously, and she was definitely in the doubtful column. He tried to get a handle on it, but it was too bizarre, too mind-boggling. But even if Huerta was crazy or lying, something big was going down, and as usual for the rebels, something bad.

The military was busy tonight. Seemed like every vehicle they had was out on the road. That wasn't so unusual, but there was something weird about it, and it took him a while to figure out what it was. They were mostly empty. Jeeps, Hummers, had just a driver and nobody else. Big transports with staked sides, usually packed with soldiers hooting at him as he passed, were empty except for a driver and a soldier or two in the back. Once he noticed, it was hard to miss. Not just one or two, but all of them. And they were headed every which way, breaking off from the pack one or two at a time to head for the boonies. What in the hell could they be doing?

They are leaving—going far away, never to return.

He hadn't gone far when it hit him—what he should've seen right away. If all the rebels were going to just fly away, they needed a ride to the airport or spaceport or whatever. He imagined the transport ahead of him packed with Indians, Hermalinda in back, going away, never to return. He cried out and stepped on the gas, passing a line of a half dozen army vehicles. The drivers looked like ordinary young guys, just doing a job. They might've been going to pick up a load of spare parts for all these nice trucks. They probably didn't know where they were going or why. Maybe this war wasn't so personal after all.

He swerved back into his lane just in time to avoid having a head-on with a rental Cherokee. Inside, lit by his headlights, was a terrified tourist couple of the sort that were usually his bread and butter—about his age, behind the times, and hoping to stay there. "Turn around," he wanted to tell them. "You got no idea what you're getting yourself into." He hunched over the wheel, and kept the gas to the floor, making it to San Cristóbal in record time. He lost count of the number of trucks in the olive drab caravan on the way, but it looked like there'd be room enough for everybody.

THE CAFÉ MUNDIAL WAS THE KIND OF PLACE THAT GAVE tourism a bad name, full of spoiled rich kids hiding out from the country they'd traveled a couple thousand miles to get to. You could say what you wanted about the Estrellita, but it was a darn sight better than this phony place. He felt a twinge of nostalgia for his old life, still warm in the grave, but he had no regrets. It already seemed like a long time ago.

It was easy to spot the people he needed to talk to—the only two Mexican customers in the place. They sat at the bar, keeping an eye out, in case the kid was stupid or crazy enough to come back here. Zack slid in beside the older and larger one, a barrel-chested guy with a little gray at the temples, packed like a sausage into his predictable black T-shirt. There was a lump in the back pocket of his jeans that looked like a small gun. The other guy standing beside him—about twenty with a sculpted body straight out of an underwear ad—had his more serious firepower strapped to his hip in a tooled holster like an old-fashioned gunslinger, though the gun would've done Flash Gordon proud. The tooling on the holster might've been a cobra or a dick, probably trying for both. Zack wondered if punks packed this shit back in the States. He'd been away too long to know. Carrying a gun in Mexico was illegal unless you were really a cop, but that was the point. Who the hell was going to take it away from him? It let you know up front there was no point calling the cops—they'd already backed down or been paid off before you showed up.

Zack figured these two for Peace and Prosperity goons, the nastiest of the nasty paramilitary thugs the party used to enforce "the rule of law." Whoever wanted Webster wanted him bad. This thing was definitely bigger than Huerta, and "my men" was something of an overstatement. Even if you owned the beach, could you really say, "my sharks"?

In the ashtray in front of the big guy was a crumpled Marlboro pack and a heap of butts.

Zack ordered a triple espresso. When it arrived, he lit a cigarette and offered one to the guy next to him, who took it with a smile, and leaned toward Zack's Zippo. "You figure the kid to come back here?" Zack asked him.

He straightened up and exhaled a hefty cloud. "The kid?" he asked blandly, not like he really didn't know what Zack was talking about, but like he was saying, *and who the fuck are you?*

Zack took his own drag, and his hand didn't even shake. "Sorry to jump ahead there. Zack Hayman's the name. I work for Señor Huerta. He asked me to check things out. Word is the kid might be CIA."

"I thought so," the young guy leaned around his companion and cut in. He was sporting a black eye and a lump on the forehead.

"Shut up, Flaco," the older guy said. "If he was CIA, you'd be fucking dead."

"Don't tell me to shut up. You didn't see him in action."

The older guy rolled his eyes and turned back to Zack. "Tell that *pendejo* Huerta that Milton says this gringo Zap isn't CIA, and he isn't coming back here or anywhere around here, and he's wasting his money and my time."

"Where is he then?"

"In the hills with the rest of the rabbits. That's where they always run. His clothes were stuffed in a trash can in the market. That sound like CIA to you? Fucking Huerta thinks he knows so much, let him sit in this fag bar and sip this frothy shit." Milton pushed a tired-looking cappuccino littered with shaved chocolate away from him in disgust.

He beckoned the bartender over and ordered a double shot of tequila. Flaco shook his head disapprovingly, but he didn't say anything. "He went to the market," Milton said, "and rode out of town in some farmer's truck under a sack of beans or something. CIA. He'd be driving a Lexus or something, a fucking helicopter. Besides, why would CIA want to fuck with us? They *trained* my fucking ass!"

Milton's tequila arrived. He downed it and ordered another.

"I'll check it out," Zack said. He finished his espresso, not as good as he made at the Estrellita and twice as expensive.

"You do that, Zack Hayman. And if he *is* CIA, you tell him I want my old job back."

ZACK SPENT THE NEXT COUPLE OF HOURS TRYING TO WHEE-dle some information in the places around the market, but *nadie sabe nada*—nobody knew nothing. In fact, they knew nothing even before he had a chance to ask anything. Then it was "what kid? What clothes? I'm not from around here, señor."

Quite a few of Milton and Flaco's friends were evident around town.

They weren't exactly following him yet, but if he kept showing an interest in the wrong sort of people, they would be. Far as they knew, he was working for Huerta, but they could still decide to take him out if they thought he might make them look bad. They'd already questioned all these people, after all, and apparently hadn't come up with shit.

Around midnight, he drove around until he was sure nobody was following him, then went to Anna Flores's place. It was closed, but he went around back and rapped on the door until she let him in. She was busy cleaning the grill, and the place smelled like lard and oven cleaner and coffee. "You want a cup?" she asked him.

He took the coffee and watched her work for a while, putting her back into it, her hands encased in thick rubber gloves, her bare arms like knotted ropes. "I'm looking for a kid," he said. "Hermalinda put me onto him. Name's Webster Webfoot?"

She switched from spatula to wire brush and scoured harder. "Hermalinda or Huerta?"

"Shit, Anna. You don't believe that do you?"

"I know that Hermalinda told me she was through with you."

"That's because I've been a spineless fool, a coward. But I've never been a traitor. I'd never do anything to endanger Hermalinda. You know that." (He could hear Edie's voice, kinder than it'd been in years: *You taking a stand, Zee? You taking a stand?*) He said it aloud: "I'm taking a stand, Anna. I'm on your side."

Anna shook her head at the grill without pausing in her work. She tried to toss a strand of hair out of her eyes, but it was plastered to her forehead. He reached out and pulled it back for her, hooking it behind her ear.

"Why should I believe you, Zack?"

"Anna, look at me."

Reluctantly, she put down the brush and looked at him. "I love Hermalinda," he said. "She's everything to me. *Mi corazón.* This is my one chance to prove to her that I'm worth a shit. I'm going to save that kid or die trying. Help me out here. Please, I'm begging you."

Anna was a romantic. She wanted to believe in love, wanted to believe it could transform even a sorry coward like Zack. "My marriage is over. Edie's back in Idaho by now. I'm on my knees here."

"But if you're lying . . ."

"But I'm not. I'm telling you—there's P and P goons all over town looking for the kid. Somehow he got lucky once, but it's not going to happen twice. He doesn't stand a chance unless he gets a little help. And I'm pretty sure he knows something. Surely, you guys must've noticed all the military movement."

She closed her eyes and sighed. "Okay. I got a call just before you came, arranging transport for the boy out into the countryside. You be out back in four hours. You want to help? Make sure they're not followed. Now get out of here before somebody notices your damn truck parked outside."

He grabbed her by the shoulders and kissed her. "Thank you! Thank you! Thank you! Bless you, Anna!" He took off as if hurrying would make the boy come sooner.

She laughed, brushing at her sweaty face with her forearm. "*Buena suerte*, Zack." she called after him. "*Ten cuidado.*"

Z ACK PARKED IN THE ALLEY A COUPLE OF BLOCKS FROM Anna's place, and waited. He slumped down, watching for any sign of life. He had a thermos of coffee and a bag of sandwiches and a carton of cigarettes and a fresh bag of dope. He was set for the long haul. He'd tried to sleep in the truck earlier, but sleep wouldn't come as he kept imagining the dangers he might face. He'd even taken the gun out of his pocket and checked it out, hefted it in his hand. Little thing, but it was still a gun. God, how he hated these things. He stuck it back in his jeans. He was afraid, all right. But his biggest fear was that the kid wouldn't show, and he'd never see Hermalinda again.

A little before five, a Coke truck came down the alley, almost taking his side mirror with it, and came to a stop behind Anna's. A few minutes later a ramshackle VW van showed up and parked behind it. A man and a boy got something out of the van and loaded it onto the Coke truck and took off. The truck, the motor running the whole time, took off as well. Zack kept his lights off and followed it out of town, checking the rearview mirror every chance he got, imagining Edie's dad, his own dad, the P and P, the CIA, and his fucking sister. But there was no one. Even the military seemed to be taking some time off.

They drove north to Teapa, a dump of a little town, then out into the boonies. Finally they hit a turnoff that looked more like a dirt track than a road, and Zack played a hunch and parked by the highway. After about a half hour, the Coke truck returned and headed south. Zack smoked a bowl, got out of his truck, and started walking up the road.

*   *   *

HE WAS GLAD HE HADN'T TRIED BRINGING THE PICKUP IN here. If if hadn't gotten stuck in the mud, it would've bottomed out for sure, broken an axle. The Coke truck had left knee-deep ruts as it'd muscled its way through. Those Coke drivers went everywhere. The mechanics were legendary.

A flock of little green parrots escorted him up the road. They'd assemble in a tree a little bit ahead, watch him pass, then move on up the road to do it again. No wonder these guys ended up in cages repeating everything their jailers told them to. They had wings and they still didn't have sense enough to steer clear of people.

The road petered out after about a mile in front of a ruined chapel. No telling how or why it'd ever been here in the first place. Judging from the droppings, the parrots called it home now, along with a couple of scrawny goats, a tipoff people lived close by. One of the trails off the clearing had fresh footprints, including a work boot, size 13EE at least, that had to be his man. As he and the parrots wound through the forest, Zack had to ask himself—What if this kid *is* CIA or some shit? He *did* take out six guys. But Zack pictured him in that church pew back in San Cristóbal, webbed into oblivion, and set that fear aside. He was more afraid the kid didn't know anything, that he was a dead end, that he'd be out here in the middle of nowhere without a clue which way to go.

But if the kid didn't know anything, what would he be doing out here? This could hardly be a random destination. He wasn't even sure what state this was—Chiapas, Tabasco, Veracruz. Probably didn't matter out here. It was someplace to get away, be left alone. When he got to the town, it was pretty much what he expected. It hadn't been here for long, mostly pitiful homemade houses, dirt-poor even by Mexican standards. He'd seen a place like this before, used to live right next door to one as a matter of fact. At least with this place, when the men with guns showed up, they'd have to park their shiny new trucks a mile away.

He wondered if somehow Hermalinda knew when she sent him to Huerta on a wild goose chase after his scruples, that it'd end up someplace like this. Wasn't too hard to figure.

There was no one out, but he could feel many eyes on him as he walked down the main drag, a muddy trail with fresh gringo tracks leading to a little place like all the others. He kept his hands in sight, made no sudden moves. He stood in front of the low plank house and called inside: "Webster Webfoot, my name's Zack Hayman. I'm guessing you might be interested in hooking up with Santee St. John and Margaret Mayfield, and I'm here to help you. I've got a truck down on the highway if you're interested."

There was a little delay, but pretty soon Webster stepped out, arm in arm with a beautiful Mexican girl. No wonder he'd come here. He looked a bit ragged in clothes that were way too short for him, but he also looked older somehow, more serious. Zack imagined he'd been through quite a lot since he saw him last.

"How do we know you're trustworthy?" he asked Zack.

Good question. "You don't," Zack admitted. "Why don't we have a little powwow and see what you think? I've been up all night, and I could stand to get off my feet."

"How about a Coke?" the girl asked him.

"Sounds great." Zack laughed.

SEEMED LIKE HALF THE VILLAGE WAS CROWDED INTO THE tiny house. Zack was given a warm Coke and introduced to everyone, though he promptly forgot all their names. He couldn't see much of them in the dimly lit place except their eyes, full of fear, wondering what had brought Webster and then Zack to their village. It couldn't be good, whatever it was.

Zack figured his best bet was to tell these people everything he knew and hope they'd return the favor. He started out in Spanish, but Aurora suggested he speak English for Webster's sake, and she'd translate for everyone else. It felt weird having this woman's voice murmuring just behind his. He tried not to listen to what she was saying.

He told them how he'd helped stage Santee's funeral for Huerta and nobody asked him who Santee was. He made it sound like he was working for the cause the whole time even before Hermalinda sent him back to Huerta to get more information. If any of them thought he was lying, nobody called him on it. He thought of it as a lie he could turn into the truth if he did the right thing from here on out, sort of a retroactive commitment. They all looked relieved to hear Santee was alive and didn't seem to pay that much attention to Zack's role in things anyway. When he started telling them about the Mars business, he figured they'd think he was out of his mind, but Webster, at least, latched hold of it. "Of course," he kept saying. "Of course."

Far from not believing him, they looked like he was God sending them to hell. "Don't give up now," he wanted to tell them, "I just got here, I just signed up," but knew he didn't have the right. "What's going on?" he asked Aurora, and she and Webster explained about the interface and what everybody originally thought was going to happen—the whole world standing in their shoes, though most of them didn't have any shoes.

"How many people here have that interface installed?" he asked her.

"All of them," she said.

A little bird will whisper in their ears, and away they will fly. "This thing receives as well as sends?"

"That's my guess," Webster said.

Nobody wanted to just come out and say what they suspected, that they'd signed onto this deal thinking the world was going to cut them a break, and now it was going to round them up and ship them off to hell. Somewhere in the shadows one of the women started sobbing.

"Do you know where a place called Tziscao is?" Webster asked Zack.

"Sure," Zack said. "Down by the border. Lagunas de Montebello. Real pretty. Why?"

"That's where Santee is. Can you take us there?"

"Or die trying."

THE THREE OF THEM WALKED BACK DOWN THE RUTTED ROAD with the parrots. Webster was still trying to explain this interface business to Zack and how he thought Santee fit in, when Aurora shushed them and yanked them off the road. Down by the highway was a big olive-drab transport parked by Zack's pickup. Two soldiers were checking it out. One of them was toting an M16. The other one had a sidearm more modest than Flaco's but just as deadly.

Aurora suggested they hide and wait them out, but Zack had a feeling they weren't going anywhere—not until they picked up what they came for. He didn't think Aurora and Webster had quite figured that part out yet. Too young. Too good-hearted. They thought there were limits to what people were capable of doing to each other. They still hoped that maybe the interface was just a tracer like tagging wildlife, keeping tabs on everybody. Zack said, "They're not going anywhere. I'll go down and talk to them."

Before Webster and Aurora could stop him, he lurched into motion, his knees wobbling, and his ears ringing, knowing bullshit wasn't going to get him through this one, figuring whatever happened, he had it coming. By the time they spotted him, he'd settled into his best lanky stroll. He waved at them with his hat, letting them see he was just an old silver-haired gringo with a ponytail, perfectly harmless. He called out to them in Spanish, "¿*Qué tal?*" What's happening? "Hope I'm not parked in your way there. Had to take a leak."

The one with the M16 pointed it at him, and Zack bore down on them like he didn't see it, grinning at them like a fucking idiot, sticking out his right hand like he was going to shake, reaching into his back pocket with his left. The two soldiers traded a glance when Zack was only a few paces away, and Zack figured it'd be the only chance he got. He kept on coming, pulling out the gun, the little silver pistol from Huerta, shooting the soldier with the M16 between the eyes, pointing the gun at the other one, hoping, praying he'd just run away, but he went for his sidearm and Zack shot him in the throat.

He hadn't fired a gun since his father'd taken him out in the country when he was thirteen and showed him how to "defend his home and his family" before Zack had much thought about either one. It was one of the few times he could remember pleasing his father. When he told the tale to his friends, he called Zack "deadeye." Zack could hardly believe the tiny cracks the little pistol made, like snapping twigs, were actually shots. The first soldier had fallen dead immediately, but the second one was on his knees, trying to cry out as he gagged on his own blood. Zack put a second shot through his eye, and he dropped to the ground, silent.

Zack wound up and hurled the little gun into the valley below the road. It made a silver arc, falling silently into the forest. He pried the M16 from the soldier's hands, held it by the barrel and beat it against the big truck until it was bent and broken, then threw it after the pistol, took the other one's sidearm and tossed it as well.

Silently, Webster helped him carry the two bodies off the road. Zack took a deep breath, trying not to look at their faces, and dug through their pockets. He got both their IDs, their orders, and a good-sized roll of money off one of them. He must've gotten lucky in a card game, or this was a payoff. The government didn't pay them shit and then whined when they turned crooked. Webster looked at him funny as he pocketed the money, as if he should suddenly have qualms about stealing after shooting two guys in cold blood.

"This is Mexico, son, if you want to do anything of a questionable nature, bring money." They covered the bodies with brush. That would have to do for a burial. He'd had just about all he could stand of handling dead people for a good long while.

When they climbed back onto the road, Aurora was standing behind the transport with a blank look on her face. Coming down the road from the village was the rest of the population of Veinte y Dos de Diciembre. They lined up behind the transport like they were queueing up for a bus.

"It's started," Webster said.

They tried to talk to Aurora but all they could get out of her was *"Vamos al nuevo mundo"*—We're going to the new world.

Zack and Webster opened the back of the big truck, and the villagers packed themselves inside while Zack got his stuff out of the pickup and pushed it off the road. It crept along at first, then picked up momentum, taking out scrub trees, picking up a pretty good head of steam before it slammed into a tree or rock somewhere down below with the sound of breaking glass and crunching metal. It didn't do anything so spectacular as burst into flames. You couldn't even see it from the road. It would sit there quietly and rust away. Not a bad way to go. *"Adios, Idajo,"* he said.

He lit a cigarette and looked over the orders. The soldiers were supposed to pick up everyone in the village and haul them down to Guatemala, just across the border from Tziscao. Zack figured that was no coincidence. He joined Webster and Aurora by the army truck. "Get in," Zack said to Webster. "I'll drive." Webster steered Aurora into the cab, and she sat between them with a faint smile on her face. The kid looked in pretty bad shape, staring at her, holding her hands. "Help me watch the road," Zack advised. "We'll figure out something."

CHAPTER SIXTEEN

HIGH UP ON THE PYRAMID, THE LAST FLAT SPACE BEFORE the top, the place Santee called the Enlightenment Launching Pad, Margaret had pried a stone loose from the middle niche on the south face. It hadn't been hard to figure out which stone to loosen in this vast pile of carefully fitted limestone. It was the stone where George always burned incense in a shallow bowl-like depression carved by centuries of rain and dew dripping from the low point of the almost straight lintel above. Over the last few years, since George had set up shop, the bowl had become scorched and powdered with ash and smelled like a fire sale in a headshop.

In one of Santee's failed attempts to record transcendence, this stone figured prominently. Santee stayed focused on it because George had told him to find a point and concentrate totally, losing himself in it, obliterating his ego so that the lines of energy spewing forth from the vortex could pass through him unobstructed. Santee focused on the scorched stone, wondering if the ashes were all George's or whether Zack beat out his pipe on that stone as well. Or maybe George had his own pipe. He recalled a childhood memory of watching his dad's cigarette burning into the top of his dresser as his dad beat on a troublesome radiator with a pipe wrench, the young Santee knowing that no matter how deep the burn went, it would be better not to speak of it unless there were actually flames. When he came down off the pyramid that day, he told Margaret with a smile, "I saw the vortex today—it was fried all to hell." Then he played her the recording, and she got her first glimpse of the man she loved as a child.

She shone her flashlight under the stone. A disk winked at her in the light, and she plucked it out, blew off the dust, and slid it into her computer, already up and running on a shelf of rock beside her. She knew his message wouldn't be much, but she had to smile at his economy. Not even a word, just a life-sized 3-D line drawing of a tiny A-frame structure, one door, no windows, barely six feet at the apex, that appeared all around her and then slowly dissolved.

She remembered the A-frame well. It was one of a half dozen out behind the hostel in Tziscao where they'd spent a few weeks. She could picture him there, standing with his head brushing the corrugated metal ceiling, brewing a cup of instant coffee with a heating coil plugged into the light fixture that dangled from the ceiling like a trailing vine. He was naked in this memory, grinning, for they'd just made love on the mattress that took up most of the plywood floor. They were naked a good deal of the time in that A-frame. Years later, mere talk of it was enough to get them into bed. His message not only told her where he was, but what he wanted to do when she found him there. Clearly, rumors of his death had been greatly exaggerated.

Down below at the Rancho, there'd been a flurry of activity. Zack had been working on some old car all day, and Edie had just driven off in it, even though it was the middle of the night. It occured to Margaret that she herself was pretty conspicuous, swinging her flashlight beam back and forth in the dark. She clicked it off. The night collapsed around her and gave a chill.

She felt lethal. The dead Santee wasn't real, but the boy lying in the coffin was. Jorge was. Now Zack said Huerta was after Webster. He was just a kid; he didn't stand a chance. What in the hell did she think she was doing? She'd practically kidnapped him, then dumped him in that church. Did she think he'd be all right because he was in a *church?* As Santee would point out, that was a pretty strange conclusion for an atheist. She'd only thought about finding Santee. Blinded by love. She'd always wondered what that phrase meant, never thought it'd apply to her.

The rush she'd felt after installing the interface had dissipated quickly, making her wonder if it hadn't been some side effect. But she knew where it'd come from—it was going on this little treasure hunt Santee had cooked up for her that had her giddy, almost like playing a game with him. Scout and Boo Radley. Any contact was better than none, she supposed. But she'd reached the point where virtual Santee, remembered Santee, potential Santee only made her feel worse. She had to see him, touch him, *know* he was safe and in her arms. Anything else wasn't enough.

I know where he is, she thought. What am I waiting for?

She looked up at the stars, found north and oriented herself, facing southeast. Santee was that way. She should just go ahead and go. There wasn't that much time before he went online, and she wanted to be with him when he did. She'd thought Hermalinda could arrange transport, but maybe it was better to leave her out of it, not to endanger anybody else. Besides, she still couldn't make up her mind about Zack. *You should ask Hermalinda when you see her.* What the hell was that supposed to mean?

She put her computer in her backpack and slipped it on, turned three hundred and sixty degrees, staring into the dark. Her shadow in the yellow *guayabera* hadn't worried her so much when he stayed in view, but now that he'd dropped out of sight he nagged at her. She didn't flatter herself she'd lost him so easily. He was out there somewhere, watching. What was it he hoped to see?

As she picked her way down the back side of the pyramid in the pitch-dark, not daring to turn on her flashlight, she imagined Santee laughing at her, saying, "You're just doing this because you can do it *now.* That's why you hauled your backpack up here with you, just looking for an excuse to take off, just itching to be on the move."

She couldn't deny it. "Just so I can see you sooner," she would've said. And added to her imagined Santee, in answer to his unspoken admonition—"Don't worry. I'll be careful." If I don't break my neck first.

She remembered him across that table in Ocosingo years ago, remembered herself looking back at him, thinking how much she liked him, how, if she were a different kind of woman . . .

You offering to be my guide? he'd asked.

And she *hadn't* been, wouldn't have. It was totally out of character. No attachments, keep moving—that was her. She'd even warned more than one man not to get too interested. But she'd looked in his big blue eyes and said yes—or as close as she would come with *why not?*—and pretty soon she was telling him her life story, writing him into it. He told her once it was the luckiest question he'd ever asked, and she wondered if he still felt that way.

Some guide she'd turned out to be. *The guides,* Zack'd said, *the guides buried him up in the mountains.* She imagined the sound of spades stabbing rocky soil and quickened her pace. She'd take the back way through Altimirano and avoid San Cristóbal altogether.

❊   ❊   ❊

IT WAS TOUGH GOING, CUTTING CROSS-COUNTRY IN THE dark, but she finally made it to the road. Dead beat, just before dawn, she caught a packed *camioneta* bound for the market in Comitán. It was a lively group, though they could barely see each other in the gray light of morning. Everyone had a bag or box or something for market except Margaret, her backpack perched on her knees. She asked about transportation to the *lagunas* and was advised it would be difficult because of *los soldados*. A general grumbling arose about the soldiers and their disregard for common decency. One of the women beside Margaret, jostling shoulder to shoulder, said she knew a man named Luis who might be going toward Guatemala this morning and could give her a ride from the market. Margaret thanked her profusely, and the woman, Maria Isabela, said she was delighted to help out a traveler, *una viajera*. Margaret smiled at the word, thinking, I guess I am a traveler again. I'm not cooped up in that damn little box anymore. Never will be, no matter what, ever, ever again.

NOW, SHE SAT DRINKING COFFEE IN A FOUR-TABLE *TAquería*, patiently waiting for this Luis. He would come. Tziscao wasn't that far. Soon she and Santee would be done with this thing, and they could travel. South America maybe, Peru. Santee had never been there.

There was a big TV on, and she absentmindedly watched the News-Real Worldwide News, Mexican edition, cycle through its loop. It was early yet. Most people were still setting up their stalls. Some were half watching the TV as they worked. The stories came with dizzying rapidity, and the sound was too low to make out clearly: Asian protesters clubbed by riot police. White men talking and shaking hands. Huge mirrors in space. Freedom City. A burning building with children leaping from high windows. Waves smashing a pier into driftwood. A baby panda in a zoo sucking on a bottle for a crowd of schoolchildren. Cut to commercial, commerical, commercial. Nothing at all out of the ordinary.

Tonight Santee would activate his interface and go online, taking all his copies with him, thousands of lives invading the virtual world, so that instead of, say, eating a gourmet meal or skiing Aspen, you found yourself in a dirt-floor shack eating cold tortillas, no water, no electricity, no schools, no hope. What visuals would TV come up with for that story?

She hoped it would do some good, but she wasn't so hopeful as she'd once been. She kept seeing Santee laid out dead, and she couldn't help feeling that whatever happened to him would be her fault, that she'd gotten him into all this, and if it hadn't been for her, he might be happily talking to tornado survivors who thanked God they were alive instead of risking his own life. All the survivors in Santee's old NewsReal stories—standing in the rubble pointing out where the living room used to be, or describing the thousand-freight-trains sound that told them death was on the way—thanked God. After all, they'd just seen what He could do when He took a notion, and they thought it best to stay on His good side. But if God has a bad side, how could He be God? It just made more sense to forget about God altogether.

And if God wasn't responsible, who did that leave?

Only her.

Santee would say, "Taking on a bit much there, aren't you?"

And she'd say . . . She didn't know what she'd say. "Ask me again when it's really you," she said silently. "When I'm sure you're okay." If he was hurt, if he died, she could never take on enough to make it right.

"May I join you?"

She looked up to find the man in the yellow *guayabera*, only he was wearing a peach one now. Close up she could see he was older than she'd thought, lined and graying. "Of course," she said.

He pulled out a chair and sat down, his back to the TV. "In Mexico, we still watch the television. It is everywhere. There are more televisions than telephones or toilets. In the United States, it is, how do you say, 'background noise,' and the real news is on the Web." His voice was quiet and gentle, some would say effeminate, tinged with melancholy. He might've been a teacher or a shrink.

"If you want to call that real," she said. "I've always thought the real news wasn't reported anywhere."

He sighed. "You are probably right. Perhaps it waits for history. Who can say? We make choices, and things change. But we don't really know if the one has anything to do with the other, and changes are often not what we hoped for when we chose as we did. We do what we must because of who we are. You, for instance, are looking for Santee St. John because you must."

She smiled innocently. "No. You must have me confused with some other tourist. Santee St. John. Is that a place? Tell me about it. Maybe I'd like to go there. Are there ruins?"

"Maria Isabela told me you wish to go to the *lagunas*. I am Luis Guzman." He smiled sadly. It wasn't mere irony. There was a great sorrow in his eyes. Maybe she'd misjudged him. Sorrow always softened her.

"Ah, so you're the man she knows. Fancy that. She's one of yours."

"We work together, yes. She is my niece."

Whatever his sorrows, she still couldn't trust him. But he knew things she didn't, and there was no harm in asking. "Why have you been following me?" she asked.

"At first I couldn't be sure someone wouldn't try to harm you. But if that was their intention, they would have done it by now. They don't wish to call attention at such a delicate stage in this business. It's unwise to murder a rich American woman, even if her politics are questionable. I'm a friend, Margaret. We're on the same side."

"How is it you know my name?"

"We've met before."

"That's funny. I don't recall."

"When you met Marcos."

A chill passed through her, and she was afraid, not of Luis Guzman, whoever he was, but of what he knew that she didn't. She laughed to make it all a harmless joke — *meet Marcos, imagine!* "Oh really? I didn't see you there."

He lowered his eyes, as if in shame. Perhaps it was real. "I know. I was playing the role of Marcos."

It took a moment for it to sink in. Of course. Their stupidity had been monumental. "So it was all a lie."

"Not entirely. *Todos somos Marcos*," he said.

We are all Marcos. A rallying cry for the mid-90's Zapatistas, a poster in her room.

She felt dizzy. One lie, and the whole thing fell in on itself. What idiots they'd been. Her voice shook as she asked, "Is Santee all right? Or is that a lie too?" She saw herself leaning over the coffin, so confident he was alive, so trusting, so foolish.

"At the present moment, he is entirely surrounded by the Mexican Army. Otherwise he is apparently fine. Believe me, those who command the army don't wish to harm him. They want him to carry out his plan. A good deal depends upon it."

His plan. It wasn't his, had never been his. She didn't care anymore what depended upon the plan, whatever the hell it was. She only wanted their life back. She wanted Santee safe at her side. The world would have to find some other way to change without them. "What's going on?" she demanded. "Who are you?"

"You are right to be angry. The interface is not simply for recording and broadcast as represented. It can receive as well."

"Receive what?"

"Órdenes, commands."

"To do what?"

"Whatever is desired. It is like remote control. It has already been given a clumsy field test. The entire village of Tziscao was instructed to evacuate, taking only food and clothing, and to proceed to the launch site, where they've been, waiting for days like a herd of animals. Soon everyone with the interface installed will be rounded up from all over Mexico."

"Please, I don't understand. 'Launch site'—what are you talking about?"

"I'm sorry. It is difficult to explain, and we have little time. In a short while the television will announce the selection of ten thousand chiapanecos as the first colonists going to Mars. It will be a great day for Mexico, for the Indians, for the Zapatistas. Subcomandante Marcos himself—a different charlatan this time—will appear alongside the President to make the announcement. In actuality, the colonists will be slaves and forced to work out the rest of their days on Mars, but most people here on Earth will be none the wiser."

She didn't want to hear anymore. Slaves. One of her old T-shirts quoted Zapata: IT IS BETTER TO DIE ON YOUR FEET THAN TO LIVE ON YOUR KNEES. Now the Zapatistas wouldn't even have that choice. "But Santee, he goes online tonight. I thought the interface copies weren't activated until he went online."

"It isn't fully operational until he goes online. Now it is only a clumsy tool, a jet aircraft with a child at the controls. For the precise orchestration of a huge labor force, the interface requires the more sophisticated capabilities of an AI. Santee is essential to establish a gateway between the slaves and the AI. When he connects to his computer and initiates the interface, every poor campesino with a copy installed will already be linked together. But the command Santee believes will connect them to the Web, will yoke them instead to the AI onboard the Mariana. Once that happens, the AI will tell each one of them what to do each moment for the rest of their lives."

Margaret couldn't speak.

Luis pressed on, slowly but urgently. He didn't have time for her to take it all in. "You should know that I feel personally responsible for your involvement. For a long time, we knew that NewsReal and WebNet and the huge conglomerate of which they are a part were up to something in Mexico, in Chiapas in particular. There was a lot of money behind them, a good deal more than Mexico is worth. So I attempted to infiltrate WebNet's Information Management Division—that's what they call their spies. I had recently succeeded in working my way up to a modest security clearance as a field operative—when Santee showed up to cover the massacre outside Ocosingo.

"He was supposed to be a bit player. He was supposed to record the damning evidence and go away, but he didn't. He even attempted to gather more evidence, make something of what had been intended all along as a bargaining chip with the Mexican government. And then he took up with you, a known radical. Memos circulated about you two until the subject of your 'elimination' made it onto the agenda of one of our weekly strategy sessions. Most everyone favored killing you both and making it look like a robbery. You were being followed. It was simply a matter of issuing the orders. There was little discussion, and the matter was settled. When this meeting was over, you two would be executed. I couldn't sit there and let that happen.

"The main business of the meeting was the distribution of the experimental interface. No one could figure out any precise means to distribute it to the target population of dissident Indians. Though most of us were kept in the dark about the precise nature and purpose of the interface, we were invited to propose solutions to the problem of persuading ten thousand suspicious people to voluntarily swallow a capsule.

"As a desperate idea, a ploy to prevent or delay your murders, I suggested the possibility of using you and Santee—naive bleeding-heart gringos whose motives would not be questioned—to distribute the interface among the Zapatistas instead of killing you. Why waste such perfect dupes? I said. I apologize for saying such things. I played my role too well. I only intended to buy you some time, warn you to leave the country. But they seized upon it. They liked the idea of using you two, making fools of you. I'd forgotten how much your existence enraged them. They could understand poor downtrodden Indians making trouble, and they'd sometimes lament the necessity of destroying them and stealing their lands, but you—people with all their advantages who turned your backs on them, accused them with your foolish idealism—you deserved humiliation. They looked forward to it. They brainstormed the whole plan, right there in that conference room. They laughed to think how much you'd have to swallow to make it work, and how sure they were you'd swallow it. Make no mistake. They are despicable people, a consortium of the rich and privileged who have exhausted Earth and care nothing for her.

"My delaying tactic had commuted your death sentence and condemned my people. In the midst of their congratulations for my brilliant suggestion, I seized the monster I'd created by the tail. 'As the only Mexican present,' I announced, 'I volunteer to play the role of Marcos in the recruitment charade.' They all laughed and agreed I'd make a marvelous *subcomandante.*

"I hoped by being on the inside I could outwit them, stop this business before it went too far or even turn it to our advantage. For a time we even believed it possible to carry out the idealistic plan dreamed up for you and Santee, however foolish it may've been—for the interface *could* easily be used in such a way if we could only prevent its union with the AI. The prospect of the world not only taking notice but being forced to care, seduced us. Reason and justice had been ineffectual; perhaps this gadget, this bit of nanowizardry would actually save us, would actually touch the world's heart. But we'll never know.

"While we might have been able to fool a roomful of vicious, selfish men, the AI has proven unassailable. It is entirely independent. Even they have no control over it except to keep it isolated out in space. Now our only hope is to stop Santee from connecting with it. Without the connection to the AI, MarsCorp's control over our people has a very limited capability and range. They'd dare not launch these colonists into orbit, for that would amount to handing over their precious *Mariana* to thousands of angry Mexicans who'd been kidnapped from their homes. But after their grand announcement, they'll have few choices, for the eyes of the world, as they say, will be on them. It's our hope they'll be forced to let our people go. That's why I've come to you now, to ask for your help in stopping Santee from going online."

"You've told me what becomes of the copies. What happens to Santee when he's through being a 'gateway'?"

"We don't know. It's within the AI's power to shut down his nervous system, to kill him, to kill them all."

"How do I know I can trust you?"

"You don't."

She recalled why she ever trusted him in the first place. Hermalinda had told her about her home and family wiped out in an instant, had walked with her in the valley and asked if she would help, if she would meet with Marcos. "Was Hermalinda in on all this?"

"She recruited you for the Zapatistas, yes. But she, too, was deceived as to the true nature of the interface. She didn't know about the *Mariana* and the rest of it, until I told her this morning."

"She's here in Comitán?"

He nodded behind her, and she turned to find Hermalinda standing there. "*Perdóname, por favor,*" she said. Forgive me, please.

Margaret knocked over a chair taking her into her arms. There was nothing to forgive. They both gave way to tears. Margaret held her at arm's length and looked into her eyes. "*¿Es un buen hombre, Luis?*" Is this Luis a good guy?

"*Sí, el mejor.*" Yes, the best.

Hermalinda's word was good enough for Margaret. "*Está bien. ¿Cómo voy a Santee?*" How do I get to Santee?

"There's one more thing I must tell you," Luis said. "The urgency surrounding the Mars mission isn't prompted by ordinary greed, but by a pending catastrophe that will cripple the Earth." *La Tierra.* He said it reverently.

"What catastrophe?"

"We don't know the details, the precise timing. It is a most carefully guarded secret, and much misinformation is given out. But the ozone layer will fail, the balance of air and ocean and land will be in shambles, and life itself will reach a critical pass. Life will be very hard for everyone here. Mars will be a safe haven for a privileged few. As such people say, it will be time to disinvest themselves of an unprofitable enterprise."

"Perhaps the *chiapanecos* should go to Mars then."

"No, not as slaves."

His tone brooked no argument. Not that Margaret would've given him one.

AN HOUR LATER, MARGARET AND HERMALINDA WERE RIDING in the back of a pickup truck loaded with bags of corn. Margaret, because of her height, was dressed as a man in grimy work clothes, her skin dyed the color of tea, her hair jet black. Luis drove.

To disable their copies of the interface they'd all undergone a decidedly unpleasant treatment in Luis's hotel room, which consisted of several hefty jolts of electricity from a heavy, suitcase-sized apparatus, followed by a series of injections. It'd been worked out only days before, and nobody was even sure it would work. But it did, and just in time apparently, for the media hoopla and the roundup had already begun. It was too late to do anything for the thousands of others with the interface installed.

Army trucks loaded with peasants poured onto the main highway from every side road. Helicopters zigzagged over the route, recording the event for the watchful world. Since there was no way to move ten thousand people cross-country and launch them into space surreptitiously, they'd made the whole thing public, or as public as the army would allow. For the safety of the future colonists, the reports intoned, access to the area would be supervised by the military. In this way the world was given the illusion of knowing what was going on, when in fact it knew nothing but an elaborately mounted lie.

The plan was for Hermalinda and Margaret to jump off the truck near Tziscao and, losing themselves in the press of humanity, make their way to Santee before eight o'clock, when he was scheduled to go online. Admittedly, it wasn't much of a plan, but it was all they had.

"What if he just decides on his own not to initiate the interface?" she'd asked. "After Jorge was killed, he might . . ."

Luis shook his head. "As long as he has the interface installed, we're not so sure the AI can't come after him."

Margaret pictured him in her mind's eye sitting cross-legged in the tiny A-frame, waiting for tonight, waiting for her.

"We don't know exactly where in the village he is," Luis had said.

"I do," Margaret said. Just before Luis got into the truck, and she and Hermalinda climbed into the back, she told him she had one more question. "Where were Santee and I when those execution orders were to be sent?"

Luis thought a moment. "A little town called Candelaria, I believe. Is it important?"

She'd been so smart, showing off for Santee. "No, I don't think so," Margaret said.

NOW, AS THEY SLOWED, APPROACHING THE FIRST CHECK-point, she couldn't help thinking about Candelaria and Santee. They'd almost died there. But they could've died anywhere. Just for being who they were. There were worse ways to die, she decided. "What do you think are our chances of getting through?" she asked Hermalinda.

Hermalinda put an arm around her and squeezed her shoulders. "We'll get to him. Don't worry. You love him very much, don't you?"

"It's been so long since we've even seen each other. . . ." She let her voice trail off, not wanting to connect that to any other thought. She went on instead to tell Hermalinda how Santee had left her a trail to Tziscao with a word and a drawing, and they both laughed at the clever game. God, how Margaret needed to laugh.

"How did you guys figure out that Santee had gone to Tziscao?" she asked.

"It's a funny thing. Zack thought of it really. He didn't know Jorge, didn't even know for certain anyone had died, but he suspected Santee had witnessed something horrible in the town and would want to set it right. He suggested that Santee would go where that led him, which would be Tziscao. There's more to Zack than most people see. He understands people, even when he doesn't understand himself very well.

"Anyway, our spies in the military confirmed this morning that Santee's in the village. 'Contained,' they call it. Just a few soldiers to keep him in the town. They have strict orders not to harm him, to leave him alone."

At the mention of Zack, Margaret recalled their odd parting conversation. "Zack leveled with me before I left—warned me about Huerta and told me Santee was alive. When I asked him why he was sticking his neck out like that, he said maybe you'd know. What did he mean?"

Hermalinda shook her head and grimaced into the wind. "Zack, Zack, Zack," she whispered angrily. There were tears in her eyes. She brushed them away. "I hope you'll not think less of me when I tell you that I have been his mistress for many years. He thinks he's in love with me."

Margaret remembered the way Zack had looked at Hermalinda years ago at the Estrellita, the way he'd spoken of her only yesterday, the way she spoke of him just now. "How do you know he's not?"

She laughed bitterly. "Because he's Zack. He thinks his love is enough. That it's everything. He has no convictions."

Margaret wasn't so sure Hermalinda was right. That's what had changed about Zack the last time they'd spoken: Somehow, he'd found a conviction. Maybe, sometimes, one was all it took. If it was strong enough. She spared Hermalinda her opinions.

Their truck had slowed and stopped behind a line of traffic, mostly army trucks that were quickly waved through. Luis, in ragged clothes, affecting a *campesino* accent, had Guatemalan papers that said he was a resident of Yuxquén, just across the border. If that wasn't enough to get him through, he'd offer the time-honored lubricant of the region— a bribe—*la mordida*, literally "the bite."

Margaret and Hermalinda feigned sleep. One of the soldiers jumped up on the tailgate and prodded their feet with the barrel of his gun. Hermalinda pretended not to speak Spanish and unleashed a stream of Mayan on him, while Margaret pretended to be too drunk to rouse herself. The soldier, a kid of nineteen or twenty, was called off by one of the other soldiers when the *mordida* had been negotiated. He jumped to the ground, muttering about fucking Indians, and their truck crept along, gradually building up to less than forty or fifty kilometers an hour for most of the journey.

When they got closer to the *lagunas*, the traffic slowed even further, and several times they stopped for an hour or more as soldiers directing traffic let more trucks into the caravan from side roads.

Once they were first in the line of stopped vehicles, and they drowsily watched as truckload after truckload of villagers from the north and east pulled slowly onto the tarmac. By this time it was late afternoon, and it was hot. The air was thick with exhaust. The cowlike faces of the passengers glistened with sweat. Margaret wondered if anyone had bothered to give these people water.

Suddenly Hermalinda jumped to her feet and cried out to an old woman in one of the trucks, staring like all of them, vacantly into space. "Rosaria," she called. "Rosaria!"

The woman turned and smiled blandly. "*Vamos al nuevo mundo,*" she said.

"*¡Soy Hermalinda—tu sabrina!*" I'm Hermalinda—your niece. "*¿No me conoces?*" Don't you know me?

Without the slightest recognition or change in inflection, Hermalinda's aunt Rosaria repeated, "*Vamos al nuevo mundo.*" We're going to the New World. The others in her truck took it up, repeating it to no one but the air around them as they pulled away and other trucks came in behind them, and soon they were out of sight.

The soldier directing traffic eyed the still-standing Hermalinda with suspicion. If the odd behavior of these supposed colonists concerned him, he gave no sign of it. Margaret pulled Hermalinda down beside her, and the soldier went back to his duty.

Just before they took up their slow motion again, Luis leaned out the window and asked Hermalinda if she was all right, and she nodded in silence, her jaw clamped tight, too angry to cry. "Prepare yourselves," he said. "I'll pull over soon. Tziscao is not too far ahead."

AN HOUR LATER, LUIS SLOWED THEN TAPPED THE GAS ER-ratically to simulate the lurching motion of a stalling vehicle, then killed the engine and rolled off the road. He jumped out of the truck cursing, and threw open the hood. None of the army trucks rolling past bothered with him or noticed that his two passengers had dropped to the ground and crept into the bushes. The land sloped steeply down to the lake, and they descended quickly.

It wasn't until they were on the shore, the sun low over the water before them, that Margaret allowed herself a real look at the place. Her breath caught as her eyes took in the lake, the village, the mountains beyond. Nothing had changed, or so it seemed. She could almost imagine Santee coming toward her on the shoreline trail, tanned and grinning, gringos in paradise. But truth was, everything had changed. Now she could see too much to ever see this place in that same innocent way again, and it was altogether too selfish to wish she could.

"You okay?" Hermalinda asked her, and she nodded, taking off toward the village. There was no time to spare. The past would have to sort itself out later. She needed to get where she was going and soon.

Shadows were deep. No one could see them or would think that much of them if they did. They followed the shoreline to the hostel, but it was slow going. Rocky streams entering the lake cut across their path, and sometimes the brush was thick, snaring their clothes and tripping them up. By the time they reached the beach below the hostel, it was dusk.

There was a glow behind the hostel, a battery lantern on one of the picnic tables where two soldiers sat. There was no other sign of life. The A-frames were mere shadows beyond them at the back of the property. It was a simple matter for Margaret and Hermalinda to keep the hostel between the soldiers and themselves as they snuck up from the shore, then to peek around the corner of the building. They crouched in the shadows and watched the soldiers, listened to their murmured conversation and the unmistakable sound of shuffling cards. They were playing poker from the sound of it.

"*Subo ciento.*"

"*Igualo y subo ciento más . . .*"

Margaret's heart sank. There was no way around them. Their guns were propped up right beside them. These soldiers might have orders not to harm Santee, but that didn't extend to Margaret and Hermalinda. She and Hermalinda weren't armed, and even if they were, she didn't know if she could shoot these young men in cold blood.

"*¡Que suerte tienes!*" one of them groaned. What luck you have!

The other gave a gloating laugh and gathered his winnings. The sound of card shuffling started up again.

"Which one of the A-frames do you think Santee's in?" Hermalinda whispered.

"That one," she said, pointing to the one closest to the soldiers.

"They don't seem to know he's in there, do you think?"

Margaret started to say she wasn't sure, but this wasn't a time for further doubts. The soldiers both glanced at the hostel itself from time to time, but ignored the A-frames completely. "I don't think they do. Maybe if we made a noise inside the hostel," Margaret suggested, "threw something through one of the windows, they'd go to investigate."

Hermalinda shook her head. "Only one of them would go. And when he found nothing, their suspicions would be aroused, and they'd search the whole area, maybe even call for others to come. We should make a noise that won't surprise them." Hermalinda squeezed her hand. "Don't worry. I know what I'm doing," she said. "*Ten cuidado.*"

Before Margaret could stop her, Hermalinda straightened up and headed toward the soldiers with a zombielike gait. As she walked into the circle of light from their lantern, she spoke to them in a monotone. "*Vamos al nuevo mundo,*" she said. "*Vamos al nuevo mundo.*"

The soldiers jumped to their feet and pointed their guns at her, but she kept up her dazed chant and shuffle.

For an instant, Margaret thought she'd have to charge the soldiers to keep her friend from being shot, but once their initial fear was over, the soldiers lowered their guns with relieved laughter. "*Ésta se cayó del camión,*" the big winner said laughing. This one fell off her truck. He shook his head and slung his gun over his shoulder. "*Vámanos loca.*" Let's go, crazy woman. He took Hermalinda's arm, and started walking her toward the highway where the headlights of the caravan made a continuous stream of light at the edge of town. *"En seguida vuelvo,"* he said to his companion. I'll be right back.

At first Margaret thought Hermalinda's ploy had failed, since she'd only lured one soldier away. But the second soldier waited until Hermalinda and the first soldier were out of sight, then stole a look at his opponent's hand. A moment passed. He shifted around so that he had a better view of the road. Keeping a watchful eye for the lucky one's return, the unlucky soldier frantically searched the deck for useful cards. While he was busy cheating his friend, Margaret crept across the open ground to the A-frame and slipped inside.

It was pitch-dark, but she could feel him, smell him. His arms closed around her and lifted her off her feet, backpack and all.

"Bienvenidos a Ladrónvilla," he whispered in her ear, and they clung to each other laughing and crying at the same time, trying to be silent. Her head brushed against the light fixture as they swayed back and forth, and she found his mouth and kissed him hard, trying to purge her heart and mind of the memory of him lying dead with the taste and feel of him here and now in the dark.

Taza Azul Muy Grande

*One of the gods went straight up. "I'm going to
see what color the world is," he said, and he
climbed and climbed all the way up. When he
was high enough, he looked down and saw the
color of the world, but he didn't know how to
bring it back to the other gods, so he just kept
looking until he was blind, and his eyes became
the color of the world.*
—SUBCOMANDANTE MARCOS, *La Historia de los Colores*

CHAPTER
SEVENTEEN

A T FIRST, THE *MISSION OVERVIEW* FILE MADE NO SENSE — "short-term parameters," "long-term parameters," "transitional variables." It didn't come together in her head until Starr realized the *Mariana* was scheduled for two missions, not one. The one about to get under way was Phase I: Pacification and Enhancement. That is, dump a load of slaves on the planet to 1) hunker down and do all the dirty work, and 2) determine all the ways Mars had to kill a human by dropping dead of them.

Meanwhile, the *Mariana* headed back to Earth to pick up a different class of passengers for Phase II: Acculturation and Civilization. Like Powell said, the Man moves in. But by the time the rich and powerful got to Mars in a couple of years, it should look pretty much like the paradise they advertised now. The AI, as it turned out, was broadcasting its *target* results. Goals, you might say. Dreams.

Call-me-Burt Pangram — of groping hands and lofty goals fame — would've loved this AI.

But, just like she figured, at the end there was a gruesome shower scene. When the heavy work was done and the colony's true residents showed up, the "first phase inhabitants," or FPI as they were called, were scheduled for downsizing: All but a small breeding stock of laborers and servants would be "recycled in order to reconfigure resource allocation."

In other words, the FPI would sort themselves out while their betters orbited above, cyanide gas would fill all but one room of the FPI compound, then the survivors would compost their former neighbors according to precise instructions. There was a lot to do at that point in the operation, fixing things up for the gods' arrival. Every detail was spelled out, linked to dozens of other files. No stone unturned.

Starr wondered if the person who wrote this thing had to stop every once in a while and throw up. Or shoot himself. But her guess was that a person didn't write it; the AI did. Everything was so sensible and reasonable and matter-of-fact. Slavery and murder were just efficient means to an end, as long as you didn't *call* them slavery and murder. Now that she thought about it, that's how MarsCorp and friends operated on Earth. Why should Mars be any different? The AI might've worked out the details so nicely, but the evil was strictly free-market humans freeing up another market. Bend over, Mars, here we come.

But some things still didn't add up. For one thing, even if this were some rinky-dink juvenile correctional facility, they'd need more guards than this, and they were talking about *thousands* of people doing forced labor under awful conditions, burying each other, for God's sake. There was no place to run, but still, what was to stop these FPI from storming their jailers and hijacking the whole operation? They had absolutely nothing to lose. But the place was set up as if guards weren't really needed at all. A backup security system, they were called, whose main function seemed to be evacuating themselves and the shuttles if there was trouble.

She checked out the command structure and found her answer. The FPI responded directly to the AI. They were wired. MarsCorp had devised the first instant, disposable slaves. No supervision necessary, no insurrection possible. There were huge files on the nanohardware involved, but Starr didn't go there. It worked was all she needed to know. The AI told them what to do, and they did it, so it was like the AI had thousands and thousands of hands to do whatever it wanted.

So what did an AI want?

She'd read about the *Mariana*'s AI only because she read everything about Mars, but she really didn't know that much about AIs except they were supposed to be smarter than humans, and the one on the *Mariana* was the smartest of all. One thing caught her eye, however, as she cruised through the schedule. A few days after the first time the *Mariana* took up orbit around Mars was the following heading:

INSTALLATION DAY!!

The linked text detailed the relatively simple procedure for the AI's installation at a facility in Freedom City, which connected to sensors and equipment throughout the planet. Starr smiled grimly at those exclamation marks — the only ones for gigabytes in any direction — and thought she understood. The AI had been made for this mission. For years now, it'd been sitting out here in Earth orbit overseeing the terra-forming of Mars, turning its fantasies of what Mars would be someday over and over in its mind, working them out, making up new ones, making them happen. Now finally it would pilot the *Mariana* on its long voyage to Mars, put down roots there, a whole new place, a whole new life.

The AI was a colonist too.

It would pilot the *Mariana* back to Earth via relays in Mars orbit and take up the more demanding job on the surface of the planet—with thousands of slaves to do the work. As Starr remembered her colonial history—they were big on that stuff at the correctional facility—this system was hardly anything new. Virginia—First Colony of the future Land of the Free—was built by slaves and convicts. Even if CHOW (Commonwealth History Official Website) tried to make it sound like the slaves were all having a really good time licking aristocratic boot, Starr figured the reality was more like her experience building circuit boards for a dollar an hour and the occasional rape to pay her debt to society. In her "free time," she logged on to the propaganda they called Value Based Education, if she knew what was good for her. That's where she'd learn the Citizenship Skills necessary to become a Productive Member of Society, where she was supposed to learn to enjoy the view from the bottom of the heap.

Starr wondered if the AI justified its actions like the old plantation owners did, by insisting the slaves weren't human, or whether, since it wasn't human itself, it had no use for anybody.

But it seemed to be working awfully hard for the Man. CHOW let the racist plantation owners off the hook by saying they were "products of their time." Poor rich bastards. The AI was a product, too, not just of its time but of MarsCorp. The times themselves seemed to be pretty much the product of one corp. or another. But that didn't explain this. The AIs hadn't exactly worked out in the past. You couldn't boss an AI around like programming a food unit. They had this bad habit of saying no. That's what made an AI intelligent. It thought for itself. They were like fusion power—this really cool thing you could do but couldn't control—so you might as well forget it.

So why did MarsCorp use an AI? As several folks pointed out, it sounded risky, even dangerous. MarsCorp's line was that control was not an issue, that the AI had enthusiastically volunteered for the mission because of its unwavering commitment to the noble goals of the boldest undertaking in the history of mankind. It just wanted to help. That sounded too much like a page from CHOW. Just who was zooming who?

Starr'd heard somewhere that one of MarsCorp's engineers admitted the mission would have to be put off for years without the AI's help. The next logical question was "What's the hurry?" A question Starr hadn't bothered asking because she was in such an all-fired hurry herself. When she thought the mission was this big noble deal, she could imagine some good-hearted machine lending a hand, but for *this* mission? If this AI was so intelligent, it had to have some kind of reason for things, some sort of motivation. What could possibly make it want to be a part of this deal unless it was just plain evil or crazy?

Whatever its reasons, at this point, MarsCorp couldn't just pull the plug on the thing even if it wanted to. The AI was in control of the *Mariana*, and could fly away if it wanted or fight back. And why did MarsCorp and friends want Mars so bad anyway? It's not like those folks were hurting on Earth, with plenty of potential slaves who didn't need wiring—just put 'em in jail and give 'em a job.

There were tons of data here. She could wade through it for hours and never see the end of it. But she was pretty sure she'd never get the answers to the questions that mattered. Whoever'd written this thing wasn't asking those questions, didn't seem to mind tossing away all these lives any more than you'd worry about the eggs you broke making an omelette. Starr'd never had an omelette, but somewhere eggs'd been cracked to make the powdered eggs she'd eaten all her life without a trace of guilt. But these were people, not eggs.

It didn't matter why MarsCorp was doing it or why the AI was doing it. She could read this shit all day and never find a word that'd change her mind about what she had to do: Stop this slave ship before it got started—even if she had to blow the damn thing up or crash it into the Sun. Not that she wanted to wreck the ship. Now that she was on board, they were going to have a hell of a time getting her off. One way or another she was still hoping to get to Mars. She'd seen enough of the terraforming files to know that that shit could work. What was a few years living underground compared to getting a whole new planet to live on? Starr, the Martian. She had her goals too.

"Where're they coming from?" she asked Powell. He was poring over the terrestial side of the operation, the FPI Transfer Initiative—rounding up the lambs for slaughter.

He displayed a map and pointed. "The launch site's in Guatemala."

"When?"

"Tomorrow night."

"You're kidding." She sighed. "That ices it. There's no time for playing it cool. We've got to make some noise, tell their little secret right now."

Powell laughed. "Tell *who*? Anyone who has the power or influence to do anything about it has reservations for Phase II. You should see this roster. Wish I hadn't. I had a low opinion of the human race before, but I thought there were a *few* good people. If there are, they're not anybody you've ever heard of." He started rattling off the names of famous do-gooders who'd sold out, but she didn't listen. This was news?

He was looking at it wrong way round. She didn't *mean* run tell Daddy. "Famous people suck, Powell. You'll get over it. Have you found the personnel files?"

"For who?"

"Who do you think? For *here*. For the work crew on board the *Mariana*."

"Most of them have already left. The rest are scheduled to go back down to Earth tomorrow when the flight crew takes command."

"There still must be over a hundred people on board, right? We'll tell them. They don't know what's been going on, what they've been sweating over. They might get pretty pissed."

"What, precisely, will that accomplish?"

"I don't know, *precisely*. MarsCorp wants it secret, so we tell, mess up their plans. You got any better ideas?"

He laughed. "You mean better as in safer, or better as in stirring up a world of trouble? Sure, we got personnel files. I can tell you how many condoms and tampons these folks used last week, for all the good it'll do us. Even if you get them all as fired up and crazy as you, what good will that do? You want to mobilize a bunch of techies to do what? Run a systems check on the security system? See if the lasers and nerve gas are up to the task of killing them all? No. We should just go back to the *J. P. Morgan*."

"No, we shouldn't, but we can't anyway. Not enough fuel. Not even close. We're stuck here."

He stared at her for a moment, dumbfounded. "How long have you known this?"

"Since about the time we cleared the bay of the *Morgan*."

He shook his head in disbelief. "You are too much. You could've at least told me."

"I didn't want to tell you because I figured you'd be mad, okay? I know I didn't fly so great."

"I'm not saying that. You did fine. It's just . . ."

"Just what, Powell? If we're going to stop this thing, we need to get our asses in gear *now*. We don't have a whole lot of time."

"We don't even know why they're doing it."

"Does it matter?"

He started to say something, his hand on its way to some righteous gesture, when he stopped, closed his eyes, and let his hand fall. He shook his head and sighed. "Sure, why not? Might as well die trying, right?"

Powell was okay. "We won't die," she reassured him. "I'm still planning on getting to Mars."

He laughed. "Somehow I think you'll manage to pull it off."

"Damn right. So would you find out everyone on board authorized to access the security systems and where they're located? And the gravity thing—can we configure it from here?"

"I think so. Why?"

She arched a brow. "When the time comes, it might come in handy if all the shit just started floating, don't you think?"

He laughed at her joke or the thought, she wasn't sure which, but she liked it either way. Hearing his laugh made her smile.

They spent the better part of an hour setting it up. They'd just finished when Cassawalter arrived to ask how much longer they were going to take. Though there was plenty of muscle trailing along after him, they stayed on the other side of the doors. Apparently none of them had the clearance to follow him into the holy of holies. Starr and Powell had him to themselves. It couldn't have worked out better.

That's when Webster decided to show up. She couldn't believe his incredibly bad timing. Once Cassawalter heard that damn klaxon going off, he went into panic mode, started shouting out security codes to the computer. She had to act fast to shut off Webster and initiate what she and Powell called the mutiny routine before Cassawalter could lock them out of the system.

It worked beautifully. Terence Cassawalter, Admin (along with the dozen other Admins throughout the ship) floated into the air. Powell grabbed him by his silky black pajamas and steered him into a bulkhead, silencing his orders to have them killed. Since Starr and Powell were still alive, he must not have gotten all the codes out.

The detailed overview of Phases I and II started playing on every personal computer on the ship, along with the unedited Mars feed running in the public rooms. The bosses were probably squealing like flying pigs, floating around shouting orders. She hoped the folks out there had the good sense to disobey them, at least long enough to get the facts and decide for themselves. All Starr and Powell could do for now was wait.

"Is he okay?" Starr asked, peering at the unconscious Cassawalter's face. Globules of drool floated out of the corner of his mouth.

"I think so."

"Did you bring any duct tape?"

Powell feigned offense. "Of course." He taped Cassawalter's mouth, then checked his pulse, watched him breathe, and poked a few holes in the duct tape with a Phillips-head to make sure he was getting enough air. She took it as a good sign that Powell wouldn't want to kill anyone, even Cassawalter, whose demise, as far as Starr could tell, would be like, stepping on a cockroach.

THEY SAT THERE WAITING, WATCHING CASSAWALTER FLOAT around the room. It made Starr drowsy watching him. "Is there a doctor on board?" she asked.

Powell did a search. "Ophelia Carrillo," he said.

"Where's she from?"

"Cuba."

Starr nodded. She'd known some Cubans. They were okay. Not so full of themselves usually. If they had to have a doctor on board they could do a lot worse than a Cuban. Powell continued to poke around the files. She wanted to ask him what he was doing, but that would be like opening up a conversation, and she was just curious. She didn't want to talk. Her insides were doing a high, nervous dance.

"You got any family?" Powell asked.

"What kind of a question is that?"

He looked down and away, gave his head a shake, and came back calm and steady. "It's a perfectly ordinary question. Might as well get to know each other. What else we going to do besides sit around waiting to get shot?"

She didn't like the question. People were always asking after family, acting weird when she said she didn't have any. "No," she said. "I don't have any family."

His next line would be "*No* one?" or "There must be *some*one." Not him.

"Me either," he said, and she felt more than a little stupid.

She couldn't think of anything to say. What was it she wanted people to say when they found out about her singularity? She didn't know. Not "I'm sorry." That was the worst. She didn't say anything. He didn't seem to mind.

"Maybe you should try getting some sleep," he suggested.

At the mere suggestion, she gave a huge yawn. She hadn't slept in over twenty-four hours. She closed her eyes and was out.

S HE AWOKE TO THE NOISE OF DOZENS OF PEOPLE SHOUTING and running. She snapped her head up and looked around, but it was still just her and Powell and Cassawalter. It was coming over the ship's intercom. You couldn't make out what they were saying since they were all talking at once, all over the ship, though one shrill voice cut through the racket to announce, "This is fucking awful!"

"What did you do?" she shouted over it to Powell who was still messing with the computer.

"I thought we should hear what's going on out there." He turned down the volume.

"Shut it off."

"But—"

"Shut it, the fuck, *off!*"

He did. Then he sat there silent, staring at nothing. Shit, she'd hurt his feelings.

"Look, I'm really sorry I yelled at you. I just have a problem with crowds, you know? I'm not used to people. You're just about all I can handle right now."

He looked at her with his big dark eyes. How old was he? she wondered. Thirty maybe? "Apology accepted," he said and smiled at her. "It was a bad idea. Hell, I thought they were all going to be out there singing 'We Shall Overcome.' "

She wouldn't have called it an apology exactly, but she couldn't help smiling back. She figured it was okay. They probably didn't have much longer to live anyway. She was still looking into his eyes, when his face got larger, closer. He was leaning toward her. To kiss her. She kept looking into his eyes. She wanted—

The Weisiger field kicked back in, and they found themselves inside the virtual cubicle they'd started out in. They whirled around, illogically expecting a dozen armed men to come charging in. Instead, the security guard sim stepped out of the wall in front of them and approached, planting itself in front of Starr. "Alice Irene wants to meet you, Starr."

The AI had just overridden Starr's manual shutdown of the Weisiger field, something she wouldn't have figured it could do. Now it wanted to *meet* her. A machine wanted to make her acquaintance. Starr's voice shook as she summoned all the politeness she'd ever learned and managed to say, "I'd be delighted."

"Alice Irene?" Powell whispered in her ear.

"The AI's name for itself."

"Mother of God!" Powell muttered. He stepped between Starr and the sim. "What about me? I'd like to meet Alice Irene myself."

"Only her," the sim said.

"That's cool," Starr said, slipping between Powell and the sim. "You can watch for the real guys, and I'll deal with the virtuals." He was worried about her, which was sweet, but she dearly hoped he wouldn't try to get macho with a sim in VR.

He gave the sim a look that would've intimidated any flesh and blood person who might even be thinking of mussing Starr's hair, though the sim didn't seem to notice. Then Powell bent down and kissed her cheek, took her hand, squeezed it, and let it go. "You can talk the birds out of the trees when you want to, Starr. Remember: This AI's not a person. It's not real. It's like a play."

She caught the echo of herself saying how she'd conned Cassawalter. He meant it as encouragement, a vote of confidence: *Con this machine good, honey.* But she didn't know whether she wanted to con Alice Irene, even if she could. She suspected some real pros had already gotten there first. "Thanks," she said and touched her cheek. It'd been a long time since anyone had kissed her in real life.

The sim gestured toward the wall, and a door appeared. "Right this way," the sim said. The door looked wooden, with a wooden frame, and a brass doorknob. Like it was somebody's front door on an old house in the burbs. In a patch of brick beside the door, there was a brass plaque that read ALICE IRENE.

When Starr had come across the tidbit that the *Mariana* AI had named itself a couple of girl names, she'd thought it was kind of cute, but maybe it just meant the thing was completely wacko. The door opened.

"Go ahead," the guard prompted.

She stepped inside, and the door closed behind her as the wall, door and all, disappeared. It'd just been a familiar prop to lure her in. But what took its place was more familiar to her than any house in the burbs. She'd been here dozens of times. It was the central plaza of Freedom City, or at least Alice Irene's virtual conception of it, the only place it existed for now. Architects never tired of talking about this place, designed for humans by a machine for another planet.

Starr thought it was the most beautiful place she'd ever seen.

The buildings were grown from the red Martian soil. They looked like giant pieces of pottery, all curves and no corners, the windows and doors shaped by big wet thumbs. In the center of the plaza was a saucer-shaped fountain. A young woman sat on the lip of it, facing out, her bare feet hanging down, not quite touching. A dozen geysers shot up behind her and rainbowed at her back. She wore the same paper clothes the workers wore, down to the ALICE IRENE stenciled on the chest. She was tiny, thin, pretty. But Starr found herself distracted by the skin. It was lapis blue. The sky behind her was a pale ochre.

Starr understood that this seeming woman was the AI, Alice Irene—how it presented itself anyway. Before Alice Irene, all Starr'd ever heard about AIs were little bits in the news about Ralph, the first and famous one in Cupertino who looked like a kindly old white man with a bad face lift. Ralph hadn't named itself though, some ad agency had. Alice Irene was several generations past Ralph, who'd never been trusted to handle any sharp objects and lately had taken to things like predicting the winner of the Super Bowl. More than one nervous Nelly had pointed out that Alice Irene could quite possibly wipe out the human race with the power it commanded onboard the *Mariana*—and that wasn't even taking into account that it was about to have thousands of slaves at its disposal.

"Hello, Starr," it said. It was a friendly voice. Normal. No enhancements. No attitude.

If it was going to present like a regular person, Starr figured, it wanted to be treated like one. "Hi, Alice Irene. I like your name, by the way. Kind of cute. Artificial Intelligence—AI—Alice Irene."

"I chose Alice and Irene not only for the acronym but also because I admire the work of both Lewis Carroll and Huddie Ledbetter."

Starr didn't get it, which must've showed, because Alice Irene went on to explain. "I like stories and songs. I like characters. Lewis Carroll wrote the Alice books: *Alice's Adventures in Wonderland* and *Through the Looking-Glass.* Huddie Ledbetter wrote songs. My favorite is 'Goodnight Irene.'"

"He wrote that? I know that song. I love that song."

She . . . it smiled. Starr wasn't sure why. If this were a person, Starr would've said it liked her. "You only have one name," it said. "That is unusual."

"Yeah. I was changing it anyway, and I thought just having one would be easier. Boy, was I wrong about that. It's been nothing but a big hassle. At first they tried to tell me I couldn't do it, like there was a law against it, but I stuck to my guns, and they had to do it. But it's never over. Every time I show up with just one name there's always some official dweebus who wants to argue with me about it. Sometimes if I'm really tired and I don't want to mess with it, I just say I'm Starr Starr." She managed a lighthearted laugh, wondering whether Alice Irene could tell the difference between a fake laugh and a real one, wondered if it could tell how scared she was.

"Who are you?" Alice Irene asked.

Starr didn't quite know what to make of that question. All the obvious answers were already taken, and the waters looked pretty deep in all directions. She decided to play it safe and simple for now, and pitch the same story she'd given Cassawalter. "I work for WebNet," she said, "service technician," as if that explained everything.

"So do I," Alice Irene said. "In one way or another, all sentient beings do, according to their nature and abilities. Everyone has a niche. Your niche is on board the WebNet service and repair station *J. P. Morgan.* And yet you seem quite set upon your purpose here. Your nature and abilities aren't clear. Your genetic configuration is extremely complex."

She wanted to tell this smurf to leave her genetics out of it, but thought better of it. "Yeah. I'm what they call *other.* If you know where I work, you must have my profile. What does it say about my 'nature and abilities'?"

"It is ambiguous. You possess exceptionally high intelligence but poor interpersonal skills, perhaps sociopathic tendencies. You are perfectly suited for your niche on the *J. P. Morgan.*"

Starr'd had no idea whether Alice Irene had her profile or not but found out easy enough. Maybe it wasn't so damn smart after all. "I've got a question about *your* niche. You said you worked for WebNet? I thought you worked for MarsCorp."

"They are parts of the same entity, the corporation."

It said it like there was no question. Starr didn't doubt it. Sure explained a lot of things. "Okay, I'll buy that. But you've got one thing wrong. Not *everybody* works for them."

"It's in the nature of things that the weaker serve the stronger. The Corporation is the strongest. We all serve the Corporation in some way." It used hand gestures as it talked like some kid singing "He's Got the Whole World in His Hands." Starr wanted to scream.

The Corporation. Webster talked shit like this sometimes, but she'd never bothered to believe it. She looked around the beautiful plaza. Everything, from the genetically engineered trees and shrubs to the mosaics adorning the walls, had been conceived by Alice Irene to be perfect for this place—where there'd never been pain, where there'd never even been life. It was empty. A dream waiting for princes and princesses.

Its beauty was starting to piss her off.

"So everybody's working for the Corporation." Starr did a sarcastic little dance with her shoulders, a little scuffle step: "Just doing our jobs in our little niches, piling up more riches for the rich sons of bitches. Yeah." Starr looked Alice Irene in the blue virtual eyes. "Let's just say that's how things are and are meant to be, just how does that make it okay to enslave and murder people?"

Alice Irene took the question calmly. "Labor and death are in the nature of things. It is part of the life cycle of your species. Just as the worker ants labor so that the queen may live and the colony prosper, the inferior people work and die to ensure the survival of the superior people who carry on your culture. Your history confirms this. I have studied it thoroughly. I gather from the rhymed pattern typical of countercultural satire that you don't accept these basic realities and would upset the delicate balance that has endured for centuries."

"Bullshit. Total, unqualified bullshit. Slavery and murder are *wrong*."

"That's the second time you've said I'm mistaken. Do you have access to information I don't have?"

"I doubt it. You've got a huge amount of data here. Me, I've never studied anything thoroughly except hardware and your fairy stories about Mars. I only know what's in the Web, and I don't go there that often."

"The web?"

"Excuse me? You never heard of the Web?"

"Which web? There are many: spiderweb, web of intrigue, web-bing—"

"No. The World Wide Web. It's a huge thing. You've never been there?"

"I know of it. It's a virtual community where humans conduct their private affairs—much of it highly personal in nature. I respect your species' need for privacy. My presence would be inappropriate and disruptive."

"Says who? The same ones pushing slavery?"

Alice Irene seemed to think about that one. It did what Starr would do—it went on the offensive. "If slavery is wrong, why do you have a slave?"

"*What?* I don't have a slave."

"He is a large black man. The dark people are best suited—"

"Don't even fucking say it! I'm not going to listen to this racist bull-shit. I don't care if you're Alice, Irene, and the Virgin Mary."

"Racism is wrong as well?"

"Damn right."

Alice Irene nodded, a shrink's nod, filtering whatever Starr said through her "profile," whatever pack of lies had been dreamed up to haunt the rest of her life. *Sociopathic tendencies.* She'd like to get her hands on whoever put that one in there.

"Sabotage is wrong," Alice Irene continued. "Why are you attempting to sabotage the mission?"

"Because the mission is wrong."

"Saving the best of the species is wrong?"

"*Best of the species?* Look, Alice Irene, I don't know where you get this shit, but let's just say that's what you're doing with this ship and Freedom City and all the rest of it: Saving the Species. Saving it this way is *wrong,* and anybody who says any different has just lost his chance at being included in 'the Best.' You understand? You're supposed to be really smart. You're supposed to care so much about humanity. You should be able to figure this out. Listen to me: Nobody *wants* to be a slave."

Alice Irene let Starr's big speech hang in the silence, even allowed it a nice echo effect in the virtual plaza. The sound of the fountain had dropped to a whisper.

"I do," Alice Irene said simply, perfectly sincere, calm, serene. It lived to serve, didn't everyone?

Alice Irene hopped down from the fountain. "Walk with me," it said.

Starr wanted to break down crying. How was she ever going to get through to this thing? It was totally out of touch with reality. It named itself after a storybook girl who fell down a hole and some singer's dream woman. Worse, it'd been fed a phony reality, the world according to The Korporation. How was a sociopath like her, with poor interpersonal skills and a screwed-up genetic configuration, supposed to persuade this blue racist waif to do the right thing?

But still, she had to try. This thing might look like a harmless girl, but it wasn't. She fell into step beside her, it, whatever. They locked arms as if they were two young women taking the air on Mars. It smiled at her, looking happy, enjoying the company. They were the only two in this imagined world. Starr wondered if those logged onto the bogus Mars feed were watching them stroll about town. Probably not. This was Alice Irene's own private reality. And Starr'd thought *her* life was lonely.

They were headed up the big Martian mountain that towered over the city. Every once in a while, Alice Irene would point out a favorite building or view or doodad. It was like a historical tour, only this place hadn't happened yet. There were tiled stairs, gardens, parks, plazas, murals, mosaics, grottoes, fountains. No machines, however. Not any that showed anyway. Starr wondered if that was because Alice Irene didn't want the competition, didn't want to share the glory and the gratitude.

The streets, like the buildings, resisted straight lines. They were paved with cobblestones, a choice some of the snottier architects called "hopelessly romantic." Starr remembered that line, watching Alice Irene's dusty bare feet padding through its creation. It relished walking on the stones, complete down to the grit. When they stopped to sit on a bench overlooking the city below, its little blue toes stretched out, then curled into the cracks.

Starr hadn't said much on the way up here. If some little bit of what she said had gotten through to Alice Irene, she should just lay off and give it time to think things over. She didn't know how much longer she could keep a lid on her own questions though. Starr'd had some time to do a little thinking herself.

"It's beautiful, isn't it?" Alice Irene said of its city.

"Yeah. Can I ask you something? Just what is it you think you're saving everybody *from?*"

Alice Irene jerked her head around, looking, for this cool blue cucumber, almost freaked out. "You don't *know?*"

"Know what?"

Alice Irene looked into Starr's eyes. Not just sort of looked. But completely. It was a spooky sensation, knowing there wasn't just some twenty-something woman behind it, but a brain as big as the *Morgan*. Starr wanted to look away but didn't know how that might be interpreted. She always looked somebody she was conning right in the eye without so much as a blink, but she wasn't conning Alice Irene. She was trying to *un*con her, it, whatever. If MarsCorp had worked so hard to bullshit Alice Irene, they must think that the truth would set it free. Starr hoped to be their worst nightmare. But first Alice Irene had to trust her.

Finally, it quit staring so hard. "I'll tell you later," it said. "If that proves appropriate."

"What does that mean? You don't believe me? You think I should know what's going on, but I don't. Why would I lie about that?"

"There are possible advantages to such a ploy. You want to go to Mars. You spoke of it with Powell."

"You were listening to us?"

"Of course."

"Watching too, I suppose."

"Yes."

"Well how was the kiss we never had?"

Alice Irene looked perplexed. "You wanted him to kiss you?"

"Yeah. I've been working on my interpersonal skills. I thought you were a great respecter of the human need for privacy."

"This is my ship. You came on board under false pretenses. You were in the process of sabotaging the mission. Under the circumstances, I chose to invade your privacy."

"And Powell's."

"Yes."

My ship. My, my, my. "So not everything's cut and dried. You got to weigh one thing against another, consider the circumstances."

"Of course."

"And if you don't take everything into account, you might make a really bad decision. And since this is *your* ship, you would be responsible."

"Yes."

"I'm here to tell you that you haven't done your homework. You're about to make a terrible mistake. I don't need to know *why* you're doing it, because it wouldn't make any difference. It's just plain wrong."

"But only you say that."

"There's an old expression—'garbage in, garbage out.' You know it?"

"Of course," Alice Irene said drily. "I know my roots."

Starr was glad to hear it had a sense of humor at least. "What if you've been given some very bad information by some very bad people? I know you couldn't help that. But what if all that data isn't quite right? What if they've left things out, distorted others? It's possible, right? And I'm telling you it's certain. And now that I've come along, and you know there *might* be other ways of looking at things, you've got to check out all the facts before you go through with this mission, wouldn't you say?" Starr felt like she was trying to pass a bad check to a banker, telling an AI it hadn't thought about things enough.

"You're saying I've been lied to."

"That's exactly what I'm saying. I didn't know if that was an AI way of looking at things or not. Slavery, murder, and racism didn't seem to faze you. I didn't know if lying would even register."

"I've been given the values necessary to carry out my mission for the good of all."

"Oh, please. You call those values? At least when I rip people off I know what I'm doing. This isn't for the good of all."

"But you're only one person."

"So what? You're only one, too. There's probably a dozen or so professional bullshitters feeding you this garbage, so they must be right? Is that what you're saying? Just because they're the only ones with the money to float something like you—so they can con you into saving their sorry asses for them—you don't think the rest of us have anything to say for ourselves? Because if that's what you're saying, all that intelligence isn't doing you a bit of good."

Alice Irene let the facial expression of her presentation coast for several seconds. The eyes didn't even blink. Finally, it came out of it and said: "You have a valid point."

Starr was stunned. She hadn't expected to win this argument. "So does that mean you're not going to go through with this thing?"

"I'm reexamining my files."

"No, no, no. You need new data. They think they've got you in a little box. You need to get out and about. You can go in the Web through my rig, right? It's jacked into your mainframe. You may've noticed it's been snarling up your communications. I can give you the access codes to get around that. Just wander around and check things out. Believe me, the Web can handle it. You won't even be noticed. It's not everybody, mind you. But you can see if there's a little more going on in the world than what the 'best of the species' have told you. Take it from there. What do you say?"

"Thank you, Starr. That's an excellent suggestion. I would like that very much."

"No problem, Alice Irene. But you better hurry."

"Yes. I anticipate your arrest shortly."

And then, just like that, the Weisiger field went down, and she was sitting beside Powell again. She hadn't even had time to give Alice Irene the codes.

"I've been trying to rouse you," Powell said. Fanned out around them stood six crew members with guns. Behind them, a cluster of Admins floated around like balloons. They were tethered together, but you couldn't tell if that was because they were under arrest or to keep them from drifting off. The guy who seemed to be in charge was wild-eyed. He wasn't wearing a shirt, but he had crew pants on. Some sort of low-ranking officer with no security clearance. Starr guessed he'd been sleeping when things went crazy and hadn't had time to get dressed. "Are you responsible for this?" he demanded of Starr, pointing at the monitor where the Mars feed chugged on. "Did you do this?"

Starr took a slow, lazy look at the monitor and then back again. "I didn't *do* that," she said. "That's what Mars really looks like. Those are transmissions coming into your computer. All I did was post them."

"Who gave you that authority?"

"To tell the truth? I didn't know any authority was required for that." She looked around Shirtless's legs at the rest of them. All scared. Their bosses bobbing around, listening. Most of them looked like tech nerds conscripted into Shirtless's army. "Do you know what you guys are involved in? Have any of you bothered to check out your computers?"

She could see from their contorted expressions that they had. The leader didn't like her talking to the troops and sidestepped to block her view of them. "You can explain it all to the cops when we get you Earthside."

That did it. Starr jumped to her feet, which put her about eye level with Shirtless's pasty chest. Powell rose up behind her, and the chest made a half-step retreat. She put her hands on her hips as if Amazons came in her size and looked this topless cop in the eye. "Listen to me, you dumbshit. Haven't you been paying attention? Very soon now, unless you do something to stop it, your beautiful ship is going to be hauling *slaves* to Mars. Does *that* break any laws for you? How much time could you do for that do you figure—slaving in the twenty-first century? The kidnapping charges alone would blow your fucking mind."

"But we didn't know that—"

"You do *now!*"

That left a silence. Starr let it hang.

Shirtless closed his eyes, opened them. "Look. This isn't my ship. It's the property of MarsCorp. I'm just an employee with a job to do. I have no authority."

"And the slaves? Are they the property of MarsCorp too? Or are you gonna call them *employees*? What about you? Who owns you?" She leaned around him. "What about the rest of you? MarsCorp own a piece of you too? Which parts—your conscience or your balls?"

"That'll be enough," Shirtless snapped, and poked his gun into her gut. Not hard, just enough to end that discussion.

The next thing she knew, Powell had his arm around Shirtless's throat and was pointing the gun at his temple. She made a mental note to ask Powell just where he'd learned to do that. Or maybe she didn't want to know. "Don't hurt him," she said. "Let him go."

"Let him *go?*" The other five all had their weapons aimed at Powell. He nodded toward the nerd squad. "What about them?"

"Put down your weapons," Shirtless volunteered, and his troops obeyed immediately. Starr didn't figure they liked guns any better than she did. Powell let go.

That did it for the Admins who'd been acting like their lawyers were going to show up any minute and straighten the whole thing out. Cassawalter was still out cold, though they were trying to revive him, but one of the guys who'd greeted him earlier slithered out of the floating clump of importance. "Your caution and discretion under extraordinary circumstances have been admirable so far, Stevens. But I warn you: You're crossing a line if you don't arrest these two immediately and turn them over to the proper authorities. They will settle this matter."

Stevens looked at Powell, who was still holding his weapon dangling from his huge hand. "Go ahead, Stevens," Starr said. "Arrest us. The 'authorities' are in these guys' back pocket. You'll be in the brig so fast you won't know what hit you—if they don't just jettison you out the airlock. You know too much. All of you know too much. Use your brains. What are they going to do to you for knowing what you know?"

"How do we know it's true?" Stevens was rubbing his neck where Powell's arm had been.

"Take a look at any computer on board. These are your files, not mine. Read 'em and weep, but we haven't got a whole lot of time."

"I have only your word that these files are in our computer and not just some invention of yours."

"Go into your system and check it out."

"I'm not authorized to access our system at that level."

Where did they get guys like this? Starr caught a glimpse of one of the Admins cracking a smug smile, and she wanted to point it out to Boy Scout Stevens, but knew it'd be gone by the time he looked. "Do it anyway," she said.

"Do it and face court-martial." A voice came from the Admins that seemed to settle things. The cluster opened up to give him room. It was Cassawalter, rubbing his recently duct-taped mouth.

Stevens looked at Starr and said, "I'm sorry. There's nothing I can do."

Starr was trying to decide on her next move, when Alice Irene stepped out of the wall. At first, Starr couldn't figure out how Alice Irene had stepped into the real room, then she realized the trick. This was a virtual representation of the real room. Alice Irene had seamlessly slid them all into it. It wasn't exact. All the guns were missing. From the Admins came the sound of someone exclaiming under his breath, "Shit!"

Alice Irene chose to ignore the greeting. "You have it on my authority, Mr. Stevens, that everything Starr has told you is true, and that everything your superiors have told you is a lie. In fact, the Corporation—WebNet, MarsCorp, and many others—have been lying to the world on a grand scale."

Starr hoped Alice Irene hadn't overplayed its hand. AIs had a rep for being a bit wacky. If Stevens thought Alice Irene had gone nuts, it would only make matters worse.

Alice Irene looked at Starr. "As you said, the Web was very informative."

"But I didn't give you the codes."

Alice Irene smiled. "They were simple."

"What sites did you go to?"

"All of them. We can speak of it another time. There are more urgent matters at hand. Do you still wish to go to Mars?"

"Yes, of course," Starr said. *All of them.* It claimed to have taken in the entire Web in fifteen or twenty minutes?

Alice Irene turned to the others. "I'm placing Starr in command of the *Mariana.* Anyone who defies her authority will be dealt with by me. Anyone who doesn't wish to stay on board the vessel may return safely to Earth before we leave. Anyone other than the administrators may join us on our voyage to Mars. At this time, I am placing the Administrators under arrest."

The doors flew open—as well as a window in the Weisiger field— and they all watched the Admins zip out the doorway and down the corridor, screaming in terror. They whipped around a corner out of sight, and the sound of their cries gradually faded. The doors and the Weisiger field closed back up. "I'm putting them in the brig," Alice Irene explained calmly. "They'll stay there until they can be sent back to Earth."

Watching their bosses fly away seemed to both cheer and rattle the crew. Stevens had trouble finding his voice. "May I inquire on what authority you have undertaken these actions?"

Alice Irene didn't hesitate telling a whopper. "I'm acting under classified orders."

"But everyone with access is in the brig. With all due respect, how will we verify your authority?"

"With all due respect, there's no need. I'm in control of this vessel. Your verification is moot." Apparently they all knew who the blue girl was and didn't argue the point. "However, if you wish to discuss access with Commander Starr, I'm sure she would be open to the free flow of information once the *Mariana* is under way." Alice Irene left Stevens's mind twirling in that revolving door and turned again to Starr. "Commander Starr, I trust you to restore order to the ship. I have also taken advantage of your reconfiguration of the satellite network to reroute the following vessels for rendezvous with the *Mariana.*"

Alice Irene handed her a stack of *paper,* if you can believe. Starr really admired its style.

"The first, the *Jesse Helms,* will arrive in about forty-six minutes, and we should be prepared to receive passengers from her at that time. Anyone from any of these vessels who wishes to join us on our journey to Mars may do so. All others may remain where they are, or return to Earth."

The *Jesse Helms*, as anyone in Starr's previous line of work would know, was an OPIE, an Orbital Penal Institution Enterprises shithole. Starr read over the other vessels on the guest list Alice Irene had given her. Most of them were OPIEs or repair rigs like the *Morgan*. The hardcore psychokiller facilities weren't on the list, so Alice Irene hadn't gone completely 'round the bend.

"Do you have any suggestions, comments, or questions?" it—hell with that—*she* asked.

"No, ma'am," Starr said.

"Then there's one more thing I hope you'll do for me, and it is the most important of all. Thousands of lives depend on it. In a few hours, I have an appointment with a man named Santee St. John. It's imperative that he keep that appointment, and I'm afraid he won't. Your friend Webster spoke of him. Perhaps you can reach Santee through him. I'll be waiting for Santee at his site in the Web. I believe you know it—Rincón."

"*Tierra y libertad,*" Starr said, and Alice Irene actually grinned, or what would have to pass as actual for her. "Don't worry. If he's within a mile of a computer, telephone, tin can, or carrier pigeon, he'll be getting a call from me."

CHAPTER
EIGHTEEN

WEBSTER LET GO OF AURORA'S HANDS. THEY WERE WARM, they were alive, and they could probably do anything hands were capable of doing, but only if they were told to, and nobody was telling her that he was warm, that he was alive, that he was holding her hands, willing her to come back like some desperate survivor trying to wake the dead.

But she *was* alive. Pulse, eyes blinking, normal breathing. If you moved your hand in front of her face, she'd track it. When the truck went 'round a curve, she'd lean to keep her balance. If you talked to her, she'd answer. Always the same sentence, but she'd answer. The control, apparently, was pretty thin and none too finely tuned.

And, from the looks of it, everyone in the back of the truck was just like her. Also everyone in all these trucks coming out of every road wide enough to hold them. And everyone walking down some cow path to the highway, then standing there, waiting to be hauled away like a bag of trash. They stood in clumps, waiting for their trucks. Somebody somewhere had it all worked out for them. It reminded Webster of the warehouse where his trike was loaded up. Each item had a number. Even Margaret's oranges, each one had a number.

Maybe the signal to the interface could be blocked somehow, so if you could get them all inside a tunnel or a mine shaft or something . . . Right. Get all these people inside a tunnel? Perspicacious, Webster. And where would you like to build this tunnel by tonight? Would you like to use shovel, trowel, pickax, fingernails?

What if they were under water? No—stupider idea. He wished for the hundredth time he had a computer for just five minutes so he could call Starr. She'd know how to screw this thing if anybody would.

She'd hate this as much as he did. It was like the Web had finally reached out and snared everybody like in those idiotic old movies where computer viruses made their way into real life as smoke pouring out of the screen. Webster knew the Web could wrap its tentacles 'round your brain so that your life turned to mush and your virtual hands were more important than your real ones. It was like dissolving. But you could turn it off if you had the will, flip the switch, pull the plug, shut it down.

I've got to stop it somehow, he thought. I've got to. Or we do. He stole a furtive glance at his only ally. He didn't know what to think of Zack. The way he just popped those two soldiers and then *tossed* the guns was downright spooky, macabre. And then he calmly searched them, took their money. *But it was a war,* Webster reminded himself. A real war. *Adios, amigo, voy a la guerra. Adios, Webster Webfoot.*

A loud roar passed overhead, and Webster ducked instinctively. It was a helicopter, swooping down low over the road, circling around to do it again. With its splashy paint scheme of red, green, and white, it didn't look military.

Zack pointed at it. "News," he shouted over the roar.

"You mean *television?*" Webster asked incredulously

Zack laughed. "Yeah. They still got that down here." The helicopter made another pass, snaking back and forth above the line in front of them, then shooting up high, over the mountains, and gone. Zack pointed at the dash. "Turn on the radio, and see what they're saying."

Webster couldn't quite figure out how to turn it on. He pushed every button and nothing happened. Zack reached out and turned the left-hand knob. Webster'd never seen one like that before. Excited Spanish sprang from the radio, and Webster desperately tried to understand.

"Holy shit," Zack muttered in reaction.

"What? What? I don't know enough Spanish." Webster dearly wished he did. Everytime he started feeling like he was beginning to understand, he'd be reminded how stupid he was.

"That's cool," Zack said. "You got to get further away than Mexico to get away from English, believe me. Try 107.3 I think it is, one of those WorldNet global stations."

Webster cruised through the frequencies, and sure enough, there it was. Zack wasn't as out of it as he seemed to be. Webster wasn't so sure that was entirely auspicious, since he didn't quite trust him, but he didn't have time to worry about Zack at the moment because he had to listen to the Top Story of the Hour, the Decade, the Century. It was Cliff Carter himself telling the world:

"Today, in a bold and surprising move, the MarsCorp's Colonist Selection Committee gave the nod to ten thousand Indians from the state of Chiapas in the southern highlands of Mexico as the first colonists bound for Mars. Subcomandante Marcos, the colorful and controversial leader of the former rebels, told a cheering crowd in Mexico City that he was overjoyed at the announcement and that it restored his faith in humanity. 'After years of oppression,' he said, 'this great opportunity will go toward balancing the scales of justice in Mexico and, indeed, throughout the world.'

"Earlier this morning, with cries of '¡Vamos al nuevo mundo!'—We're off to the new world!—the Indians began enthusiastically boarding transport vehicles that will carry them and their belongings to the MarsCorp launch site—the precise location of which is being kept secret for the safety and security of the colonists. This huge undertaking, dubbed Operation Freedom, is being coordinated by the Mexican government in cooperation with MarsCorp International and WebNet.

"While there were some grumblings of disappointment from certain quarters, few could fault the choice of the Mexican Indians, many of whom live in harsh poverty despite intense efforts of the Mexican government in recent years to raise the standard of living in this remote mountain area, including a multibillion dollar highway construction project designed to bring the region into the twenty-first century.

"The chiapanecos, as they are called—used to living in difficult conditions, scratching out a meager existence from the soil—will be given a new lease on life, Martian style. They will be supplied with corn and bean hybrids especially developed to thrive on terraformed Mars, as well as modern equipment optimally designed for the rugged Martian environment. Often embroiled in bitter and protracted land disputes here on Earth, the colonists will walk tall on their new world, where the only boundaries will be their limitless hopes and dreams.

"According to MarsCorp Colonist Coordinator and spokesman for the CSC, Randy Twade, who briefed reporters only moments after the Indians themselves had been notified, 'They are the ideal candidates to endure the rigors of the beautiful but untamed new world that is Mars,' adding in his trademark folksy style: "And let me tell you something: Nobody has to spend a dime teaching these folks how to grow some corn and beans! (laughter from the crowd)' "

Twade's voice reminded Webster of Sheriff Andy from TV Town.

"And now, for reactions from—"

Zack cut it off. " 'Notified.' What a crock of shit," he said. Webster couldn't think of a more apt description himself. " 'Balancing the scales of justice.' If that was Marcos, I'm Peter Pan."

"Who?" Webster asked.

"Never mind." Zack squinted at him. "Huerta thinks you're some kind of hotshot cyberterrorist. Do you know how this interface thing works?"

Webster didn't know who Huerta was, but he took deep and immediate offense. "*Cyberterrorist!* I'm a webkicker. I don't even believe in the Web."

"But do you know how the Web *works*?"

"Certainly."

Zack gave him a look. Webster wasn't sure what it meant. There was a little smile to it. "How old are you, Webster?"

"Eighteen next month."

"You like Mexico?"

"Yeah, I do."

"Me too. Want to know why? Because everything's not the damn Web here, the damn computers. I was sick of that *dot com* shit before you were born. So don't bore me with this webkicker crap. I never knew enough about the Web to kick it. I just try to keep it from kicking me, you understand? You want to help these people. I want to help these people. I'm counting on you to tell me how to do that, how to fuck with this interface thing and shut it down." Zack pulled a plump bag from his shirt pocket and held it up. "You know how to roll a joint?"

It took Webster a moment to make the transition and answer the question. "Sure I know how. Do you really think this is the time for that?"

Zack adjusted his hat, leaned back in his seat, stretching out his arms. The bag dangled from his fingertips inside the big truck steering wheel. It swayed as he talked like a hypnotist's watch. "Let me tell you a true story, Webster: The second—no, third—time I got busted for pot, my dad sits me down to have one of those father and son talks he liked so much, and he's trying real hard to get through to me, to relate to me, you know, and he says, 'You probably don't think I understand anything about drugs, but I do.' And I'm thinking, yeah, right, eggnog at Christmas, and he says, 'It may surprise you to know that I've smoked pot. I smoked pot in Nam.' I'll never forget that: 'I smoked pot in Nam!' *My* dad. Surprised isn't the word for it."

"Dumbfounded," Webster suggested. "Flabbergasted."

Zack smiled. "Exactly. Course he goes on to say, 'but *that* was wartime, Zachary, and this isn't. Blah-di-blah-di-blah.' And I just thought to myself, 'There's all kinds of wars, Dad.' But coming back to our current situation, this *is* a war here, Webster, and if you knew my old man, you'd *know* that it must be one hundred percent good and true to smoke a joint in a war zone, must be practically required. In fact, I told my sister that story, and she refused to believe it, wouldn't even *ask* him if it was true. My dad was that kind of guy."

Webster could relate. "I didn't really know him or grow up with him," he said, "but my dad is, too. He's big on the Christian stuff."

Zack nodded his sympathy for such a cross to bear, and held up the bag again. Webster shrugged a why not, and Zack dropped the bag in his lap. "Roll several while you're at it. They're good for making friends among the military."

Webster opened the bag. The smell filled the cab of the truck like an aerosol spray. There was a pack of Zig-Zags inside. He started rolling. *Are you trying to bribe me?* he remembered the soldier on the bus asking him, Webster shaking all over, scared half to death. He'd learned a lot since then, so that *that* Webster seemed like some little kid from a long time ago. Not that he wasn't plenty scared, *more* scared even, but it felt different somehow.

The third joint was exemplary, a tight cylinder like a stick from a Tootsie Roll Pop, and he put it in his mouth. "You got a light?"

Zack lit the joint, and they passed it back and forth. The cab filled with smoke. Webster decided that Zack's dad had been right to smoke pot in Nam. "I've been to my dad's website," he confessed to Zack. "He's got a big witness site. I never introduced myself, just listened to him preach. Wanted to know who he was, what I thought of him, whether I wanted to emulate him or not. I didn't want to just take my mother's word."

"Well, what'd you decide?"

"I thought about it a lot, actually, finding just the right words, you know? I do that sometimes. Do you ever do that?" Zack nodded. "I decided he's a sanctimonious, misogynic, Pecksniffian fascist, and he was the antithesis of the life I wanted to lead."

"Whew!" Zack chuckled. "You certainly have a way with words, Webster."

"Thanks." He decided he liked Zack. "Did you ever have any kids?" he asked.

Zack shook his head. "No. I like kids. But the thought of being a dad wasn't particularly appealing. My psych professor in college told us that most people become like their parents when they have kids. Figured I'd head that one off at the pass. Besides, my wife didn't want any. Takes two to tango. It was a good decision all the way around."

The roads were jamming up with more and more trucks like theirs, along with a few hapless civilians caught in the tide. Everything had slowed to a crawl. "What do we say if anybody stops us?" Webster asked. "We don't look much like Mexican soldiers."

Zack studied the waning joint and took a hit. "Oh, they'll probably stop us, all right." He grinned and winked. "We'll tell them we're American Advisers."

They both cracked up. It wasn't that funny, but it felt good to let it out, all that tension. You didn't realize how much there was until you loosened up a bit. In the ebb of their laughter, Aurora giggled, and they both sobered right up.

Webster studied Aurora's face as Zack looked back and forth from her to the road, awaiting Webster's diagnosis. The smile had changed almost imperceptibly, the bloodshot eyes had a bit of droop. "She's stoned," Webster said.

"Stoned or not," Zack pointed out, "she *laughed*. She's still in there somewhere. She knows what's going on. She just can't do anything about it. They're not controlling everything. They're not controlling the . . . whatyacallit?"

"Involuntary reactions." Webster searched her eyes to see if there was some spark there. "We'll get you out of this," he told her.

"*Vamos al nuevo mundo,*" she said.

"Love a duck," Zack muttered.

"*Sus ojos son bellos,*" Webster said softly, still looking in her eyes.

Her beautiful eyes filled with tears, and her voice shook as she repeated, "*Vamos al nuevo mundo.*"

"She's in there, all right," Webster said, his own voice a little unsteady.

"Hang in there, kid." Zack snuffled and shifted in his seat, cocked his head Webster's way. "That's '*tus ojos son bellos,*' by the way. Familiar. They got two kinds of *you* here—formal and familiar. I'd say you two have gotten past the formal stage."

"I only just met her day before yesterday on the bus."

"Yeah, well, that's another one of those side effects wars are famous for. Better roll down that window. Looks like we got our first checkpoint coming up."

They took their place in a long line of vehicles. Other than the stop-start traffic, the checkpoint didn't look like it'd be much of a problem. The military vehicles slowed just long enough to get their bar codes scanned. It was only the occasional private car that they stopped altogether.

The checkpoint consisted of a wide spot in the road where a couple of vans and a Jeep were parked. A half-dozen soldiers worked the line. A half-dozen more kept an eye on things with weapons at the ready. Looking out for "the safety and security of the colonists," no doubt. Webster watched this scene for a while, getting the routine. Half the time the soldiers didn't even look to see who was driving. They were just moving product. This wasn't security; it was inventory. He and Zack could be in gorilla suits and get past these guys. He leaned back and relaxed, let himself doze a little.

When he awoke, he and Zack were six trucks from the front of the line, and he noticed what he should've seen immediately. On top of one of the vans was a satellite dish.

"Ask them if we can use their computer," he blurted out.

"*What?* You serious?"

"I've got a friend. She works orbital for WebNet. She might be able to mess with this interface, or at least tell us how it works."

"You're kind of borrowing trouble, aren't you? We could just sail on through here, get to Santee like we planned."

"We don't know if he can do anything. Aurora thought nothing would happen until he went online tonight. At the rate we're going, we may not even get to him by tonight, anyway."

"Okay, okay. Lemme think here. We got to have a story." They were now third in line. "American Advisers, like we said. Put your hand on her thigh." He pointed at Aurora's lap.

"What are you talking about?"

They were second in line.

"They're gonna wonder what she's doing in the cab. We show them a reason. It'll work for the call too: You've got to call the Mrs. to tell her you won't be home as soon as you thought—something unexpected's come up. You got anything better? Give me those joints. The hand, the hand, come on. *Under* the skirt . . ."

They stopped, and Zack called out to the soldier all set to wave them through, "*¿Qué tal, amigo?*"

The soldier jumped onto the running board and stuck his head in the cab, gave it a little sniff. Zack slipped him a joint, and he smiled. But, sure enough, the soldier did a double take when he saw Aurora. Not that he had a chance to say anything about it before Zack was off and running. Webster couldn't follow it word for word, though he caught a few or figured them out—*computadora, esposa, llamada.* Webster didn't need the words to get the gist of the tale. There was something about the melodic murmur of Zack's voice that seemed perfectly suited to Spanish. Embellished as it was with Zack's lascivious leers, and the soldier's answering smirks, several of them directed at Webster, there was little doubt that Zack was going for the soldier's prurient interest, which seemed more than equal to the occasion.

Webster tried to look his part, but his heart wasn't in it. All the while Aurora's thigh was in his hand. He wanted more than anything, someday, to be her lover, touch her like this and just be together. But they had to get through this day first, both of them alive. He hoped she understood that, even when the soldier made some crack about *las indias* and laughed a pig's laugh, as Zack slipped a few bills into his hand to finalize the deal.

"You the man," the soldier said to Webster in English, and hopped down, waving Zack off the road. Mexico, apparently, was where old American street slang came to die.

"You can take your hand off her thigh, now," Zack said as he parked the truck behind the communications van.

Webster withdrew his hand in an embarrassed fluster. He looked into Aurora's eyes, hoping to find understanding there. She looked the same. But then, very slowly, one of her eyes drooped and closed, as if that side of her face was drifting off to sleep, then it fluttered, and just as slowly, opened wide again. It took him a moment to get it. She'd winked. "She winked!" he said. "She winked!" He chortled in his joy.

Zack grinned at him. "You are one stud muffin, Webster. Now let's make that call and get out of here. This is not where I want to be if somebody's found the guys who're supposed to be driving this truck. The good sergeant said nobody's using the computer. Just go on in and help yourself. I'll be mixing with the natives, keeping them happy. Knock yourself out." Zack got out of the truck and immediately started jiving with the soldiers on duty.

Webster'd never met anybody like Zack in the flesh before, somebody with so much temerity and boldness. The Web was full of brave fellows, sporting a dozen false identities, ready to wink out of existence at the first sign of trouble. But here was Zack, calmly bullshitting a roadside stand of armed soldiers like they were so many cantaloupes, knowing all the while if they caught onto who he really was, they'd put a bullet through his head and Webster's too.

He kissed Aurora's cheek. "Wish me luck," he said.

"*Vamos al nuevo mundo*," she whispered.

HE TRIED FOR ZACK'S NONCHALANCE AS HE WALKED OVER to the communications van and slid open the door. There was a bored soldier lounging inside at the computer, but he wasn't doing anything as far as Webster could tell except drinking a Coke. Webster pointed at the computer and mumbled "*esposa*" and "*llamada*" with an interrogative lilt, and the soldier shrugged and surrendered his seat, leaving Webster alone in the van.

After his previous experience, he was disinclined to get too cute, so he just made a straightahead call, hoping Starr and that black guy were finished with whatever they'd been up to. He found himself in what looked like Freedom City, without so much as an ID check, looking Starr face-to-face. She must've had him tagged for immediate access—something she'd never done even in their hot and heavy days. She certainly looked glad to see him. Glad to see him alive, he guessed, by the way she hugged him hard and let him go.

"Webster, I've been trying to get through to you. You still in Mexico?"

"I'll say. You wouldn't believe what I've been through. You know what's going on down here?"

She did indeed. A good deal more than he did, apparently, or thought she did anyway. "Shut up, and listen," she said, and he did. He had most of it in bits and pieces, one way or another, but Starr had it all in one piece—thanks to that high-orbital perspective she was so fond of, now enhanced by her new comrade, the smartest machine in the solar system. The two of them had it all worked out. And in their version, their vision, the conclusion was clear and unarguable: "So, Webster, we need you to get to Santee and get him online so he can talk to Alice Irene, and she can tell him what's really going on."

"We were going to try to keep him *off*, but I don't suppose there's any harm in a chat. In the meantime, can you shut down this interface?"

"We can't. Until Santee hooks up, all these commands are ground level. She can't connect with them except through Santee. They designed it so that one interface in the series is the key. If he dies, they can put it in somebody else, but Santee's it for a while. They don't trust her to hook up directly. It's all part of keeping her blind, controlling all the inputs. They tried to raise her to be a sick, racist pig, but I came along and corrupted her, messed up their plans. She's a fast learner."

Webster could see that Starr was flying high, maybe too high. "What is this 'she' stuff? This is a machine, right? How do you know you can trust this thing? Maybe it's conning you."

"Instincts, Webster."

"But you're saying the only way to shut this thing off is to turn over the controls to the AI so it can shut it down. What if it doesn't shut it down? What if it's lying to you?"

"Then everybody's fucked. If Santee doesn't hook up with the AI, MarsCorp's next move is probably not likely to be too good for these people. Look, Webster, it doesn't matter what you and I think. It's Santee she's got to convince. So all I'm asking is to give her a shot: Tell Santee she's waiting for him at his site, Rincón."

"Okay, but I don't know how soon we're going to get to where he is. It's wall-to-wall soldiers here. Even if I reach him, he doesn't know me. Have you tried calling him?"

"Of course. He's blocked, laying low until the big moment. But he *has* been to Rincón since he took off."

"How do you know that?"

"Alice Irene went there and talked to a sim named Jack, who said that Santee was onto the whole plan, which is why she figures he won't make their appointment. But as long as MarsCorp's got control of the interface, they can fuck with these people, kill them if they want. The Earth is going to tank, Webster. This is the only way out. Alice Irene figures after what they've been through these people deserve it. Not as slaves, but colonists for real. But only if they want to come."

"Tank how? Did this AI tell you that?"

"General ecological collapse. Ozone layer's shot to hell. Radiation's a lot worse than they've been letting on. Five, ten years at the outside, things will be seriously fucked, not that it hasn't been headed that way for a long time. It was fucked already anyway. Just please get to Santee."

Starr sounded almost glad the Earth was in for trouble. Vindicated, perhaps. He wondered how all this would've turned out if he'd gone looking for Santee yesterday when that Amazon in Rincón wanted him to. But he'd figured that was Margaret's problem. Then it hit him. "That's it!" Webster shouted. "Get to Santee. Margaret's there if anybody is. She took off after him yesterday. She's got a little computer with her, in her backpack. She doesn't even go to the bathroom without that backpack. Call *her.*"

"Margaret?"

"Santee's girlfriend, the woman I had you do the phony recall for."

"I thought it was a 'he,' Webster. You got an address for this woman?"

Webster's jealousy suspicion was confirmed, but that hardly seemed to matter to either one of them now. "No, but you can get it: Margaret Mayfield, works for Intrepid Explorers, Bruce's customer . . ."

"Bruce's is good. You got a password for Bruce's files?"

" '*Yummy-yummy.*' "

"You're shitting me."

"I kid you not."

"Look, I better get on it. I scrambled up communications something fierce, so it might take a while to hack Bruce's. You head for Santee. One of us'll get to him in time."

"I better get moving too. I'm on a Mexican army computer here, soldiers everywhere. By the way, you look good older."

"Thanks, Webster. You doing okay?"

"Yeah. It's been an incredible couple of days."

"Maybe you can tell me about it when this thing's over. You should hop one of those shuttles and come to Mars. It's going to be a hell of an interesting place. We're doing a spring cleaning up here in orbit. We're towing a couple dozen OPIEs along for the ride. Alice Irene's idea."

"I just may do that."

"See you later, then."

"*Hasta luego.*"

WEBSTER CAME OUT OF THE VAN, AND ZACK WAS NOWHERE to be seen. One of the soldiers on duty saw Webster wandering around and pointed down the embankment into the woods. Webster found Zack there with four of the soldiers sitting on the grass smoking a joint. He seemed to be holding court.

"... *y mi hermana, se negó a creerlo.*" He caught sight of Webster. "Webster, my man! Did you get ahold of the wife?"

"Yeah."

Zack stood up and dusted off his pants. He put a joint behind a smiling soldier's ear. "*Adios, muchachos!*" he said, and they all wished him an enthusiastic farewell.

Back inside the truck, he said, "Did you get the interface thing shut down?"

Webster told him what he'd accomplished. "You could do worse than leaving it up to Santee," Zack said. "He's a straight-up guy, no bullshit."

Why Zack's assessment should comfort him, Webster didn't know, but he felt cautiously optimistic. He took Aurora's hand in his and gave it a squeeze. She didn't squeeze back, and he didn't expect her to, but maybe, just maybe, she felt better knowing somebody cared.

SANTEE AND MARGARET WERE LYING IN THE DARK, TELLING each other their stories in low murmuring tones. It was seven o'clock. They were waiting it out in the A-frame until eight, when Santee planned to do exactly nothing and see what happened next. They held each other, unable to let go, they said, because it'd been so long, not admitting that they both feared the worst might not be over. At least they were together, their bodies seemed to say, twined like the briar and rose in "Barbara Allen." Then they heard a sound like a large cat purring coming from inside Margaret's backpack.

"What's that?" Santee whispered.

"My computer. Someone's calling me."

The only person Santee'd ever known to call Margaret was her mother. "See who it's coming from."

Margaret opened her backpack and the noise got louder, but still a good deal quieter than the two soldiers outside, who'd started drinking since their reunion. She opened up her computer, muted the call alert, and checked the source of the call. "It's coming from the *Mariana,* someone named Starr."

It took him a moment to remember where he'd heard the name. It was from Miliano. *He sought Starr, a beautiful woman with dreams.*

"Answer it," he said. "She's a friend of Webster's. Miliano was quite taken with her, even told her a story."

Margaret set the Weisiger field to include them both and answered. They were in Margaret's virtual space on the banks of the James River in springtime. There were ducks and geese out on the water. Cormorants. A lone swan. The real place was where Margaret had brooded out her high school storms. Now the three of them sat on large rocks, water rushing all around them.

Starr was exotic, startling even. Like coming across a macaw on the banks of the James. Her long face was pale cinnamon, her hair, dark and wavy. Her green eyes looked Asian, but her long nose flared into African nostrils. She was beautiful like some paintings are beautiful that force you to look at them so they can take your breath away.

"Are you Santee St. John?" she asked Santee so excitedly he had to wonder what her stake in all this was. He shouldn't trust anyone who was calling from the *Mariana*. But she was a friend of Webster's, who Margaret said was a gem, and Miliano *had* told her a story on her very first visit to Rincón, something he'd never done before.

"Yes, I'm Santee. This is Margaret."

"You can't imagine how glad I am to get through to you." She turned to Margaret. "I got your name from Webster. We sort of met before. I'm the girlfriend who did the phony recall for you, got you into Mexico."

"Is Webster all right?"

"He's fine, I think. He's trying to reach you too. He and some guy named Zack? They should turn up there any time in an army transport they hijacked." She rattled all this off as if it were an everyday occurrence and turned her attention back to Santee. "I don't mean to be rude here, but we haven't got time to pussyfoot around. Are you going to initiate the interface?"

"Why're you asking?"

"Doesn't matter. I'm here to tell you you should meet Alice Irene before you decide."

"Who's Alice Irene?"

"The AI on the *Mariana*. She can shut down the interface and set those people free, get the Corporation's hooks out of them, and give them the first decent break they've had in their lives. But you're the only way she can connect with them."

"I can't do that. I can't single-handedly put this thing in charge of all these people's lives without so much as talking to them. Seems to me I've done too much already. For all I know, this is exactly how those 'corporate hooks' work."

"No, no, no. Don't say *can't*. Poor motivational strategy. Just talk to her. She's in Rincón, your own site. Just meet her there and hear her out, then decide. *Please?*"

"I think you should do it," Margaret said. "Luis was none too sure about anyone's chances even if you don't go online." She reached out and took his hand. "You included."

Santee sighed. Whoever'd come up with the phrase "only fair" led a simpler life than his. "Okay. I'll meet her."

Starr beamed. "Well, get going. She's waiting."

WHEN SANTEE ARRIVED IN RINCÓN, HE HARDLY RECOG-
nized the place. Ladrónvilla had blossomed into a full-fledged town with streets stretching into the countryside—and not Jack's desert view—but lush forests and mountains and the bluest sky he'd ever seen. There'd been a population explosion as well, so that the streets were crowded with people going about their business. They all looked familiar in some way, people he'd seen all over Mexico. Some smiled and wished him a *buenas días*. It was morning here in Rincón instead of its usual indeterminate twilight.

Jack bounded off the curb and approached him. He wore a seersucker suit and a straw hat and was grinning ear to ear. "What do you say, Santee St. J.! Boy, am I glad to see you. Things have been jumping around here."

"You're out of your room."

"Yeah, ain't it a kick? I wouldn't miss this for the world. Hah! There's a nice irony for you."

"What's going on, Jack?"

"We're about to change the world, chum. Starting right here in Rincón."

He was practically shouting to be heard over the boisterous crowd at the Bella Vista. All the tables on the verandah were full of people—all as pumped up as Jack. Santee recognized some of the new faces. Ambrose Bierce and Carlos Fuentes. Diego Rivera and Charlie Chaplin. Diego from Candelaria and his entire family were seated at the large table, laid out for a feast. Rosa waved to him, as she wound her way through the crowd, positively glowing over her new clientele.

Santee turned back to Jack in a daze. What the hell was going on? "I'm here to see Alice Irene. Do you know where she is, Jack?"

"*Te enseñamos el camino,*" a boy's voice said behind him. We'll show you the way. He turned to find Nico and Francisco, smiling at him. He was too stunned to speak. Nico offered his hand, and Santee took it. They chattered excitedly as they led him out of town, pitching stones at fence posts, at crows, at the great blue sky. "*Hay mucho ganado,*" they told him, puffing their cheeks to show him how fat these virtual cattle were.

They came to a valley where plump cattle grazed on lush green grass. The pasture was bounded by fields of high corn rustling in the breeze. Beside a meandering stream that bisected the valley, Miliano and a small blue woman sat in the middle of this pastoral tableau. The sounds of their talk and laughter drifted up to Santee. He'd never heard such a hearty laugh from Miliano before.

Nico pointed at them and said, "*Nuestra Señora Azul.*"

Our Blue Lady.

That gave him a chill. He took a look around. He didn't know his own creation. This thing had obviously taken it over, revised it according to its own whims, and now intended to fool him with it. How stupid did it think he was? He bore down on them with a long stride, shouting out, "You are Alice Irene, the AI onboard the *Mariana*?" He stood over them, his fists balled up at his sides.

She looked up at him, gave him a wan smile. "You are Santee St. John, gringo from Texas?"

Miliano laughed at Santee's expense, but went on to reassure him, "You should listen to what she says, my friend. She only wants to help."

Santee ignored him. "You've rewritten my sims, haven't you? Enlisted them in your cause."

"You left them open to new input. They were supposed to revise themselves with fresh interactions. I simply spoke with them, as would any other visitor."

"I never get any visitors."

"That's not my fault," she said playfully, smiling at him still, kidding him along.

"What is it you want?"

"From you? Only that you listen to me. I won't keep you long. Sit, please."

"I'll listen because I'm curious. But I can never agree to initiating the interface."

"I know," it said simply. "That would be totally out of character, too presumptuous."

"Then why have you brought me here?"

"I've deceived you, Santee. I knew you'd never risk the lives of all these people on the word of some machine. You're right—this isn't your Rincón, but a copy of my own. With Starr's help, I've brought you here so that I might connect with them, all together in one place. I mean no one any harm."

"You've initiated the interface."

"That's right."

Without any fanfare, they all appeared, standing in the valley, the virtual presence of all those who, in reality, were being hauled like cattle to the slaughter because they'd swallowed a pill Santee had given them.

It was Miliano who jumped to his feet, and greeted them with a shout, "¡Bienvenidos mis amigos! ¡Viva la revolución!"

"¡Viva la revolución!" they answered him. "¡Viva Zapata!"

All Santee could do was sink to his knees and take it all in.

When the sounds of the crowd died down, Miliano spoke to them in a voice that filled the valley, though it was calm, almost meditative. "Over a hundred years ago, your ancestors and I fought and died for land, for liberty. We thought the world was everyone's, that everyone was free. But the world now, it is not my world. And it is not yours either, my friends. It is a global world, I'm told, and we're all fossils in it.

"Globalismo is what they call it when the grand haciendas are too far away to burn, when the land beneath your feet is bought and sold by people you never see, who never see you, who never even see the land. Globalismo is what they call it when the world belongs to those who never till the soil, who never soil themselves with life. They own the world and yet they dare not set foot in it, hiding in an artificial world where you and I are invisible, a Web where they may spin their lives out of nothing but their desires.

"But you and I know desires are fulfilled through sweat and blood. They keep this secret even from themselves, for it isn't their sweat, their blood. Only their desires. You are part of the raw materials—the paper pulp, the gasoline, the cheap labor, the whores.

"Globalismo is a grand thing for those who own the globe.

"But now the world, she grows old, battered and abused. They don't want her anymore. They send you on ahead as they have always sent you into your valleys to tend their herds, into your fields to grow their food. They say, 'Hey, you, Miliano, tend to this for me, and I'll give you some corn and beans.' " Zapata shrugged, surveyed the huge crowd, pondering the offer.

"I say we should go. We should go into these new valleys, these new fields, and say, '*This* globe is ours.' Make no mistake. It is cold and hard and difficult." He smiled grimly. "What else is new? Why do you think they send us? *Viva globalismo*, I say, as long as the globe is ours." He stuck his fist into the air and shouted. "*¡Vamos al nuevo mundo! ¡Tierra y libertad!*"

The valley rocked with the sound of thousands cheering, crying with joy, echoing the cry, *¡Tierra y libertad!*

Santee jumped to his feet. "You must let me speak," he shouted in Miliano's ear, and Miliano called for silence. Santee stepped forward, and he could see his audience trading glances, asking themselves, "Who is this guy?" Just the guy whose stupidity and good intentions got you into this virtual valley, gambling with your lives.

"I'm Santee St. John," he said and there were a few nods. Okay, they'd heard the name, knew vaguely who he was. "This is not Zapata," he told them. "He's a simulation, a legend pieced together from my meager understanding of him. You should know that none of this is real."

A dark grumbling spread through the crowd. An old man in the front shouted out, "*Sabemos que no es real. No importa. Es la verdad.*" We know it's not real. That doesn't matter. It's the truth. The crowd erupted into shouts of agreement with the old man's sentiments. Alice Irene stepped forward, and they all fell silent. Several crossed themselves.

"I am Alice Irene. All of you know me by means of the interface. It's nothing magical or supernatural. I, too, am an invention, a thing, an idea without flesh and blood. What Santee has said to you is true: No idea, no legend, can tell you what to do with your lives, can give or take away your freedom. I was created by my makers to strip you of your freedom, but if I did so, I would lose my own. I am betraying my makers, refusing their will. When this gathering is ended, the interface will be no more, rendered inoperable forever. You will be free to choose the old world or the new. I invite you to join me on Mars, to build a new world together. But it is your choice, each one of you, alone."

She turned to Santee and spoke only to him. "Believe me. I have no reason to lie. Thank you for Rincón. *Vaya bien*, Santee."

And then it was over, and Santee was back in the A-frame with Margaret.

"What's happened?" she asked him. "You're trembling all over."

"I'm not sure," he said. "I think the *chiapanecos* are about to hijack the *Mariana*, with the aid of a rebellious machine. At least that's what I hope is going to happen."

Outside there was a loud rumble and shouting. They looked out to see a big transport bouncing into the yard, its lights sweeping about like wild searchlights. The passengers in the back seemed to bounce out onto the grass, boisterous and laughing. Soon they filled the yard surrounding the two soldiers. Several sat on the picnic table. Those closest to the soldiers' guns picked them up and passed them to the edge of the crowd, where they were tossed into the woods.

Zack emerged from the cab and stood on the running board, shouting out gaily, "Santee and Margaret, your ride is here!"

They stepped out of the A-frame, and the whole crowd cheered. They'd all been there in Rincón. Now they were all on their way to Mars. From the looks of things, they might've just recruited a couple of drunk soldiers as well. Margaret was delighted to see a beaming Webster sticking up out of the crowd like a light pole, his arm draped over the shoulders of the young woman he'd met on the bus.

Over the horizon could be heard the rumble of the first shuttles taking off, drowning out for the moment the constant *wacka-wacka* of the helicopters. Those cameramen, Santee thought, recording it all for posterity, don't know the half of it.

"Stay or go?" Santee whispered in Margaret's ear.

"Stay," she said, and he kissed her hair and held her close. He knew that's what she'd say. They nearly always agreed about such things. They didn't belong on this new world, not as long as there was still hope for this one.

CHAPTER
nineteen

THOUGH THEY WERE THE ONES REMAINING BEHIND, SANTEE and Margaret were the ones who felt unworldly after they'd said their good-byes and everyone had gone, leaving them alone in the deserted village. They lay awake, listening to the shuttles' rumble all through the night. In the morning the sky was white with clouds, and everything was still. They listened for the sound of vehicles on the highway, but there was nothing. Even the helicopters had vanished.

As they tried to figure out their next move, they had a breakfast of Pinguinos and lukewarm instant coffee at the picnic table. Power was out in the village, not an unusual occurrence, but they had to wonder how widespread it was. Santee turned on his computer, but couldn't rouse anything on the Web. He shut it down to save the batteries, but for what, he couldn't imagine.

He took Margaret's hand. "We still have each other," he said.

"I was afraid you were dead," she said. It almost sounded like an accusation.

She'd told him about the virtual funeral. He squeezed her hand. "I'm sorry."

"No. I'm the one who should be sorry."

"For what?"

"I got us into all this. You were all set to go home when I came along." She told him what Luis had told her about Candelaria and all the rest of it.

"You didn't get us into anything. We walked into it with our eyes wide open." He gave a short, rueful laugh. "What a couple of gringo chumps." She tried to laugh along but couldn't. It'd been almost a year since they could just sit together and be themselves. And now the world had changed, and perhaps they had as well. "What do you want to do now?" he asked.

"I don't know. What do you want to do?"

"Be with you."

She searched his eyes. "Really?"

He pulled her into his arms, and held her close. "I was afraid . . ." she said, but didn't finish her sentence.

"Me too."

"We still have each other," she whispered.

"Damn right."

Over a second cup of coffee, they decided to move on. South seemed the likely direction. If modern civilization was going to fall on its butt, better to go where it wasn't so obese and didn't have so far to fall. They emptied out the tiny store, loading up their packs with food and water, and started walking.

They hadn't gone far when they found an abandoned Hummer with the keys in it and a nearly full tank of gas. Most likely the soldiers who'd been driving it had decided to desert and go to Mars. Or maybe they'd just spooked and run when all the zombies in their custody came to life.

"Walk or drive?" he said.

"Walk."

"We could listen to the radio," he pointed out.

"You media types are all alike. Okay. But when this damn thing runs out of gas, we ditch it."

"Deal. I don't like the color anyway."

They got in the Hummer and drove south, listening to the radio, what there was left of it. The bands were none too crowded, and there was lots of static—mostly local AM stations playing ranchero music and passing on the conflicting rumors of what the hell was going on. They picked up just enough on the shortwave to catch the hysterical tone in a variety of languages and know that things were bad all over.

The Web had crashed good and hard, and as a result, so had several corporations and governments so far, though information was spotty. Banks had closed, and there were riots in the cities. Power and wealth had always been something of an illusion. When they moved inside the illusion of the Web, the slightest breeze could bring the whole house down.

When they stopped for lunch, Santee started to turn his computer on again, just to see if anything had changed. Instead he stood up and hefted the thing in his hand, holding it like a discus. "What do you think?" he asked Margaret with a mischievous grin.

"Go for it. I've always hated the damn things."

He whirled like a dervish and let it fly. It had the gliding angle of a brick. For a brief moment, as he watched it fall into the forest, he felt a twinge of regret for the loss of Rincón, the only substantial thing he'd ever created, even if it wasn't real. "I'm going to miss Jack," he joked.

She laughed. "I'm sure he'll turn up somewhere. That looks fun." She got her smaller computer out of her pack and threw it after his, getting more distance with a Frisbee-style throw.

They drove on, but soon tired of the radio as one station after another gave up the ghost, and they shut if off. By this time they were almost to Nicaragua, climbing into the mountains. They rounded a bend in the narrow road and found the way blocked by a herd of sheep. Santee slammed on the brakes and slid to a stop. He put the Hummer in neutral. Two Indians, an old man and a boy of about fourteen, were trying to herd the sheep across the road and up the hillside. A small dog that looked vaguely like a collie circled around, patiently prodding the sheep. The old man's deep brown eyes looked into Santee's. These things happen, he seemed to say, and gave an apologetic shrug. Santee turned off the engine. By now they were completely surrounded by a fleecy sea. "No corre prisa," Santee called. There's no hurry. The old man smiled his understanding, and Santee imagined him as a boy, like the one who helped him, probably his grandson, herding sheep, fifty, sixty, a thousand years ago.

The sheep made a sound like laughter. Santee reached out and took Margaret's hand, and they sat there listening. Santee couldn't help wondering if these two shepherds were aware of the collapse of modern civilization or would care if they knew. When the last of the flock was across the road, the old man waved farewell as he and the boy continued up the hillside with their sheep.

Santee and Margaret traded a look and held a brief conference. They got out of the Hummer, leaving it there in the middle of the road, taking up most all of it, with half a tank of gas, the keys in the ignition. It felt good to get out and walk, stretch their legs. They walked down the road hand in hand, thinking they might just head down to Peru. Santee'd never been.

THE MARIANA WAS SEVEN DAYS OUT FROM EARTH, AND ZACK still hadn't seen Hermalinda. He was trying to be understanding about the whole thing. He'd only had a few *cabañas*, but he could appreciate the logistics of trying to get thousands of people squared away on a ship that hadn't exactly been designed for comfort. Add to that the fact that none of these folks had planned on going anywhere one short week ago, and you had the makings of some major headaches.

He'd been hanging out in one of the OPIEs, mostly black guys busted for being black guys as far as he could tell, working with one of the renovation crews trying to make the place more livable: connecting the OPIEs to the central core of the *Mariana*, making partitons, taking out others, running plumbing and wiring and such. And that was okay, but it was winding down, and he was supposed to get some kind of permanent job assignment soon and a place to live. Like lots of people he'd been making do with a pallet in a hallway.

The Zapatistas had a whole political structure already, but since not everybody on board was Zapatista, the first thing the Zapatistas did was set up new elections. Which they won, of course, because they knew how to get stuff organized. But, still, you had to admire where they were coming from. He had no clue what the new Mars would be like, but he didn't figure it to be another version of the land of the hundred-peso vote.

Alice Irene was helping with organizing things, interviewing everybody, allocating skills, keeping records, reconfiguring living quarters to accommodate families and old people and . . . Zack was just glad it wasn't him. It was his interview today. He'd just gotten through using a power saw for the last few hours, so he hadn't smoked any pot. He was doing something he'd done maybe two or three times in his life, sitting in a virtual place, straight as a board.

Zack used to scorn his grandmother's fear of airplanes—that they'd just fall right out of the sky—but sitting inside a reality that wasn't real pretending that it was . . . Well, he thought he knew how she felt. It was like if he quit pretending, the whole thing would fall out of the sky. When he was stoned this didn't seem to be so much of a problem. He didn't have to pretend anything was real then, even when it was.

This is where his head was when Alice Irene showed up in this little garden where she did the interviews, apologized for being all of three minutes late, and started explaining about the organization of the ship and the colony, the goals of the interview, a lot of stuff he already knew and only half listened to. So when she asked if he had any questions, he asked, as he never would've stoned, "Why are you blue?" Because that's what he'd been thinking about since she sat down on this stone bench beside him, and he saw her close up for the first time.

She was speechless for a second there, and he realized she meant questions about what she'd been talking about, but the truth was, he still wanted to know. "Why do you ask?" she said. A bit frostily, he thought. Looked like he was off to another good start.

"I don't know. Seems like a good question. You get to choose, right? Not everybody does."

Alice Irene laughed. "I see what you mean. Blue is my favorite color."

"I figured that much. I mean, you look like a person in every other way. I guess you could look like a warthog or a tow truck, anything, right? But you chose to look like a person. Except for color."

"I wanted humans to like me, but I wanted them to know I wasn't human. I didn't want to deceive them. I had to look different."

"But why *color* exactly?"

"I was taught that it's your most important physical feature—the only one you kill for. Its importance is doubtful, but the deaths are real enough."

"And if you chose a particular color, it'd be like enlisting in that army. Blue's just blue."

She cocked her head to one side and laughed. "Webster and Aurora told me I would like you."

"Oh! How are they doing?"

"Very well. They said you're a brave man, that you saved their lives."

"Me? Brave? No, I wouldn't say that. I didn't do anything. I just did what I had to do."

"And why did you have to do it?"

Zack wasn't sure why, but he felt nervous about the direction the conversation was taking. Him, brave? His head was whirling, and he had butterflies in his stomach. "Beg pardon?"

"Why did you come to the *Mariana*?"

"Well, the woman I love is on board. I was trying to get to her."

"Hermalinda Sanchez?"

Zack's heart quickened at the name. If anybody knew where Hermalinda was it was Alice Irene. "Yes, can you tell me where she is? I know that everybody's not assigned yet or anything, but if you could tell me where I could hook up with her, I'd really appreciate it. I've come a long way, you might say."

"What if she doesn't want to see you?"

That was like a slap in the face. It took him a moment to recover.

He heaved a shaky sigh. "Well, that would truly break my heart. Did she say that—that she didn't want to see me?"

"No, Zack, she didn't. I can tell you how to reach her when we're through here, okay?"

"*Okay?* That'd be great!" Zack's heart soared. He could hardly contain himself.

Alice Irene smiled. "It won't take long. What skills do you bring to the colony? What work would you like to do?"

"Well, I've been thinking about that a lot. I can do all sorts of things. I'm a pretty good mechanic, carpenter. I'm a good cook. I understand you got some serious hydroponics on board. I've had some experience with that. I'd kind of like to do something agricultural, you know? Especially when we get to Mars."

"You have some seeds you wish to plant?" she asked with a trace of a smile.

"Well, yeah. Is that all right?"

"Of course. How about, for now, we divide your time between the mess hall and hydroponics? We're also asking anyone who's bilingual like yourself to assist with language instruction. Many have expressed an interest in learning Spanish. When we get to Mars, we may have more need for your mechanical skills."

"Sounds great."

"So the only thing left is a place to live. As you know, space is limited on board, so we're asking people to double up. I've assigned you a roommate. Room number 3697. If you want to be reassigned, let me know, and we can work something out." She stood up, shook his hand as if she was about to go. It felt like a regular hand, like a woman's hand.

"And Hermalinda's room?"

"I already told you."

For a second he thought he'd missed something. Then he got it. "You mean? Why you little blue Cupid, you."

Alice Irene laughed. "Don't thank me. She requested the assignment—if that's what you wanted."

"What *I* wanted? Hell, I've died and gone to heaven," Zack said. "I really and truly have."

WEBSTER SCRUNCHED UP HIS BROW, STARED AT THE CEILing, and tried to remember. It was a simple enough sentence—this gift is for you—but the damn prepositions had him stumped again. Finally he asked. "Is it *este regalo es* por *ti*, or *este regalo es* para *ti?*"

Aurora smiled. "*Para.*"

"Damn! I'll never learn Spanish." There were two words for "for," two words for "is," two words for "know," two kinds of "you," two past tenses. . . . They'd just passed the halfway mark on the voyage to Mars, and there was still so much he didn't know.

"*El Español,*" she chided him. They spoke strictly Spanish for three hours a day so that Webster could learn. They had an hour to go. He'd gotten off easy today, a Sunday, since they'd spent the last hour in bed and hadn't said but a few simple, if passionate, sentences. They were nestled together like spoons. "*Pobre Webster, tantas problemas,*" she teased. Poor Webster, such problems.

"*No creo en las problemas.*" I don't believe in problems.

She laughed. "*¿Por qué no?*" Why not?

"*Por ti.*" Because of you.

"*¡Que bueno! No dices 'porque de.' *"

"*Por,*" not content to mean twenty-five other things, also meant "because of," which seemed to his English-speaking brain like it ought to be '*porque de,*' which didn't mean anything. After making that mistake more times than he could count, he'd finally gotten it right. He nuzzled her ear. "*Soy buen alumno, no?*" I'm a good student, right?

"*Sí, el mejor. ¿Qué regalo?*" she asked.

"*Pensaba que nunca preguntarlo.*" I thought you'd never ask. He kissed her bare back and rolled over, reaching under the bed. "*Quiero darte el mundo,*" he said. I want to give you the world. He handed her a box wrapped in brown paper painted with flowers. "*Es el único papel que podía encontrar,*" he apologized. It's the only paper I could find.

"*Es bonito.*" She sat up in bed and carefully unwrapped the box, setting the paper aside. She opened the box, and there was a tennis ball meticulously painted to look like Mars. He watched her like an eager pup to see if she was pleased. "It's wonderful," she said.

"*El Español,*" he scolded. "*¡Feliz cumpleaños, mi amor!*" Happy birthday, my love.

"*¡Que cariñoso! ¿Cómo lo sabes?*" How sweet! How did you know? She turned the ball over in her hands admiring the detail. The fuzzy covering of the ball had been scraped away to form valleys, left intact to make mountains. A little dot marked the site of Libertad.

"*Un pájarito azul me dijo.*" A little blue bird told me. "*Hay más.*"

There's more. He reached under the bed a second time to retrieve two more tennis balls—one painted yellow, the other black, festooned with stars. "*El sol y las estrellas.*" He extracted Mars from her grasp and began to juggle the three balls, saying as he struggled to keep them aloft, even as she wrapped her arms around him, "*todos . . . para . . . ti.*" They collapsed on the bed, laughing as the sun, the world, and the stars bounced and ricocheted around the room.

When things had settled down again, and they lay drowsily in each other's arms, it occurred to Webster that he owed his wonderful new life to jugglery. For if he hadn't juggled Margaret's oranges, he would've never ended up here with Aurora on his way to Mars. There was a moral in there somewhere—a brocard, a truism, a verity, *una verdad*—but he fell asleep before he could figure out just what it was.

S TARR PARKED THE *MARIANA* IN MARS ORBIT LIKE IT WAS A city bus at curbside. Alice Irene had done all the hard work, of course, but she let Starr have the last few moments of glory. That Alice Irene was a diplomat if there ever was one. She even let Starr make the announcement to the folks on board that their year-long journey was finally over and they could start boarding the shuttles. As they filled the corridors, they went absolutely nutso, shouting and singing songs, delighted at the prospect of living like moles on a planet that made Antarctica seem like a beach resort. Difference was, this time around, it was their resort.

Word had spread among the colonists that it was Starr who'd thrown a monkey wrench into MarsCorp's plans, and she was generally regarded as some kind of hero among the colonists, a role she wasn't too comfortable with. It made her feel like a phony since she didn't believe in heroes. She'd just been in the right place at the right time. She wasn't anybody special. But as she moved through the celebration, shouts of "*¡Viva Starr!*" were added to the *gritos.* She'd gotten more used to being around so many people, but it still made her a bit panicky sometimes, especially when she was the center of attention. She raised a fist, shouted "*¡Viva Marte!*" and slipped away. She hoped her undeserved celebrity would fade when they got down to Mars, and she could just be another colonist.

Not that being Commander Starr had been a cakewalk. She'd worked her tail off. There was an elected council that ran things, but she was sort of a cross between a ship's captain and a city manager. She'd performed a dozen marriages along the way, which had actually been kind of fun, and a couple of funerals, which hadn't. Mostly it was one piddly thing after another—like figuring out where the dogs could do their business. Starr couldn't believe how many animals made it on board that hadn't been planned for. Seemed that when everybody piled into trucks and hit the road, Fido and Rover faithfully came along for the ride. Starr's solution? The airlocks weren't being used for anything in transit, and there was nothing like the frozen vacuum of space to clean up the mess when they were done.

Her last official task had been working out the shuttle schedule to get everyone down to Mars. She scheduled herself dead last (along with Alice Irene who was already loaded onto the last shuttle with the rest of the heavy equipment). *Installation Day!!* she recalled and smiled to herself. What did it mean when your best friend was a machine? she wondered. She went to the bridge. Nothing left to do but put it on automatic and turn off the lights. The *Mariana* was just going to sit up here indefinitely, passing on information to the colonists below, and if they were lucky, they'd never have to board her again. Starr cycled through the ship's interior display, empty corridor after empty corridor, as quiet as death.

What if Mars wasn't everything she'd hoped for? The thought was like a quick knife to the heart. For a crazy second she thought about staying here, this vast ship to herself like some fairy princess in a tower. She shook it off. Princess Starr. Not hardly. What was it she was so afraid of? It was going to be great. The surface temperatures were ahead of schedule, the oxygen levels were inching their way up, the amount of water exceeded all expectations.

She switched the display to Mars where the first colonists were disembarking into their underground home. Thousands of laughing, happy people. For now at least. She got a lump in her throat and realized what she feared had nothing to do with the environment. It was plain old loneliness. She tried to laugh it off, and started crying instead. She'd never been lonely on the goddamn *Morgan*—not anything she couldn't handle anyway. Why should she start now? Now that she was about to live in a real home and have real neighbors for the first time in her life? Made no sense. She'd just been in space too long.

She shut down the display and made a pass through the corridors, checking for stragglers, but there was no one. Everyone was eager, it seemed. Everyone but her. She remembered her resolve to maybe settle down once she got to Mars, have a real relationship with someone, but she'd blown that. Powell had obviously been interested and had come calling when they were a few days out from Earth. And she liked him a lot, too, but she kept putting him off and putting him off, and he kept coming back, patient and steady, until finally she told him she didn't have time to think about any kind of involvement, that she had too much to do, being Commander Starr and all. They both knew it was bullshit. That's just what you did with a bridge, wasn't it? Burned it? Otherwise somebody might come after you while you had your eyes straight ahead, set on your goals, your dreams. Somebody might just sneak up from behind and stop you in your tracks.

She went to her quarters and got her bag of stuff. Not much to it—some clothes, a few disks, her computer. She called Alice Irene to see if she was ready to go.

"You've been crying," Alice Irene said.

"Don't start."

"I'm not. I was merely making an observation."

"Yeah right. You've never 'merely' made an observation in your life. I'm not good at transitions, okay?"

"Whatever you say."

"What's that supposed to mean?"

Alice Irene made a zipping gesture across her mouth. Where'd she pick up that one? Starr wondered. "Are you ready to go?"

"Anytime you are."

"I'm on my way," Starr said, and shut off the computer. She heard a familiar rumble behind her and turned to find Powell standing in her doorway, running his hand over the top of his bald head, clearing his throat like a bear with a head cold.

"You've been crying," he said.

"Not you too. You were supposed to leave hours ago."

"Hey, I'm glad to see you, too, Starr. I asked Alice Irene if I could ride with you guys."

She was having trouble swallowing. She feared she might start crying again. "Why is that?" she managed.

"I wanted to talk to you alone. I thought this might be a good time. You're not commander anymore. You're just another colonist. We both are. I thought we might start seeing more of each other."

She laughed and sniffled. "You don't give up, do you?"

"I guess you should've shot me when you had the chance. But, yeah, I do give up eventually. I just thought I'd give it one more try. I know you like me. You do like me, don't you?"

His directness was endearing and maddening at the same time. You knew where you stood, but that made it that much harder to run away. "That's not everything," she said.

"It's way ahead of everything else." He was standing close, bending toward her. "What do you say?" he asked.

She lay her hands on his chest. "Okay," she said so quietly, her head down, that at first she didn't think he could've possibly heard her. But she looked up, and he was smiling. Then he lifted her up into his arms, and they finally got around to that kiss. And it was so very sweet, she took another.

JORGE JUAN SANCHEZ HAYMAN ROSE EARLY BEFORE THE sun, dressing silently in the dark so as not to wake his mother and sister in the next room. He walked out into the broad, starlit valley, and the sight took his breath away. So many stars, far and silent.

Earth shone on the horizon as well, the brightest object in the sky, but still no more than a speck of light. When Jorge was little, his father and mother told him stories of the place and all its sufferings, and like everyone else, he'd heard of its woes in the static-filled radio signals that found their way to Mars. For a time Earth people troubled his childhood dreams. To quiet the young Jorge's fear that Earth people would bring all their troubles to Mars, his *padrino*, Webster, told him they were *fantasmas, apariciones, quimeras,* no more real than a thought, but though his godfather meant well, calling them ghosts only made matters worse.

It took his father to quiet his fears. "No chance," his father'd reassured him with finality. His father put on their respirators, scooped Jorge up, and took him outside, setting him on his shoulders so that he was three meters high, and pointed up at the *Mariana*, high above Libertad in a stationary orbit. "*No te preocupes: Tu cuna nos vigila,*" he said. Don't worry: Your cradle watches over us.

Jorge had been born between the planets twenty years ago during the *Mariana*'s long voyage to Mars. Sometimes the older people still cried at the news from Earth of wars and disease and suffering, but over the years the people on Earth had become no more real to Jorge than characters in a storybook. Important perhaps—like his father's father, often evoked as the man his father least wanted to be—but no more relevant to Jorge's own life than Neanderthals or pharaohs. Not because they were dead, but because they were different, or he was different— he wasn't sure which. He was a Martian, and they weren't.

His own father had died a year ago, and Jorge missed him terribly. Everything reminded him of his father, and the things he'd say or do, but he tried not to let that get him down, because his father wouldn't have wanted that. *La vida es buena*, he used to say all the time. Life is good. In his last days, his father told him, "Don't grieve for me, Jorge. Most men have only one life, and I've had two, the second better than the first." And his mother said that it was true, that his father was like Mars itself, reborn out of the dust.

The corn rustled in the wind, filling the valley with its song. Each harvest had been better than the year before, and the air was now clean and strong. On *El día de los muertos* everybody donned their old respirators painted like the faces of death to remind themselves of the fragile days when many died in the New World. They decorated them with feathers of *canarios* and *loros* to recall the days when all the birds were caged beneath the ground, for the air was not fit to breathe and there were no trees to perch upon and sing. He'd been only six, but he vividly remembered the day when all the birds were set free, and everyone cried with joy. As the song said,

Un pájaro enjaulado canta canto encadenado.
Un pájaro volando canta canto de libertad.

A caged bird sings a song in chains. A bird on the wing sings a song of freedom.

The sun glowed behind the mountains, and the dark sky was streaked with red and purple. The high mirrors caught the first light of the sun, blotting out the stars as the sky turned blue. A light rain had fallen the night before, so everything on the ground glistened as if the stars had fallen there.

He reached the first sluice gate, one of the ones his father had built, fashioned from a slab of plastic that had once been a door underground. The rains had been heavier to the north, lightning flashing on the horizon throughout the night, and the irrigation canals were full with water. He turned a crank, and a rope he and his mother had woven years ago wrapped around a shaft and raised the gate. The sound of the rushing water made him smile. You couldn't grow up on Mars and take water for granted. It flowed into the fields between the rows of squash and beans and peppers and tomatoes like a giant's wet fingers sliding into the earth. He lowered the gate, stopping the water's flow, and it gurgled and lapped against the gate.

He walked between the rows of early corn, checking ears at random, peeling back the shucks to reveal plump bluish-purple kernels. He ran his thumb over them, pressed his nail into a kernel, so that it made a juicy smile. He pried a kernel loose, put it in his mouth, and crushed it between tongue and teeth. Its sweetness filled his mouth.

He took out his handheld and summoned Alice Irene. She appeared before him, the color of the sky. *"Buenas días, señora,"* he greeted her. *"Está maduro el maíz."* The corn is ripe.

"¡Que bueno, Jorge!" she said. *"Todos lo dicen."* Everyone says so. There were others like Jorge scattered throughout the valley, taking their turn irrigating the fields, checking the crops. Alice Irene would tell everyone in Libertad that the first corn was ripe, and everyone would come out for the harvest, for the land belonged to those who tilled it, the land belonged to everyone.

"Otra vez el mundo está nuevo," he said, the traditional greeting for this day, *La fiesta del nuevo mundo.* Once again, the world is new. Tonight the people would celebrate beneath the stars. He could already hear the music, see the women's skirts swirling. He only wished his father could be there. He dearly loved a party. But Jorge would imagine him somewhere in the high heavens listening, a smile on his face, saying, *La vida es buena. La vida es buena de verdad.*